DEATH NEVER SLEEPS

Roger—
You are a great host! *(signature)*

DEATH NEVER SLEEPS

A Novel

E. J. SIMON

Dear Linda,
You are a great host, too!
Thanks so much for a lovely stay.
Best,
(signature)
October 12, 2018

S/Z

DEATH NEVER SLEEPS

Simon/Zef Publishing
For more information about this book and its author, visit www.EJSimon.com

Edition ISBNs
Trade Paperback 978-0-9912564-0-2
Hardcover 978-0-9912564-1-9
E-book 978-1-4759-8622-8

Cover design by Jeffrey Michelson
Book design by Catherine Leonardo

This edition was prepared for printing by The Editorial Department
7650 E. Broadway, #308, Tucson, Arizona 85710
www.editorialdepartment.com

Printed in the United States of America.

For Andrea

I believe we all have a story; most never get written.
Without her love and encouragement, this one
would have remained a dream.

Chapter 1

Whitestone, Queens, New York
October 31, 2009
5:45 p.m.

Alex Nicholas had often wondered what the last moments of his life would feel like. Would it be a shortness of breath, a cold sweat, a stabbing pain near the heart? Or perhaps a tender piece of Smith & Wollensky's New York strip lodged in his trachea, refusing to go down. He was in a dangerous business, which might have been what led to this morbid fascination. More likely, Alex thought, it was the result of attending all those gloomy Greek Orthodox funerals as a kid.

Or was it that shadow of a person nearby, someone watching or following him that he had caught a glimpse of a few times over the past few days? He wasn't sure what it was, but something was wrong.

He sat in his den, admiring his sleek Apple laptop. Although it looked like the same computer owned by millions of people, it was far more powerful. Inside the polished aluminum case and underneath the smooth white keyboard were over a million dollars of state-of-the-art upgrades and enhancements sourced from diverse specialized companies located all over the world and combined together by an obscure but strangely talented computer genius who just happened to live across the street. The combination had resulted in a breakthrough, Alex knew, that would change everything.

For a full minute, Alex just stared at his image on the screen. Using his laptop, he had taken the photograph of himself, and now he thought carefully about which words he wanted to place at the bottom of the screenshot. Then it came to him, the phrase that he had read days ago and that had stuck in his mind ever since. He began to type, watching the words appear below his image: *Life is a dream; death is waking up.*

Alex laughed. *That will get their attention,* he thought. *Someday, hopefully not anytime soon.* Alex smiled at his mirror image. *I can't wait to show this to Michael.*

Alex often thought about his brother, Michael, the only remaining link to the family of his childhood. He wished they were closer, though there were plenty of reasons why they weren't. Alex suspected it was either the business he was in or the women he married. He knew Michael wasn't comfortable with either. But now that he had completed his secret project, Alex Nicholas was determined to get closer to the brother that he sorely missed. Alex decided he would call Michael later—as soon as he'd had something to eat.

Moving quickly now, he signed off and closed the laptop. Alex carried the computer into his master bedroom and entered the spacious walk-in closet, quietly closing the door behind him. Inside there was a row of custom-made wooden shelves, running from the ceiling down to the floor, each shelf jutting out at an angle, designed to hold and display two pairs of shoes. He removed the shoes sitting on the fourth shelf from the bottom and, gripping the polished teak, pushed it upward. The specially designed panel easily lifted up, revealing a hidden compartment. Alex placed his unique laptop snuggly into the empty cavity and returned the shelf to its original position.

As he headed down his stairway and out the front door, Alex thought about the amazing breakthrough that was contained inside his computer and lightened his step. He was no genius when it came to electronics, and he didn't understand how it worked—or even *why* it worked—only that it did.

And because it did, Alex knew now that he would live forever.

Chapter 2

Despite the uneasy feeling that had plagued him over the past few weeks, tonight Alex had no complaints. He was almost feeling good.

Grimaldi's, an old Queens bar and restaurant, was buzzing despite the early dinner hour, an ominous sky, and the first snow falling outside. Frankie Valli's hit song "Sherry" played for the thousandth time on the jukebox.

Veal parmigiana sizzled on the plate, the cheese and rich, red tomato sauce bubbling, a work of old-fashioned Italian-American art. Alex was about to cut into his first slice, when Maria came over to his table.

"Alex, how are you? You've been a stranger the last few weeks."

Maria was one of the sexiest women Alex had ever known—tall, slim, long dark hair, and exotic Mediterranean looks. Her deep, smoky voice only added to her unique appeal. She was forty-eight years old but exuded the confidence of a good-looking woman who knows she doesn't need to conceal those years.

5

"I've been busy," Alex groaned. "Everybody owes me money. I'd be rich if people would pay their fuckin' debts." He had sold Grimaldi's to Maria twelve years earlier. She still enjoyed seeing him every time he came in.

"I think you're still rich. Someone must be paying up," Maria shot back. "And I don't think that sport coat is from Walmart."

Alex looked down at his custom-tailored navy sport jacket as though it was the first time he had seen it. "What? It's from the Korean tailor in Flushing. I don't think it even fits right."

Alex Nicholas ran one of the largest sports gambling and loan-sharking operations in the city. He had that outer-borough, tough-guy appeal that women like Maria found irresistible, despite the fact that his body was showing the toll of fifty-five years of too many fast women, marriages, double scotches, and evenings that stretched out to early mornings. There had been many times Maria and Alex had longed to go to bed together, but somehow, between the business, the scotches, and their spouses at any given time, it just never happened.

Maria sat down with her gin and tonic and joined Alex while he devoured his veal. She wore a tight, clingy black dress that showed just enough cleavage for him to enjoy the view. "Alex, you know if you'd stop complaining all the time, you might find your life's not so bad."

"Oh yeah, you think so? I'm supporting everyone I fuckin' know or ever met, including three wives—and I'm only married to one, and she goes to bed at nine o'clock," Alex replied with his mouth full.

"You love it and you know it, Alex," Maria said with a laugh and a sly smile. "People need you, and I think you like it that way."

"Hmm," was all Alex could muster while he continued to methodically work through his meal. Two Chivas Regals had begun to soothe his edgy nerves, and the veal parmigiana was having the same effect on his stomach. Maybe Maria wasn't too far off, and maybe life wasn't so bad.

"You know, your brother told me once that he thought you never really recovered from losing that girl Molly when you went away to college."

"Who knows? It might not have worked that well either. I was crazy, and she might have been too." Alex's face and expression turned reflective, almost sad. "I'm not sure I was ever cut out to be married. I'm never getting fuckin' married again, that's for sure."

"I was also surprised when he told me the story. I didn't even know you went to college, Alex."

"In my business, the dumber people think I am, the better. I don't exactly brag about it. I was only there three years. I played baseball and fooled around. After high school, I had an offer to sign a minor league contract with the Pirates, but, you know, my parents were Greek immigrants. My father was a furrier, had a shop on Fifth Avenue but wanted his kids to go to college and become bankers or whatever corporate shit. Anyway, it wasn't for me."

"So what happened?"

"I went to Miami and played ball until I blew out my knees. Then I came home, got my insurance broker's license, took bets on the side, and finally found the closest thing I could do to playing ball—I became a bookie. That's how it all began."

"Jesus, Alex, that's some story. I can't believe you never told me this before."

"Yeah, well, not everyone thinks it's such a great thing."

"It's funny how your brother went so corporate, working for a big company. You two are very different, aren't you?"

"I guess so. He heads up some big company in the city. I'm proud of him. My parents never lived to see him like this. They died when he was in his thirties or so. He's always traveling all over the world. I couldn't do what he does, even if I knew what it was that he does."

"Well, Alex, he couldn't do what you do, either. Plus, despite your son-of-a-bitch persona, everyone—or almost everyone—likes you."

7

"I don't really give a shit whether people like me or not. I don't think about stuff like that. I got other things to worry about."

"Look around, Alex. Half the guys in this place tonight are your friends, even the cops. How many people in your line of work get along well with cops?"

Alex looked around the restaurant, silently counting the number of police officers. "They're all big shots now—detectives, narcs, captains. I knew them when they were on the beat, in their uniforms. I treat people well. I play by certain rules. No drugs, no dealing. And I've never hurt anyone—not seriously anyway."

"You just scare the shit out of them." Maria giggled.

"Sometimes that's the only way I can get paid, you know?"

"What I know, Alex, is that underneath this tough guy is the nicest person I have ever known." Maria reached over the table and caressed his cheek.

He turned away, gave a sideways smirk, and with his best touch of sarcasm said, "Well, you don't know that many people."

Maria rolled her eyes.

"You know what? Maybe I'm feeling pretty good tonight." He was finally smiling.

Alex turned back to his dinner, and Maria signaled the server for another round of drinks. He felt a chill run through him as a cold draft swept through the restaurant. He looked up in time to see the front door closing and a young man wearing a bright blue Mets cap moving, hesitantly, toward the bar.

Chapter 3

L uke Burnett knew he was a long way from his home in Green-ville, South Carolina. Although Grimaldi's was just a local Queens neighborhood bar and restaurant, Luke didn't fit in. His blue jeans were too baggy for his tall but skinny frame. The Mets cap was too new. He felt like a redneck or, worse, a hillbilly. Luke looked around the bar. He was surrounded by tough-looking hefty guys, all seemingly in black leather jackets, talking, shouting, or arguing. They spoke English, yet their New York accents were foreign to Luke. No one was as thin or as slight as he was. Even the women looked tougher. This gritty, blue-collar section of Queens was nothing like Greenville.

Luke's mind was spinning in all directions. He was nervous and insecure, yet excited about the people he had met in New York and the turn his life had taken.

He thought about his last meeting yesterday with the mysteri-ous man who had now become his employer. He recalled that when he asked this strange, dark man whom he had come to trust for the reason behind his assignment, he was told, "When you find the right woman, Luke, you'll do things, things you might not have done before. Someday, you'll understand what *obsession* means."

As he scanned the dining area, Luke recognized Alex Nicholas seated at a table twenty feet away, and a woman was sitting opposite him. Luke could only see her from the back, but his eyes caught a glimpse of her long black hair and well-formed bare shoulders. She worked out, he thought. Any other time, he would have just stared at those shoulders until someone gave him a dirty look or the guy with her hit him hard in the face.

He felt sick. Everything was moving too fast. His heart was racing, and he needed to sit down quickly to steady his shaking legs.

"What'll ya have, buddy?" asked the bartender. It sounded like an echo to Luke. He was facing away from the bar, taking in the room, stealing a quick glance at Alex's table in the process.

Luke checked his back right pants pocket and could feel the reassuring bulge of his wallet. *For the first time I have real money,* he thought. *I've got a fucking job.* He felt a rush of excitement, of energy, like a drug racing through his entire body.

He heard the bartender saying, "Hey, fella," then felt the room closing in on him and sensed faces turning his way. He didn't want to answer, didn't want anyone to hear his voice, his slow southern drawl. Luke looked around. In the periphery of his vision, he could see patrons going about their business, apparently oblivious to his presence. Maybe everyone wasn't watching him after all.

His cell phone was ringing. He opened it and placed it to his ear. The waiting bartender turned away, rolling his eyes. Luke whispered into the phone, "I'm here, at the bar."

"Is he there?" said the voice on the other end of the line.

"Yes, sir. He's having his supper," Luke said, glancing again at Alex and then quickly gazing off in the other direction.

"Luke, we call it dinner here but don't worry about that now. Just do your job. Then, you'll be able to take care of your obligations, and you won't have to worry anymore. Everyone will be proud of you. You'll have work, and you'll have money. Hey, then maybe we'll even find you a girl. I got one in mind for you; she'll even let you use her service elevator. Ha. You understand what I'm saying, Luke?"

"Not exactly. She lives in a high-class building, I guess."

"Oh, Christ. No, it's a type of sex. Never mind, kid. Just get your work done and call me when you're on your way home. I'll teach you everything you need to know."

Luke turned back to face the bar as he imagined having sex in an elevator. Then he caught the attention of the bartender and ordered a Budweiser.

The bartender took a long look at Luke and said, "I gotta see some ID."

Chapter 4

Whitestone, Queens, New York
6:15 p.m.

Alex always enjoyed getting his brother on the phone, finding him wherever he was in the world and, however briefly, connecting with him. But tonight he had even more reason to find him.

Alex looked at his watch and then to Maria. "Speaking of Michael, I need to call him tonight before it gets too late. I think he's in Paris."

Alex followed Michael's pursuits and was proud of his brother's achievements. He admired his ability to navigate a world that Alex had only ever seen from the outside. At times, Alex even yearned to live Michael's life. He was certain the feeling wasn't mutual.

Alex was anxious to share his discovery with his brother, but he knew it couldn't be tonight, in front of Maria. In fact, he thought, it was something he had to do face-to-face so Michael could see it with his own eyes. But he could drop a hint, and tonight he would do just that. He had already set in motion a series of other messages to Michael; he knew he was teasing him, but he also needed to ensure that Michael would find Alex's secret should something occur before he had a chance to show it to him.

Almost as an aside, Alex continued speaking while turning on his cell phone and waiting for the indication that he could begin dialing. "We're different. Same fuckin' parents and all, but he's more of a loner, more introverted. He loves books ... He's strange that way. Our whole family would be playing poker or whatever, and Michael would be in his room, reading."

Maria gave a sympathetic smile. "You know, Alex, that's not so odd. He's just different than you that way."

"It's not just that. Listen, I love him, but he's always stayed away from a lot of our family and even some of the friends we both grew up with. These people all ask me about him. 'How's Michael? Where's Michael?' I think some of them follow him through me. I tell them, 'Listen, I don't see him that often myself.' He's a good guy, but I've never been able to really figure him out."

Maria appeared puzzled. "But anytime I've been around him here, he's always very nice, very sociable. He couldn't be that introverted or a loner if he runs a major corporation."

Alex shrugged. He knew Maria was right, but for him, it didn't change the mystery of his brother's personality, a mystery that only those closest to Michael could see.

As Alex looked around the room, that uneasy feeling that someone was watching him returned, despite the otherwise secure sensation he had from being in the familiar confines of his regular hangout.

With his cell phone pressed tightly against his ear, he waited anxiously for Michael to answer. He wondered what the time difference was between Queens and Paris and then felt a flush of relief when he heard his brother's voice.

"Hi, Alex," Michael answered. "For you to be calling at this hour, either the Yankees signed a big free agent or some old ballplayer died." Alex chuckled, remembering that Michael was critical of his habit of forwarding the e-mail link to the obituary as soon as any celebrity or sports figure died.

"Michael, first of all, I'm surprised you're awake. It's good to hear your voice. Maria here wants to know where the fuck you are now. I think she likes you." Alex laughed and looked at Maria. "Are you in France again? What the hell do you do there all the time? Your wife must do all the talking; you can't speak French. Of course, she does all the talking anyway."

"Never mind *my* wife, I'm trying to figure out why you never marry the women you seem to enjoy being out with." From the noise in the background and the tone of his brother's voice, Alex could tell that Michael was enjoying himself.

Alex's voice shifted to a near whisper. "Listen, Michael, when the hell are you coming home? There's something I have to show you. I can't talk about it on this fuckin' phone. You won't believe it though."

As he waited to hear Michael's reaction, Alex's gaze shifted from the outline of Maria's breast, visible through her sweater, to what was at first just a blur of movement coming from over Maria's left shoulder in the bar, maybe fifty feet away. He saw the skinny young man with the Mets cap who seemed to be staring, eyes unnaturally wide, right at him.

Something was wrong, very wrong. His mind raced, trying to locate or identify the tormented face he realized was focused on him. He flipped through a virtual filing cabinet of acquaintances, enemies, people he might have crossed, guys who owed him money—but nothing registered. He quickly looked behind him to see if maybe this kid was focused on someone else, but no one was back there. No, this crazed kid was coming at *him*.

Alex had been in many fights over the years, although not in the last ten or even twenty. Still, he felt he could hold the kid off until the crowd at Grimaldi's, many of whom knew Alex, could overtake him.

He heard Michael's voice on the phone, his mind now relegating the conversation to the background. "Alex, I can't really hear you."

Alex saw the stranger pull the gun from his coat pocket. Well, this would be different from any fight he'd ever had.

Clear and defined as if a spotlight had been shining on it, Alex saw the bright silver barrel and the opening from which would come the bullets he knew would end his life. His mind went into slow motion.

In a succession of helter-skelter images, Alex watched the highlights of his life flash before him: his parents; the Dodgers baseball camp in Vero Beach; his first car, the blue Buick convertible; the Tudor-style home he grew up in; his first, second, and third wives; a well-worn Rawlings infielder's glove; his laptop computer; flashing images of the day's pending bets; his son, George, and grandson, Pete. He wondered what would become of them. He saw his current wife, Donna, and a series of his friends and wondered if she would wind up marrying one of them when he was gone.

It was strange, he thought, there was still so much time left. He remembered hearing about how time stood still in a dying person's final moments. And so it seemed now. He looked into the young stranger's eyes. "What the fuck do you want?"

But the kid said nothing. He was closing the gap between them rapidly. Now, Alex knew, there was little time.

"Shit."

He thought of trying to lift the table over him for protection, but he knew it was too late, and even as he calculated his chances, he worried about injuring Maria if he threw over the heavy table toward her. He knew that was an odd concern, considering the circumstances. Maybe he was a nice guy, as she said. His eyes darted toward Maria who had only just sensed his distraction. She turned around, seeing the stranger close in. She screamed.

Alex could still hear the tinny voice of Michael on his cell but dropped the phone as he saw the skinny young man approach.

Why? What did I do? Who did I piss off? He was trapped, wedged in between the table and the wall behind him. There was no room. There was no time.

In those final seconds, he thought of the secret he had not had a chance to tell Michael. It was too late now, he realized, but Michael would find it. Michael was smart; he would figure it out. Michael would find him.

Chapter 5

Whitestone, Queens, New York
November 4, 2009

Greek churches are designed to make you feel like you're in God's waiting room.

It begins as soon as you enter, with the musky smell of incense; the feel of the red velvet cushions on the hard, varnished dark wood pews; and the larger-than-life ancient icons of Jesus and all the saints gazing out at the mortal world. With its Byzantine architecture, monumental stained-glass windows, and ever-present gold religious statues, the Greek Orthodox church on a quiet Queens street provided an unlikely backdrop for Alex's polished mahogany casket, the center of everyone's attention.

"Alex is on his way to heaven," proclaimed the large, bearded, and gloriously robed Father Papadopoulos near the end of his eulogy. Many of Alex's friends and loved ones sitting in the pews were not so sure.

"Did we walk in on the right funeral?" asked Lester Fink, also known as Skinny Lester.

"Alex's having a fuckin' shit right now listening to this crap," said his cousin, Fat Lester, also known as Lester Fink (but only on his driver's license). Skinny Lester and Fat Lester had known Alex since they were all kids growing up in Queens and were loyal employees of his betting and loan-sharking business. Despite his tough-guy demeanor, Alex had always taken care of his friends and employees.

In his midfifties like his cousin, Skinny Lester was tall and lean, with a former college basketball player's frame and the look of someone who struggled to fill out his clothes. He wore a dark brown suit under his tan overcoat, both of which seemed to hang loosely on him.

Fat Lester was five foot six and weighed nearly three hundred pounds. Unlike his cousin, he appeared to be bursting out of his unfashionably wide-lapelled sport coat. The sleeves were two inches too short, and the coat had not been buttoned in the last decade. But Fat Lester's girth had provided Alex with at least the appearance of a physical enforcement threat for those clients who might be delayed in paying their debts.

"I can't believe he's in that box," said Fat Lester. He eyed the casket with his typical sense of suspicion and doubt about anything beyond the daily observable and routine activities of his unconventional life, including eating, drinking, occasional cocaine, and collecting the betting slips from drops across New York City. "I'm just waiting for him to put his fuckin' leg through the fuckin' lid and then get up and look at us like we're nuts sitting here."

"Les, if we don't figure something out pretty quick, we're goin' to be in the same box," Skinny Lester whispered to his cousin.

"What do you mean, the same box? How we goin' to be in the same fuckin' box? We couldn't fit even if we wanted to, and I don't."

"Asshole, I don't mean literally. I'm saying that we got some clients that are looking to get paid. The big one being Mr. Sharkey. We've got no money to pay anyone. Alex had all the receipts, and I don't know where all the fuckin' cash is now. The ones that owe Alex money don't give a shit. But Alex owes Sharkey seven hundred grand. He's going to be looking at us."

"Holy shit," groaned Fat Lester, gazing toward the cross above the altar, as though the Crucifixion had finally become real to him and the heavens suddenly seemed within reach.

"We have to talk to someone. I don't know if it's Donna. I mean, she's a widow now, for Christ's sake. Maybe Michael," Skinny Lester said. "We've known Michael since he was a kid, but he's never had anything to do with the business. I don't know how much Donna knows."

"Alex always said that Donna didn't know shit."

"Well, someone's got to know something because there's got to be at least a few million that Alex has stashed somewhere. Some of that was for Alex. Some of it's to pay off in case anyone hit big," Skinny Lester said.

"Jesus, I'm going to get an ulcer from this shit," Fat Lester said, breathing heavily now. "I got that pain in my stomach again, and I got a bad taste in my mouth, like that acid coming back up."

Skinny Lester thought about Michael. The last time he'd seen him was ten years ago at a birthday party for Alex when Michael made one of his rare appearances. All he knew about him now was that he was very successful, traveled a lot, and had a nice family. Despite the awkward timing, he knew that he would have to at least let Michael or Donna know today that they needed to talk about Alex's affairs.

Skinny Lester could hear the growing stress in his cousin's voice; he knew he needed to reassure him, despite his own nervousness. "Relax, Les. I'll take care of it."

"Take care of it. How the fuck are you going to take care of it?" Fat Lester said, a bit too loud. Several heads turned their way.

"I have a plan." Despite his reassuring words, Skinny Lester knew he had no plan, except that they had to locate Alex's cash so they could settle the accounts. "I just wish I could talk to Alex one last time." But as he sat back in the pew, he thought about that night several months ago, drinking with Alex in his den, and the strange thing that Alex had showed him. It was a scene he hadn't been able to get out of his head since then.

Chapter 6

Alex's immediate family filled the first two rows of pews. On the left side, facing the altar, Michael sat with his wife, Samantha, and their nineteen-year-old daughter, Sofia, who had just flown in from college at Notre Dame.

Directly across in the front right row were three women, all of whom had been married to Alex. On another occasion when all three of his wives were together, Alex referred to them as "Murderers' Row," a reference to the hard-hitting New York Yankees lineups of the twenties.

Seated first, on the end, was Alex's current wife, Donna, who was thirty-five with long, straight black hair. She was a well-built woman with firm, prominent, and expertly stylized silicone breasts that were spilling out of the top of her short black dress. A shapely yet slim pair of legs showed underneath dark black stockings. Donna was followed by Alex's two former wives, both of whom would fit the exact same description as Donna's with the exception of their ages. Greta was forty-six, and Pam was fifty-four. All three were scented with the same fragrance—Alex's favorite, Chanel No. 5—and all three were devoted clients of Dr. Armando Simonetti, a prominent Park Avenue plastic surgeon. And all three loved—and hated—Alex. Somehow, these were not mutually exclusive passions where Alex was intimately involved.

Next to Alex's second wife, Greta, sat his only son, George. At twenty-three, he was a large, hulking presence, underdressed as always in a black-and-silver heavy-metal-themed sweatshirt barely concealed by his dark green, ill-fitting sport jacket. His black wavy hair and a ponytail gave him a Christ-on-steroids appearance. Next to George was his own son, Alex's only grandchild, Pete, a five-year-old seemingly oblivious to his immediate surroundings and circumstances, if not the entire planet, while glued to his electronic game.

Suddenly feeling his BlackBerry vibrating, Michael reluctantly reached into his pocket for it, catching Samantha's attention.

"Jesus, Michael, put that thing away. It's a funeral, for God's sake," she whispered.

Michael looked pained. "I know, but this is crazy. Someone just sent me Alex's picture."

"Alex's? Well, that's nice," she said.

"I'm not sure. This is more strange than nice."

"What do you mean? What's wrong?" Samantha now turned toward Michael.

"Well, the picture is okay. It's just Alex behind his desk, in his den."

"So, what's wrong?"

"There's a quote or some saying, underneath the picture." Michael was straining to read the small print without attracting the attention of the others in the pews.

"What does it say?" Samantha asked.

"It says, 'Life is a dream, and death is waking up.'"

Samantha turned back, an expression of confusion on her face. "That is so odd. Who would send something like that?"

"I have no idea. I don't recognize the sender's e-mail address." But as Michael continued to stare at the small screen, the e-mail began to dissolve until it disappeared. The screen went blank. He clicked onto "Recently Deleted" mail, but there was no sign of it there either. "That's strange. It's gone now. It just disintegrated right on the screen."

"Michael, are you sure it was there in the first place?"

"Yes, of course. But I can't imagine who would have sent it."

Just before turning her attention back to the altar, Samantha smiled and said, "Maybe Alex did." Michael nodded and, perplexed, stared ahead at his brother's coffin.

The pews behind him were packed with a broad assortment of cousins, nieces, nephews, Alex's devoted employees, and a colorful spectacle of his "business associates," most of whom appeared to be genuinely saddened by Alex's death. Michael could hear the low murmurs of grief and an occasional sob coming from a group of women sitting behind him; an unknown hand had given him a sympathetic pat on the back as he'd entered the church.

As Michael watched and listened, his mind sped back to the years when he and his brother were home and very young. He wondered if Alex had been happy or at least content with the life he had lived. He tried to imagine how things might have been different if Alex had married a different woman—or different *women*. Or, Michael thought, was he simply projecting his own preferences and prejudices onto his brother, who was clearly different than he was?

Nevertheless, he was intent on *not doing* what he believed most people did at funerals: flashing back through one's memory of the person inside the casket. For, despite the day-to-day distance he had kept from his brother, the memories would be too painful to relive now. But, as he always did at funerals, even as a child, he couldn't help asking himself as he looked at the casket, *Where is this person now?*

Michael always believed, from too early an age, that one's whole life was almost irrelevant without the answer to that question. Too much of life, he thought, was simply a race to a finish line with no clue as to where that line was or what was on the other side of the tape.

All this uncertainty was likely the source of that persistent feeling of angst that he had; that shadowy fear of something he couldn't put his finger on. But he knew what it was. It was his inability to juxtapose this beautiful life with eternal extinction. What was the point of a great dinner in Paris with people you loved, when you were all going to wind up in a box? How strange that all the buildings and houses would still be standing, yet everyone who ever breathed would be gone.

Michael was awakened from his nightmare by Samantha's gentle tap on his arm; it was time to file by the casket and leave the church. The Greek custom was for the casket to remain open during the funeral service at the church and then, in full view of all the mourners, for it to be shut—forever—at the conclusion of the service. Michael always felt this was undue torture for those left behind, but perhaps it allowed the deceased a final view of everyone in attendance. Fortunately, Michael thought, his brother's casket was closed. Alex never cared much about traditions or customs.

As they began their exit, Michael took his sister-in-law's arm. "Michael, I need your help," Donna whispered. "I need to speak with you alone. Please. You have no idea how important it is."

"Okay, don't worry, Donna. Let's talk while we're at the wake after the burial. We'll just find a quiet table at Grimaldi's away from everyone for a few minutes."

As Michael approached the church's door, Greta Garbone, Alex's second wife, caught his arm. He turned around and looked closely at her. Her hair was disheveled and her blue eyes appeared to be bloodshot. She seemed unsteady. Michael was unsure whether she was gripping his arm to catch his attention or to keep her balance. Despite moving to within inches of his face, she was nearly screaming.

"You got my name wrong in the obituary." Her words were slightly slurred.

Michael could feel Samantha pulling on his other arm, trying to keep him moving toward the doors, but Greta's grip only tightened. He turned to face her. "Whatever happened to 'I'm sorry for your loss'?" he said softly.

"*Your* loss? Where the hell were you all those years? And I read the fucking obituary, Michael; you know my name's Greta, not Rosemary. You did it intentionally." Greta's face was red, twisted. In fact, Rosemary Garbone had changed her name to Greta just before marrying Alex, figuring it was a better stage name and assuming that Alex would bankroll her into a career as an actress.

"Greta, I didn't write the obituary. I never even saw it. I don't care about obituaries, they're all too late, if you know what I mean." He knew she didn't.

Greta's face came even closer. "I'm only sorry his fucking casket was closed. I wanted to see him dead. I wanted to see the last look on his face, the one when he knew he was going to die."

Samantha, watching the exchange, pulled Michael more firmly now. "Ignore her, Michael; she's crazy and drunk. Come on, please."

Michael moved away, hoping that Greta would release her hand from his arm. But as he moved in the opposite direction, she tightened her grip again, forcing him back toward her and now catching the attention of the surrounding mourners.

"Your brother used me. He wouldn't go to LA; he wouldn't leave fucking Queens—and then he dumped me for Donna."

Michael knew the story differently. As he watched his nephew, George, pushing through the crowd around them to rescue his mother from her tirade, Michael thought about Alex's distress when Greta left him for the lure of a Las Vegas magician whom she believed had Hollywood connections.

A teary-eyed George Nicholas finally reached his mother, pulling her away from Michael and off to the side of the church. "Mom, what are you doing? Let's go."

But Greta Garbone wasn't quite finished. "You're no better than your brother," she called out in Michael's direction, her words echoing off the marble floors and stone walls, as all eyes inside the church now followed her. "And if you'd spent any time with him at all you'd know he didn't want to be in any goddamned church—"

Sounds of *shh* and assorted protestations swept through the crowd.

Her son pulled harder, almost lifting her off her feet. "Let's go. Please, Mom, stop."

But as George led her toward a side exit, Michael thought he heard Greta say to George, "I want you to go to Donna and find—" But he couldn't hear the rest and wasn't even sure that what he thought he heard was what she said. Nevertheless, as he exited the church and squinted at the afternoon sunlight, he wondered what it was that was so important for Greta to find that she had asked her son to talk to Donna after years of acrimony and resentment.

Michael turned around to accompany Samantha and Sofia for the walk out of the church, and to observe the somber scene of the hearse and the black limousines waiting to take them to the cemetery.

But Donna, who had been separated from him in the progression, suddenly appeared by his side. She gently touched his shoulder, and pulling closer, whispered in his ear, "Michael, just be careful."

As he proceeded down the church steps outside, thinking about Donna's words, he noticed the license plate of the hearse carrying Alex's body. It read, "Rest in Peace." And, knowing his brother, he found that highly doubtful.

Chapter 7

"I'm not sure which is worse, a funeral or a wake," Samantha whispered to Michael as he clutched her hand.

"I guess that depends on whether you're the one who was just buried," Michael answered wryly, "in which case, you only get to go to the funeral."

"Michael, I hate it when you get flip at times like these. Sometimes I think you just use your slightly sarcastic sense of humor as a shield."

"You're right, I know. I will miss him—I'll miss him a lot. He would have done anything for me. We grew up with the same parents, in the same house, and yet we were so different. He tried to get closer with me. I know he was disappointed that I wouldn't bring us all over to his house for every holiday. But I just didn't want to go there. It was all too different, beginning with his wives and their families. I didn't enjoy myself, and I knew neither you nor Sofia would either. I don't know, over the years we drifted away ... yet, I thought of him all the time."

"You loved him as best you could, Michael. Life isn't perfect. You were a good brother to him, and you were there when he needed you, even if we didn't spend our Christmas dinners together."

Donna and Michael had arranged with Maria to take over Alex's former restaurant for his wake immediately following the funeral. As they all entered Grimaldi's, Michael thought of the happy times right after his brother purchased the restaurant and the many dinners he shared there with Alex and their parents. He recalled his father half-jokingly asking Alex why he opened an Italian restaurant instead of a Greek one. Michael had only been to Grimaldi's a few times since his brother had sold the restaurant to Maria. Each time he met Alex there for dinner, Maria would join them at their table for cocktails. Michael understood again why Alex found her so alluring.

Oddly, Michael thought, he could understand his brother's attraction to most of the women in his orbit—except his three wives.

As soon as Michael and Samantha walked in the door at Grimaldi's, followed closely behind by the two Lesters and Donna, Maria ran from behind the bar to greet Michael. She embraced him warmly. "Oh Michael, it's a sad occasion, but it is so good to see you." She hugged Samantha and greeted both Lesters with a hug and a kiss on the cheek.

Michael noticed that her greeting to Donna was much cooler. Clearly, there was no love lost between the two women. Michael instantly realized why Donna had said she would have preferred the wake to be at another restaurant. He speculated that Maria had probably felt that Donna was not a good wife to Alex. Alex, as a form of psychological torture, played mind games with his wife and enjoyed leading her to believe, incorrectly, that he had slept with Maria.

"Samantha, please excuse me for a few minutes," Michael said. "Donna asked me to speak with her privately. Maria, do you think you could get us a small table away from the crowd for just a few minutes?"

Maria showed Michael and Donna to a table hidden from the collection of strangely festive mourners. She appeared to carefully avoid the table that Michael knew had always been Alex's favorite.

Now unset and the only table with a "Reserved" sign on it, Michael assumed it was where Maria had sat with Alex when he was shot. He tried to imagine the scene that night before forcing himself back to the present.

Once they were seated, Donna appeared to relax. Michael struggled to ignore the images he was still constructing in his mind of his brother's final moments, while fighting the urge to glance again at the table, just a few feet away.

"You're so lucky, Michael. Besides being a beautiful woman, Samantha is just so sensitive. I mean, she is really a nice lady. I wish I could be that nice—I'm just not." Michael sensed a certain refreshing honesty in Donna; she wasn't apologizing, just stating a fact.

"Listen," Michael interjected, trying to keep the conversation from getting too emotional or psychological. "Alex wouldn't have been attracted to you if you were all that sweet. And you would have never been attracted to him if you were all that sensitive. So, you two were a great match."

Donna, appearing suddenly distracted, glanced at her gold-and-diamond-studded Rolex watch. "Michael, I'm sorry, but I just need to make a quick call, and I know my cell's battery is dead. Can I borrow your cell for a minute? I'll just run out to the ladies' room where it's quieter."

"Sure," Michael said without thinking. Donna thanked him and vanished for a few minutes.

"Everything all right?" Michael asked her when she returned with his phone.

"Oh, fine, fine," Donna said, quickly downing a double shot of Grey Goose vodka. Likewise, Michael finished his martini uncharacteristically quickly, waiting for the effects of the drinks to work their magic and loosen up the evening and the conversation.

"Alex loved you—you know that, don't you, Michael?"

"I do, and I loved him."

"He was never quite sure of that," Donna said.

31

"I know. I always kept some distance." Michael was feeling almost apologetic. He remembered the times his brother and parents would try to bring them all closer together, but Michael always resisted. He wanted to go his own way. He also knew the two worlds they lived in could not mix easily.

"Listen, Donna. It's complicated. My brother and I were different in some obvious ways. I couldn't do what I do and earn a living if I mixed at all in Alex's world. Have you ever seen the security and background clearance you have to go through today to be a senior executive for one of these companies? It takes weeks to do. They actually look at every place you've ever lived, every driver's license you've ever had; they check court records. It's crazy."

"Michael, no offense, but the people you hang out with are bigger crooks than Alex's gang. It's just not the type of shit that shows up on background checks."

The drinks were kicking in. Michael laughed knowingly. "I forgot how crazy—but good and honest—you were, Donna."

"He was proud of you. I think, on one level, he admired your family life and he always bragged to his cronies about how well you were doing. You know, the CEO thing and all that." Michael felt that Donna meant this, but he sensed she also needed to say something to soften what she had just said in case she had offended him. "It was something Alex knew he could never do. It just wasn't in him."

"Donna, when we were leaving the church earlier you said, 'Be careful.' What did you mean by that?" Michael asked, looking right into Donna's eyes.

"Listen, Alex was not one to tell his wife everything. But I know he was worried. First, he had some guys trying to take a cut of his business. I don't remember how much they wanted, but Alex said they approached him back in September and wanted either some big payment up front or something every month."

"How did Alex react?"

"You know your brother. He told them to go fuck themselves. He told me they just looked like a bunch of kids, and he wasn't about to just start paying them his hard-earned money."

"Could one of those kids have been that guy Luke who shot him?"

"I don't know because I never saw any of these people. Alex only said that they were Italian and then he said maybe Portuguese. You know your brother; he was never good with accents, let alone languages." As she spoke, Donna's eyes darted around the room watching the parade of friends and acquaintances in the restaurant behind Michael. It was a practice that had annoyed Michael in the past. He remembered it now.

"The police think this Luke guy was just a punk who needed money, and someone paid him to kill Alex. He couldn't have been the brightest crayon in the box to have shot Alex in Grimaldi's with all those off-duty cops around. Many of those guys were Alex's friends—they shot that kid like fifteen times. He's dead, but finding who hired him might be impossible now. I don't think the police have any real clues."

Donna paused to reach for her glass, realized it was empty, and took a deep breath before continuing. "Michael, I know you can't get in the middle of all this now, but I have no one else to turn to. George certainly can't handle this. Alex always said his son just had no touch for the business. Plus, he's only twenty-three, for Christ's sake."

"And you think I do?" asked Michael, almost laughing but at the same time feeling a deep sense of doom approaching.

"I know this is ridiculous but, yes, I do. Who else can I possibly turn to? Also, there's more. Skinny Lester just cornered me at the cemetery—he's so nervous he couldn't wait until the dirt even settled on the damned casket. Alex owes one of the bettors seven hundred thousand dollars!"

"You've got to be kidding." Michael began to sink deeper into his seat.

"It's not as bad as it sounds, Michael." Donna began to lay out the pressing issues confronting Alex's business. "Alex has people who owe him money. From what Lester told me, he has about half a million out there that is owed to him right now. Some of these people will pay Lester out of loyalty to Alex. Some won't pay anything until they see someone with some presence who makes them understand that the debt still has to be paid, Alex or no Alex."

"Well, that at least closes some of the financial gap," Michael said, partially relieved since he suspected that Donna was going to ask him to help pay the seven hundred thousand dollars in order to keep everyone safe from harm. At least the gap now appeared to be only two hundred thousand dollars. But Donna's expression about the need for "someone with some presence" was giving Michael an instant migraine. His throat was tightening and a familiar pain deep down in his stomach began to assert itself.

"Michael, relax. It gets better."

Michael couldn't read Donna well enough to know whether that was a joke or whether there really was good news to follow. He suspected the former.

"Alex had, but now *we* have plenty of money. I think there are millions stashed away."

"You think? Or you know?"

"I know," Donna answered quietly.

"Well, that's a relief. At least we—or you—don't have to worry about money," said Michael, almost able to exhale.

Donna repeated her point. "I know there's plenty of money. I just don't know where it is."

"Oh, Christ. Then who does?" Michael said.

"Only Alex, I think." Donna smiled and took a healthy sip from another vodka, which Maria had replenished.

Michael looked around at the restaurant, partly to relieve the pressure from the intensity of their conversation. As he did, he realized that many of the men were eyeing Donna with a look of lust that certain women inspire, if not command. She had a presence and the rare ability to look sultry and sensual in mourning. Her short black dress and dark stockings barely concealed the tan legs that Michael knew were carefully nurtured recently under the Miami sun. She showed just enough cleavage to ensure attention—too much, perhaps, for such a recent widow. Michael's mind, he realized, had wandered too far.

"You must have some idea, Donna. How about the Lesters or George?"

"No way. Alex was always afraid someone would beat it out of them. He loved both Lesters, but he knew neither of them could stand up to too much pressure. He certainly loved George, but he wanted to be sure his mother never got her hands on any more of his money than she got out of the divorce."

"Where do we start?" As soon as the words left his mouth, Michael wished he could take them back. He realized he'd said "we" instead of "you." He also knew it was too late. The life that he so carefully insulated from Alex's was about to be merged.

"I'd like both of us to talk with your old friend Russell," Donna answered. Russell Munson was an old friend, originally of Michael's, since grade school. As was typical, Michael moved on and had almost no contact with Russell, while Alex and Russell became close friends. Russell was smart, a graduate of the exclusive Brooklyn Tech High School and City College. Like Alex, he wasn't interested in the traditional white-collar world, and he became a very talented carpenter and mason.

"How would Russell know?" asked Michael, trying to figure out the possible connections and implications.

"Alex would always have Russell do work in the house. I don't know for sure, but I remember years ago Alex told me that, before I knew him, he would hide money in the woodwork and drop-down ceiling of his apartment with Greta. Russell seemed to be doing a lot of work in our house, especially when I happened to be down in Florida and Alex was home alone."

"Do you need me to speak with Russell?" asked Michael, beginning to look for what was known in his world as an exit strategy.

"Michael, Russell trusts you. Someone has to deal with Fat and Skinny Lester too. Not to mention the rest of his crew, probably twenty more guys. They're devastated and they don't know what the hell to do. And I need you now—just for a short time to unravel this whole thing … and to keep the family safe. That includes keeping you and your family safe too."

Michael knew that her words had made their intended impact. His head jolted back ever so slightly. He felt like he'd lost his focus momentarily as the realization of real danger to him and his own family sunk in. He could see Donna looking right into his eyes as though she was trying to look behind them, to see how much havoc she'd caused. He knew he needed to recover.

"Donna, everyone around Alex knows I've never been involved in his business."

"Some know. Some don't. Some don't care. In their world, Michael, you're family so you'd have to know. Whether you are or you aren't, they're going to assume you are. So whoever had your brother killed probably did it over money or something having to do with his business. These guys are going to figure you're brothers, you're tight, and you're involved."

She stopped, reached over, and gently placed her hand on top of his. It was a loving gesture from a hardened woman, making it so much more effective. "He loved you, Michael. He was hurt by your absence. Your mother and father would have wanted you to do this for him. They believed you did whatever was necessary for your family."

She knew how to manipulate men, Michael thought. After all, she'd had years of practice. A decade of dealing with Alex had made her capable of turning the less volatile, more even-tempered Michael into putty in her hands. He could feel her pulling him into her world.

"Just help me find Alex's money, let's pay off his debts, and then help Fat and Skinny Lester collect the money that people owed him. That's all I ask. Then you go back to Connecticut." *Donna makes it sound so simple,* he thought.

But Michael knew his life was about to change.

"The Lesters can hold on for a few days—but, please, I need you as soon as possible. This is for your brother, Michael."

Michael sighed, knowing he was about to make a mistake but unable to stop himself.

"Michael, it's for your brother, God rest his soul." Her words pierced the same opening in his chest through which her earlier carefully crafted approaches had already blazed a path.

Later that evening, Michael and Samantha finally left the restaurant arm in arm. Michael was checking his BlackBerry as they approached their car. Suddenly, he stopped in his tracks.

"What's wrong?" Samantha said, looking concerned.

"Oh, it's …" Michael stared blankly into space. "Someone sent me another celebrity obituary."

"Who sent it?"

Michael looked puzzled as he tried to reconcile what he was looking at on his BlackBerry screen. "How the hell should I know?"

"Well, what e-mail address is it from?"

"Jesus, it's from Alex's. I know that's not possible. Someone must have hacked his e-mail account."

Samantha moved closer to Michael. "Yes, but that's still very unusual, to say the least, that they would then be sending you an obituary for some famous person. I mean, hackers usually just send requests for money or offers for Canadian Viagra. They don't pick up where a dead account holder left off."

"I know; this makes no sense," Michael said. "It's like that message, the picture of Alex that I received on my phone during the funeral."

"Michael, I was thinking … since Alex was sending all those obituaries, do you think there was something your brother wasn't telling you? I mean, could he have been ill?"

"I don't know. Just before it happened, he was acting a bit strange, like he was at the end of his life instead of in the prime of it. And I told you how the last few times we had dinner, he would keep mentioning our parents, and particularly their final days. It's like he'd become fixated on his own mortality."

"He'd never taken good care of himself. I know he quit smoking ten years ago, but he was a heavy smoker for so long. That, and all the liquor …" Michael's voice trailed off, as though he didn't want to complete his thought.

But Samantha filled the void. "Maybe it was just the type of life he lived—out all night, not sleeping much, not to mention the un-savory characters he associated with. My God, his work alone had to fill him with stress."

It all rang true. Michael had been troubled by the increasingly somber, if not morbid tone of his brother's most recent communications. It was odd and disturbing, he thought. Yet Michael, at times, had the same troubling thoughts about mortality or, as he thought of it, the preciousness of time. But he generally kept them to himself. And he was sure that he could trace his issues to an event in his childhood, one that changed his perception of life.

Once inside their car, Michael started the engine, but before pulling out, he glanced again at his cell phone and then looked up with a puzzled expression.

"Is something else wrong?" Samantha asked.

"I don't know. When I was sitting with Donna, early in our conversation she said she had to make a call and that her phone was out of juice. It didn't seem spontaneous; it was as though she planned it purposely. She borrowed my cell and said she was going to the ladies' room to make an important call. But I just checked the call history, and it doesn't show that any calls were made."

"Maybe she changed her mind," Samantha said.

"I guess that's possible. She was gone quite a while though. She wanted my phone for a reason, and it obviously wasn't to make a phone call." Michael sat motionless in the driver's seat, staring out ahead at the darkness through the windshield.

"Well, what are you thinking?"

"I'm thinking that now I realize I never trusted her."

Chapter 8

Whitestone, Queens, New York
November 12, 2009

Michael felt a chill as he and Russell Munson entered his brother's den.

"This is like entering Cooperstown," Michael said to no one in particular as he examined Mickey Mantle's pin-striped Yankees uniform, framed in glass, hanging on the wall. Alex had taught young Michael to admire Mantle. In Michael's mind, it was his brother who had worn it instead of the legendary Mantle himself. *Now they're both gone,* he thought.

The large room was a shrine to American sports. Its custom cherry walls and shelves were filled from floor to ceiling with hundreds of glass-encased baseballs, autographed by virtually every modern-day New York Yankees baseball player. Framed photos of famous athletes lined the walls. Muhammad Ali's bright red boxing gloves, protected under glass, added an unexpected, violent splash of color in a room otherwise devoted to bygone events captured mostly in black and white.

"I can't believe Alex is gone." Russell was visibly upset as he gazed around the room in the den where he had spent many hours with Alex. He took a generous swig from the glass of scotch Donna had just brought him. "Remember when he coached our team, the Flushing Royals? He was a pisser."

"I know," said Michael. "You were a great friend to him. Alex was one of a kind. We all go way back. Those were good times, so innocent."

"On the phone, Donna asked about all the work I did in the house for Alex. I wasn't sure whether you guys knew what it was all about or not. I was going to wait a few days and ask whether you wanted to know about what Alex had me do for him."

"Thanks, Russell," Michael said. "The truth is we don't know very much. You can help us."

"Listen, I don't know what's in those secret places I built for Alex—but I know where they all are." Russell continued, "I did some interesting things for him. I know Alex would want you two to know now. I'll fill you in on everything."

Michael wondered what *everything* might be but decided not to ask any questions until tonight when he hoped to speak with him in private at some point.

"Thanks, Russell." Donna kissed Russell on the cheek. "You were always there for Alex when he needed you."

"We suspect Alex hid cash in the special places you built. We don't have any idea how much. Hopefully, it's a lot. If there's anything Donna or I can do for you or your family, we'd be happy …" Michael was searching for the right words to show his appreciation; then Russell interrupted the awkward moment.

"I don't want anything. You know I wouldn't take anything for this. It's just the right thing. You guys know I don't give a shit about money. Uh, maybe a case of Bud. That would be great."

Michael remembered what a great friend Russell had been to him so many years ago. Russell was always a different breed; he never cared what people thought, was tough as nails, and had a big heart.

"Okay, when can we start?" asked Donna.

"I need to get to a job I'm committed to finishing this afternoon a few blocks from here. How about if I come back here with my tools after dinner, around eight thirty tonight? I can show you where all the compartments are and open them enough so it'll be easy for you guys to open them all the way and get whatever's inside. I don't want to see what's in them."

"Russell," said Michael, "that's terrific. We'll see you at eight thirty. I'll have the case of Bud for you."

Michael had never seen Alex's business office. Above the Mediterranean Delicatessen on Northern Boulevard in Flushing, Queens, it looked like any other small-time accountant or insurance office from the outside.

Inside were two rooms. The larger room was set up with three identical large flat-screen televisions hanging from the ceiling; ten desks, each with multiline black phone consoles; and several chairs scattered around the desks and randomly placed throughout the room.

Alex's private office was in the second room, behind a simple hollow wooden door. Inside, Alex had Russell custom build an ornate wet bar, which, at the touch of a button located within easy reach from Alex's seat, would miraculously rise out of a wooden cabinet, showcasing a very respectable selection of scotch, whiskey, vodka, gin, and rum brands along with the usual necessary bar glasses and accessories. Alex's desk had a twenty-button phone console; a computer; a framed photograph of his son, George, and grandson, Pete, in their season seats at Yankee Stadium; and a sheath of neatly stacked papers.

Alex was always neat and meticulous, Michael thought, and would have left his desk exactly this way even if he knew he would never return to it.

43

The blinds were drawn, the phones were silent, the television screens dark. Michael sat in his brother's chair behind the desk. Fat and Skinny Lester sat in what appeared to Michael to be their usual seats on the other side of the desk. Everything was as it used to be—except Alex was gone and Michael was in his seat.

The discussion had already lasted two hours. The first hour was spent with Skinny and Fat Lester telling old stories about Michael as a little kid, and newer recollections of Alex and his more colorful escapades.

As Michael listened, he realized that, for both Lesters, their daily lives revolved around working with and for Alex. Fat Lester played the role of tough "enforcer" while Skinny Lester was the "brains." Although Fat Lester had an unpolished exterior, he was, like his tall, slim, smarter cousin, truly a gentle soul underneath it all who would prefer never to harm anyone unless provoked.

Now Lester and Lester began to fill Michael in on the details of Alex's business.

"Michael," Skinny Lester began, "most of the money that's owed us seems to be coming in. I met with Ralph yesterday. He'll pay his twenty-three thousand this week. Steady Eddie is meeting me tonight. He's good for almost thirty grand. It's a little tough because they didn't figure on the game ending. You know, usually these guys roll over some of the bets and assume they'll make some of it back on next week's games, so they don't figure on paying everything off all at once with no chance to win it back. But most of them are okay. They liked Alex."

"Yeah, they know Alex couldn't help getting shot. I mean, like, it wasn't his idea. You know what I mean?" Fat Lester was obviously confident in his logic.

"But," interjected Skinny Lester, "a few big ones aren't paying."

"Who and how much?" Michael shot back. As he did, Michael felt a strange sensation, almost a sense of familiarity with the discussion, if not the approach and subject matter. It was a bit disconcerting. *How can this feel comfortable?* he asked himself. It was not that different, he reasoned, from a discussion he could have with his finance head or collections group back at Gibraltar.

"Johnny Rizzo—we call him 'the Nose'—owes about eighty grand. He's an asshole. He and Alex tangled a few times. Alex and I threatened him once when he claimed he hadn't put as much on a Giants game as we had him down for. He finally paid."

"How'd you threaten him?" Michael was waiting for this as he began to feel like he was now at least scratching the surface of his brother's business. Not much different, he thought, than when he stepped into a new, troubled company and had to quickly grasp the essence of the business, determine which executives he could trust, and then put a plan together to turn the situation around.

Fat Lester chuckled. "Your brother told him that I was going to waterboard him. Alex was funny. You know, he had just read about it or saw it in the news with those fuckin' terrorists. You know how we torture those creeps. I wasn't even sure what the hell he was talking about. But he tells Rizzo that if he doesn't pay that I'm going to put him under the sink or something. He tells him that I did it when I was in the service.

"I'm thinking, holy shit. I don't know about this shit; I don't know how to do it. But your brother stares this guy down. You know how when Alex got mad he looked fuckin' dangerous? Well, he scared the shit out of Rizzo. He did this in the fuckin' men's room of the Palm in the city. I said to him when we left, I said, 'Alex, you gotta tell me about this shit before you tell some guy I'm going to do it to him, because I don't really know this shit.'"

"What did Alex say?" Michael was glued to his seat.

"He said he didn't plan on saying it. It just came to his mind on the spot. He said don't worry, we'd figure it out if we had to. You know, just bang his head around a bit and then put his mouth under the sink for a while. Just scare the shit out of him if we had to."

"Did you ever really have to do any of this stuff to anyone?" Michael was worried about the answer.

The question appeared to take Fat Lester by surprise. His head twitched slightly like a dog does when it doesn't understand something. "You know, we never really did anything. Alex just scared people. We never had to do anything like that."

"Well, that's good, I guess." Michael was clearly relieved, actually feeling that tightness in his stomach loosen somewhat. But he could see the stress on Skinny Lester's face as he was about to speak.

"First of all, Michael, this guy—Mr. Sharkey—is waiting for me to tell him when he's going to get his seven hundred grand that he's up." That sense of relief that Michael felt began to quickly dissipate. "Also, whoever had Alex shot is still out there."

"Do you guys have any idea who it could have been?" asked Michael. "What about Rizzo or this Sharkey guy?"

"Rizzo's a former cop—crooked, but not a murderer. Plus, just a few weeks ago, he was up fifty grand himself," Skinny Lester said.

"And what about Sharkey?"

"No way," said Skinny Lester. "He knew Alex was good for the money. He'd be the last one to do it. Now he's gotta worry about how he gets paid."

"By the way," Fat Lester said, smiling, "open that top right drawer." He pointed to the desk drawer on Michael's right. "It may come in handy."

Michael feared he knew what he'd find as he slowly opened Alex's desk drawer. Nevertheless, seeing the .38-caliber pistol sent a shudder through his entire body.

"Jesus, Lester. What am I supposed to do with this?" Michael carefully closed the drawer.

"Your brother kept it just in case," Skinny Lester said almost apologetically.

"Is it registered?" Michael asked. Just as his intuition told him what was in the drawer, he also knew that it was highly unlikely that the weapon he was not about to pick up was registered with the New York City police department.

Neither Lester answered; both just gave him a quizzical look reflecting the absurdity of his question.

"I have to go, guys. I'm supposed to be at Alex's by eight thirty."
Michael was uneasy but didn't let it show.

His cell phone rang just as he was leaving. "Take Me Out to the
Ball Game," the ringtone Michael had assigned for Alex's calls.
Now, Michael thought, the ringtone was no longer cute, but bizarre. Donna must be using Alex's cell. He quickly flashed back to
the last time he heard that ring, when Alex called him in Paris,
minutes before the shots rang out.

He put the phone to his ear and heard Donna screaming, "Michael, oh my God. Oh my God. Where are you? Come right away,
please … It's Russell. He's dead."

Chapter 9

As Michael rushed in his car to Alex's house, he could see the flashing red-and-blue police lights from blocks away. Donna was hysterical on the phone and with good reason. Once Michael cleared through the initial police blockade, he was quickly waved into the house. Donna nearly collapsed in his arms when she saw him.

"I had just come home from shopping when I saw the front door partly open. I thought maybe you or Russell had gotten here early. I called out but no one answered, and then I saw him on the floor in the kitchen. They shot him with his own goddamned nail gun. Michael, the cops said he had at least thirty nails in him. They tortured him first, and then finished him with two in his head."

"But why?" Michael was trying to make sense of it. "What's going on?"

"Someone must have known that Russell knew where the money was. They were trying to get it out of him."

"But how could they have known that Russell knew about all this?" Michael wondered how someone else was putting all these pieces together. "Did they also know we were all going to meet tonight? I never even told the Lesters I was coming until I got up to leave."

"The police think whoever was here rushed out the back door when they saw me drive up the driveway. Maybe they figured he'd talk easily, and they could get in and out quickly," Donna said.

"Do you think they got him to talk? Is anything missing or ripped open?" Michael was scanning the immediate area to see if things were out of place, hoping he would not have to go into the kitchen, where he knew his old friend was still sprawled on the floor, pierced by multiple nails.

"I don't think so. Nothing seems out of place except the mess in the kitchen." Donna was clearly distraught, her eyes red and puffy, but she seemed to be gaining control over the trauma of finding Russell's body.

"Have the police questioned you?" Michael anticipated the complexity of the discussion that might take place once the police began asking questions. He knew Donna could not acknowledge that Russell was coming to the house to uncover the secret hiding places he had built for Alex to hide his cash.

"So far, they've only asked who Russell was and why he was in the house. I just said he was a close friend and frequently dropped by, and that the three of us were going to have a drink to reminisce about Alex. They also asked if I had any idea who may have killed him." Michael was impressed. Donna had explained Russell's presence with as much of the truth as possible without mentioning the lure of hidden cash.

"They don't suspect me, do they?" Donna asked.

"Right now, I'm sure they suspect everyone. You just have to stay away from any further questioning until a lawyer gets here. I called Larry Rothberg, my attorney. He's on his way. Then, we'll let him handle it and buy time. We need to talk this thing through."

Michael could see that he was no longer just an observer trying to clean up loose ends. He felt the sensation one gets when stepping over a threshold, one with no safety net and a life-threatening drop below.

"Michael, who's doing this? What's going on? I can't stay here."

He first thought he should take Donna up to his home in Connecticut but quickly came to his senses. "Don't worry. I'll get you a room in the city, at the Carlyle. You'll be safe there. I'll hire some security to guard the house and someone to guard you. Whoever is behind all this must be looking for Alex's cash."

"Well, that makes two—" Donna hesitated and locked eyes with Michael before continuing, "three of us."

Michael averted his gaze, as though trying to release himself from Donna's power. "But I don't understand why they needed to kill Alex to steal the money. And, what's most frightening, I don't know what danger we are in from these people."

Donna didn't appear to miss a beat. "I don't understand what's going on either, Michael, but I've been around enough to know it's just a matter of time before they get to us."

Chapter 10

Westport, Connecticut
November 12, 2009

Michael and Samantha's home was a forty-five-minute drive from Queens, over the Whitestone Bridge and then up the Connecticut coastline. Situated along Long Island Sound, Westport was a picturesque Connecticut town with one of those charming main streets filled with little shops and trendy restaurants.

Formerly the home of celebrities like Paul Newman and Martha Stewart, it was fast becoming a suburban hub of hedge-fund headquarters.

"You can spot them around town, the guys wearing baseball hats, blue jeans, and then custom shirts with their sleeves rolled up and thousand-dollar loafers," Michael would often comment.

The house was a large but unpretentious gray colonial behind a manicured lawn and near the water. It was only a five-minute drive to the beach. High, thick hedges concealed a lush private backyard and a swimming pool covered for the winter.

As Michael drove into his garage and entered his house, he had a sense of stepping from one life and into another, the process of disarming and then rearming the alarm system giving him permission to pass through. Yet he was no longer sure which one he was visiting and which one was home.

During his drive, he had begun to think more about Samantha and how she would feel about his involvement, however temporary, in Alex's business. He knew he had to bring Samantha up to date on a lot of what he had been doing the past few days. So far, he had been somewhat vague on many of the details. He hadn't mentioned Russell's murder to Samantha when they spoke on the phone earlier in the evening. He wondered whether that alone was some sort of transgression, a temporary breach of faith. He decided to tell her tonight, in person.

He knew the murder and its grizzly details would be like a stick of dynamite going off in her psyche. He wondered why it wasn't equally so for him. Samantha would be highly skeptical—if not petrified—of Michael's participation in a life he had so adamantly rejected for so long. He was too … or was he?

They had not made love since Paris, but as soon as Michael entered the bedroom and laid eyes on Samantha standing in the black, short sheer negligee she had purchased on the Rue Saint-Honoré, he knew that drought was about to end. The negligee fell to the floor as they collapsed into a passionate embrace. They were on the bed in less than a minute. As Michael watched her below him, he marveled that she could look so good at nearly fifty. But, as crazy as he knew it was, he struggled to stay in the moment and tried not to think about the conversation he knew they needed to have. It was over quickly, neither of them having the patience for leisurely lovemaking.

As Samantha began to cool off, she sat up in bed and pulled her beige cashmere Hermes throw over her shoulders and breasts. "I think we needed that."

Cautiously, Michael began to recount the last few days' events including the details of Russell's murder, Donna's earlier plea for Michael's help, and his reluctant consent to do so.

Samantha tilted her head slightly, her mouth dropping open. "Michael, are you out of your mind?"

Before Michael could formulate his response, he saw Samantha's eyes fixate on the alarm panel near the bed. The series of tiny red lights that indicated the system was armed had turned green.

"Michael, I thought you turned the alarm on when you came in."

"I did. Those lights were red a few minutes ago." Michael bolted out of bed, locked the bedroom door, and pushed a large, low dresser several feet so that the door couldn't be pushed open. In a series of visual flashbacks, he mentally retraced the brutal events of the past few days. "Call 9-1-1."

But just as Samantha picked up the phone to dial, it rang. Flustered in her attempt to dial out, she answered on instinct, "Hello, who is this?"

"Yes, Mrs. Nicholas, this is your alarm service. We understand there has been a breach. Is everything okay?" The voice was loud and deep; Michael could hear everything from where he stood.

"No, we're not okay. Send the police. Someone is in our house." Her voice was cracking.

"Don't worry, Mrs. Nicholas. We'll be upstairs to help you in just a minute." Michael could see that Samantha was momentarily comforted, but he then saw a look of confusion on her face.

"Michael, how did he know I was upstairs?"

Michael looked closer at the multiline phone. The numerous buttons and lights showed which telephone lines and extensions in the house were being utilized. A paralyzing chill darted up his spine. A red light was flashing, indicating that the telephone extension in the downstairs library was being utilized. The caller was inside the house.

Michael reached for his cell phone on the bureau near his bed. But before he could press in 9-1-1, a voice seemingly coming from in the bedroom stopped him in his tracks. "Don't touch that cell phone, Michael."

Samantha appeared to bolt upright. "Michael, it's the same guy I just heard on our phone. But where is this coming from?"

Before Michael could answer, the stranger spoke again. "I'm here with you."

Without moving from where he stood, Michael looked around, his eyes scanning the large bedroom. He looked at Samantha. "He's not here. There's no one here."

The voice echoed through the room again. "Oh, but you're wrong, Michael. I was here before you moved the furniture against the door. I didn't want to interrupt your screwing around." Michael again reached for his cell phone.

"If you want to die right now, go ahead and get your phone. By the way, Samantha, I just loved your little nightgown, although you look even better in that blanket."

Michael continued to look around the room, unable to find any-one—or anything—unusual. "What do you want? Who the hell are you? Where are you?"

"Where am I? I'm here, Michael. You can keep looking around, but you won't see me until it's too late. By the way, I enjoyed the show."

Michael rushed toward Samantha, taking her in his arms. She whispered closely into his ear, "What do we do?"

The phone rang again. They both stared at it, sitting on the table by their bed, the blinking red light indicating the incoming call. The first ring seemed to last forever. And again there was another red light glowing on the phone panel, indicating that someone was on another line in the house. But this time the call wasn't coming from the library downstairs. Michael stared in disbelief at the indi-cator light signifying "Guest Bedroom #1." The caller was on the second floor, in the room next door, just five feet away from their bedroom.

Michael whispered to Samantha, "But how can he see us in here?" He scanned the room again. Connecting to their huge bed-room was a large bathroom and two dressing rooms. The doors to each of those rooms were open. Four large windows were, as always, obscured by thick fabric drapes behind which were blackout shades. The lighting was soft, coming from the dimmed lamps on either side of their bed and from recessed spot lights, also dimmed, illuminating the several pieces of fine art, mostly fashion photographs, each framed in either black or silver, on each of the white walls.

"I don't see anyone here—unless they're hiding in the dressing rooms or the bathroom and peeking in," Michael said after checking one door after another, looking for movement or, worse, a pair of eyes staring back.

The distinct squeak of a turning brass door handle interrupted their hushed huddle. They both looked at the bedroom door. The shiny gold brass knob, just visible above the dresser, was turning back and forth. "I locked it, but that lock won't keep anyone out for long," Michael said. "It's just to keep little kids out."

"Oh my God, Michael. Do something, please."

"We've got to take a risk. I'm going for the cell." Michael broke away from Samantha and headed again toward the bureau where he had left his cell phone. But before he could reach it, all the lights went out. The room turned black. "He's cut the power."

As Michael groped in the sudden darkness to find his cell, the stranger's voice let out a piercing, horrific laugh. It reverberated through the room. Michael finally grasped his cell phone. It was then that he saw the unfamiliar tiny blue light near the floor at the other end of the room.

Chapter 11

Michael knew he had to call for help. As he dialed, he whispered into Samantha's ear, "Check out the little blue light near the bathroom door." The cell phone keyboard lit up as soon as he hit the 9.

But before Michael could finish dialing 9-1-1, the bedroom phone rang again.

Michael looked at Samantha. Finally, he checked the caller ID. "It's Fletcher!" he whispered to Samantha as he switched his cell into his left hand and picked up the receiver with his right. Fletcher Fanelli was a close friend and the police chief of Westport.

"I'm two minutes away, but we've already got three patrol cars approaching your house right now. Where exactly are you?"

Michael could hear the police sirens in the near distance, and soon the red-and-blue flashing lights were reflecting through the windows and partially opened curtains, creating a light show on the walls. He felt a flush of relief.

"Samantha and I are locked inside the master bedroom." Michael moved toward the other end of the room. "I'm looking out the front window. I see the patrol cars out front. But, Fletcher, someone's inside the house. He actually called us, first from the library downstairs and then from the bedroom right next to us here upstairs."

"Okay, Michael. Just stay where you are. Don't leave the bedroom. I'm on the radio with my men now. They're going to enter the house through your front and back doors. We've got officers all around the house. They know you're in the master. Just stay there. I'm pulling up to your street myself. Just don't leave the bedroom and don't open the door until I tell you to."

"Fletcher, there's something else—he spoke to us, from *inside* our bedroom."

"What do you mean, from inside your bedroom?"

"I don't know, Fletch. We could hear his voice like he was right here in the room. But I don't see anyone. The doors to the dressing room and the closet are open, but I haven't gone in there to look."

"Don't. Don't go into the closet or the dressing room. We'll do that. Stay put until I tell you otherwise."

"Fletcher, another thing." Michael looked again in the direction of the blue illumination. "There's a strange blue light, like an LED or laser or something. It's coming from the other side of the room. I didn't notice it until the power and the lights went out. It's very small. I haven't gone near it yet."

"Is it flashing?"

"No, it's a steady blue glow." Michael felt like he could read Fletcher's mind.

"Michael, is it ticking?"

"Jesus, Fletcher. No. There's no sound that I can hear from it. And there are no little digital numbers counting down, if that's what you mean."

"Okay, Michael, we're just turning down Imperial Road, we're a minute away."

It seemed like a very long minute before Michael could hear a commotion downstairs as half the Westport police force, led by Chief Fanelli, entered the house.

"Police! Don't move," the command repeated as officers moved throughout the house. The police radios were abuzz with chatter and static. Looking out the window, Michael saw the lights from the surrounding homes, one by one going on. He recognized several neighbors standing on their front porches. He realized too that this was the second police scene he had been in the middle of in less than four hours.

But as he retrieved his cell phone from the night table where he had left it, he noticed something unsettling: the screen was still lit up, indicating the last digits Michael had tapped in when he had begun dialing 9-1-1. And only a flashing 9 appeared.

"How did Fletcher know?" Michael said to Samantha.

"What do you mean?"

"How did Fletcher and the police know to come to the house?"

"You called him, didn't you? On your cell, I saw you."

"Samantha, the call never went through. I only got as far as the 9—see?" Michael watched as Samantha stared at his cell phone screen, the 9 blinking, a stark reminder of the unfinished call.

Chapter 12

Samantha was trembling. She looked stunned by what was happening but alert to every sound, her eyes darting from the blocked bedroom door to the opened doorways leading to the dressing room and closet. While keeping an eye on the strange blue light, Michael took her again in his arms. "Don't worry. The cops are here. Fletcher's here too."

"But, Michael, how did they find out? What's going on? I don't understand."

"We'll deal with that later. Right now, let's be thankful they're here." He handed Samantha her robe and put on his trousers and a sweater. "Come on, let's get dressed."

The bedroom lights came back on. Michael looked at the spot where the blue light had been. It was nearly impossible to see now. His cell phone rang. "Michael, it's Fletcher. We're outside your bedroom door."

"Did you find anyone in the house?" Michael asked anxiously.

"No, not yet anyway. You can open your door now. We're going to secure you guys and search the rooms off your bedroom—and check out that light. Samantha must be crazy in there."

Michael pushed aside the bureau as he unlocked and opened the door. Samantha, in tears, hugged Fletcher as four uniformed policemen with guns drawn walked swiftly by them and proceeded to check out the rooms off the bedroom.

"Oh my God, Fletcher. He was here, on the phone, in the house, and then … We heard his voice—and that laugh, that horrible laugh, here in the bedroom." She looked around the room, as though she was now unsure of what she had seen and heard. "Somewhere here. But I don't understand."

"Where's this light?" Fletcher asked, his eyes scanning the room. Michael pointed to the far end of the bedroom, to a spot near the door to the bathroom.

"Over there, around the sculpture," Michael said, pointing to a white polished-marble sculpture at the other end of the room, near the door to the bathroom. "But once the lights came back on, I lost it."

He watched as Fletcher walked to the spot and stared at the Picasso-like cubist rendition of a woman's head sitting atop a glossy white wooden pedestal. It was twice the size of a normal head and distorted, with only one giant eye. Michael could see that Fletcher had spotted something else. It appeared to be a small white box, about the same size as a pack of cigarettes. It was cleverly camouflaged, wedged securely inside the white marble cubist sculpture. Fletcher cautiously moved to within inches of the mysterious box, pulled it out of its crevice and then examined it, turning it over in his hand.

"It's one of those home monitoring devices. It's got a camera, a speaker, and a microphone all built in. It connects to someone's computer through the Internet. They can see everything going on and even carry on a conversation with you. If the light level gets too low, as it did when your power was cut off, it has an infrared blue light that kicks on, enabling it to see in the dark. I've seen these used by law enforcement to monitor people on home confinement or early release programs."

"So someone actually broke into our house, planted this monitor in our bedroom, connected it to his own laptop through the

Internet, and then went around the house and called us on the phone?" Michael said. His mind wandered back to Russell's murder earlier in the evening, and in another part of his brain, he wondered when to break that news to Samantha.

"You got it," Fletcher said. "But he must have come into your house earlier to plant the device. He then either left and returned, or …" Fletcher stopped, looked at Samantha, and took a deep breath, "he stayed in the house and hid out waiting for the right time."

Samantha let out, "My God, I was out most of the afternoon. Do you mean he may have been in the house for a while, just watching me and waiting? He was here while I was alone, before Michael came home?"

Fletcher and Michael exchanged concerned glances. "Right now, Samantha, we're not sure exactly what happened here." Fletcher said as he watched the faces and signals of the parade of officers as they approached after checking out every corner of the house. He stepped aside and conferred with the one who appeared to be his next-in-charge. The officer spoke, loud enough for everyone to hear. "It's all clear; no one's in these rooms, Chief."

Fletcher resumed speaking with the officer and then turned back to Michael and Samantha. "As he said, everything's okay now. But not only didn't we find anyone hiding, we can't even find any indication of a break-in. The doors to the outside were all locked, although with most of your locks, they could have been relocked easily by someone on their way out. Except for some damage we did to your doors getting in, nothing appears to have been disturbed.

"We'll let you look yourself in just a few minutes in case you see something out of place that we might have missed. Other than the monitoring device, there's no trace that an intruder was here. For all we know, he came in, planted the electronic devices, left the house, and controlled everything, including your phone system, from a car a block away."

"Maybe, but we heard someone actually trying to turn the door handle," Michael said, pointing to the bedroom door.

Fletcher appeared stymied until he appeared to have a revelation. "It was probably a clever sound effect that they piped through the system."

"But, Fletcher, we *saw* the knob turning," Michael said.

Fletcher's face tightened. "Listen, I have to admit this is the strangest thing I've ever seen. Even from my days in New York."

The unfinished 9-1-1 call was eating away at Michael and, he guessed, at Samantha, too. He was sure Samantha understood that he was perhaps treading carefully, waiting for the right time to pose the question to Fletcher as to how he knew there was an emergency at their home.

But before Michael had the chance to ask, Fletcher posed his own question. "Michael, when did you get a police scanner, you little devil?"

"What do you mean?"

Fletcher smiled, a sarcastic look on his face. Michael recognized the look, the one Fletcher used when he was sure Michael was trying to put something over on him. "Come on, how do you think we got the emergency call? It came through to headquarters on a two-way transmitter, the kind they sell with the police scanners."

"But, Fletcher, I don't have a scanner or transmitter, whatever the hell they are, and I never sent any message to you guys. I did start to dial 9-1-1 on my cell phone, but you called on the house line before I ever finished dialing. I'm serious."

Fletcher appeared confused. "That's impossible. Who called in then on our police frequency?"

Michael thought for a few seconds, unable to process another strange occurrence. "I don't know. I can only imagine," he said.

Fletcher looked totally perplexed.

Michael was silent, his mind now wandering back to Queens. He was hesitant to bring up Russell's murder now with Samantha already in shock.

"This is just too bizarre," Fletcher continued. "You know all we get in Westport are either burglaries or kids causing trouble. But this doesn't fit either of those. Samantha's jewelry here wasn't touched, and no burglar is going to call you on the phone and install an expensive monitor in your bedroom—and I can't even begin to think about how we were notified. It's all too dangerous and sophisticated for a juvenile prank. This guy was a pro. Who would want to do that?"

Samantha looked at Michael and said exactly what he was thinking from the moment he realized the alarm system had been disabled, "This has to be connected to your brother."

Fletcher jumped in, saving Michael from having to speak. "Michael, you always purposely stayed clear of anything to do with Alex's business though, didn't you?"

Michael knew Fletcher was in a delicate position as both his close friend and a local law enforcement officer. Not that Michael had done anything illegal, at least not yet.

After an awkward silence, Michael looked at Fletcher, then at Samantha, and said, "We need to talk. There's another murder I need to tell you about."

Chapter 13

New York City
November 13, 2009

The Carlyle had hosted presidents, dictators, kings, queens, divas, and princesses, but tonight it sheltered Donna Nicholas in a junior suite and her private security guard in an adjoining room.

Michael stood in the lobby and watched as Donna emerged from the elevator, each step loudly announcing her arrival as her heels seemed to prance to a silent marching band on the white marble floor. All she needed, Michael thought, was a baton or a stripper's pole.

She was dressed to kill—another short black dress showing off her long, slim legs and thigh-high leather boots with six-inch black-and-silver stiletto high heels. A diamond necklace drew the eye to the center of attention: Donna's perfect breasts, a triumph of silicone technology and Dr. Simonetti's genius. As always, she showed just enough cleavage to attract every male set of eyes in the lobby. Her Chanel No. 5 preceded her by just a few seconds and followed her for much longer. Michael took in her scent.

Until now, he felt he had never really noticed her before. She looked enticing, even seductive. He put that thought quickly out of his mind.

"Donna, you look great." As he said it, Michael wasn't sure he was comfortable with how it came out. He helped Donna put on her full-length mink coat, which she was carrying over her arm.

"Well, thank you, Michael. That's unusual for you to say. I'm flattered."

Michael was unsure how to take that remark and decided he really didn't want to know. He figured it would have something to do with the distance he had always kept from his brother and any of his wives. "Let's get out of the hotel. How about Cafe Boulud across the street? I have a reservation for us."

"Michael, that's perfect."

Fortunately they didn't have far to walk. Manhattan was bitter cold, made worse by a strong November wind blowing through the streets. As they crossed Seventy-Sixth Street and then Madison Avenue, the entrance to the discreetly elegant restaurant was just a few doors ahead on the left. As they entered under the green canopy and into the small reception area of the restaurant, a breeze of warm air enveloped them. It felt comforting and secure. They were both efficiently relieved of their coats and shown to a quiet and private table in a cozy alcove off to the left.

The waiter, obviously assuming they were a couple, politely offered to seat them side by side. It was a favorite choice for Michael when he dined here with Samantha. Besides the natural intimacy of the arrangement, they both enjoyed the view of the room and the ongoing show of New York nightlife that paraded by. Before Donna could respond, however, Michael quickly interjected, "No thanks, we prefer to face each other."

The restaurant had a full house of well-heeled and smartly dressed New Yorkers. Michael watched as Donna took in the room. "Michael, that's Regis Philbin and his wife, Joy, over there on your right. Oh God, I see Mayor Bloomberg and Oprah sitting in the back. This place is unbelievable."

"I've always enjoyed it. The food is great and it's just quiet and calm, yet it has an East Side buzz about it. I know that's a contradiction. Anyway, Samantha and Sofia love it here too."

"Oh, Michael, I do miss Alex, but he hated places like this. Too many ties, too many suits, too many hushed conversations. He said he didn't like going to restaurants where everyone looked like they had a rod up their ass."

"Alex did have a way with words." Michael's sarcasm, he knew, was lost on Donna.

Michael had called Donna early in the morning and told her exactly what had happened at his home the night before. He expected her to have brought it up for discussion by now. He was anxious to get her thoughts on what she thought was going on.

"Donna, do you realize all the shit that's been going on here? This is dangerous stuff." Michael needed to try to get Donna to focus on the total picture of everything that had happened. "Someone had Alex and Russell murdered, and they've got to be connected to whoever broke into my house. Samantha is hysterical. I have private security guards watching the house twenty-four hours a day. Where is your guy, by the way?"

"He's having dinner in his room. I told him to just stay there. I figured I'd be okay with you, and I preferred that he keep an eye out on my room instead. He's also got hotel security watching us like a hawk. Every time I go to the elevator, it seems like there's a plainclothes security guy somewhere in the hall."

"How do you know it's hotel security if he's in plain clothes?"

"Michael, you can't miss them. They've all got radios and earphones in their ears. You can hear the radios going even from the room sometimes. Either they're all security, or there's a goddamned deaf people's convention at the Carlyle."

Touché, Michael thought. "And what about the police investigation? Have you heard anything new?"

"Not really. They called me this morning. They have gone through Alex's insurance office and the computer he had there.

Naturally, they found nothing unusual. Let's face it, whatever is happening is not a result of the shitty little insurance brokerage he had. Even the cops know that was just a front. It gave him enough legitimate income so the IRS wouldn't get suspicious."

"What about Alex's real office?" Michael was suddenly concerned about the police finding Alex's bookmaking and loan-sharking records—and his handgun in the desk drawer. He was also trying to remember whether he ever actually picked up the gun. His mind raced through the implications of his own fingerprints being discovered by the police.

"They don't know about his other office. You know, only the Lesters and a few others of his closest guys were ever allowed into that place."

"But, Donna," Michael interjected, "the cops know Alex was a bookie; they're going to want his records. They're going to need to know who he was doing business with, who may have wanted him dead—"

Donna interrupted. "Of course the cops know Alex was a bookie. Some of his best customers were cops. I just said he was an insurance agent as far as I knew. I played the dumb wife who knows nothing about her husband's business—or businesses. These guys have all seen *The Sopranos*. They believed what I told them, or it was what they wanted to believe. I also gave up Alex's home computer."

"I'm sure they'll go through that pretty thoroughly. Do you know if there's anything on it?" Michael had not really thought much about Alex's computers, and he had never even been to the insurance office, which was just a few blocks from Alex's home. He knew that Alex rarely spent any time there.

Michael felt better, seeing that Donna appeared to be pretty well informed now that her mind was focused on the situation.

"Well, Alex was no fool. His insurance office computer was strictly for his insurance records—and the cops found some porn sites. Alex would be bored stiff, excuse the pun, whenever he went to that office. And to be honest, I was never sure what he had on his home computer. The police said all they found on it was a lot of seemingly innocent personal stuff and a lot of sports.

"Michael," Donna continued, "the police are not going to solve this. The answers are only going to be found where the cops aren't going to go—Alex's real business. We can't let them go there."

"I think I know the answer to this, but just out of curiosity, why can't we let the police go down that road? Maybe they can solve this thing—find out who killed Alex and Russell and who's out there who can kill us."

"Michael, well, let me think." Donna placed her hand on her forehead, a mocking gesture as though she had a sudden revelation. "Why wouldn't we want to just open everything up to the cops? Could it be that Fat and Skinny Lester would be arrested? Maybe I'd be too. Maybe even you, Michael. Or could it be that if the guy behind all this is more than a little crazy, then we both might wind up dead too?

"And then there's the money—the money Alex's clients owed and the cash that Alex has probably hidden somewhere in our house. And I know your situation is different, but I need that money. By the way, I have torn the fucking house apart. All I've found so far is about a thousand bucks—pocket change—that Alex had in various places."

Michael had already thought of all the reasons Donna just set forth, but it was unsettling to hear it from her lips. He also knew that the slightest publicity linking him to any sort of scandal would mean a swift end to his career. As he began to sink into some sense of despair, Michael's cell phone rang. It was Skinny Lester.

"Michael, we've got trouble. Mr. Sharkey wants to meet. He wants his money. *Now.*"

Michael's first thought was to question why this had now become *his* problem. But he knew he had somehow walked through a door, one that had quietly but permanently closed behind him.

"What did you tell him?" Michael asked.

"What do you mean, what did I tell him? I had to tell him we'd meet—on Thursday."

"And Lester, who exactly is 'we'?"

"You, me, and Fat Lester. Anybody else you wanna bring is okay with me, Michael."

Chapter 14

Whitestone, Queens, New York
November 13, 2009

For Michael, Grimaldi's would always be his brother's final resting place.

And tonight, as Michael walked into Grimaldi's, a stunned Maria met him immediately. She was standing, frozen, in front of the bar. She had apparently been on her way to the kitchen and, as she passed by the front door, saw Michael walking in.

"Oh my God, Michael, I thought I saw a ghost. I never realized how much you resemble your brother. When I saw you walk in I thought I was going to faint. I swear, I almost lost it." Maria ran up to Michael and hugged him tightly.

"I'm sorry, I should have called to let you know I was coming, but I was on my way back to Connecticut from dinner with Donna and thought I'd just drop in. There's something I wanted to talk with you about."

"Of course, Jesus Christ, please, sit down. How about a drink or something to eat?"

Maria brought two chilled glasses of wine and joined Michael at a quiet table off to the side. "Here, try this. I know you enjoy your wines. This is a new sauvignon blanc from Chile." They both took a generous swallow. Michael noticed that Maria seemed to be staring intently at him.

"Maria, do you remember, right before Alex was shot when he was on the phone with me in Paris? He said he had something to show me, something important, that he couldn't discuss over the phone."

Maria's expression was pained, as though she knew right away she didn't have the answer. "Yes, I was waiting for you to ask me. It was odd when he said it because Alex never used those words, you know, that something was important. He wasn't into secrets, either. In fact, I was going to tease him, ask him what it was about, as soon as he hung up but …" Her voice trailed off.

"I know, you never got the chance." Michael could tell he had brought her back to a painful memory, but he needed to push a little further. "And he never hinted what it might have been?"

"No, Michael, I'm sorry." Her hand gently brushed Michael's arm. It was a simple but touching gesture.

"I know. It's okay, Maria, I just thought I'd take a shot that he may have said something."

"Michael, you know your brother was the sweetest guy I ever knew. He did so many things for people around here, people in trouble or just going through a rough time. He'd rarely talk about it. In fact, you just missed someone who said she knew Alex from high school. Her name was Germaine, Germaine Strauss."

"Oh my God," Michael said, "I remember her."

"She knew your brother in high school. She was a … small person."

"A dwarf. We used to call them midgets back then, I guess. I lost track of her completely."

"Well, she'd been in Florida and just came back and heard about Alex. So she came in here, and we talked for a while. She told me about how Alex was this great-looking jock in school and how, despite having his pick of any girls, he took her to the prom. He knew she wouldn't have a date. I mean, it's so nice it sounds corny. Yet, never once in all these years I knew him, did he ever even mention it."

"I remember her so well. She had a tortured life because of her condition. I think Alex always kind of protected her."

"You know, he'd come by here a few times a week. We'd sit together, have dinner, talk. There was something so different about him. So tough on the outside but like a little boy underneath. He always had this crankiness about him, yet all of a sudden, he'd make some wisecrack and then break out into one of his mischievous grins. I just loved it when he'd show up." Maria's voice was breaking. She stopped speaking as she struggled to regain her composure.

"I'm so sorry, Michael. It's just so strange to one night be sitting across from a person at dinner, having an intimate conversation, and then just a few days later, see them at their funeral—not moving, not smiling, in a casket."

"I know, Maria, I just try not to think about it."

"I'm sorry to do this to you, but Alex was such a character. I loved him. It's funny, too, I always felt so safe around him. I knew he would protect me—against what, I don't even know. But Alex watched out for the people he cared for."

Michael knew he had to ask. "Were you guys, ever, uh …" but as he began, he lost his nerve. Maria was an open person, it appeared, but he could tell there was a private side one didn't go to without either knowing her better or having her permission.

"Were we ever *together*? It's okay, Michael. You can ask. No, we never went to bed. It's probably how we managed to stay good friends for so long. I think we were both attracted to each other, but we both knew better than to ruin it by going any further."

"I think you were one of the few women that he trusted."

"Thanks, Michael." Maria stroked Michael's arm again. "Your brother really loved you. He never actually said those words to me, but I could tell. Whenever he spoke about you, I knew. He had a certain sparkle in his eyes. He was proud of you. I hope you know that."

"I do, thanks, Maria." As Michael looked at Maria and felt the warmth from her hand on his arm, a touch that seemed to deliberately linger for an extra second or so, he felt an odd sensation that Maria was attracted to him, but not because of any sex appeal of his own. He looked at Maria, into her dark eyes; they seemed to be searching. Michael knew she was searching for Alex.

Chapter 15

Newport, Rhode Island
November 14, 2009

"Just seconds before he was shot, when I was on the phone with Alex, he told me there was something that he couldn't wait to show me, something that would shock me. It was almost the last thing he said to me."

"What do you think it could have been?" Samantha said.

"I don't know. I almost forgot about it with everything that happened, but of course, I can't get it out of mind. Whatever this thing of Alex's was, assuming it wasn't just some joke, I'm sure he kept it close to his vest. I've broached it with a few of the people he was close with, but no one seems to have a clue what he could have been up to—or they're not saying. If anyone knew anything, it would have been Russell but …"

"Have you asked Donna?"

"No, I guess that would be a logical place to start, but first, I don't think Alex would share some big secret with his wife. He wasn't that type of guy. He obviously didn't even share with her where he's hidden his money. Second, I don't want to arouse any more suspicions or curiosity on her part. I guess I just don't trust her, and I don't think Alex completely did, either."

Michael and Samantha had decided to head off to Newport for a night, a favorite retreat and an easy two-and-a-half-hour drive north from Westport. Michael knew that Samantha needed to get out of the house, and it was a good time to visit one of their favorite French restaurants, Bouchard.

There were only a few other diners, giving the restaurant a softer, yet more formal feel than during its busy summer months.

"I love Newport in the winter. It's quiet, serene," Michael said as he carefully extracted the olive from his half-finished martini. He looked over at the large, predominately sea-blue mural of the port of Saint-Tropez, just above Samantha's shoulder.

"I know it's months away, but I can't wait for us to be back in Saint-Tropez again," he said, referring to their annual August vacation. Michael relished the taste of one of Bouchard's signature dishes, a coffee-crusted breast of duck.

"Michael, how did you really feel about your brother? You know, it's odd that all these years we've discussed Alex, and I know you loved him, but beyond that, you've never really spoken about how you felt."

This was typical Samantha, Michael thought. She had a way of drawing people out, to open up about their lives, their innermost secrets. She knew how to ease their pains and their fears. It was a quality she had that Michael had never seen in another woman.

Michael had to think. In truth, he'd never really synthesized his thoughts about his brother. They were all just a collection of fragments of feelings. But now, Michael knew, it was time to more neatly categorize them, for Samantha—and for himself.

"As a kid, say through my teens, I certainly looked up to him. He was like a sports idol too. He was such a great athlete; you could tell that he had kind of an aura around him that other people and kids saw. Other kids, older than Alex, were also afraid of him. He was a tough guy, and so quick."

Michael paused, his spirits sagging. "But then, I guess sometime after he was injured and returned from college, it was like his mission in life was over. He wasn't going to be a professional ballplayer. The aura around him was gone. People can smell it when your run is over."

Samantha looked into Michael's eyes. "So things changed?" she said.

"Not to me, but I think to himself. He had to earn a living. Yet, I don't think traditional success, the way society sees it, meant anything to him. My parents were great about supporting either of us, but you know, eventually you've got to find your way. For Alex, that was rough. Baseball had been his life, and there was no reason to think he wouldn't be playing in the majors. He had been so much better than other kids his age, at any stage of his life, at least until it all fell apart."

"So what happened then?"

"My father called some of his friends, executives that he knew, and arranged interviews for Alex. But he really wanted Alex to go back to school to get a degree. He figured he'd show Alex what life without one would be like, so the first job he helped him get was with one of the big airlines. My father had a friend there. Alex probably thought he was going to have a cushy desk job, but when he showed up for work, they had him cleaning the toilets in the aircraft lavatories. I think he lasted a day."

"Did he go back to school?"

"No, you know that Alex hated school. Don't forget, he'd been thrown out of two high schools until he finally graduated from Rhodes Prep in Manhattan."

"Yes, the school for misbehaving rich kids."

"Anyway, we had good family friends who owned a major insurance brokerage firm in Queens, and they took Alex on. He was pretty good at it, eventually earned his own brokerage license and set up his own small business in Whitestone. It gave him some decent income—and eventually served as the cover he needed to be able to pursue his real business. It also allowed him to show enough legitimate income so he could buy a house and spend some of the money he earned in his illegal business without attracting the attention of the IRS."

Michael looked at Samantha. She was listening intently. "But he changed. He started running around with these shady types, and his girlfriends were no longer nice, smart college girls but hard-edged bimbos."

"Michael, are you sure he changed, or did the people around him just reflect who he was? Wasn't he always just a hard-nosed tough guy with no patience for any crap, including the niceties and hypocrisy that most of us just tolerate?"

"You may be right. Listen, for many years I never thought that much about Alex. I mean, I was pursuing my own career. I couldn't afford to be seen with a lot of his friends, and I certainly couldn't get too close to his business. I'm actually not sure I remember all my feelings at that point. I just had to stay clear. I didn't tell any of my business associates what he did. Some only vaguely knew that I had a brother. Don't forget, he was busted a few times. What company was going to hire or promote a senior executive whose brother was what they considered to be a mobster?"

These were arguments Michael knew Samantha had heard in bits and pieces over the years. "I guess I knew all this, although it's funny how seldom we've discussed it."

Michael continued, "Maybe the problem too was that I started seeing Alex through the lens, so to speak, of his wives, each of whom I detested. Maybe I had no right to judge. Alex was always the first to say he was a terrible husband. But in any case, I always thought his wives made him worse, either encouraging or enabling his unhealthy behaviors while enjoying the fruits of it—the money."

"Your brother always had a big circle of friends that he seemed to enjoy," Samantha said.

"More than that. Although he was antisocial in some ways, it didn't apply to his friends. He'd do anything for them, and they'd do anything for him. Alex was the most loyal guy I ever met. Remember when he was having some heart problems, and we brought him to see Dr. Roney?"

"Yes. Hadn't his own cardiologist—I forgot his name—some doctor on Long Island, actually been arrested for hiding a video camera in the ladies' room of his office?"

"Yes, and despite that and seriously misdiagnosing him, Alex still wanted to go back to him. He said he felt sorry for the guy. I miss him, Samantha. He's the last link I had to my childhood, and all that history went with him when he died."

"I know, dear. I know how you feel." Samantha made an understanding nod.

"But there's something else I want to tell you. When we were speaking about Alex and his wives, I thought about us, you and me. I wanted to say something."

Michael's voice broke, ever so slightly, and he knew Samantha had caught it, just as he knew that she could sense the churning of his emotions. He could feel the hint of moisture in his eyes, something that would usually cause him to veer away from whatever discussion had caused it. But tonight was different.

"What is it, darling?" Samantha said.

"I was thinking as we were talking before about how Alex's wives brought out the worst in him."

"Yes, I know."

"Well, you brought out the best in me. You found the best things in me, and you wouldn't quit until you brought them out, no matter how much I protested. You've made me happy—in a way no one else ever could. You've been an unbelievable mother to Sofia. What we have is priceless. I don't say it to you often enough."

"I know you don't, Michael. But I cherish our relationship, beyond words. Sometimes, though, no matter how content I feel with you, I do miss having Sofia at home."

"I do too, but right now, I'm happy she's away at Notre Dame.

At least she's missed all the craziness at home, and I feel like she's safe, away at school."

"Michael, I really love you. You know that," Samantha said, although as Michael watched her, it was clear there was more. He waited as she finally formulated her thoughts. "But sometimes I wonder if this is really enough for you."

Samantha's question took him by surprise. "Sometimes you come out with the oddest—but most accurate—observations. I've got to think about that, but I've had enough emotion for one night. I'd like to enjoy my duck." He felt a sense of relief as he looked at the beautiful arrangement of dark pink, thinly sliced duck breast.

But as Michael sliced through the tender meat, he couldn't help but think about Samantha's question. He knew she was right. His life as it was today was not enough. But the source of his restlessness had nothing to do with Samantha—she and Sofia truly were the joys of his life. No, there was something else happening. *It is ironic,* he thought, *after so many years of keeping my distance from Alex, now that he's gone, I can't get him out of my mind.*

Chapter 16

Saint Michael's Cemetery, Astoria, New York
November 16, 2009

"I hate hospitals and cemeteries. You get into one when you're sick and the other when you're dead. I guess I don't like the admissions requirements," Michael said as he and Skinny Lester approached Alex's grave.

Michael often wondered whether the living went to cemeteries to visit the dead or to ruminate about their own lives and mortality. He suspected that as people aged, they were more naturally drawn to where they were ultimately headed.

Since Alex's murder, Skinny Lester looked to Michael as if he was worn down and rapidly aging each day. Although only in his midfifties, his health was fragile. Two heart attacks had left him weaker than his tall and lean body appeared to those around him, most of whom seemed to be more horizontally built. Although it was clear to even the most casual observer that his cousin, Fat Lester, was neither in good shape nor good health, Skinny Lester was falling apart, despite looking good and fit.

Lester took Michael by surprise this morning when he asked if he wanted to visit Alex's grave.

Except for an actual funeral, Michael did not go to cemeteries. He remembered taking his father to Saint Michael's Cemetery several times over the years to visit his own parents' graves. He would watch as his father would plant flowers near their headstones. As he stood a few feet behind him, he tried to imagine what his father's emotions were at that moment. He remembered wondering whether he himself would do the same when his father passed away. He didn't. Most who knew Michael assumed that he simply wasn't thoughtful enough. Michael allowed and even encouraged that assumption. In reality, however, he knew it would be just too painful to stand over a slab of granite and contemplate the loving parents who had raised him.

As Michael looked out over the cemetery's hills, he was filled with angst. He stared at the endless landscape of neatly placed grave markers in a perfect geometrical pattern. If life was chaotic, noisy, and random, certainly death appeared to bring perfect symmetry, order, and silence.

But for Michael, the noise was deafening. Just being in Astoria always brought him an uneasy sense of nostalgia. Although he had never lived there, it was filled with the memories of all the long-departed Greek relatives he would visit as a child.

He stood side by side with Lester, gazing at Alex's grave. But Michael was distracted by the blizzard of thoughts—an attack of memories—brought to his consciousness by this bizarre place and scene. He believed that although people may come to graveyards to speak with the dead, instead, the dead speak to the living. And as Michael stood staring at his brother's gravestone, he felt an overwhelming barrage of messages and recollections coming from every person now buried who ever touched his life. He now knew why he stayed away.

In order to keep his emotions in check, Michael allowed his mind to wander to other simple, mundane topics. Although he felt intense emotions, he was never comfortable allowing them to show. He remembered how, at his father's funeral service, sitting in the front row of pews and listening to the eulogy, he had to divert his mind to scenes from the World Series so he wouldn't risk breaking down in front of his family and friends. He didn't know exactly where this need to control the exhibition of emotions came from, only that he rarely saw his own parents cry.

Michael had turned off the ringer on his BlackBerry, but he could now feel the vibration indicating an instant message. He took the phone out of his coat pocket and read the one that popped up.

"What are you doing here?" It was from Alex.

Michael continued to look at it until he was sure he had read it correctly. His eyes then moved to his brother's grave, as though expecting some signal or apparition to appear. He turned to Skinny Lester who appeared to be somewhere else, lost in his own thoughts or memories.

Not finding any clue or verification that the haunting message that he had just seen was either real or imagined, he looked back at his BlackBerry. He clicked on "Reply" and tapped out, "Who is this?"

Seconds later, he watched the screen and felt the BlackBerry vibrate. "Trying to reach you. You must find my—"

But the message stopped there. Michael felt a certain light-headedness as he waited for the remainder of the communication. His mind was racing. *How could it be from Alex? It's impossible. And what did it mean that I need to find something—what? Who is behind this?*

Michael kept glancing down at his phone, hoping there would be more to the message, but nothing else appeared. He scrolled back to reread what had been sent, but it was gone. He felt disoriented. Had he really seen it? He was sure he had, yet ... Maybe it was all too much. Maybe he was feeling the strain. He would keep this to himself for now.

He would have preferred not to speak, but it was apparent that Lester needed to. Michael had tuned him out, until something Lester said captured Michael's full attention.

As he spoke, Lester's eyes darted between Alex's gravestone and

Michael. It was a nervous gesture, as though Lester was looking for Alex's approval before continuing his story.

"It was several months ago, maybe three in the morning. We were in Alex's den, at his house. Just the two of us. We'd polished off almost a whole bottle of Dewar's. Alex was like a little kid. All of a sudden, he tells me he wants to show me something he's been working on. Then he turns on his computer. He says that he had Russell help him purchase some fancy new artificial intelligence software from one of those high-tech companies in Silicon Valley, and that he had another company in Scotland that recreated his actual voice, and then another one somewhere else for the imaging or something. I think Russell spent a lot of time putting this all together for him.

"Alex got all excited. I thought he was going to show me the week's results from the games or something. But he tells me to look at the computer and—holy shit—it's him on the screen. Alex then asks him a question—and the Alex on the computer answers him. Not only that—but it was in Alex's voice, and it was Alex looking at you. He was so real, even the facial expressions were perfect. I've never seen anything like it. Alex talking to Alex. I couldn't believe it. They had a conversation with each other. It was funny—no, actually it was scary. Very scary."

Michael could see that Lester was unnerved, but he didn't know what to make of his story. "Lester, wasn't Alex one of the first to use computers in his business?"

"Yeah, Alex was always a little ahead of his time. Alex used computers for two big reasons. First, it allowed us to track the bets, and we'd get up-to-the-minute feeds from Vegas on the odds for any game or event. Knowing when something happens to change the odds on a game is a big edge. We also had each customer's status at our fingertips. The computer tracked who owed what and exactly what bets they had pending, up to the minute. It was great. Most bookies have everything on a million little slips of paper; it's crazy."

"What was the second reason he used computers?"

"Sex, of course. Alex loved porn. He'd actually 'dated' some of his favorite porn stars. He really liked that one, Jenna Jameson. I wouldn't mention that to Donna, by the way."

"Believe me, I won't," Michael said. "But, Lester, let's get back to what you saw that night. Did Alex ever bring it up again?"

"No, and I never thought much about it after a while myself."

Michael wondered if this could have been what he wanted to tell him on the phone or was it just another of his toys? Russell was known to be a computer genius. What exactly was he doing for Alex? It appeared he was doing more than just building hiding places for Alex's cash. But didn't Donna mention just last night that the police found nothing of interest on Alex's home computer? "Maybe there was nothing to this, but it sounded odd.

"What was the point of it? Was it a game?" Michael asked.

"I'm not sure," Lester said. "I would have easily said yes except, a few minutes into it, Alex suddenly got real quiet. He shut the computer down and muttered something about how he and Russell still had a lot of work to do on it. And then he looked at me with that real serious look that he'd get and told me not to tell anyone.

"He said, 'Lester, I mean no one, ever.' I remember thinking it was as though he'd had too much to drink that night and was sorry he'd shown it to me. That's why I'm not sure it was just one of his computer games. Plus, it was damned good. This didn't look like some off-the-shelf computer software."

Lester looked down again at Alex's grave. "There was something else, too. Your brother was afraid of only one thing."

"What was that?"

"He was afraid of dying. It was the one thing he couldn't control. And maybe more than that, I don't think he could imagine the world going on without him."

"Lester, did you ever tell anyone about what you saw that night?"

"Not a soul. When Alex tells you—or told you—not to say anything, you kept your mouth shut." Lester looked down again at Alex's grave. "In fact, I'm still nervous about it."

Chapter 17

It was just a blur, but Michael was sure he saw it.

"I just saw someone move, over there," Michael said, pointing to a spot over Lester's right shoulder.

Lester jumped, turning around to look. "Christ, no one moves in a cemetery."

"Well, someone's here. I have a bad feeling. Maybe it's nothing, but whoever it is, they didn't drive up. There's no car around."

"Michael, all the people that live *here* had drivers." Skinny Lester's voice cracked as he spoke.

"Someone's watching us," Michael said as he scanned the area and then looked back at Lester. He realized that Lester was too weak, if not fragile, to be of any real help if physical danger threatened.

"You don't happen to carry a gun or anything, do you?" Michael knew better.

"You've got to be fuckin' kidding," Lester said nervously.

"Let's get to the car and get out of here. Just go nice and slow, not like we're running away," Michael said, almost in a whisper. Although logic might have dictated a hasty retreat, Michael's instinct was to move slowly, showing no fear. Perhaps, he thought, if it worked when confronted with wild dogs, it would also work with bad guys chasing you.

Michael's black BMW sedan was parked on the narrow, winding road, less than fifty feet away. He glanced quickly over his shoulder. There was only Lester walking behind him at a slight trot. He reached the door and then grasped the handle and opened the door, quickly sliding into the rich black leather driver's seat. He looked around, fearing his pursuer was close, but he saw no one.

"Let's get the fuck out of here," Lester shouted as he pulled his own door shut.

Michael firmly pressed the ignition button, expecting the usual powerful but quiet start to the 740's German engine. But there was nothing, not even the problematic clicking sound.

"Shit. This has never happened." Michael checked the gauges and clicked his seat belt in place in case something missing in his usual routine had caused the car's complex computer to shut down. Still, not a sound.

Michael looked up into his rearview mirror and saw a shadowy figure passing behind the car. "Lester, someone's coming behind the car."

Lester turned around, and his eyes appeared to be following someone now. "He's coming around to your door."

Michael now turned in the same direction and saw the tall stranger as he approached his driver's side window. "Lester, do you recognize this guy?" Michael said, trying not to move his lips.

"I don't think so, but I can hardly see his face. Who the fuck wears sunglasses in a fuckin' cemetery in November?"

Michael knew he was trapped. There was no point in either staying in the disabled car—or in getting out. If this guy meant them harm, he would certainly be armed. Michael turned to Lester. "What do we do?" But Michael could see that Lester was mentally immobilized.

There was a tapping on the driver's side window, and Michael turned to his left. He looked at the stranger, and then he pressed the automatic window button. The window wouldn't go down. The man was inches away, separated by a thin—and not bulletproof—layer of glass. He was trying to say something to Michael. Although his looks were menacing—black attire, pockmarked face, big hands, black sunglasses—his manner seemed calm, if not helpful. Michael opened the door halfway.

"Looks like you need some help." His voice was gravelly and hoarse.

Michael didn't know what to make of this. But he did need help. "Yes, I can't get the car to start."

"I can have a tow truck come by. I know a lot of people here."

Lester murmured to himself, "Of course you do."

Michael didn't know what to say. He had his own cell but knew he would probably just have to call the BMW roadside assistance 800 number he had somewhere. That didn't look too promising inside a cemetery at the moment.

"Sure, that would be great. Do you work here?" Michael hoped the man was a cemetery administrator.

"No."

Michael hesitated; he looked at Lester.

"Who cares, Michael, let him get us a tow truck so we can get the hell out of here. We're surrounded by dead people."

Chapter 18

Mario's had the best meatballs in the world. But tonight, Michael had another dish in mind.

Inside a quaint old building near the Westport train station, Mario's old-fashioned, polished mahogany bar was always bustling with a lunch and dinner crowd of locals and daily Manhattan commuters. The shots weren't premeasured, the tablecloths were still pressed white linen, and a cash register, not a computer, sat on the counter. Whiskey, scotch, gin, and vodka flowed from eleven in the morning until two in the morning.

Dinner at Mario's was comfort food that warmed your soul even before the food arrived. Michael loved the restaurant and its owner, Tiger. He had owned and operated the venerable Westport establishment for over forty years. Tiger was a short, bald barrel of a man well into his seventies—a no-nonsense but lovable teddy bear.

Michael and Tiger would lament that many new chefs looked down on the traditional dishes like lasagna or spaghetti and meatballs. Tiger was proud of those dishes. Michael also liked Mario's clientele—just good, hardworking people of all income brackets and walks of life, without an overabundance of chardonnay-drinking, overindulgent investment bankers. Tiger took care of his restaurant and his customers. Michael always felt at home whenever he walked in the door. It was a clubby atmosphere, without the club.

Tiger saw Michael seated at a quiet table near the window. "I didn't know you were coming tonight. Where's Samantha?"

"She's in South Bend with Sofia at Notre Dame for a few days. I'm solo tonight." Michael realized that although he'd eaten at Mario's hundreds of times, this was the first time he'd been there alone. He needed time to just think about the next few days' challenges. Even though Tiger was the proprietor—and a good friend—he knew that Tiger was, in some ways, like himself. He liked to say hello, make a little small talk, and then move on.

"Jesus, Michael. If you're going to get in trouble this week, just don't do it here. Samantha will kill me."

Tiger, Michael thought, as he watched his friend's eyebrows arch up, was one of those guys who are naturally funny. *He doesn't try; it just comes out of him.*

"Don't worry, Tiger. You know me, I like being alone more than I like other people. Plus, this way I can taste the food. I'd rather eat than talk."

"I wish more people were like that. If people would eat more, they'd *have* to talk less and I'd make more money. And, I wouldn't have to listen so much. How about your usual martini?"

"Sounds great."

Mario's cocktails filled a proper martini glass, but they also arrived at your table with the glass shaker, which contained a second full drink. Michael knew he was at that optimum point, where the drink opened up his mind and thoughts beyond what they seemed capable of without the gin—yet he was still sharp and incisive. The veal parmigiana sizzling in front of him helped too. Maria had mentioned that this had been Alex's last meal that night at Grimaldi's. Michael leaned back and began to think about his brother.

Michael had always felt that Alex's personality was pretty straightforward. What you saw on the surface was what was going on underneath; it was all up front. People who knew them both always assumed, as did Michael himself, that it was only Michael whose personality had layers of complexity. Certainly Michael knew there was always a lot going on under the outward and most visible layer of his own personality or what he showed the world. Beneath the easy smile, there were tensions, strains, hopes, doubts—almost other lives going on simultaneously.

Could Alex have been the same—did his gruff exterior and rough-and-tumble lifestyle mask a similar complexity? Clearly Alex was not only smart but shrewd. He could not have succeeded in his business without those skills and a highly developed emotional intelligence. But if all that were true, what did it mean? What was going on under all the simple sentences and frequent antisocial behavior? Were there nuances that no one really had picked up on? And what did that mean in the context of Alex's life?

Michael's thoughts focused on that last phone call. *And what is the secret that he couldn't tell me over the phone? Is it connected to what Skinny Lester saw on Alex's computer that night? But the police had checked all Alex's computers. If there was something unusual on them, the cops would have found it. And what about the instant message at the cemetery?*

He had spent the last week with uncharacteristically little communication with his office. Michael had that nagging tug in his gut that told him he was going to need to quickly reengage. His role was too high profile and visible—and the problems at Gibraltar too severe—for him to be able to coast, let alone disappear for any extended period. The death of his brother had kept other executives and staff away for the time being, but that time was coming rapidly to an end. Without his active presence back in the office, questions would, subtly and cautiously at first, be asked. He knew he needed to reestablish his presence back in New York. He also knew he could not just walk away from the new life he had entered, even if he was only visiting.

He wondered how far through his veal his brother had progressed before the gunman struck. Knowing Alex, there was probably a split-second where he would have been annoyed at not being able to finish his meal. His brother, he thought, had an uncanny ability to alternate between issues of life and death—and those of the immediate satisfaction of his next bite. It was a trait, Michael realized as he savored the contrasting tastes of thinly sliced veal, sweet tomato sauce, and melted mozzarella, that they both shared.

Michael allowed the gin to open up his mind and the meal to satisfy his hunger. He waited for some inspiration, an insight into his brother and the secret Alex couldn't wait to reveal. He ate his dinner, absorbed in the past and his memories of Alex. As he finished his dinner, he realized the absurdity of his hope that a dinner reminiscing would unveil any mysteries about his brother's life. But nothing came ... other than the check.

But as he put the credit card down on the table and waited for the bill to sign, Michael thought more about the scene Skinny Lester described with Alex and his computer.

Then Michael heard the familiar ringtone he had programmed into his BlackBerry to notify him of a text message from a member of his family. It must be either Samantha or Sofia, he thought. But as he checked the screen, it was a message from Apple:

The owner of this Apple device has requested that you be notified in the event that it should be located. Here are the longitude and latitudinal coordinates, representing the current location of the Apple product named, "Alex's Apple": latitude: 40.76626; longitude: -73.89695

Confused, Michael's attention momentarily drifted to the television monitor hanging above the bar. The news anchor was reporting on a recent *Jeopardy* quiz show contest, featuring a battle between Watson, a computer armed with specialized artificial intelligence, and a human contestant. Apparently, the newscaster stated, the computer won handily.

His mind spinning, Michael punched in the speed-dial number for his administrative assistant.

Chapter 19

"Hi, stranger. Are you okay?"

Karen DiNardo had worked for Michael since he joined Gibraltar. She was a smart young woman in her early thirties, a devout Catholic, conservative Republican, and a Rutgers graduate who commuted into Manhattan each day from her home in New Jersey. Michael trusted her implicitly, and he knew that Karen was totally loyal to him. She was intelligent and knew the volatile politics of the organization, but more importantly, she had great street smarts and was not afraid to tell Michael things others wouldn't tell him or that he didn't want to hear.

"I'm doing fine, Karen. It's all still just a little crazy. Listen, I'm going to need to be out for a few more days, but I want to catch up. Can you meet me in the city tomorrow? I'll treat you to Lattanzi." Michael knew Karen loved Italian food, and the restaurant on West Forty-Sixth Street was one they had both enjoyed during a number of business dinners over the past year.

"Just tell me what time, and I'll be there!"

"Let's meet early—noon. Karen, just two things before you go. First, if I give you a latitude and longitude coordinate, would you try to figure out where exactly in the world that point is?"

Karen didn't answer. Michael could picture the expression of bewilderment on her face. Better, he thought to just keep going.

"You may want to write these down. The latitude is 40.76626 and the longitude is minus sign, 73.89695. I vaguely remember this stuff from geography class. There must be some way to find out where the heck this is."

"O-kay," she said. Michael recognized the expression. "And what's the second thing?"

"The second one should be a lot easier. Would you do some research for me on artificial intelligence?" Again, there was a silence. Michael knew Karen would be frustrated until she figured out the point of his questions.

"I can see you've had maybe too much time to think."

"Listen, Karen, I know this might be a bit strange. I'll explain it all to you tomorrow." Again, there was just the slightest delay before he heard her response.

"Boss, before we go, while we were speaking, I Google-mapped those coordinates and then I went onto this thing, iTouchMap.com. I have the location you wanted. It's in Queens, looks like Astoria."

"Jesus, that was fast. Do you have an address by any chance?"

Karen's voice was suddenly tentative. "I do. I do …" Michael felt like she was stalling, perhaps thinking. "Hold on."

"What's wrong? Did you find it?" he asked.

"Yes, Michael, I did."

He was becoming impatient. She was hiding something. "So, where is it?"

"It's Saint Michael's cemetery. Isn't that where your brother is buried?"

Chapter 20

New York City
November 18, 2009

Wednesday was a matinee day on Broadway, so Lattanzi was nearly filled with an unlikely pairing of out-of-towners and the "women who lunch" crowd. Michael led Karen to a table off to the side, away from much of the bustle. The soft lighting and the rich wood paneling provided a serene backdrop for their conversation.

Seeing Karen with her office attire and briefcase full of folders was an unwelcome reminder to Michael of the world he would soon need to reenter with all his energy and attention. Michael was aware that he was, uncharacteristically for a supposed business meeting, attired in a sport shirt and black woolen sweater instead of a suit and tie. He wondered how that would register with Karen. He felt different and was sure it was obvious.

He ordered a bottle of Antinori brunello and a bowl of linguine with *fra diavolo* sauce over fresh lobster, mussels, calamari, and shrimp. Lattanzi was like being in Rome for lunch, he thought to himself. The room was relatively dark, the waiters Italian, and with no windows to the outside world, you could just as easily be on the Via del Corso as Forty-Sixth Street. As he completed ordering, he could see the expression of surprise on Karen's face.

"Wow, I don't think I've ever seen you order such a full meal at lunch. That's a change."

You have no idea, Michael thought.

While picking at her crisp calamari salad, Karen took Michael through the topics summarized in great detail in each of the manila folders. Michael watched her watching him and knew that Karen would have an uncannily accurate idea of what was going on inside his mind, at least to know when he was bored or unengaged in the subject matter, as he certainly was now. So as Michael's attention was wavering, he knew Karen would pick up on it in just a few more seconds if she hadn't already.

"Michael, is it too soon? I know you're upset about Alex ..."

"No, that's not it. I mean, I'm upset, but that's not what's on my mind. The other thing I asked you yesterday to research was artificial intelligence. What have you got?" Michael knew he hadn't made a smooth transition, but he couldn't help the curiosity tugging at his mind after his discussion with Skinny Lester at the cemetery.

Karen was clearly surprised, but she appeared to recover quickly. "I can see that you're not interested in this part of our agenda, so let's move on before you fall asleep."

Michael tried to control his amusement.

"Okay, here's the story." Karen handed Michael an inch-thick file filled with detailed analyses and studies, most printed from the Internet.

"Now, of course I know you won't read all this, but take it in case you change your mind. Let me take you through it verbally."

He opened the "Artificial Intelligence" folder immediately but listened as Karen summarized the reports.

She began, glancing occasionally at her handwritten notes. "You have a lot of very sophisticated research going on all over the world on this—from high-tech companies like Google and GE to major universities. The centers for all this are Silicon Valley and various places in Europe—"

"What the hell is it, exactly?" Michael interrupted.

"Okay, Boss. I can tell I'm missing something here. But here goes. Artificial intelligence is the use of computer technology to simulate the human mind. It's supposed to eventually be better than the human mind because the computer can store an endless amount of information and can be programmed to make better use of logic than most humans. There is supposedly some very sophisticated software that replicates the human mind and its reasoning and judgment."

"Does it replicate the human mind in general—or a specific person?" Michael's mind was overheating as he tried to guess what his brother had been up to.

"Both. The material I've read and printed out for you mostly talks about the human mind in general. But you'll also see some work that's being done to really emulate a particular person and, in a sense, create a computer model of that individual's mind.

"They do it by feeding into this software millions of bits of information, the person's past decisions, and all kinds of data. There is a very complicated questionnaire, with thousands of theoretical situations and questions that the subject person would have to feed into the software. Then it constantly gets updated by new events, and the person keeps interacting with it so that eventually, the computer can pretty much predict or emulate the behavior, actions, or decisions that the person would make in real life. I understand that they are also working on simulating a person's emotions."

Michael pressed further. "What do you mean, simulating the emotions?"

"Well, as you know from your own peculiar political tendencies, we don't always make decisions or have beliefs based upon common sense or logic. Sometimes what we do or what we believe defies logic, or is just plain stupid." Michael could see that Karen was obviously feeling more comfortable again, poking fun at his left-leaning politics. He just raised his eyebrows ever so slightly and let the remark go.

She glanced at Michael, and he noticed the beginnings of a repressed smirk, but she continued on. "The point is, part of what makes a person unique is the emotion—as opposed to just the abstract logic—that goes into that person's belief and decision systems. So if you are going to, in a sense, replicate someone's mind, you have to also build in their emotional state."

"I guess this could be powerful stuff if you were trying to predict the behavior or decisions of a competitor or an enemy, in business, in the courthouse, or politics or wars." Michael was grasping the point of it all. What he couldn't figure out was whether it had any applicability or value to Alex.

"It's none of my business, but where are we going with all of this? What does this have to do with Gibraltar's business?"

Michael ignored the question and pressed on. "What about the image of the person? Can the computer show the head or body of the individual?"

"Well, there have also been great advances in computer imaging, sometimes even 3D imaging. There are programs being developed that continually photograph a person using a camera—called a webcam—attached to a computer monitor. Eventually, the computer learns to accurately reproduce at least the facial qualities and expressions of the person in a way that is compatible with the feelings or verbal communications coming out of that person."

"What else? What about the voice? Can the computer speak?"

"Yes, Boss, with what they call voice replication technology, the computer learns to reproduce the subject's voice, perfectly. That part is pretty easy."

"And can this artificial—or re-created—person recognize who he's talking to?"

"My goodness, you are on a roll today. That part is trickier. You'll see from the reports, if you read them, that there have been some breakthroughs on this. Through the latest voice and visual recognition technology, this artificial person, in a sense, cannot only recognize who is speaking to him—or her, by the way—but can also visually recognize the other person. All of this technology, the software at least, is pretty exotic and is being created and perfected, separately, in various parts of the world. But what's interesting is that it's all done through a computer with a webcam, microphone, and speakers, which are pretty much standard these days."

Michael nodded, his eyes drifting off. "I see." He could see from Karen's expressions that her curiosity was killing her. He was also thankful that she hadn't asked about the coordinates that turned out to be Saint Michael's cemetery. After all, he still didn't know himself what to make of that message from Apple.

"Does this all make sense?" she asked.

"Yeah, it does," Michael answered, trying to figure out if all this had anything to do with what Alex and Russell were working on. "Has anyone put the computer imaging, voice duplication, and recognition together with the artificial intelligence?"

"Yes, he was called Dr. Frankenstein. Is that what you mean?"

Chapter 21

New York City
November 19, 2009

I t was time to get acquainted with Sharkey.

Michael chose to meet him at Pete's Tavern in Manhattan's Gramercy Park neighborhood. Michael had eaten there many times over the years, starting after college when he lived a block away on Irving Place. It wasn't exactly his home turf, but it was a place where they at least *used* to know his name.

The tavern was likely to be unfamiliar to Sharkey, the crowd there was too young, the owner Irish, and its legacy was literary, not mobster. Michael appreciated its history: it had been around since 1864 and stayed open, disguised as a flower shop, during Prohibition; and O. Henry wrote one of his famous short stories there, in his favorite booth by the front door.

Michael walked up to the redbrick building and passed under the black canopy reaching out to the end of the sidewalk. Forever etched in his mind was the memory of one particular dinner here, the last one he would ever have with his father, just before he passed away.

The bar was busy with hard-core drinkers from the afternoon and a younger crowd that just arrived as their workday ended. Michael walked past the old zinc bar lined with endless rows of bottles and polished glasses waiting for the thirsty neighborhood dinner crowd. He wished he was still part of it. He longed for the carefree times he enjoyed at Pete's so many years ago.

Michael sat down at one of the tall private booths just past the bar, ensuring that, even though he was in a public and well-exposed place, he and Sharkey would have reasonable privacy. Fat and Skinny Lester were in a car less than a block away, south on Irving Place. If he needed them, Michael knew two things. First, he was in serious trouble. Second, they would be too late.

As he waited, Michael felt the same nervousness he felt before meeting with an important client. But he knew today's meeting would be different. He thought about the extensive briefing about Sharkey that the Lesters gave him last night.

Sharkey had been a Mafia "made" man at twenty-six, by which time he had made his mark with several hits. The most notable was the one he did alone, leaving a former wiseguy turned police informer with five bullets in his face from Sharkey's silenced pistol. It was a brazen murder performed in classic Hollywood-Mafia style, inside an Upper East Side Manhattan beauty salon while his stylish victim was having his hair washed.

Sharkey, dressed in an immaculate black silk suit, white shirt, and black tie, took over the gentle massaging of his victim's wet head, then just before shooting, whispered for him to open his eyes. As Sharkey was leaving, he turned to the terrorized hairdresser and politely said, "He's all yours. Sorry about the mess." Sharkey calmly exited, his white shirt splattered red, smoking gun in hand.

The next day, the *Daily News* had a graphic picture of the scene in its centerfold showing the lifeless body with a bloody towel covering its head still in the salon chair, as though awaiting the final rinse. The *New York Post* dubbed the unidentified killer "the Clairol

Gunman" and heralded the murder itself "a hair-raiser." Sharkey reveled in the notoriety.

Sharkey's flair for the dramatic, with its resulting publicity, caused him to be shunned by many of his crime family's leadership, leaving him mostly on his own for his income and survival. Although a blow to his ego, Sharkey had survived. Using his talent for local business shakedowns and his thriving prostitution houses, he prospered. And with the extortion of several of his high-profile prostitution customers whom Sharkey captured in living color on his hidden cameras, Sharkey created lifelong annuities.

Christ, who the hell am I meeting with? Michael thought. *I need a drink.* Just as he ordered a martini, Joseph Sharkey appeared through the front door.

Although now nearly seventy and slight—if not fragile—in stature, Michael could see why Sharkey was still feared. Michael took a deep breath. *This guy looks like a psychopath.*

Seeing him approach, Michael remembered Fat Lester's story about the poor soul who had unintentionally collided with Sharkey in a bar men's room and was later found dead, his head in the toilet. "Just making people piss in their pants is all this guy needs to be happy," Skinny Lester had said.

Sharkey's eyes were sunk far back in his head, his hair coiffed into a receding white pompadour that matched his thin moustache. Michael figured that Sharkey had to use hair spray to keep it that stiff. He wore a heavy diamond-studded gold watch and a diamond ring with a gold band that even a hip-hop star would have envied. He was deathly pale, seeming to have been already embalmed, giving him a corpse-like sheen, especially when contrasted with his all-black attire: black turtleneck, black pants, pointed black shoes, black silk sports coat, and black leather jacket.

"Joseph, it's good to finally meet you," Michael said, trying to break the ice after what seemed to be an unusually long initial silence. He felt awkward, and he knew his words sounded stiff, too formal for this man.

Sharkey looked around, scanning the restaurant. Michael wondered whether he was looking for undercover agents or if this was simply a habit that developed with the territory. Michael watched, intimidated yet fascinated. Finally, Sharkey spoke, slowly and deliberately, with a strong Brooklyn accent.

"Michael, please accept my condolences regarding your brother. He was my friend. He was crazy, but he was someone I could trust. He could be difficult, but he was good for his word. God rest his soul."

"Thanks. He was a good brother," Michael said, trying to stay grounded in the ridiculous situation he found himself in. It felt like a Hollywood scene, without the cameras and with only one actor. Michael could sense the disconnect he felt as though he was a viewer in the audience, not an actor in the scene.

He hoped to first try to establish some sort of relationship, to size up Sharkey. The wild card was whether Sharkey was violent. His history certainly suggested it. Was this going to be a confrontation or a meeting with a business associate? If it were the latter, he would begin to feel more at ease. If there was a physical element to this, it would be a brave new world for Michael, one he knew he was not yet prepared for. Worse, he suspected that Sharkey also knew it.

Michael remembered Skinny Lester's suggestion that he try to talk about baseball. So, trying to lighten things up, Michael said, "How about those Yankees this year?" As soon as he said it, he knew it sounded contrived, off.

Suddenly, as though on cue, Sharkey's mood visibly changed. It was apparently time to get serious. Sharkey's facial muscles tightened and a vein in his forehead magically appeared under his skin. At the same time, his smile disappeared, his forehead furrowed, and the lines around his mouth tightened as his eyes narrowed. It was a sudden and frightening transformation.

"Michael, you seem like a good man. I know you want to do the right thing here. I'm worried though. I know this business is not in your blood. It doesn't come naturally to you; you know what I'm saying? Your brother, God rest his soul, he understood that certain obligations have to be met. Whether you have the money or not, no one wants to know. You find it and take care of things; you see what I'm saying?"

"I understand." Michael did understand, but he doubted whether it was coming across at that moment. He felt like he couldn't get his footing; he was slipping.

Sharkey was tightening further, his face becoming almost grotesquely contorted. "Michael, don't you fucking patronize me." He leaned onto Michael's side of the table, his face inches from Michael's. Sharkey's left hand gripped his wineglass so tightly it looked like the stem would shatter at any moment. Michael noticed that Sharkey's right hand was missing from view.

"Michael, I've been at this maybe fifty years longer than you. I know you picked this place because you wanted to be sure we were in a public place. It don't matter to me."

Sharkey gave a slight smile as he continued. "I have a pistol under the table pointed at your balls. It has a silencer. If I put four or five bullets in your crotch right now, you won't even be able to scream. You'll want to, Michael, because the pain is excruciating, but you won't be able to make a sound. After the last bullet, I'll slowly get up and leave the restaurant. You'll be in agony. Eventually the waiter will come, but it'll be too late. You won't even live long enough to pay the bill."

Michael was sure he felt the barrel of the gun brush lightly against his knee.

"Michael, do you understand me? Have we bonded, as they say in your corporate world? I think so. We have to do this again. Maybe have your secretary call my secretary. You know? It's a great life, Michael. Don't fuck yourself now. Bring me my seven hundred thousand and the interest—I think another hundred thousand—by Wednesday next week. Otherwise, Michael, you better wear a cup next time."

Sharkey got up from the table and walked out of Pete's Tavern.

Chapter 22

Westport, Connecticut
November 20, 2009

"So, how was your dinner with Mr. Sharkey last night?" Samantha said, just as they were seated in the rustic, Tuscan-style restaurant, Rustico, nearby their home in Westport. "After spending all this time with Sofia at Notre Dame, I feel like I've missed all the excitement."

"Brief. I had a drink and left. We never even ate."

"Well, it was a little early for dinner, don't you think? I mean, who eats dinner at five thirty?"

"Actually, meeting him was helpful. He clarified some confusion about how much Alex owed him. We didn't stick around long. He had to go." Michael knew he could not mention the gun to his groin. Instead, he said, "You look beautiful tonight," which had the desired effect of changing the subject.

"Michael, I wish you'd wear a sport coat when we're out to dinner. You look so good in them."

He was dressed in his typical casual dinner winter attire: tan slacks, blue button-down shirt, and a black crewneck cashmere sweater. He knew that it was rare when he was able to escape the house with Samantha and his initial choice of attire intact.

"You realize that not one guy in this restaurant has a sport coat on?" Michael said.

"I realize that, but you'll notice I didn't marry any of those men," Samantha answered, apparently unfazed.

Michael and Samantha shared many traits, including a certain playfulness and an easy sense of humor, which characterized their dinners. When they were joined by others, dinner conversation resembled a husband-and-wife comedy routine.

"How did Sofia react to the break-in?" Michael asked, turning serious.

"She's okay. I'm not sure she's connected everything yet. Neither have we, for that matter. You know, she's kind of in her own world at school. As sensitive as she is, at that age we're all a bit self-centered. I think she's very upset over Alex's murder though, and of course she doesn't have any idea that you're doing anything with his business affairs."

"Good, she doesn't need to know," Michael said.

"Yes, I suppose so. It would be even better, however, if it was the truth." She cast a suspicious look in Michael's direction, just avoiding a direct stare. Michael got the message.

Samantha finished her first cocktail. It was just enough for her to go where Michael hoped she wouldn't.

"Michael, why do I get the sense that you're not telling me everything?"

Michael bought time by lifting his martini up to his lips and taking a long sip. "Believe me, you don't want to know everything."

"I don't know whether I do or not. You may be right. But I also don't want us to be in any more danger, and I don't want to have to worry about you."

"There's nothing to worry about." As soon as the words left his lips, he wished they hadn't. He knew better.

"Michael, I don't know how you can possibly say that as long as the people who are behind all these horrible things are still out there. You can't be serious."

"No, you're right. There is danger, obviously. But that's one reason I have to stick with this. The police may never figure it all out. I get the feeling they're overloaded already, and all this stuff is just too complicated. The answers are buried somewhere beneath the mysteries of Alex's illegal business and the people he did business with. Samantha, I need to fulfill my obligation to Alex—to help Donna wind it down and to maybe, in the process, uncover who killed him. That may be the best way to be sure we are safe."

Michael took another sip. He believed everything he had just said, but he knew there was another voice deep inside him—the one that whispered that he had to keep going, but not just for the reasons he just gave to Samantha. Maybe it was an excitement he hadn't experienced in years. Then there were the strange but so inviting characters—the Lesters, Maria, even his somewhat mysterious and sexy sister-in-law. People, he realized now, that he would miss.

Or was this an impulse, a need, driven by something deeper, something in his makeup, his genes? Those were the same genes as his brother, and that was a worrisome thought. Either way, Michael couldn't explain exactly why, even to himself, but he needed to do whatever was necessary to continue down the path of his brother's old life, wherever it might lead. At least for now.

"Michael, you're so engaged and engaging, yet at the same time, so removed. I still sense there's more going on in your head."

Michael knew she was right again, which is why he was particularly relieved to see Rustico's head chef and owner, Miguel, come bounding out of the kitchen to their table, his arms spread open.

"Ah, Michael, Samantha, my friends. I love to see you."

Michael enjoyed Miguel and his energetic, warm-blooded Brazilian personality, but tonight, as he hugged Miguel, Michael's mind wandered. He tried to quickly sort through his brain to make sense of what it was that drew him to Alex's treacherous life. For as long as he could remember, Michael saw himself as living two different lives: the obvious one that everyone saw, and then another life. A life that was strictly his, that no one else inhabited. It was his private life, the one he lived inside his own mind, like that unsettling dream he often returned to yet couldn't always remember. At certain times, those two existences didn't seem to connect—or worse, were fighting each other. This was one of those times.

Michael knew that the steps he was taking to enter his brother's life were in conflict with the external world that he inhabited. He wondered how he could possibly reconcile those conflicting realities to Samantha.

"Michael, I love you. You and Sofia are everything to me. You're my world, and I'm behind you, no matter what. I know that you've become disenchanted with your business life. But you've worked so hard to get where you are. Be careful that you don't throw it away. You're not your brother, you know."

"I do know, Samantha. We were very different." But of that, Michael was less sure than he had ever been. It was an unsettling thought.

"And don't let yourself be persuaded to do things you don't want to do—or you know you shouldn't do—out of guilt. I understand obligation, but you have nothing to feel guilty about."

"I know you're right. I've just got to go with this a little longer. I've got to see it through, and ..." Michael hesitated.

"What is it?" Samantha asked.

"I can't help wondering what it was that Alex was so anxious to show me. It was so out of character for him to hold back some surprise, or whatever it was."

"Michael, I know how you feel, but sometimes you just have to let things go. You'll probably never find out."

"It's funny, but I feel I will," Michael said, unable to stop thinking about his conversation with Skinny Lester and Karen's briefing on artificial intelligence. He wanted to mention both to Samantha—along with the message he had received under Alex's name at the cemetery. But this wasn't the time. He had to find out more; it was probably just a hacker. Yet the message, though incomplete, seemed to hold out another puzzle, not the usual work of hackers. To mention all of it now would only further frighten Samantha and perhaps even invite her skepticism over his sanity.

Their plates had arrived. Michael looked at his plate of fresh fettuccine with lamb meatballs in a rich tomato sauce, topped with goat cheese, and said, "Some needs are easy to satisfy. I do love dinner."

As she picked up her fork, Samantha looked around at the busy dining room. "God, I don't remember the last time we had a quiet dinner at home." Samantha had calmed down and seemed reflective; it was very unusual for her, Michael thought.

"Neither do I. But let's face it, we've always enjoyed eating out."

A smile electrified Samantha's face. "Remember when the Realtor was showing us homes in Westport and she took us to the one where the kitchen was being redone so there was only a telephone on the wall—no appliances, counters, or anything?"

"Yes." Michael smiled, his body finally relaxing.

"And you walked in and pronounced, 'This is the perfect kitchen! All we need is the phone for reservations.' That was so funny."

Michael's cell phone buzzed. It was Jack Benoit, the head of technology at Gibraltar Financial. Suddenly Michael's muscles tensed again. "I'm sorry. I'd better take this call. It's a guy from Gibraltar. He wouldn't call at dinner unless it was important," he said to Samantha as he pressed the phone to his ear.

"Hi, Jack, what are you doing at this late hour?"

"Mr. Nicholas, I'm sorry to bother you, but there are some strange things going on with your e-mail account."

"Strange things? What do you mean, Jack?"

"There have been some highly unusual—and sophisticated— attempts to break into your e-mail account. It's not the usual spam attacks or viruses. I hate to admit it, but I've never come across anything like this before. Neither has anyone on our IT staff."

"Well, what does it mean, Jack? Am I the only one who's being attacked?"

"Yes, just you. At least in this manner. And I'm not sure that 'being attacked' is even the right way to describe it. It looks as though someone is trying to communicate with you from some type of server, or source, that we can't identify. I thought perhaps you might be aware of anything unusual. Maybe one of your kids is a real high-tech genius and is showing off?"

"Well, I have a daughter, Sofia. She's pretty damn smart, but not a techy type. She's away at college. I'm sure it's not her. I have been receiving some odd messages since my brother, uh—"

"I'm very sorry by the way to hear about your brother's death."

"That's okay, thanks. But I have been getting some unusual e-mails and messages. In fact, a few days ago, I received an instant message that seemed to have been cut off in the middle."

"That may have been a result of the actions we've taken here to block these intrusions."

"Oh, good, I appreciate what you're doing." Michael didn't want to mention that the e-mails and instant messages all revolved around—or appeared to be sent by—Alex. He didn't want to draw any more attention within Gibraltar to connections to his brother's life than was already obvious from the news accounts of his murder. But now he wondered again what the rest of the message was and, of course, who really sent it.

"Jack, you didn't happen to save the remainder of that instant message that was cut off, did you?"

"No, as I said, we were able to block the full message from coming through at all. Listen, Mr. Nicholas, there's no cause for concern. We're on top of this. We've been able now to deny access so there should be no further breach. Don't worry. I just thought I'd check in case you were aware of anything unusual going on."

"Okay, thanks." Michael exchanged glances with Samantha. "There's nothing unusual that I'm aware of." *No, just two murders, our house broken into, strange e-mail and messages, a gangster with a gun in my crotch, and a missing Apple device that seems to be located in the cemetery where my brother is buried.*

Chapter 23

M ichael looked out of Alex's kitchen window at the small in-ground pool, now hidden under its green winter tarpaulin. He remembered how, in the summer months, Alex loved to lounge in the shallow water, the Yankee game playing loudly on his transistor radio nearby as he soaked up the sun. It was all the vacation he ever needed. It was his version of Saint-Tropez. "Everyone speaks English here," he would say. "And after a few drinks, Donna goes topless."

Sitting around the kitchen table were Skinny and Fat Lester, Michael, and Donna who had taken a taxi from the Carlyle back to her home for the day. Michael had filled everyone in on the details of his aborted dinner meeting with Sharkey.

"We all know what happened with Sharkey. I figured we should sit down together and discuss where we go from here." Michael knew the heat was on. Things had to happen in the next few days, but he was unsure what their options were.

"Sharkey wants his money—not to mention another hundred grand in interest—by Wednesday."

Fat Lester's face became distorted with rage. "Wait a minute, Michael. First of all, Sharkey is full of shit. Alex never paid anyone interest on bets. As long as Sharkey gets his money, there's no fucking interest. I'd like to break Sharkey's fucking neck. He had no right to treat you that way last night. Alex would have killed him if he had seen it. He would have broken him in two."

"Lester, you told me you guys never really even touched anyone." Michael was trying to keep Fat Lester calm.

"We did some stuff. We did some good stuff. I didn't want to scare you." Fat Lester, with a mischievous smile, looked first at his cousin and then Michael. Michael wasn't sure what to make of the remark or Lester's facial expression.

Skinny Lester, characteristically, appeared calmer than his cousin. "Alex charged interest when he *made* loans. He never *paid* interest. If we owed money, we paid right away. We're not crooks. This isn't Bank of America, for God's sake."

"Okay, Sharkey knew he had a rookie with me the other day. I figured the interest was bullshit. Let's worry about that later. How do we deal with the seven hundred grand that he actually won?" Michael was trying to keep this discussion as clear and concise as he could. "But first, what's our cash situation? Have we collected what these guys owed Alex?"

Fat Lester jumped in. "We've collected some of it."

"We've collected about three hundred and fifty thousand of the five hundred grand that we were owed from sports," Skinny Lester said, "and we paid out about fifty grand on bets we owed. Plus we had about a hundred and twenty grand lying around from before."

Michael was always astonished at how his brother handled cash. He remembered Alex always having a wad of fifties and hundreds in his pocket. Alex used to joke to friends, "My little brother here carries a fuckin' black American Express card. I just carry fuckin' cash."

Michael did a quick tally. "So we have four hundred and twenty thousand in cash, is that right?"

"That's right, Michael," Skinny Lester answered. "But we've got to come up with at least seven hundred to pay Sharkey."

"Unless we kill him first," Donna said. Michael wondered whether it was obvious that his jaw had involuntarily dropped.

Fat Lester smiled again, ever so slightly.

Chapter 24

New York City
November 21, 2009

Michael decided that he needed to stay in New York for the next few days. The trip back and forth to Connecticut was becoming tedious, and he had convinced Samantha to take off again and bring Sofia to Chicago where he would meet them for Thanksgiving.

He booked a junior suite at the Carlyle, specifically requesting a room on a different floor than Donna's. He treasured what little privacy and solitude he had left. The suite, with its soft lighting, beige walls, and views of the Manhattan skyline, gave him a sense of detachment, beyond the street and above the fray. He was to meet Donna shortly for a drink downstairs in Bemelmans Bar.

Michael longed for the quiet evenings at home with Samantha across the dining room table at home or in their familiar restaurants in Westport. Now his life had become an endless stream of Donna, drinks, and dinners, babysitting the Lesters, and being terrorized by the likes of Sharkey.

With an hour to kill before meeting Donna, he had spoken at

length with Samantha and Sofia. It was an awkward conversation since they did not want Sofia to know the whole story of what was going on.

Michael's cell phone rang; it was Karen. "Hi, Boss. Just thought you might want to know that Chairman Dick called for you. He asked if I knew when you were expected back."

Karen and Michael unaffectionately referred to Michael's boss, Dick Applegarden, as "Chairman Dick."

"Karen, did I ever tell you my theory that executives fall into two categories?"

"No, Boss, I don't think you did. Is this a joke coming on?"

"No, not at all. I'm serious. There are two types of business executives. I call them Velcros and Teflons. The Teflons do little, blame others for their mistakes, and take credit for successes, whether theirs or not. The Velcros generally do the work for the Teflons, get saddled with the failures (whether theirs or not), and never get credit for their successes. Our good Chairman Dick is a Teflon."

"And I guess that makes you a Velcro?"

"Actually, no. But that's a very good question. I should know better than to tangle with you."

Finally relaxing, Michael stretched his legs out on the coffee table. "Karen, you have to buy me another week or so. I'm trying to clean up a mess here with my brother's affairs and my sister-in-law. Just get back to Dick and reassure him that I'm in touch daily, and that I'll definitely be at the global business meeting in Beverly Hills on the second, so he doesn't have to worry. I'm supposed to be a speaker—he's probably worried that he may have to fill in for me."

"That reminds me, Michael; we haven't discussed the speech yet, have we? Any thoughts? Do you want me to have marketing put an outline or some ideas together?" Karen, as usual, was on top of things. Michael believed she could do most senior executives' jobs better than they did themselves.

"Don't worry about it. I need to think it through on my own

first. I want to do something I've never done before." Michael was scheduled to speak on the topic of "corporate cultures." The last two weeks had given him a fresh perspective on a lot of things. As he thought about reconnecting with his business life, he was determined to do things differently moving forward. He wished he had a video of his discussion with Sharkey. It would be a great lesson for corporate executives on negotiation skills. The world no longer looked the way it did before Alex's murder. If he was going back to his old world, it would be on different terms. Karen's next comments, however, brought him back to Alex's world.

"Michael," Karen hesitated, "I thought you mentioned that your car broke down and was towed from the cemetery."

"Yeah, it was. I was astonished at how quickly this guy got the tow truck there. Why?"

"Well, the police just called. They found the car."

"What do you mean, the *police* found the car? It's supposed to be at some garage in Astoria. I have the name somewhere. They're working on it."

"Oh, they worked on it all right. The police found it just off Chelsea Piers."

"You mean at the police pound there?"

"No." Karen paused. "Not in the lot. In the Hudson River."

Bemelmans Bar was a Manhattan landmark and glorified watering hole for visiting movie stars, New York socialites, politicians, and Wall Street titans. Ludwig Bemelmans was a famous *Vogue* and *New Yorker* magazine artist, and also the creator of the classic Madeline books for kids. In 1947, he painted the bar's walls with clever, whimsical murals and scenes in exchange for his hotel bill. The legendary New York pianist and entertainer Bobby Short ruled the bar's piano for decades.

Tonight Michael Feinstein held court at the piano with his own selection of jazz-inspired, classic songs. As Michael felt the warmth of his first sips of his martini, Feinstein sang an old Sinatra tune, "Strangers in the Night." It was a perfect backdrop for a strong drink and a light bar meal while seated at one of the chocolate-brown banquettes. The dark art deco decor and soft lighting made it difficult to see the other patrons, a likely reason for the bar's popularity with celebrity clients.

Donna's face, however, was clearly visible to Michael. He struggled, as he had since the day his brother married her, to understand what lurked inside, underneath her good looks.

Michael needed to discuss Donna's comments this morning about eliminating Sharkey. He now also wanted to break the news to her about his car showing up at the bottom of the Hudson River. He was getting frustrated by her apparent indifference to the events unfolding and her somewhat erratic, if not incendiary comments. She couldn't have been serious about Sharkey, he thought—and hoped. Michael was gaining a newfound respect for what his brother must have had to deal with every day.

"Donna, what in the world were you thinking this morning when you talked about killing Sharkey?" Michael was straining to keep his composure.

"Shh, Michael, that's Rudy Giuliani at that table in the corner with his wife." As usual, Donna's eyes and attention were not focused on the conversation but on a celebrity watch around the room.

"I don't give a shit about Giuliani. What the hell did you mean this morning? And in front of Fat Lester, of all fucking people." Michael heard Alex in his own words. It surprised him and made him uneasy.

"Michael," Donna was now speaking as though she were the sane and calm one instead of her increasingly volatile brother-in-law. "You have to relax and calm down. You're overreacting. I wasn't serious; I was just suggesting that it was one way to eliminate a seven-hundred-thousand-dollar problem, that's all. I'm sure there are much better solutions. You're going to get high blood pressure like your brother."

"Shit, listen, I'm expecting the police to call me here shortly. My secretary called a few minutes ago while I was in my room. They found my BMW at the bottom of the Hudson River."

"Michael," Donna said with a straight face, "did you leave it there?"

Just as Michael rolled his eyes, his cell phone rang. After a weary sigh, Michael accepted the call. "Michael Nicholas."

"Michael, it's Fletcher. I just spoke with the Manhattan police. They want to question you tonight. They know you're at the Carlyle. I told them I would call you to be sure you knew they were contacting you and that you stayed put until they called. I just tried your room."

"I'm in the bar," Michael said.

"I should have figured."

Michael anticipated that Fletcher was letting him know what he had already heard from Karen. "I understand they found my car—which had broken down at the cemetery the other day and was towed—under the Hudson."

"Michael," Fletcher's tone turned more serious, "it's more than that."

"What does that mean?"

"They also found a body in your car."

And then, as if in a scene from an old James Bond movie—a tuxedoed waiter appeared with a phone from the bar. "Mr. Nicholas, I believe this call is for you. They said it's a detective."

Chapter 25

Westport, Connecticut
November 22, 2009

M ichael knew he was in over his head. He needed Fletcher's advice—and a bowl of spaghetti with Tiger's special meatballs. They sat down for both at their regular table inside Mario's large front window.

"Jesus, Fletcher. My car turns up at the bottom of the Hudson, someone breaks into our house and terrorizes us and then calls your cops on a scanner, my brother and Russell are both murdered, I've got a Mafia psycho pointing a gun at my balls and demanding eight hundred thousand dollars by Wednesday, and I'm dealing with my sister-in-law who's either a nut job or scary, most likely both."

"Imagine what next week could bring," Fletcher said while sipping his cocktail.

Michael let the remark sink in. "The thought of next week gives me a strange mix of fear—and a rush of adrenalin."

"I hope it's more fear. Listen, Westport isn't exactly a hotbed of criminal activity, but between my time here as chief and my days with the NYPD, I've seen a lot of shit. This isn't good, Michael. You're getting caught up in something neither of us understand at this point. Something dangerous and violent. The city cops told me they think the dead guy in your car was some thug the mob must have knocked off for some reason they don't yet know. You didn't recognize him though, right?"

"No, I never saw the guy before." Michael couldn't get the images the police showed him last night of the dead body out of his mind. "The cops said they were pretty sure he was shot and killed somewhere else and then placed in the car before they rolled it off the pier. But the other crazy thing is that my car broke down at the cemetery on Monday. Some guy who I first thought was chasing me winds up approaching Skinny Lester and me in the car and offers to have it towed to a nearby garage in Astoria. Five minutes later, the tow truck shows up. I thought, *Wow, that was fucking fast.*"

"The police checked with the garage—they claim they never towed your car in and didn't know a thing about it," Fletcher said.

"Why would they bother to dump the car in the river anyway?" Michael asked, his mind replaying the day in the cemetery.

"Who knows? Could be they thought it would make it harder for the cops to get any fingerprints or evidence. Or maybe they wanted to send you a message. Sometimes these guys don't act logically or have reasons we'd understand. They may have had a few to drink or were a little nuts, and they felt like doing it."

A smiling Tiger appeared at the table, jolting Michael's attention back to the world in front of him. "Drinks are on me, guys. Michael, I hear you had a rough week. You better get Samantha back home. You're dangerous home alone. Remember that movie?" Tiger was laughing.

"Tiger," Michael protested, "that was about a little kid left home alone at Christmas."

"Well, it's just about December, and you're like a little kid." Fletcher and even Michael had to laugh.

The evening progressed over Michael's martinis and Fletcher's manhattans. Michael recounted in great detail the amazing events of the past week, including Skinny Lester's revelation at the cemetery.

"He said he saw Alex having a conversation with himself on his own computer. He said Alex had Russell do some computer stuff for him. I'm thinking it might have to do with artificial intelligence. But I doubt Alex even knew what that was, and when the police scoured his computers, they didn't find anything unusual."

"Your brother was definitely a character. It was probably just one of those new apps or games."

"Most likely, but there's more. At Alex's funeral, I received an e-mail with his picture and some saying about death—which then disappeared. It just dissolved. I couldn't find it again in my e-mails. Then at the wake, I got one of my brother's famous e-mails announcing the death of some celebrity, like he used to send me when he was alive—and it came from his own e-mail address. Also, at the cemetery, I received a partial instant message that also appeared to be from Alex. Plus, my e-mail account at Gibraltar has been under an unusual but sophisticated attack. Then, listen to this: I'm having dinner here at Mario's the other night, and I receive a notification on my BlackBerry that some lost Apple device has been located."

Fletcher scratched his chin. "Okay, that's a lot of weird stuff. I don't know—"

Michael interrupted, "It gets weirder. The message about the lost device gave its location; it was at Saint Michael's cemetery."

"Maybe they buried your brother with his iPhone?"

"He didn't have an iPhone. He just used some basic cell phone that Donna's now using. I know because Donna called me on his phone recently—long after Alex was buried."

"Okay, I admit all this computer stuff is definitely unusual, but from my experience, there's a lot of odd things that go on. Sometimes you get hacked, and then all of a sudden shit happens. But, you're lucky, no one's gotten hold of your credit card or bank information."

"I suppose so." Michael wasn't convinced, although Fletcher's explanation sounded plausible.

"Listen, Michael, let's get back to your involvement in your brother's business. You're in deep here. You've jumped into a world that you know little about. This isn't a Fortune 500 boardroom. These guys play in a different sandbox. You can get hurt, physically. Can't you get yourself out of this whole thing? I mean, what do you want to do?" Michael could see the expression of deep concern on Fletcher's face.

"I can't abandon my brother's wife. How's she going to work out of this mess? And I've known Fat and Skinny Lester since I was a little kid. They can't deal with this on their own. They'll wind up dead or broke," Michael said. "And I'm already on someone's radar due to this whole thing."

"Okay, for now at least, let's take it one step at a time. You've got to get a few big things done. First, help these two Lesters collect the remaining money that's due your brother, then find a way to either pay off or deal with Sharkey—by Wednesday—and finally, figure out who's messing with you now. And that may or may not be the same people who had your brother murdered. Right?"

"I think you've summarized the situation perfectly," Michael said. "Here's what I've been thinking. I could just 'loan' Alex's business enough money—it'd be three or four hundred grand—out of my own savings to pay off Sharkey on Wednesday and then get it back when Lester collects the rest of the money owed."

"What if they don't collect the balance?" Fletcher said, adding, "Samantha will have your head."

"There's more, Fletcher. We believe Alex stashed a couple of million dollars somewhere in his house. Russell built secret hiding places for him. Of course, now they're both dead. Donna's been trying to find out where these secret compartments might be, but she hasn't found anything yet. She's even ripped up some of the construction or improvements that she knows Russell made in the house. Nothing has turned up."

"Are you sure Donna hasn't found any of Alex's money in the house?" Fletcher was skeptical.

"I can't know for sure, but I highly doubt it. One of the reasons she's moved back to the house is to stay close to it and try to figure out where the cash is hidden. I think Donna's a manipulator, and I'm sure she's a good liar, but I don't think she'd deceive me. At least not right now. She needs me."

"I have to tell you, Michael, I'm almost in shock here. This just isn't like you. I mean, you're almost like a Boy Scout. Most normal people, just seeing this guy Russell *literally* nailed dead, would be running the other way. What's going on with you?"

"Fletcher, I'm not exactly sure myself. I know that I'm doing this for all the things I've said already, for my brother and Donna and all that. But there's more. I can't exactly understand it myself. As crazy as it sounds, I feel like this is something that I *want* to do. This business, I mean. And it's more than just the business; it's also something about the life or some of the people. There's an odd attraction here, but I'll be honest, I'm not sure exactly what it is. But for now at least, I've got to at least keep my commitment to Donna."

"You realize that, at some point, you cross over the line legally." Michael could see that Fletcher was putting on his law enforcement hat.

"At what point is that exactly, Fletcher?"

"Certainly when you either take money out for yourself or put your own money in, it's a problem. Also, anytime you engage in bookmaking or loan-sharking, you've crossed over the line."

"What about if I'm simply collecting money owed to my brother or paying off his debts?" Michael asked.

"Jesus, Michael. When did you become a criminal attorney? You probably are in trouble if you pay or collect and you had—or should have had—knowledge that they represented illegal activities. I think any reasonable person who knows about your meeting with Sharkey with a goddamned gun pointed at your balls under the table is going to assume that you know you're in the middle of illegal activities. Not to mention a few murders happening all around you."

"Is there any other risk?" Michael continued to try to evaluate where the week had taken his formerly respectable, traditional life.

"Yes."

"What is it?"

"That you wind up like your brother."

Chapter 26

New York City
November 23, 2009

"Y**ou're probably wondering why I called you. Your brother was more than a client to me. I don't want to hurt his wife or family in any way, but Alex told me some things I think you'll want to know. I didn't know who else to tell."

Jennifer Walsh was beautiful. In her early thirties, with high cheekbones, a permanent tan, and blonde hair tied back in a pony-tail, she wore tight-fitting designer jeans that accentuated her long legs. Jennifer's turquoise-blue eyes competed for attention with her perfectly aligned breasts that jutted out beneath her thin red sweater, the point of her nipples visible through the fabric.

Michael had seen those breasts before. They were the same ones proudly displayed by each of Alex's three wives. Dr. Simonetti's handiwork was hard to miss, particularly on Jennifer.

"Michael, thank you so much for meeting me here. It was nice of you to suggest lunch." He caught the familiar scent of Chanel No. 5 as it wafted in the air around Jennifer.

Michael had no idea when Jennifer called him earlier in the day that she was someone who would turn every male—and female—head in the restaurant as she strolled by the bar and approached his table. He was curious as to why Jennifer wanted to meet with him. She was Alex's hairdresser, or "barber" as Alex preferred to call her. But Jennifer was anything but just a barber. She worked for one of the highest profile hairdressing salons in downtown Manhattan. Her clientele included some of the hottest, most glamorous starlets. Alex was her only male client.

"It's great to meet you. I hope this place was convenient for you. It's one of my favorites."

Mia Dona was a good-looking restaurant, highly stylized yet comfortable, on Manhattan's East Fifty-Eighth Street. Jennifer ordered a glass of champagne. Michael followed with a glass of Riesling, partly so Jennifer wouldn't feel awkward drinking alone—not that it appeared she would.

Jennifer proposed a brief toast. "Here's to Alex, a good guy who didn't want anyone to know it." They clicked their glasses and both took a good swig.

Jennifer looked directly and intensely into Michael's eyes as if to emphasize her point. "Alex and I were lovers. We have—had—been lovers for over three years. Your brother could be a tough son of a bitch. But I never met a man with a bigger heart. He concealed it well. He was complicated, but I loved him and I know he loved me."

Although Jennifer also had a hardened exterior that she showed to the world, she appeared to Michael to be vulnerable underneath. Maybe, Michael thought, it was that vulnerability that appealed to Alex, in addition to Jennifer's stunning looks. But knowing Alex and now watching Jennifer, inhaling her scent and feeling the gaze of her powerful blue eyes, Michael concluded that her personality may have only played a secondary role in his brother's attachment to her.

Michael was unsure where this was going. Was she looking for money? Or were there more problems or unpleasant surprises coming? He continued to sip his wine and noticed Jennifer had already finished her glass of champagne. He ordered another round, figuring they both could benefit by breaking the ice a little quicker.

"Michael, first, I want you to know there is nothing that I want from you. I loved your brother. He had actually taken very good care of me already. There's nothing that I need. I'm successful on my own. I make unbelievable money doing hair. I just want to do the right thing by Alex. I know he trusted you."

"Thanks." Michael could feel himself begin to relax, a result, he figured, of her words and his second glass of wine. "I really didn't know what to expect, but I can see you're a good person." Michael realized that he had never thought about whether his brother trusted him. He wasn't yet sure about Jennifer Walsh, but she had just made him feel pretty good.

"Michael, I was more than just your brother's girlfriend or something. I mean he would come to my apartment just about every night, for hours. Most of the time, he'd stay until around three or four in the morning and then go home. Some nights he just stayed. I don't know how Donna never figured it out. I've never met her, but she must have been blind."

"Alex and his wives always seemed to have a combative type of relationship," Michael said.

She smiled; her perfect bright-white teeth and blue eyes reminded Michael of a cheerleader he managed to date once. "Alex loved women, especially beautiful ones. He collected wives, but they were like a separate species to him."

Michael sat, trying to absorb Jennifer's stream of perceptions, surprised by her insights and the apparent complexity of her personality.

Jennifer broke out into a laugh. "I'll never forget one night, he was half in the bag, and he looked at me, kind of staring into my eyes, and then he called me his 'muse.' I said to him, '*Muse*, where did you get that word? It wasn't an Alex word, if you know what I mean. He said he'd just seen a Woody Allen movie. That wasn't Alex either. Donna must have made him go. Alex was a riot; sometimes, at least."

Michael sensed that, like all of Alex's wives, Jennifer had a short attention span. Perhaps, he thought, it was a useful trait for anyone who had spent a lot of time with Alex. But, unlike Alex's wives, Jennifer Walsh had a certain spark, a high energy level, and a head on her shoulders.

Jennifer lifted her champagne flute and finished her second glass. She appeared nervous and tense and obviously was looking for something to relieve her anxiety. As he watched and listened, he sensed her insecurity but began to believe in her sincerity.

"Michael, there's a very important reason I asked to meet with you today."

"What is it? Is something wrong?" Michael could see Jennifer struggling, but he really had no clue what it could be, unless … But he quickly forced himself to stop speculating and turned his total attention to this beautiful woman who was now leaning in closer to him, her face only several inches from his, as he inhaled her Chanel scent.

"Here's the thing. I don't know if you know any of this already, but Alex had this obsession with living forever. He never believed in that stuff like where they froze Ted Williams's body."

"You mean cryonics?" Michael and his brother had once discussed the sad situation where the great baseball star's son actually had surgeons first decapitate and then preserve Williams's body in two pieces, frozen in liquid nitrogen.

"Alex said that was total bullshit, and he didn't like the idea of being split in two. But he was always talking about some way to live forever or something like that, you know?" Jennifer ordered another glass of champagne. Michael could see the tension beginning to lift as she began talking about Alex and perhaps unburdening herself.

"I know," Michael said. "I often thought he had too much free time on his hands. Sometimes, though, he had some really good insights."

"Well," Jennifer continued, "he really got into this artificial intelligence thing with computers. He had Russell do a whole lot of work for him on his computer, along with some imaging stuff so that *he made another real Alex on his computer.*" She was watching Michael's face and expressions as she was describing Alex's uncharacteristic foray into sophisticated technology and the afterlife.

Michael wanted to reassure her that he wasn't questioning her information. "I've heard a little about this from Alex's friend, Skinny Lester. Do you know him?"

"I met him a few times. Mostly by accident when Alex and I went out to eat. I didn't think Alex had told anyone about this except, of course, for Russell ... and my God, I read what happened to him."

"Well, I don't think he really meant to tell Lester, but I think they were sitting around Alex's house one night, and Alex had too much to drink and showed it off. But Lester didn't really know what to make of it. By the way, the police found nothing unusual, other than some porn, on Alex's computer."

Jennifer looked puzzled. "Which computer did they check?"

"Donna told me the police downloaded everything from Alex's office hard drives and his home computer that sits in his den," Michael said.

"Was it a regular big computer with a separate monitor and all that?"

"Yes. It's got a pretty large screen or monitor attached. Alex's was larger than most people's television screens." Michael was laughing.

"A lot of Alex's things were bigger than other people's." Jennifer leaned into the table, slightly invading Michael's private space, making him feel just a bit uneasy. "That's not the computer he used for real personal things—or for his artificial intelligence stuff."

"Oh my God, that's it." Michael brightened up with the

revelation. Now he knew what Alex had wanted to show him. "I never thought of that. There's another computer?"

Jennifer appeared to relax, ordered her fourth glass of champagne, and continued enthusiastically. "Alex never wanted to leave real personal things on his home computer. He also even set up a separate e-mail account just so we could e-mail and message each other. He was always nervous that someone would get on his home computer and see stuff."

"Who was he worried about?" Michael could see several more layers of Alex's life and personality being unraveled.

"Well, he was worried about everyone. Alex always worried about everything, you know. He was obsessed that someone might go on his computer—even innocently—while he was at work or out at night. He certainly didn't want Donna getting into it—especially if anything about me was in there. But he was also very concerned that this artificial intelligence stuff stayed a secret."

"So he had *another* computer ..." Michael was now the one leaning into the table.

"Well, Alex was also absolutely in love with Apple computers. He had an iPod, you know, for years. He had twenty thousand songs on it. Then, when he saw this Apple laptop—I think it was called a MacBook—he fell in love with it. After he got it home, he had these really smart people customize it or something. Alex said he owned the most powerful Mac in the world. He called it his 'Big Mac.'

"But here's where it got real interesting. He then had Russell do all this research and contact companies that specialized in artificial intelligence. One of them was in Europe, I think, some others in San Francisco or Silicon Valley. Alex spent a shitload of money on all this. Then Russell loaded all this new experimental artificial intelligence, and voice and imaging software onto the laptop.

"Alex brought the Apple over to my apartment one night. I swear he was obsessed with it. He said that, in the process of working with all that expensive software, Russell had made some big breakthrough, something that had never been done before. This laptop was unbelievable though. It weighed a ton, too. I told him, I thought those things were supposed to be light, but this was some special machine. I called it his 'mini Alex,' you know, like 'mini me.' He thought that was funny."

"Jennifer, where is this laptop now?"

"Michael, you have to promise me one thing."

"What's that?"

"You know that porn you mentioned? On Alex's other computer?"

Michael's imagination began to soar, despite his best efforts to stay focused. "Yes. I never saw it though. Donna just mentioned that the cops had found it."

"Oh, I don't care about that. It's the porn on his Apple laptop that I need your help with."

"What do you mean?"

"Well, it's pretty kinky. I'd hate for it to get out."

"What difference does it make? Why do you care?" Michael had already guessed the answer.

"I'm the star. It was meant to be private, just for Alex."

"I'll take care of it. I promise. But, Jennifer, where is the laptop?"

"It's where no one would ever find it." Jennifer's electric-blue eyes lit up. "Shall we order lunch?"

Chapter 27

Michael let himself in through the front door using the key
Donna had given him after Alex's murder. He entered the
security code, disabled the alarm system, and then walked
through the entry hall and up the stairs into the master bedroom.

Alex's house was dark. Michael knew that Donna was out to
dinner at a nearby Queens restaurant. He walked across the room,
switched on the lamp by the bed, and then turned and walked several steps over to Alex's personal closet, opening the double doors
and walking into the huge wardrobe.

In an odd flashback, he remembered, as a teenager, searching
his brother's closet, looking for Alex's collection of *Playboy* magazines. Tonight, as he turned on the closet's many recessed lights,
Michael was astonished by what he saw.

The closet was empty; not a trace of Alex was visible in the
dark-red mahogany shelves. Not a pair of trousers or a shirt. In
fact, the cabinetry looked brand-new, as though it had been built,
or rebuilt, quite recently. The walls had been freshly painted and

the carpeting, although the same design as the rest of the master suite, was clearly new, its color tones slightly brighter than the surrounding areas.

Michael pulled out his cell phone and dialed Jennifer's number. She answered on the first ring. "Michael, is everything okay? Did you find it?"

"Everything is fine, I guess. I'm in Alex's closet. I think we're too late though. Everything's gone. All his stuff is gone. In fact, it looks like the whole closet's been redone. It's all new, the shelving, everything. The paint's all fresh.

"I didn't think Donna knew about the laptop, but if it was here as you said, she must have found it. Everything's been ripped up."

Michael left Alex's closet and stood, gazing at Donna's bedroom in the soft light. Unlike when Alex was alive, the bedroom was a mess, with Donna's nightgowns, lingerie, and several pairs of shoes on the floor. The bed was unmade. Used bath towels rested on one of the chairs. A half-empty bottle of chardonnay and a single dirty wineglass stood on the table beside Donna's side of the bed. Michael checked the glass carefully. There was lipstick on the rim. It appeared that Donna was drinking alone.

"She may not have known about the laptop," Michael whispered to Jennifer as he continued to walk around the room. "I think Donna was just looking for some cash we think Alex hid somewhere in the house. If she found the laptop instead, she may not know what's in it unless she was able to figure out his password."

"Wow," Jennifer exclaimed, "how much did Alex hide?"

Michael felt a twinge of concern over the question. He wasn't about to tell Jennifer that the amount Alex stashed away could be millions. After all, he thought, how well did he know Jennifer? For that matter, how well did he really even know Donna?

"I don't know," Michael answered, doubting Jennifer believed him.

"It doesn't matter to me, Michael. I was just curious." Her tone turned curt. "Maybe the laptop is somewhere else in the house, particularly if Donna doesn't know about the AI stuff. Maybe it's just lying around there somewhere."

"It's possible. I'll take a quick look, but I need to get out of here before Donna gets back and finds me in her bedroom."

Michael was becoming more unsure about whom he could trust. Donna had, after all, mentioned to him that she had looked through the house for Alex's hiding places. Michael was still surprised, however, that she had completely ripped up Alex's massive closet and already had it totally rebuilt. It all seemed a bit too much and too soon.

He continued to look through the mess in the bedroom, carefully replacing each black lace bra, pairs of black stockings, purple thongs, garter belts, Spanx, and other lingerie to where he found them, but there was no trace of the laptop. He could smell Donna's Chanel perfume as his fingers touched each intimate item. Feeling like a voyeur, Michael rifled through her drawers and armoire. *It's like Frederick's of Hollywood in here. Lots of panties but no computer,* he thought as he left the bedroom.

The light reflecting from the outside street lamps illuminated enough of the hallway so that Michael could see where he was going. He wasn't sure why he was so concerned about the lights since his car was parked right outside anyway. If Donna did arrive back home while he was still in the house, she would recognize his car and know he was there. He would have to explain that he dropped over for some reason. He knew that he could never acknowledge that he had been in her bedroom.

He entered Alex's den, turning on the overhead recessed lights. The room looked much as it had when he met there a few days earlier with Donna and the two Lesters. His eyes immediately focused, however, on Alex's desk. There was something new: the brushed silver laptop with the Apple emblem sat on the top of the desk, next to Alex's other desktop unit.

Beside the laptop was a yellow legal pad filled with numbers and letters. Michael studied the notations. The page was divided into two sections, one titled "UN" and the other "PW." Underneath each column were hundreds of various potential user names and password combinations of names, numbers, and letters. The handwriting was not Donna's. It was clear that someone was trying to figure out Alex's user name and password in order to gain access to whatever was on Alex's laptop. Michael noticed that many of the combinations were well-educated guesses, including numerous variations of "121354," "117247524," and "5149149," which represented Alex's birthday, social security number, and street address.

Michael sat at his brother's desk and opened the laptop, waiting for the home screen to appear. He understood Alex's fascination with the Apple. It was a sleek, finely crafted machine. Suddenly a bright blue screen appeared with the logo of the New York Yankees off to the right, alongside a photograph of Alex, George, and Pete, three generations, on the beach in Miami. Finally, a series of icons appeared.

Michael's eyes passed over the twenty icons neatly displayed in four symmetrical rows of five. The first one to catch his attention was a miniscule image of a pretty blonde face. As Michael brought his face closer to the screen he recognized the blinking blue eyes. They were the eyes of Jennifer Walsh. This was likely the "private porn" he had promised to erase. *I'll keep that promise, eventually,* he thought to himself, aware that he was now sidetracked.

But as he moved the cursor to her image, another icon caught his eye. It was a small gold cross, antique or Eastern Orthodox looking. This had to be what he was looking for. He clicked on it and typed in the user name, "57chevy," and password, "triplecrown7," Jennifer had given him at lunch.

Slowly a new scene unfolded on the laptop screen. It was Alex, seemingly alive, smiling broadly, sitting behind the very desk Michael sat at right at that moment. The camera zoomed in. Alex's eyes stared right back at Michael as though they were speaking to each other across the dinner table. It was a miracle and bizarre—but real.

"My God, it's you," Michael said.

It was as though Moses had parted the Red Sea. The camera zoomed in even closer, and Alex's voice answered back, "No shit. I must be dead."

"You are dead."

If Jennifer was correct, Alex had totally integrated an intuitive system of artificial intelligence, computer imaging, and voice duplication and recognition programs. Michael thought too about Karen DiNardo's research. It was likely that the state-of-the-art technology had been supplemented with personalized input that allowed the software to replicate Alex's thinking, emotions, and logic patterns, and even duplicate his voice. Visually, it perfectly re-created his physical image, attributes, facial expressions, and other mannerisms.

When there was no dialogue, Alex just stared back. It was a cold, blank stare—so far, the only uncharacteristic attribute.

Michael continued, "So, how does this work? What can I ask you?"

Alex's eyes came alive. He definitely recognized Michael's voice. Jennifer said that Russell even had Alex record phone conversations with people that Alex wanted his system to recognize. Russell then programmed the system to acknowledge when a familiar voice spoke.

"Michael, you can ask me anything. Make believe we're at Peter Luger's having lunch—except there's no steak. Your old friend Russell loaded hundreds of thousands of different types of data and had me answer thousands of questions. This computer is me now—actually even smarter than me. Russell added a lot of 'intelligence' features—stuff I never had before." Alex laughed.

"Has anyone been able to open this program up since you died?" Michael wondered whether Donna and whoever was helping her with the user names and passwords had been successful.

"No. You're the first," Alex answered. "Michael, what happened to me?"

"This kid Luke shot you, but we still have no idea who hired him. Do you know who would have hired him to shoot you?"

"No. I don't have enough information. You can help me, but you will have to input more data. How did you get my password, Michael?"

"From Jennifer," Michael answered.

"Oh. You've met her then."

"Yes, she's beautiful and seems like a good woman." Michael was also testing Alex's reaction to Jennifer.

"She is. We had a good time together. She's full of surprises." Alex's facial expression loosened up; he appeared to relax.

Michael wanted to follow up on Alex's comments about Jennifer when he saw a low-battery warning appear in the lower right-hand corner of the screen. He noticed that the laptop was not plugged in and obviously was no longer fully charged. The power adapter cord wasn't attached or visible in the room. Michael also became concerned about the time he had now been in the house. Donna could return at any moment. Yet, he had so much to ask.

"Alex, you have to help me with this guy Sharkey. I'm supposed to meet with him on Wednesday. He wants his seven hundred thousand and another hundred grand for interest." Michael gave Alex more detail about the Sharkey situation, including their meeting last week at Pete's Tavern.

The camera zoomed in on Alex's face. There was intense anger in his eyes, a look Michael rarely saw in his brother.

"Michael, Sharkey is scum. He's the dregs. He's also chickenshit. He hides it by walking around in all that black leather shit. If he's by himself, he won't do anything. He did all the bad stuff when he was young, and he had a lot of goons hanging around with him. He's a has-been now. He's not connected the way he used to be. I'm not saying he's not dangerous on some level, but you can't be afraid of him or he'll walk all over you."

The low-battery warning light was now flashing rapidly. Michael knew he didn't have much time. "Alex, what do I do about Wednesday?"

"Go to Peter Luger's in Brooklyn. Get a private room. Invite Sharkey, but have Fat Lester nearby in case you need him. Have Fat Lester frisk him and take the fucking gun if he's carrying. Then he should stand outside the room when Sharkey walks in. Have him leave and close the door so it's just the two of you. The moment the door closes and it's just the two of you, when Sharkey sits down, you quickly get up—like a madman, like you're nuts, out of control—you jump over the table at him. Throw him down in his chair and grab his neck. Choke him enough to scare the shit out of him. It won't take long—he's old, Michael. He weighs a hundred fucking pounds. Tell him he's misjudged you and that you'll kill him if he messes with you again.

"When you've got him totally scared—let him go. Pick him up, straighten him up, help him. Like you just turned Jekyll and Hyde. Go back to your seat. Give him a briefcase with five hundred thousand. Tell him that's what's left of my 'estate'—otherwise, if he's not satisfied, to let you know and you'll have someone finish what you started. He'll piss in his pants."

"Do you think I can do it?" Michael wasn't sure what was taking his breath away, seeing his brother or the plan of attack with Sharkey. Both seemed unbelieveable.

"I know you can, Michael. He has to think that you're crazy, that you're capable of anything. He'll believe it because you're my brother. He'll know there's got to be something more than that corporate shit in you."

The low-battery warning flashed more rapidly now. Michael still had not asked Alex where his money was hidden; he wanted to know more about Jennifer—and Donna. He wanted to know ... about life and death.

But Michael heard a noise downstairs. Was Donna back, opening the front door?

"Alex, I've got to run. The battery is almost gone, and Donna may already be downstairs."

As Michael mentioned Donna's name, the camera again zoomed in to a close-up of Alex. "Michael, about Donna ..." But before he could finish his sentence, the screen went blank.

"Michael, is that you? Are you upstairs?" Donna was downstairs.

Michael shut down and gently closed the laptop. "I'm up here, Donna, in Alex's den." He could hear Donna's six-inch spiked high heels rapidly climbing up the hardwood steps. Michael had no idea what to expect as she reached the top of the steps and walked into the room.

"Michael?" Donna looked at him with a look of confusion that appeared to be turning to anger. "What are you doing here? I didn't know you were coming."

Michael had to think quickly. "I'm sorry, Donna. I just wanted to look myself for signs of where Alex may have hidden his money. If I'm going to meet with Sharkey on Wednesday, I've somehow got to come up with seven or eight hundred thousand dollars. Unless we find it, what are we going to do?"

"I understand that—but why didn't you call and say you were going to come over?" Donna's facial expression tightened; Michael could see a fire in her eyes.

He was battling to keep his credibility and relationship with his sister-in-law. "I'm worried. Somehow, I've taken on this responsibility. This isn't my world. You know that. What the hell do you expect me to do on Wednesday? The Lesters are trying, but they can only go so far. They're role players here, not principals. I'm the one hanging out to dry. When I got here tonight, you were gone. I couldn't wait. I was going to call you on your cell, but to be honest, I just got sidetracked once I got into Alex's den, looking at all his stuff."

"Okay, Michael. Fine. I guess I understand. But you know, this is my house. You're always welcome, but somehow I feel like you intruded by not at least calling. Just call next time."

"You're right. I will. I didn't mean this the way it looks." Michael wanted to shift the conversation to the money and the laptop sitting almost in front of them. Pointing to the Apple, Michael asked, "Was this Alex's?"

Donna seemed defensive. "It must have been. I had never seen it before, but when I took Alex's closet apart, we found it. Alex had obviously hidden it inside a compartment in the woodwork for some reason I can only imagine. The cops haven't seen it. George offered to help with the carpentry work in Alex's closet, and after we found it, he tried to figure out the password and user name. So far, no luck. I was hoping to find money, but this is really all we found."

"I didn't know you and George got on all that well." There had always been a lot of tension between Donna and Alex's son from his marriage to Greta.

"Well," said Donna, "I guess everyone got shook up when Alex was shot. Evidently, after Russell was murdered, Greta told George to come over and offer his help. She figured I'd need to find out where Alex hid the money. I guess all of his wives knew Alex hid money all over the house. We just never knew exactly where. Only Alex and Russell knew—and neither one of them are talking now. Greta, whom I despise, obviously wanted to make sure she'd know about it when we find any money. But I'll take any help I can get."

Michael needed to get the laptop out of the house. "Listen, Donna. Let me take the laptop. I've got some real pros back in my office. They can crack anything. Maybe this can tell us where Alex hid the money."

"Okay, Michael. I have to trust you. I have to trust someone. I'm not as tough as you think, and I feel lost. Go ahead and take it. I didn't mean to give you a hard time. I just don't know where to turn or who to turn to. I appreciate all you've done. I know this has turned your life upside down." As she spoke, Donna's face became flush and her eyes filled with tears—tears Michael had always assumed she was incapable of shedding. It caught him by surprise.

Donna reached out to embrace him in what Michael hoped was a hug based on need and not lust. Donna's breasts pressed hard against his chest. He wondered if it was intentional. She appeared distraught, yet the press of her breasts implied a different script. His thoughts returned to the delicate lingerie he had handled only minutes ago. Her scent was the same as he had inhaled when touching her lace bra. Michael pulled back ever so slightly, just enough to interrupt the warmth pressing through her fine cashmere sweater. Donna certainly was alluring, but this was not a path he had any intention of pursuing. Worse, Michael thought that he might, on some level, fear her.

"Donna," Michael said, "everything will be okay. I'm going to help you. I've been here so far for you. I'm in too deep now, even if I didn't want to continue. I'll get this thing cleaned up, get your money out for you, and get these people off our back so we can move on with our lives."

As she put her head on his shoulder, Michael was again unsure of the meaning of her gesture. She didn't speak.

"Donna, by the way, has this laptop been anywhere near Alex's grave recently?"

She pulled her head back, a look of confusion or surprise on her face. "At Saint Michael's? What an odd question. No, it hasn't left the house since we found it in Alex's closet."

Chapter 28

Westport, Connecticut
November 24, 2009

"Where am I?" Alex asked as he stared out, his voice sounding weaker, not as confident as Michael was accustomed to hearing from his brother. For once, Michael thought, Alex sounded tentative, unsure of himself.

"I was going to ask *you* that question, but right now I'm—we're—sitting in my library at home, in Westport," Michael said, his voice subdued. "It's three in the morning. I had to charge the computer; it took a while. Samantha's upstairs asleep. I haven't said anything to her about this yet."

It appeared as though Alex was actually looking around, trying to scan the surroundings from inside the computer screen. "You have a lot of fuckin' books. Anyway, it's probably a good idea not to let her know about this too quickly." Alex seemed to be regaining his footing, Michael thought.

"More important—did you meet with Sharkey yet?"

"No, it's tomorrow—actually, tonight at eight, at Luger's, just like you said. I couldn't wait though; I had to contact you again to be sure I didn't just dream this whole thing."

"You mean like I said in that e-mail at my funeral: 'Life is a dream, death is waking up'? You liked that shit? You didn't think I could come up with this, did you?"

"Listen, who would believe anyone could come up with this? But what is this? I mean, Alex, is this really you?"

"What do you mean?"

"What do I mean? What the hell do you think I mean? Are you just a bunch of computer software that was made up of who you were, or is this the same Alex who used to coach my baseball teams—the one who died? Are you two separate things, or are you the same person, or what?"

"What do you think, Michael? Do I look and sound like I'm a piece of software?"

"No, of course not. It's just that, I don't know. I guess my question is, are the two of you connected?"

"Michael, everything is connected. You'll learn that ... someday. It's complicated. Too complicated to explain to you now. You'll see. I promise you—one day, you'll see."

Michael noticed the red low-power warning light had reappeared and was blinking. "It looks like this laptop is running out of juice again. It took hours to charge it even enough to just turn it on. I couldn't wait for it to get to a decent power level."

"Michael, as you know now, this is no ordinary laptop. It's got so much stuff loaded into it that uses a lot of fuckin' power. That's also why it weighs so much. Since it was so drained, you'll need to charge it for a full day."

"Don't get me wrong, Alex. I'm really happy about all this. It just takes a while to understand what's happened."

"You better shut it off now. Do exactly what I told you tomorrow night."

"Okay—" Michael said as reached for the "power-off" button. But he could see Alex begin to speak again.

"I know this is hard to understand, especially for someone as smart as you are, Michael. But what you see is real. And, before you go, there's one more thing I want you to know."

"What's that?" Michael answered.

Alex looked straight ahead, his face expressionless, yet Michael felt as though their eyes had locked together. "Your life will never be the same again."

Chapter 29

Brooklyn, New York
November 25, 2009

At eight at night, Michael and Fat Lester pulled up in Michael's new black BMW 740i to the front of the Peter Luger's Steakhouse on Broadway in an old, dilapidated section of Brooklyn. Michael immediately caught the eye of John, the valet, an older man who had worked there forever. Although the valet charge was five dollars, Michael handed him a twenty, which ensured that his car would stay right in front of the restaurant.

Michael had arranged a private room, to which he and Fat Lester were immediately shown. He checked his watch. Sharkey was to arrive in half an hour. Michael surveyed the room and reviewed the plan in his mind. The dining room was designed to hold at least twenty people. Michael would be waiting there alone for Sharkey. Fat Lester would greet Sharkey when he arrived at the desk downstairs, escort him up, then request his gun and frisk him. He'd then open the door, usher Sharkey in, close the door behind him, and wait outside—but within earshot in case Michael should need help.

The table was twenty feet long, but was set for only two people to dine. Michael would sit at the head of the table, Sharkey just a few feet off to his right. Michael had choreographed the scene just as he had done for major board or client meetings. He'd outlined in writing the plan for the evening and rehearsed the scenarios with an impatient Fat Lester at least three times. Yet, Michael knew his role had to appear totally unrehearsed and spontaneous. He had to look homicidal and violent. It was, as he used to tell his staff at Gibraltar, *showtime.*

Michael had secured five thousand crisp one-hundred-dollar bills, packaged in neat stacks and secured in an aluminum steel suitcase. Fat and Skinny Lester had been successful in collecting nearly all the remaining debts owed to Alex. If Michael was successful in getting Sharkey to agree to $500,000 in full payment of his winnings with Alex, then Alex's business issues were all but settled. Sharkey's greed made Michael feel justified in turning the tables on him.

Both Fat Lester and Donna had recommended that Michael bring Alex's gun as additional insurance. Michael had never fired a gun. He also knew there were strict penalties in New York for carrying unlicensed firearms. He wasn't ready for that step yet.

He sat alone in the large, empty room thinking about his life, his brother, and how their relationship had been so distant over their adult years. But Michael forced his mind to focus on the present. He had come a long way in the past two weeks. He would now threaten and beat the shit out of Sharkey if he had to. Michael thought about Donna, still unsure whether he trusted her.

Fat Lester knocked on the door, opened it slightly, and stuck his large head in. "Sharkey's here, Boss. I'm going downstairs to get him." This was the first time anyone other than Karen called him "Boss."

In a low but firm voice, Michael said, "Bring him right in. Make sure you get the gun. It's showtime, Lester." Fat Lester nodded, smiled, and securely closed the door.

Alone, Michael stood up and adjusted his turtleneck and sport coat and sat back down in his chair at the head of the table. Moments later there was a sharp knock on the door. Fat Lester opened the door just enough for the diminutive Sharkey to walk through. "He's clean, Boss," Fat Lester said proudly. Michael knew he had heard that line in countless old gangster movies. *Now, I'm starring in one,* he thought.

Fat Lester closed the door as soon as Sharkey entered Michael's dining room. Sharkey looked around the large room and at the enormous dining table set up for only two diners. Michael had placed the aluminum suitcase with the crisp currency closed on top of the table. Sharkey stared at the suitcase and smiled.

"Michael." Sharkey smiled. "It's so good to see you again. I can see this will be a much better meeting than our last one." He was dressed exactly as he had been last week. Yet, Michael thought, Sharkey seemed much smaller now and more, as Alex had described him, just a fragile, pathetic old man.

"Yes," Michael said, "I'm sure it will be." He thought about how Sharkey had humiliated him at that first meeting. Now, he felt an unsettling desire for revenge. It would make things easier.

As Sharkey settled comfortably and confidently into his seat at the table, Michael stared at him, working himself into an irrational fit of aggressive anger. He pursed his lips and let a sudden unhappy frown almost distort his face. Sharkey watched, uncertain.

Without warning, Michael leaped up from his seat, sending his chair flying backward. He catapulted over the table onto a stunned Sharkey. He placed both hands around Sharkey's throat and pushed him backward onto the floor. He could feel the tendons in the old man's neck, but Michael continued to press in with both hands, even tighter.

Despite the violence of the moment, Michael could feel his mind detaching itself from his body, breaking away, watching over the scene. A familiar voice inside him said *What are you doing, Michael?* Doubt was creeping into his consciousness. Michael shut it off. He had no doubt about his superiority. As he tightened his grip around Sharkey's neck, Michael knew he could easily kill Sharkey. Sharkey began choking. He spit up and wheezed. Michael was sure that it was the sound of a man beginning to die. *How could this be so easy?* he thought. *This is how they do it, simply hold it like this just a little longer. Now I understand.*

Finally Michael's hands eased up slightly, just enough so that Sharkey could get enough air not to die but not enough to speak or even think of fighting back.

Michael's eyes were bulging with fury as he held Sharkey's slender neck in his hands and pinned his shoulders against the back of the chair with his knees. Sharkey appeared to be helpless. Michael knew he had taken him totally by surprise.

"You'll be able to last until you use up whatever air you have in you. And then you'll choke because you're not getting another breath," Michael said, his face inches from Sharkey's. Whatever Sharkey might have wanted to say could not come out; he was lucky to have enough air to stay alive. Michael looked into Sharkey's eyes, and in a fit of rage recited the script Alex had recommended two days before. The words flowed naturally as Michael added his own.

"You fucking son of a bitch. I'm going to kill you right here. Then Fat Lester's going to take your fucking body downstairs to the butcher, and we'll grind you into fucking Luger burgers. You'll never walk out of here, and no one will fucking miss you. You want another hundred grand, you piece of worthless shit? You think you can intimidate me? Your days are over. You're a fucking weak old man. I'm going to fucking kill you now." He tightened his grip again.

Michael no longer felt that he was acting. He knew he could kill Sharkey; he could have just choked him to death right there on the carpet. Yet, he knew that he wouldn't. Was it just that he didn't see himself as a killer? *Stop thinking so much,* he told himself. Nevertheless, Michael sensed that he had crossed some invisible line in his life. It was a fleeting but troubling thought.

Then, as though he flicked a switch, Michael felt the tension leaving his body. With his eyes still locked onto Sharkey's, he relaxed his hands. He could feel a wave of relief pass through Sharkey's body, as though Sharkey sensed his life might not end there on Peter Luger's carpet.

"I'm going to let you live this time. Next time, you'll die. There's five hundred thousand in that suitcase. That's what's left of Alex's estate, so to speak. That's what I'm going to give you. Let's say I'm charging you two hundred grand for being an asshole and trying to rob me. I'm giving you this—and your fucking life. As they say in those commercials, 'That's priceless.' You're a piece of shit. You misjudged me—Alex was the easygoing one. Five hundred. Just nod up and down if you agree." His tone was now measured and unemotional.

Sharkey could hardly move, but he managed to nod ever so slightly and moan.

Michael smiled, releasing his death grip. "Looks like we have a deal." He saw his fingerprints imprinted in red on Sharkey's neck. Sharkey tried to catch his breath. He was still choking and coughing. Michael stood up straight and looked at Sharkey, who appeared to stare back in utter disbelief—or, Michael thought, was it gratitude?

Michael lifted Sharkey and his chair up off the floor. He returned both to their original position at the table, just as before Michael's attack. He smoothed out Sharkey's jacket and, using Sharkey's linen napkin, cleaned up the spit around his mouth. "There," he said, very upbeat, "now I think we have a good understanding. How about lunch? The Luger burgers are great."

Chapter 30

Westport, Connecticut
November 25, 2009

Michael drove home immediately after his meeting with Sharkey. He was anxious to return to his library where he had placed Alex's charging laptop. Samantha was asleep upstairs as he anxiously opened the computer and clicked on the icon.

It was as though Alex, too, had been impatiently awaiting his brother's return. "Where the fuck have you been?" he said to Michael. "How long does it take to charge a computer?"

"Between the Lesters, your wives and mistresses, and one aging but scary gangster, I haven't had a minute alone, or of peace, for that matter."

"Did you do what I told you with Sharkey?"

"Yes," Michael said, "and it went well—if you can call assault and battery going well. He took the five hundred grand and was happy to get out of there, just like you said he would."

"Good, but be careful now. He's pissed. You cut his balls off. He'll try to get back at you."

"Oh, that's great," Michael said, although he already suspected he had not heard the last of Sharkey. But Michael's mind shifted back to the miracle before his eyes. He had to go deeper, much deeper.

"Alex, what's it like to be dead?" Michael was uneasy with his own question.

"What the fuck kind of question is that?" Alex first appeared to be annoyed, but his composure quickly seemed to loosen as though he recognized the inevitability of the question. "Well, it's not the end of the world—although, actually it is. It's funny, all those nutcases who thought they knew when the world was going to end. They had it all wrong."

"What do you mean?"

"When you die, Michael—when you *really* die—the world ends. It ends for *you*. So all these apocalypse crazies that thought it would end for everyone at the same time, like *they* were just coincidentally going to see the end of the world happen on their watch—after all these fuckin' millions of years. I mean, give me a break."

Michael wondered what exactly Alex meant when he said, "really die." Was he implying that now he wasn't really dead? There were so many questions he needed to ask.

"You didn't answer my question."

"Which one?" Alex asked.

"What's it like to be dead?"

Alex looked straight ahead and into Michael's eyes. "I can't answer that. Nothing that's been programmed into this system is relevant to that question, Michael. But each time we speak, I gain more knowledge, so it's possible that I'll be able to give you more information as time goes on. This software is designed to learn faster than we do when we're alive—especially me, since I didn't learn too quickly in the first place."

Michael was skeptical that any further conversations would open the doors to the ultimate mystery of what happens when you die. Computer software couldn't possibly unravel the afterlife, he thought. But he would keep those thoughts to himself.

"What happens between our conversations, when I've got your laptop shut down?"

"Probably the same thing that happens when you go to sleep. As far as I know, nothing. I guess it's when I rest."

"Do you dream? Do you feel or sense anything during that time?" Michael asked.

"Yeah, I have nightmares that I'm getting married again."

"No, seriously, what's this all like? I mean, can you see or speak with other people who are dead?"

Alex's face was blank. He appeared to be processing the question.

"No, not yet anyway. But things will change."

Chapter 31

Sofia Nicholas had her father wrapped around her little finger, and Michael Nicholas liked it just that way.

"I still don't really understand why we're having Thanksgiving dinner here in Chicago instead of Connecticut. I was looking forward to being home. Not to mention, Dad, they're not even serving a traditional turkey here tonight."

She looked like the classic American coed. Preppy but with a sophisticated sense of style, wearing a simple black Ralph Lauren dress and black high heels, she was inches taller than either of her parents. Her hair was a longer and brighter version of her mother's medium blonde with even lighter highlights. Sofia's athletic build fit the image of the new captain of the freshman women's tennis team at Notre Dame. She had particularly light skin, rosy cheeks, and like her father, a vivacious smile. Sofia inherited both a sharp sense of humor and a slight but noticeable edge to her personality from both Michael and Samantha. She was normally even-tempered and easygoing, but with a little provocation, she could direct a single retort or a machine-gun-like stream of subtle mockery—sharp projectiles striking her antagonist.

"Chicago was so close to your school, and I admit, we wanted to get away for the holidays, so I thought this would be a good solution," Michael said, twirling his fork around Spiaggia's al dente spaghetti, delicately covered with a simple tomato and basil sauce. Just before placing the fork in his mouth and with a mischievous look, he added, "And, to your point on the turkey, this is what we'd eat in Italy when we would happen to visit there on Thanksgiving, which as you know we did a number of times."

But Michael knew better. Thanksgiving in Chicago was all about shielding Sofia and Samantha from the surreal world he was embroiled in back east.

"Very good, Dad, an Italian Thanksgiving. Also, I wasn't born yesterday. I know what's been going on—after all, you've told me some of the news already. Plus, I get our local papers online. I mean, our house break-in—or whatever it was—was in the *Westport News*." Sofia showed off a self-satisfied smile as she sipped her dirty vodka martini—another inherited custom, if not craving.

"Not to change the subject, Sofia, but I'm still finding bottles of vodka in our bar at home that seem to have been diluted. How many of them did you and your friends empty when your mom and I were away?"

Michael too was smiling. The subject was a source of humorous needling since Sofia confessed to raiding the liquor cabinet and replacing the vodka with water during a small party she hosted at home the year before with her closest friends in high school.

"Oh Dad, I don't know. But it sounds like you must have a lot of bottles of vodka in your bar, if you're still discovering them. You don't have an alcohol problem, do you? I mean, how much vodka does a household need?"

Michael Nicholas knew when he'd been bested.

"Sofia, don't look at me. Your mom's the one with the vodka

obsession," Michael said, raising an eyebrow in Samantha's direction.

"You're right, darling. Sometimes being married to you, I wonder if I can ever get enough of it." Samantha was feeling the effects of her second cosmopolitan. "I'm so glad Fletcher introduced me to these," she said, holding up her martini glass with its pink concoction.

"By the way, Dad," Sofia continued, "didn't you used to tell me that one of the reasons we never saw Uncle Alex a lot was because he hung out with a bunch of shady characters?"

Michael could see trouble coming. "Yes, why?"

"Why? Because it looks like *you're* hanging out with them now."

Michael was relieved as he watched Samantha intercede. "First, Sofia, some of your father's new friends, like Lester, are people he's known since he was a child."

"Mom, there are two Lesters, Fat and Skinny. Don't you think that's a little odd, to have names like that?"

"Somewhat, but it's just a reflection of their different physiques and a good way to tell them apart," Samantha said, somewhat flustered.

"Sofia, they may be odd characters, but they're not bad people. Really, just the opposite," Michael said, before being cut off by a now-agitated Samantha.

"This is all temporary. Your father is just trying to help Donna sort out your uncle's affairs."

Michael knew he had not yet told Samantha about his second meeting with Sharkey. Although he felt guilty about the omission, he was now even more convinced of its necessity.

"Uncle Alex did have a lot of affairs, I'm sure. I loved him, but he was some character. Do you realize I've had three aunts from him alone?" Sofia said, before rolling right into her next topic. "Do you guys know the actual criteria for sainthood in the Catholic Church?"

"I haven't checked it lately," Michael said.

"We're just studying this now in my religious studies class. One of the things that has to happen for someone to be made a saint is that the candidate has to have interceded on someone's behalf *after* the potential saint has died," Sofia said.

Michael thought about the help he received from his brother in preparing for yesterday's meeting with Sharkey.

"That's fascinating, Sofia, and maybe if we can get your Uncle Alex to magically help me straighten some of his affairs out, we can nominate him for sainthood," Michael said, knowing he was the only one who would catch the irony.

Later that evening while Samantha was watching a movie in Sofia's room down the hall, Michael gazed out his wide hotel window at the falling snow illuminated by the night-lights of Chicago. It reminded him of the effects of a strobe lamp, capturing still fragments of moving images, each captured snowflake getting its two seconds in the spotlight.

The aging elegance of the Drake Hotel suited his mood tonight. He thought about the many times over the years that he had stayed there while on business or on vacations with Samantha and Sofia. Michael looked around at his suite; he was sure he had stayed in this same room at least once before.

He checked his watch. It would be at least an hour before he would expect Samantha back, assuming she watched the entire movie with Sofia. He finally had some time alone. He opened his briefcase, pulled out Alex's laptop, clicked onto the Byzantine cross icon, and typed in Alex's user name and password. Once again, Alex appeared, the camera moving in for a close-up.

"I don't suppose you celebrate Thanksgiving?" Michael said. He wondered whether his attempt at humor was a good idea. And then, he thought, *Am I really worried about hurting my brother's feelings? This is absurd, I think—or maybe it isn't. I just don't know.*

But Alex quickly put his mind at ease. "I hope you brought me some turkey."

"Actually, we mostly had pasta. I guess it wasn't a traditional Thanksgiving. You don't really have an appetite, do you?"

Alex appeared to be processing the question. "I don't feel hungry in the sense that you might, but I miss food and I know what I like ... or liked."

Michael felt unsure again. He wondered about Alex's range of capabilities. *Can he experience physical activities? What are his emotional capabilities? Were they built into the software? If so, is it just how he used to feel about things, or is he capable of changing his feelings?* Michael realized that his mind had wandered. Alex was staring at him, almost as though he could read Michael's mind. Then he remembered reading in Karen's research about a computer program that could detect a person's emotions based upon their facial expressions.

"What's wrong?" Alex interrupted Michael's thoughts.

"Nothing—but let me ask you, can you look at my face and know my emotions? Can you tell what I'm feeling?"

"Yeah, I know everything, Michael."

Michael didn't know what to say, but Alex's answer was disconcerting. He wanted his brother back, but not on steroids and not with powers that were abnormal. Because then it wouldn't really *be* his brother. But before he could react, Alex spoke up again.

"Michael, relax, I'm kidding. I can read your mind the same way I always could. The same way you can read mine. I can make guesses based on your expressions, that's all. Just like everyone else."

The answer, Michael thought, was the perfect response to his concern. *Except,* he thought, *I never verbalized it. I only thought it. How did Alex know what I was thinking?* Now wasn't the time to worry about it.

"Have the police made any progress on figuring out who hired that kid to shoot me?" Alex said. Michael noticed that Alex said, "to shoot me" instead of "to murder or kill me," or was he simply reading too much into each word?

"I personally haven't heard anything much from them. Donna told me they've asked her for a list of people that may have owed you money. The detective assured her that they weren't interested in your illegal businesses; they just wanted to find whoever was behind your murder. So Donna called Skinny Lester to get the names, but Lester told her it wouldn't be a good idea to give the police the list. So, she just gave the detective a few names, relatives mostly, some of our cousins who owed you some small amounts."

"Good idea. I'll have to think about that list, but I can't really see of any of those guys who owed me being killers."

But as Michael's mind focused on his brother's words, he was startled by the suite's door swinging open as Samantha swiftly entered, a look of confusion on her face.

"Michael, what's going on, who are you talking to?"

He quickly pushed the "Escape" button on the laptop and shut the lid. He could see that he had further aroused Samantha's suspicions.

"Oh, I'm sorry, I didn't even hear you at the door," he said.

"Obviously." Her tone was curt. "What were you so absorbed in? Were you Skyping with someone?" Samantha was staring at the closed laptop. "You sure ended it rather quickly, didn't you?"

Michael was thankful for the Skype idea. He hadn't thought of using that as an excuse, especially since he rarely used a computer for video calling.

"Actually, I was playing around with it."

Samantha was still staring at the laptop. She seemed to be half listening to Michael's answer, speaking over him. "And I noticed that you brought Alex's laptop with you. How come?"

Michael took a breath and tried to look as nonchalant as

possible, shrugging his shoulders. "I've always wanted an Apple, so I've been playing around with Alex's. It's a great machine."

Samantha appeared to be skeptical. He hoped she wouldn't want to handle the laptop. Michael knew its weight alone would raise more questions.

"So whom were you speaking with on it?" she said. "You know, if the voice had been a woman's, I'd be suspicious."

Michael was relieved. "Well, it certainly wasn't a woman."

Samantha smiled and let out a slight laugh. "If I didn't know better, Michael, I'd have thought it was Alex on the other end. The voice sure sounded like his."

Michael looked away, as though his attention had moved on to something else. "I guess that's not very likely, now is it, dear?"

Chapter 32

New York City
November 29, 2009

Perhaps it was the allure of the still-unopened Jennifer Walsh icon with the blinking blue eyes that Michael couldn't get out of his mind. Or was it that he sensed she represented a new doorway to other layers of Alex's personality? Or, Michael thought, was he simply attracted to his brother's lover? The reality was that Michael didn't understand the nature of his attraction to her, and he was comfortable with the uncertainty.

Although Michael usually drove his own car, "Deacon Dan" had been Michael's driver for nearly seven years. Michael and Samantha would hire Dan for certain occasions so Michael could enjoy his cocktails, or when the drive, such as the one back and forth from Westport to lower Manhattan, was a long one.

Besides being a driver, Dan was a friend and an occasional spiritual adviser to Michael, Samantha, and Sofia. A former athlete and coach, he had been a starting guard on the basketball team at the University of Nebraska in the late sixties. Now sixty-five, he worked more than ever as a deacon at the Basilica Assumption Church in Westport and was the owner of Dan's Driving Service. He presided over Sofia's baptism and would likely do the same whenever she married.

Michael sat in the backseat of Dan's Lincoln Town Car. He thought of Jennifer Walsh and how instrumental her information had been. Without Jennifer's help, Michael would not have known about Alex's Apple laptop, and without the password, George would likely still be trying out the thousands of word-and-letter combinations in order to gain access to its contents. Without Jennifer, Michael would never have been able to speak with his brother again. He needed to formally thank her, maybe stop by her salon and see if she was free for lunch.

It was almost noon. The city air was cool and brisk, despite the blue sky and bright sun. Michael took out his cell phone and dialed Jennifer's number. "Jennifer, it's Michael Nicholas. Listen, I'm in the city. I'd like to fill you in on what's happened since we sat down. You've … you've really helped me out. Any chance you're free for me to drop by?"

"Michael, oh, that's so nice, and it's so nice for you to think of me. I'm staying at the Gansevoort downtown. Just give me an hour, and why don't you come up for a drink or some breakfast or lunch, or whatever. I'm here with a friend. We're in the penthouse; the room's under the name of Saint-Laurent."

"Great," Michael said. "I'll be there in an hour." Michael wondered who Saint-Laurent might be. The only Saint-Laurent Michael was aware of was the recently deceased French designer.

An hour later, Michael took the elevator to the penthouse suite. As he exited the elevator, he noticed that the door to the penthouse was slightly open. Room service was being delivered to the room. Michael knocked on the half-open door.

"Jennifer, it's Michael. Are you there?" Before Jennifer could respond, the door opened as the room service waiter was leaving with the remaining empty trays. Smiling, he held the door open for

Michael to enter the room. He entered a grand living room with an elaborate breakfast spread across a dining room table, anchored at both ends with a silver ice bucket holding the familiar yellow-labeled bottles of Michael's favorite champagne, Veuve Clicquot. For an instant, Michael thought of Paris and Samantha. The grand living room, with its high ceilings and a wall of floor-to-ceiling windows, overlooked a dramatic view of the Hudson River and New Jersey beyond.

"Jennifer, it's Michael. Looks like your breakfast is here." The door to the bedroom was slightly open, although Michael couldn't see anything from his vantage point.

But the unmistakable stirrings of a couple in the throes of love-making stopped Michael in his tracks. Over their moans and sighs, Michael announced, "Jennifer, I'm going down to the lobby. I'll be back in a little while."

Jennifer, perhaps finally recognizing that Michael was indeed in their hotel living room, called out, "No, Michael, oh my God. We'll be right out. Just give me one minute. Don't move." Michael wondered exactly who Jennifer meant when she said "we." He was curious to see whom Jennifer had chosen to take the place of his brother.

Michael could hear giggling and sensed some sudden movement from the bedroom. After another brief pause, the bedroom door opened all the way and out walked Jennifer, her blonde hair mischievously astray, but looking tanned, radiant, and beautiful. She was wrapped in the hotel's white terry cloth bathrobe and tying a belt securely around her waist as she strolled out of the bedroom. She hugged and then kissed Michael on both cheeks in the European style.

"How great to see you, Michael. I'm so sorry; we kind of got wrapped up in everything. I didn't realize you were here. I want you to meet a good friend of mine."

Michael realized that, in fact, he was not anxious to meet Jennifer's lover. But he could not have anticipated the figure who now strolled out of the bedroom, also wrapped in another of the hotel's robes. Although at first he couldn't quite place her name, he had seen the aging but still beautiful French movie star in many films over the years. She was a glamorous legend.

"Michael, so nice to meet you. I'm Catherine Saint-Laurent. Please, help yourself to a glass of champagne." Her English was perfect, although she spoke with an unmistakable French accent.

"It's an honor to meet you, Miss Saint-Laurent. I've enjoyed so many of your films. I hope my timing wasn't a problem. I just wanted to say hello to Jennifer and thank her for some nice things she's done for me."

"Michael, Catherine is aware of my relationship with Alex. In fact, your brother was also a big fan of Catherine's. The three of us went out together many times." Jennifer was obviously relishing breaking this news to Michael and appeared to be cleverly leaving to Michael's newly energized imagination all the titillating possibilities.

"Please accept my sincere condolences over the loss of your brother. Jennifer is correct; we enjoyed each other's company many times. The three of us had an extraordinary time together. We shared many dinners and late nights. Alex loved women—and women loved Alex. He didn't care whether you were famous or had money. Even cultural differences were meaningless to him. He was a unique man—a very generous man. I will miss him."

Michael poured himself a glass of champagne. The scent of Chanel No. 5 filled the suite.

Chapter 33

Michael recognized an increasing and troubling pattern of deception in himself. Samantha had always been his closest confidant. Now, in the space of less than a month, he had delayed, downplayed, or never even told her about the bizarre series of events that seemed to be a pattern of his life and that he no longer found to be unusual.

Samantha had just arrived back again from her extended stay with Sofia. Michael had intended to correct it all tonight. It was a rare dinner at home, with candlelight and fine crystal in their dining room. The spotlighted contemporary art contrasted with the otherwise soft hues and lighting.

But as Michael began to lay out the corrections and clarifications, he saw panic in Samantha's eyes. And he had only begun to tell her about his discussions with Alex.

"Michael, why didn't you tell me all of this until now? My God, you had a virtual séance with your brother, who was having an affair with a lesbian, who in turn is having an affair with a French movie star … and in the meantime, you've had guns pointed at you, and now you've almost choked to death some old Mafia guy? *What's going on?*" Samantha was distraught. "And what are you trying to say, that Alex is somehow still alive? Have you lost your mind?"

"It's not exactly like that," Michael protested, but he knew it was like that and more. It was now clear to Michael that if he was going to continue to clean up his brother's affairs, he would have to keep more of the details to himself. In fact, he would have to keep more of his life to himself until he could make Samantha more comfortable—at least temporarily. Unless, of course, it wasn't temporary. But his mind couldn't go there just now. He feared he may have already told Samantha too much. It was a habit, an openness they both had with each other—but that would have to change, he thought.

"How much longer are you going to have to be involved in Alex's business affairs?" Samantha asked.

"I need another month or so. That's all. It looks like we've collected most of the money Alex was owed, and now that Sharkey has taken our 'settlement' offer, we've paid off most of Alex's debts."

"So, what's left? And, Michael, what about Gibraltar? When are you going back to your office? What's going on there? I thought you felt so vulnerable. How much longer can you afford to be away?"

Michael had hardly thought about Gibraltar and the job that, until Alex's murder nearly two weeks ago, had consumed him virtually day and night.

"Dick knows I need another week or so. Next week, we are all flying out to Beverly Hills for a big financial services conference, on ethics no less. I'm giving one of the keynote speeches. Here, we still have to find Alex's money. Donna needs that to live comfortably, and George is entitled to a good part of it. I may not have been close with any of them, but I owe it to Alex to finish all this and be sure his family is taken care of. There are millions of dollars hidden somewhere."

"How are you possibly going to find it?"

"I've got Alex's laptop now. The answers may very well be there."

Samantha had not yet actually witnessed the miracle of Alex's virtual resurrection. Michael had significantly downplayed some of the imaging and artificial intelligence aspects to her, so she had not pressed Michael to actually see Alex on the computer monitor. And Michael was not yet ready to have her meet the new version of Alex.

"Michael, no one was ever more practical—if not downright cynical—than you. You can't seriously believe in this 'artificial intelligence' scheme or whatever it is. How could your brother have had the means to really put this together, when our own government with all its resources hasn't done it?"

Although Michael knew he had again given Samantha too much information, he now wondered if she had also heard more than he thought when she surprised him during his last conversation with Alex at the Drake. Either way, he would have to be more careful in the future.

"But they have, Samantha. You just don't read about it. They've kept it pretty secret. The CIA has already replicated the personalities of many foreign leaders. They created an artificial model of Saddam Hussein. They tested his reactions to our threats and sanctions. They were then able to predict that Saddam would never allow full UN weapons inspections."

"Michael, you're telling me that our government staged the whole weapons thing, knowing that Hussein would never want the world to really know he didn't have them and, therefore, would never let the inspectors in to prove it to the world?"

"Exactly," Michael continued. "The CIA could see from Hussein's model that first, he wouldn't believe we would really invade his country and start an unprovoked war, and second, his own pride would lead him to want the rest of the world to believe that he actually did have the weapons and, therefore, was stronger than he was."

"How do you know all this and the *New York Times* doesn't?"

Michael took a deep breath. "Fat Lester read it somewhere."

Chapter 34

Westport, Connecticut
November 29, 2009

Michael sat alone in his library, surrounded by the hundreds of books that had meant so much to him during his life, the very volumes he had read and relied upon since his childhood. They were his history, the input of his life so far, and his serenity and security. Michael knew he could always be entertained and educated—even if he was alone—as long as he had his books. They were an antidote to any stress or strife of the moment.

Alex had also been a source of security to Michael. From childhood, Alex, the older brother, had provided an introduction to the adult world, a more relevant one than his much older parents represented. Alex was Michael's protector in the schoolyards or on the baseball diamond. Alex's hidden *Playboy* magazines, which Michael would examine when Alex was not home, were Michael's first introduction to the sensual world of the opposite sex.

And so, while Samantha slept upstairs, Michael clicked on the icon, typed in the password, and stared at the laptop where, in just a few moments, he would see his brother again.

"Next time, do me a favor and don't slam the fuckin' computer shut without warning me," Alex said.

"Sorry about that. Samantha surprised me in the hotel room. She's not ready for you yet."

"She wasn't quite ready for me when I was totally alive. That's the problem with Jewish girls, they think too much. Jewish guys, too, for that matter. You're smart to go slow on this with her. Of course, if it were me, I wouldn't tell my wife anything. I don't marry a woman to talk to her and tell her everything."

"We're different that way, to say the least."

Alex gave a sarcastic smile. "Well, we'll see how different. You may be surprised. Anyway, what's going on?"

"Well, now, I'm not only tied up with one of your wives, but two of your girlfriends," Michael answered.

"Which two of my girlfriends tied you up?" The expression on Alex's face showed genuine curiosity. From his question, it was obvious that Alex had more than two girlfriends.

"Neither of them tied me up literally, although nothing would surprise me. I went to thank Jennifer for letting me know about this laptop and giving me the password. When I met her at her hotel, she had just left the bedroom with Catherine Saint-Laurent."

"Christ, you hit the jackpot already."

"I didn't hit any jackpot. I'm not even looking to hit a jackpot. I just want to clean up your affairs for Donna."

"So you went to Jennifer's hotel room to do that?" Alex was smiling at him with his best dirty-grin expression.

Michael knew he needed to get to the heart of some major mysteries. "Alex, I need to find some things out. A lot of things have happened since you were murdered. I'm trying to be sure Donna's fixed financially."

"And George too," Alex quickly interjected. "I know you hardly know him, but without me, he's lost. Greta can't help him; she can hardly take care of herself. He's my only kid, don't forget. He's a good kid."

"I know, Alex," Michael said. "That's why I'm trying to help with all this. Donna has asked me to get involved. I'll see this through and take care of Donna and George. I promise."

"Listen, Michael. You may enjoy it too. It's a lot better work than all that corporate shit you've done all your life—working for all those lowlife suits."

"I know. You're probably right. But it's been a pretty good ride, and the money's been good. I have to admit, though, I'm a bit fed up with all the bullshit, the hours, and the travel. I'm never home."

"Yeah, well, I was always home—or a few blocks away in a bar—and, believe me, the money's better; it's tax free." Alex laughed.

"It's tax free—but you can't spend it," Michael responded. "But listen, I don't know what's weirder, that I'm having this conversation with you or with a computer. Anyway, here's what else has happened. Someone murdered Russell just before he was going to show Donna and me where he built secret compartments in the house to hide your money. So, as far as I know, whatever cash you had is still sitting somewhere, and without tearing the whole house down, I don't know how to find it."

"That's not the only money, you know," Alex said.

"Where else do you have money hidden?"

"My cash is in two places. First, the house. There's exactly one million dollars hidden in a compartment under the carpet and wood flooring in the dining room. When you pull the rug up, you'll see a section of the wood flooring that is a slightly lighter color. You'll have to pull up the wood planking to find the compartment. Russell was the only person I could trust. He was a good carpenter. He knew his shit. Have they figured out who killed him?"

"I don't know, Alex. Someone is out there who wanted both you and Russell dead. They probably figured out that Russell knew where your money was stashed. I don't think he gave up the information before they killed him."

"He only knew about the hiding places in the house. The rest of the money is in a bank safety deposit box in the Citibank branch on Main Street in Flushing. The keys are in a false compartment in the kitchen cabinet just to the left of the refrigerator."

"Who has access to the box besides you?" Michael asked.

"No one. Just me."

"Oh, shit. How the hell am I going to get into that box?"

"You're probably the only one who can pull it off. You used to forge my signature when we were kids. You'll get past them at the bank. We don't look that different. You'll just use my IDs from my wallet, sign my name, and they'll let you in."

"And what if the bank has been notified of your death?" Michael felt that sinking feeling in his stomach.

"Listen, it's a risk, but a small one. They don't know me there at all. That's not my regular bank; I hardly ever go in that branch. I only have the box there, not my checking and savings accounts. Plus, you're thinking of one of those old wives' tales. There is no formal, automatic notification process to banks when someone dies, unless maybe when there's a lot of money involved."

"Jesus," Michael moaned, seeing himself getting in even deeper and with another unlawful transgression on its way. "How much is in the box anyway?"

"A little over two million," Alex said proudly.

"Holy shit, Alex. You mean you've got over three million dollars stashed away?"

"I told you, it's better than your corporate shit. And by the way, the issue of my 'death' as you call it, is still open now, isn't it?"

Michael wasn't sure what to expect. "What do you mean?"

"What do I mean? I mean, how could I be dead if you and I are having this conversation? That's what I mean." Alex arched his eyebrows.

His brother might be right. Michael felt a surge of adrenaline. It had been a long time since he had felt it coursing through his bloodstream. The virtual reappearance of his brother, the danger, the promise of instant caches of cash—it was a thrilling week. Michael realized that he thought less each day about Gibraltar Financial. But before he could reflect further or respond to Alex, Michael heard Samantha's footsteps; she was coming down the stairs. It was time again for "Alex" to leave.

Chapter 35

Whitestone, Queens, New York
November 30, 2009

Michael opened the drawer in the coffee table where his brother's wallet still rested, as though it expected to be reclaimed by its owner at any moment. He was sure that Alex never figured it to outlast him. Well-worn, soft black leather—it looked frozen in time, almost shriveled. Michael remembered seeing it as Alex would pull it out after every restaurant lunch or dinner, peeling off large bills to pay the tab. Inside were the typical remnants of a life: a New York state driver's license, a few credit cards, and a wrinkled photograph.

Donna had placed the wallet in the drawer after collecting it back from the police detective and then removing the substantial amount of cash Alex always kept in it

Since his brother's death, Michael had made no grand decisions about the direction of his own life. Yet he knew that each small daily choice would eventually move his life in a certain path. As he replaced his own wallet with that of his brother's, he knew that he was also burning the bridges behind him.

Accompanied by Fat Lester, Michael left Donna's house with Alex's wallet and his large navy-blue gym bag that had a New York Yankees logo emblazoned on its side.

Main Street in Flushing, New York, looked like a lot of small cities across the United States until the 1990s, when an influx of Korean and other Asian immigrants settled there. Now it looked like a typical street in Seoul. The Citibank branch on Main Street, with its modern blue sign, looked out of place amongst all the Asian symbols. The branch was not one of the more attractive storefronts, with a sterile exterior and inhospitable interior, made more so by the presence of thick, bulletproof glass partitions separating the bank's employees from potential bank robbers and its customers alike. Today, as Michael entered the bank, he was thankful for the lack of intimacy.

Fat Lester double-parked outside and waited anxiously for Michael. Once inside the bank, Michael approached a young lady sitting at a desk near the entrance.

"I need to get into my safe deposit box, please."

Michael realized that he was again breaking the law by misrepresenting himself and showing false identification to gain access to the box in order to obtain the cash his brother had earned illegally and, perhaps worse, not reported as income to the Internal Revenue Service.

He thought of Al Capone, who had died in prison for less than what Michael was doing today. What if the branch had somehow been notified of Alex's death and had impounded the box? Although highly unlikely in just a few days, Michael would be caught red-handed. He was relying on the guidance and wisdom of his brother, or some version of his brother, and taking risks he would have thought unimaginable just weeks ago.

The middle-aged bank clerk looked at Michael, and rising from her desk said, "Just follow me. I'll need two forms of identification, one with a picture." With his empty gym bag folded under his right arm, Michael followed her to the rear of the bank and through a door leading to a small room, behind which was a huge vault with its thick steel door wide open. Inside he could see a series of safe deposit box doors, each with an engraved number and two keyholes. Michael handed over Alex's driver's license and a gold American Express credit card.

"Here, I also have my Peter Luger's credit card if that helps." As soon as he said it, he knew it was a silly attempt at humor since few bank clerks in Flushing had likely heard of Peter Luger's. The woman just looked at Michael with a quizzical expression. She checked the driver's license, looked at Alex's picture, and then looked up at Michael. She nodded; he had passed the first test.

"Please sign your name on the card."

Michael looked at the signature card, which already had Alex's signature on it from three previous visits to the box. Michael saw that he could easily replicate his brother's signature. He signed Alex's name below the other three signatures and handed it back to the clerk. She glanced at it quickly and said, "Follow me."

Before she could lead Michael into the vault, however, the phone on her desk rang. As she picked it up and listened, Michael began to perspire. Had someone recognized him as Alex, knowing that Alex had been murdered weeks before? Had the bank been notified of Alex's death? He tried to gauge the situation by watching the expression on the clerk's face. She was listening intently and did not make eye contact with him.

Finally, she spoke into the receiver, "Okay, I'll do my best." She hung up, looked at Michael, and said, "Please excuse me for just one minute; my manager needs me in the front. I'll be right back. I apologize."

Michael's mind and heart began racing. This wasn't good. His only backup plan was to try to leave the bank quickly, but that wasn't a very promising strategy. Even if he made it outside, he would be easy to identify and track down. He sat down on the chair at the desk. He envisioned the worst, that the police were on their way or already in the bank discussing the best way to apprehend him. He continued to wait for what seemed like an eternity.

Four minutes later, he heard footsteps approaching the door. The door opened and inside stepped the bank clerk. "I'm very sorry," she said. "Let me show you to your box." Michael was relieved but still suspicious.

They entered the inner vault. The clerk glanced up and, locating the number, walked swiftly to the box. She inserted her key into one of the locks, took Michael's key and inserted it into the adjoining lock, then opened the steel door and pulled out a large gray steel box. She handed the box to Michael and led him to a tiny room adjacent to the vault. "Just let me know when you're finished. I'll be at the desk right outside."

Michael closed the door behind her, turned around, and for a moment stared at the box sitting on the Formica desk in the small, bare room. He undid the small latch at the top of the box and opened the lid. A copy of an old *New York Daily News* stared back from the box. It was the back page from several years ago, with the headline announcing the Yankees as the World Series winner. For a split second, Michael feared he had been lured into either a hoax or, worse, a trap. He fingered the newspaper and lifted it up out of the box, where it had been snugly secured. As he did, he saw what he had hoped to find.

The box was tightly packed with one-hundred-dollar bills in bundles of one hundred, each one containing $10,000. There were too many packets to count. Michael unzipped the gym bag and dumped the contents of the box into the bag. He then placed the copy of the *Daily News* on top of the money and closed the bag. He didn't know yet if he was home free, but the presence of the cash was certainly a good sign. Now he still had to leave the bank and get safely into Lester's car waiting outside.

He opened the door. Everything looked normal. When he saw the clerk in the adjacent office, he said, "I'm all set."

She looked up at Michael. "Good, let's put the box back." She walked back into the vault with Michael following close behind, holding the bulging gym bag and the closed but now empty box. Michael carefully slid the steel case into the slot. The clerk closed the door, turned the locks, and returned one key back to Michael. She took the second key and proceeded back out of the vault and into the area where Michael had initially signed in. "I just need for you to sign out."

As Michael signed alongside his own signature from fifteen minutes earlier, the clerk seemed to have something more on her mind. Michael was waiting for another ball to drop. "I noticed," she said, "that your yearly payment is due at the end of the month. Would you like to pay it now?"

Michael wanted to leave the bank as quickly and unobtrusively as possible. Although he had two million dollars in his gym bag and had placed a few hundred dollars of his own cash in Alex's wallet, he didn't want to prolong his visit any longer than absolutely necessary.

"No, thanks. I'm in a bit of a hurry now. I think the bill is sitting at home, so I'll just send it in this week, if that's okay."

He proceeded out the door, gym bag firmly in hand, toward the bank's lobby. As he entered the lobby, Michael saw two New York City policemen speaking with the bank's private security guard, none of whom he had seen when he entered the bank. They seemed absorbed in conversation, although one of the police officers turned his way as Michael entered the lobby. Michael continued to walk swiftly through the lobby, past the barricaded tellers, the cops, and the security guard. He tried to be aware of movement around him while making eye contact with no one. The glass doors to the sidewalk were now in front of him. He didn't hesitate, although he expected someone to call out or take him by the arm at any moment.

He opened the glass doors and walked outside. Fat Lester's black Cadillac was still double-parked in front of him. He heard the locks open from inside. He looked both ways but saw no one approaching, so he grasped the silver door handle, opened the door, and sat in the front passenger seat, putting the multimillion-dollar gym bag on the floor in front of him. Lester put the car in drive, the doors locked, and they took off for Alex's house, where Donna was anxiously awaiting them.

As he pulled out onto Main Street, Fat Lester checked his rearview mirror. "Looks like we may have company. I'll lose him."

Michael turned around and saw a black Lincoln Town Car. The driver was wearing sunglasses. "Do you recognize the car or the driver?" he asked.

"I don't think so, but my fuckin' eyes aren't that good," Lester said as he put his foot on the gas and made a sudden left turn across two lanes of traffic and then completed a full U-turn so that they were now watching the stunned Town Car driver as they passed each other going in opposite directions. *Sometimes being nearly blind helps,* Michael thought. Lester then made a series of turns through a back alley and several Flushing side streets. Michael checked the rearview mirror again. There was no sign of the Town Car. They headed again for Alex's home.

Michael and Fat Lester walked through the front door. Donna saw the bulging Yankees gym bag and hugged Michael warmly. Skinny Lester and George were right behind her.

"Michael, I'm so glad to see you walk in that door. Did you guys have any trouble?" Donna asked.

"No, the bank went fine. I was just nervous. Every time someone blinked, I thought it was all over. The only suspicious thing is that it looked like someone was following us as we left the bank. Lester almost killed us, but he lost whoever it was."

"Was all the money there?" Donna and Skinny Lester asked,

nearly simultaneously. George seemed curious but characteristically quiet.

Michael opened the bag and the tightly wrapped bills spilled out. "I haven't had a chance to count it, but my guess is that there's two million dollars here."

Donna was finally smiling, obviously relieved. "Now what do we do?"

"Well," Michael continued, "we need to get this money someplace safe. I'm going to arrange for our own new safety deposit box, but before that, we need to rip up your dining room floor."

Chapter 36

Beverly Hills, California
December 1, 2009

Michael and Samantha arrived at LAX and whisked past the paparazzi looking for celebrities. Spotting their waiting driver, they got in the limousine and went directly to their favorite Los Angeles hotel, the Peninsula in Beverly Hills.

As they drove up to the entrance to the hotel, Michael felt a rare sense of calm. Finally locating his brother's hidden cash would allow him to take care of Donna and George and perhaps have a good amount of money left over. It was better, he thought, than winning the lottery. Also, tomorrow's speech would allow him to publicly take a position regarding destructive practices that he believed were destroying American business. And having Samantha at his side made the future seem that much brighter.

The driveway of the Peninsula was lined with exotic cars. As their limousine stopped in front of the main entrance, the bellman stepped out and opened the car door. "Welcome back, Mr. and Mrs. Nicholas. We missed you."

As they approached the reception desk, Samantha whispered

into Michael's ear, "How do they know who we are? I know we've stayed here a number of times, but it's been over a year since we were here."

"Each morning they probably have a meeting with the whole staff and review each incoming reservation. Sometimes they even have pictures of their repeat guests," Michael said.

"Seriously, Michael. Did you have to take the mystery away? I thought they were just good."

"Don't worry; I have the feeling there'll be plenty of mysteries to solve."

Michael knew he needed to reengage with his staff at Gibraltar before the whispers about the absent or detached CEO began circulating amongst the never-ending line of corporate busybodies or those hoping to fill his shoes. His speech before the international business press was tomorrow afternoon at the UCLA Business School auditorium. It would be an appropriate way to demonstrate his return to the tortured situation at his company.

Michael always liked to arrive early for his major, high-visibility meetings or events, get there before the other participants, and dine either alone or with Samantha if she was accompanying him. It allowed him to organize his thoughts, prepare for "battle," and put the situation in his own organized perspective. Dinner at the Grill on the Alley in Beverly Hills, one of Michael's favorites, was a routine when he was in Los Angeles.

"You know I hate this restaurant, but I know how much you like it here," Samantha said as they sat down to an early dinner. They had a coveted booth near the entrance, an accommodation the maître d' was happy to make in view of Samantha's stylish attire and good looks. After cocktails, Michael ordered his favorite dish, chicken potpie, while Samantha ordered her usual salmon, grilled very rare.

Michael watched as Samantha eyed the waiter suspiciously. "See, this is what I don't like about this place. The waiters are all these old, gruff guys who look right through the women as though we don't exist. They ignore women, unless, of course, they're filled with silicone. He's made no eye contact with me; he's just ignored me. They fawn over all the men. If I was here alone, he'd never come to the table."

"Samantha. This is your imagination—you're too sensitive. He loves you. It's just that this is Hollywood, and guys run things out here."

"Well, that may have been true years ago, but now some of the major studios are run by women."

Michael decided not to agitate his wife any further. The last time they had eaten at the Grill, Samantha refused to eat her meal, stating it was overcooked, but she had watched while Michael devoured his cherished potpie. He was surprised she had even agreed to return, and now he needed to prepare her for the possible fallout from tomorrow's speech.

It had been two years since the chairman of Gibraltar Financial hired Michael to turn the business around. Now the board that carelessly sanctioned the bad decisions over the two years before he was recruited expected him to work miracles overnight. Worse, they were beginning to try to shift the blame to Michael himself.

Michael knew he was becoming increasingly uncomfortable with the evolution of business over the last several years. Starting with the leveraged buyout movement through to today's private equity and hedge fund craze, the world was changing, and not always for the better. Michael seemed to be able to function, albeit not always comfortably, with this strange new breed of financiers. He knew how they operated and what they expected. But Michael feared that they sensed his ambivalence toward their world and that his heart and passion were in building or rebuilding organizations—not stripping them out for short-term profits.

"Samantha, this speech tomorrow is high risk." Michael felt he had to let Samantha know that it was possible the speech could be his swan song. "I don't know how Dick or the rest of the board will react. I purposely didn't allow Karen to circulate a copy of the speech. They'd all have a nervous breakdown if they saw it in advance. They'd never let me do it." Michael proceeded to summarize the main points to Samantha.

"Michael," Samantha said, "you can't change the world. I know you don't like the direction of all this merger and private equity and hedge fund world, but you can't change it."

Michael's cell phone rang. "Karen, what are you doing this late? It's ten o'clock for you."

"I just want to be sure you're all set for tomorrow. Did you get the FedEx with some mail and your speech?"

"Yes," Michael replied softly into the phone, not wanting to disturb the other diners. "I've got it, and it looks perfect. Thanks for making the changes—and keeping it out of Dick's hands."

"Boss, the speech looks great, but I sure hope you know what you're doing. This will be like a bomb going off to Dick and some of the board members. And you know that you've got to read it from your script. I would have had to give the marketing department the speech yesterday in order for it to be loaded onto a teleprompter. I can sure as hell see that we didn't want to do that."

"That's okay. I'm not crazy about those teleprompters anyway," Michael said. "I've practiced it enough so that I'm very comfortable with my delivery."

"Also," Karen said, "Mr. Applegarden wants to meet with you tomorrow before you go on. He's going to call your room, so be ready. You're supposed to be at the UCLA business auditorium at three."

"I've got it. I'll see Applegarden at some point before. I just want to keep it brief so we don't get too deep into the details of the speech, and I've got to be sure we don't meet too early so there's no chance he can force me to rewrite or change anything."

"Oh God, I'm glad I'm not going to be there. They're all going to have a fit—although the press may love it."

"You're right on both points, Karen."

"Yes, but remember, Boss, it's the board that pays you. Not the press."

"Karen, that's why I love you. You're just like Samantha. Always right."

"I know. Good luck. Please call me when it's over."

Michael turned off the phone and looked at Samantha She was not eating her salmon.

Chapter 37

Los Angeles, California
December 2, 2009

"Michael, God, it's good to have you back. I know this has been tough for you." Dick Applegarden had finally caught up with Michael. It was ten minutes before Michael was to step to the podium in front of a crowd of over two thousand reporters, executives, and business students. "Are you ready for this? I never actually got a copy of your speech, but nobody does this sort of thing better than you do."

"Oh, I'm ready. Hopefully everyone is." Michael knew that Dick Applegarden was uncomfortable around him.

"Anyway, we can get together later at the hotel. You're just about to go on. Good luck. I trust you." Michael knew that Dick Applegarden didn't trust anyone.

Michael was dutifully introduced by the master of ceremonies, and he walked up the four steps to the stage and headed for the podium to a polite round of applause. He thanked the speaker who gave the introduction, took a deep breath, and gazed out at the audience hidden in the subdued light. As the applause from his introduction subsided, he began his speech.

"America has led the world in innovative business practices, but it has initiated a cancer, which, if allowed to grow unchecked and unregulated, will destroy the very fabric of our great industries. Hedge funds and private equity investors have mandated the relentless purchase and merging of companies, many of them industry leaders with long track records of success. These investors, driven by the need for fast, short-term gains, force the supposedly cost-efficient restructuring—or, as we so often call it, 'right-sizing' of these companies. We say it's to make them more cost-efficient or competitive. But we all know we're sacrificing long-term sustainability and competitiveness for a quick return, which can then be leveraged for a profitable sale of the organization.

"It has resulted in the destruction of hundreds of excellent companies and hundreds of thousands of American jobs. It has torn apart the bedrock of great organizations: the implied contract and trusting relationship between a business entity and its valued employees. Great companies are never run by accountants or consultants. How can we look at ourselves in the mirror when we strip out the more seasoned and talented employees—who happen to logically earn the most—in the name of so-called right-sizing?"

Michael tried to gauge the reaction of the audience as he looked up from his speech notes. It was difficult with such a large crowd sitting mostly in the dark. They seemed, however, to be listening intently and staring back at him with unusual focus and interest, at least for a business speech.

Energized, Michael continued. "Whatever happened to building a great product and a great company, investing in the future, having the patience to invest in research and development and in your people, even though the financial payoff may not come within the next quarter? Why are we allowing financial deal makers and traders to purchase our companies; pull out the equity built up over years; sell off the assets; eliminate its pension, health, and other employee benefits; load the business up with debt—and then sell it for a quick profit, crippled and loaded with debt payments, to another investor, while earning millions more in fees?"

Michael paused and made eye contact with Dick Applegarden sitting in the first row. Dick's eyes were like lasers staring back at Michael. Michael glanced down at his notes and delivered his coup de grâce. "Our new business titans have become the financial technicians, or as I would affectionately call them, plumbers, who neither know nor care how to run a business or even understand the company's products or services, but who are expert at the manipulation of the financial architecture of the organization. And, ladies and gentlemen, this financial architecture has become a sophisticated way to simply rape a company."

Michael concluded with the outline of a solution. "I propose a new standard of regulation to limit the ability of corporate raiders to purchase a company, devalue that company, and then steal its assets—and a new leadership paradigm whereby CEOs are not only challenged with short-term financial performance, but long-term business growth and sustainability. Finally," he concluded, "I fully expect my organization, Gibraltar Financial, to be a part of this new direction, and I will do everything to lead by example. Thank you."

After a moment of shocked silence, a few brave souls in the audience applauded. Slowly, the few became many, and the room erupted in a spontaneous and exhilarating roar of applause—except for the stunned members of the Gibraltar's board of directors surrounding Michael's boss, Chairman Dick.

Michael waved and smiled to the appreciative audience, turned around, and stepped down the same steps he had walked up twenty minutes before. He then attempted to take his seat in the front row. But before he reached his seat, Dick Applegarden jumped up, took Michael firmly by the arm, and led him to the nearby hallway and exit.

"Are you fucking crazy, Michael? No wonder I never saw the fucking speech. What the hell is wrong with you? You just committed suicide, my friend." Dick's face was red and contorted. "The board will have your head. I'm not going to let you damage me with this disaster, but mark my words, *I will destroy you.*"

Chapter 38

Beverly Hills, California
December 2, 2009

I t had not been a good day for Dick Applegarden.

Still in his forties, he was extraordinarily successful. Tall and wiry, with prematurely gray hair and wire-rimmed glasses, he looked more like an accountant than a chairman. Early in his career, he had toiled as a salesperson selling mortgage services to corporations for its employees, achieving success at a time when the real estate and mortgage markets were booming. As he rose up the executive ranks, he proved to be an adept political player in the big corporate world.

Dick was frequently critical of Michael, who was trying to fix the mess he had inherited. But Chairman Dick's memory was short. In the frequently contentious board meetings, Michael was interrogated by Applegarden, who did not want to hear that the company he had purchased and that Michael now led was a godforsaken disaster needing a total and costly overhaul.

Dick needed a scapegoat to deflect attention away from his ill-conceived acquisition, and Michael's explosive speech had just presented the perfect opportunity.

Now, nearly inebriated after an evening of scornful discussions in the Peninsula Hotel bar with Michael and the angry members of the board, Dick was in his suite and about to retire to his bedroom when he received a call from his own boss, Richard Perkins, the chairman of Gibraltar Financial's parent company.

"Richard, I've got it under control. I have the agreement from our board members to remove Michael from his position. We just need to let a discreet period of time go by so it won't look as if we fired him over this goddamned speech. In the meantime, I will make his life a living hell before I kick his ass out of here. Maybe we can get him to resign, and we won't have to give him a severance package. When I'm done with him, he won't know what hit him."

Applegarden took the two Ambien he had earlier placed on the night table by his king-sized bed and washed them down with the remaining Bushmills single malt whiskey in the glass he had brought up from the bar.

Within five minutes he was sound asleep, lying on his back and snoring heavily, his mouth wide open.

At midnight, the power mysteriously went off throughout the Peninsula Hotel, shutting down the security cameras and casting the hallways in near darkness except for the glare of emergency lights placed at various positions.

Minutes later, two men in dark, well-tailored suits and ties, and one woman in a long black evening gown walked casually through the hotel lobby. They passed the bustling bar and two sets of doors until they approached the door to Suite 134, at which time they each put on gloves. They ignored the "Do Not Disturb" sign, expertly disabled the electronic lock on the door, and without making a sound or uttering a word, entered Dick Applegarden's suite. They carefully closed the door behind them and stood inside, stopping briefly to adjust their eyes to the dark and to survey the room layout. The only noise was Applegarden's tortured breathing and gasping coming from the open door of the bedroom.

One of the men nodded to the rest of the team, and they all entered the bedroom. They rushed to Applegarden's bed and removed the covers over him, causing him to stir. For a second, he opened his eyes wide and appeared to try and raise his head from the pillow. He was able to utter only one word, "Who—" before the men held him down and pulled off his boxer shorts. The tall woman in the long black dress jabbed a needle into his upper thigh near his groin.

In the next moment, every muscle in his body went limp, and although his eyes were wide open and his mouth seemed to form a scream, he was silent and totally paralyzed.

As the others watched, one of the men placed a pillow over Applegarden's face, leaving only his eyes exposed. "Don't fight it," he said. "Just go gently into the night and it won't hurt a bit." While holding down the pillow, the killer was careful not to bruise his immobilized victim. For two or three minutes, he watched as Applegarden continued to stare at him in uncomprehending disbelief. Finally, Applegarden's eyes took on the unmistakable look of the dead.

The three then carefully put Applegarden's boxer shorts back on his body and pulled the covers back to their original position. They opened two of the suite's windows slightly. Then, one by one, each of them silently climbed out one of the windows and onto the isolated flagstone path outside, just a few feet below.

Applegarden's body, neatly tucked back in under the covers, would be found the next afternoon when his fellow board members notified the hotel that he had not shown up for their meetings and that calls to his room and cell phone had gone unanswered. The coroner would attribute the death to a case of sleep apnea, whereby he stopped breathing in his sleep, aggravated by a combination of

Ambien and the consumption of a large quantity of alcohol. There were no signs of a struggle on the body. There were no reports of suspicious people in the hotel around the time of death, and the door was securely locked and latched from the inside. The police believed that the deceased had opened two of the windows sometime before he went to bed to allow fresh air into the room.

Officially, Chairman Richard "Dick" Applegarden had died of "natural causes."

Chapter 39

Queens Village, New York
December 3, 2009

I t was a short detour, maybe ten minutes out of his way, but it would take Michael Nicholas back a lifetime. He steered his car off the Grand Central Parkway and headed toward the quiet suburban street in Queens Village where he and his brother had grown up. It had been over twenty years since the last time he had passed by it, and even then, he had not paused to sift through his memories.

He drove up to the house, a two-story Tudor-style home on a manicured lawn, still looking like it did when he lived there. He parked across the street and reached over to the passenger seat for Alex's laptop.

"What are you doing back there at the house?" Alex said.

Michael was taken back. "How do you know where I am?"

"I have a GPS system that allows me to track your location when you log onto me. I've just figured it out."

As Michael began to speak, he thought about what an incredible advance this software—his brother—had just made.

"What am I doing here? I don't know, I just thought that coming here, with you, maybe I could discover some insights, something to help me understand what is happening," Michael said. He sat behind the wheel, alternating between looking at his childhood home and watching his brother on the laptop screen. "I guess I'm waiting for some revelation, something to connect the dots from a time and place where we once were together, to now, where we're together again, but differently."

"I wouldn't waste your fuckin' time."

So much for deep insights, Michael thought. Alex didn't appear interested in an emotional experience or the "awakening" that Michael had intended for their visit. But he wasn't going to give up.

"Alex, can you speak or communicate with the dead? A few days ago you seemed to indicate that you might at some point."

"Michael, you know how you used to say that life is complicated?"

"Yes, I still say it. More than ever now."

Alex's face was blank. "Well, death is even more complicated. Believe it or not, the world here, if you can call it that, is divided into two groups: BI, Before Internet, and AI, After Internet. Finding or communicating with people is very different depending on *when* they lived and died."

"You mean kind of like BC, Before Christ, and AD, the year he was born or whatever?"

"Something like that. I'm still trying to figure it out myself. I'm getting smarter, but it takes time. I was programmed to keep learning, you know. Unlike when I was alive."

Michael sat back, trying to make sense of what Alex had said. But, as he played back the words and looked again at his old home, he felt a wave of memories passing through him.

"My first contact with death or even its very existence came the day our Uncle Tom died," Michael said. "I thought of that day last week while I was watching Sharkey choking."

"You were just a little kid. You were at home that day, weren't you?"

"I was five. I remember it, Alex. Forty-five years ago, but I can see every minute detail. I can replay it, like a video in my head. I can see each room—his bedroom, ours, and then our parents' bedroom, where I heard it all. It's engraved in my brain, and I can feel it in the pit of my stomach, just as though I'm there right now and it's happening in front of me.

"In some strange way, I cherish the memory because it's always allowed me to put myself back in that precise moment, to remember everything around me on a particular day so early in my life. I've got a permanent picture, more vivid and precise than I ever could have had if hadn't been so traumatic."

"Uncle Tom was like another father, except he was home all the time. I always went to him whenever I did something wrong—which happened a lot. He was my protector as a kid," Alex said.

Michael resumed his story. "It was an ideal world, to have two good parents and an older uncle living with you. He wasn't that old, maybe late fifties when he died. He was a tall man, in good shape. I remember his frameless glasses and his short white hair—he had a crew cut. Mom said Uncle Tom had been a captain of a big Greek cargo ship. He used to take me everywhere. I hadn't even started school yet. I remember he'd taken me for a few practice walks for the three blocks to my school, I guess so I'd be more comfortable on the day he would actually walk me there. But, looking back, it was like he was preparing me for the walk without him." Michael paused and looked at the computer screen. He could see that Alex was processing the story from so long ago that impacted both of them.

"I was out playing ball that day. It was a summer morning. I've never heard you talk about it. Everything I remember, I heard from our mother," Alex said.

Michael continued. "I was in the kitchen. He had made me my

breakfast, soft-boiled eggs, and then he went upstairs to his bed-room. He told me he wasn't feeling well, but the way he said it, it didn't sound like any big deal. The next thing I knew, Mom was with him in his room upstairs—she was by his bed. He was having a heart attack. She ran to the phone to call an ambulance, and in the rush, forgot about me for a minute or so.

"So I watched him, from his bedroom door. I was scared. I didn't understand what was happening, but I knew it was terrible. Mom called out to Peggy, our housekeeper, to take me away, but I ran to join her in her bedroom. She was on the phone, fighting with the operator who evidently wasn't going fast enough or tried to put her on hold. And I was standing there, by her side, watching and listening. I was worried about catching germs. I was so young."

"What happened then?"

"She went back to his bedroom, and they made me stay in Mom's bedroom, but I could hear everything. She was asking if he wanted water, telling him help was coming. I could tell she was helpless. I don't think he was saying anything. And then I heard it. The most terrifying sound I have ever heard, even today."

"What was it?" Alex said. He looked somber, as though it had just happened.

"He was kind of choking. I couldn't understand what the sound was then. I had no idea, although it was so gruesome I knew it was bad, very bad. I know now it was his death rattle."

Alex stared ahead. He showed no reaction. Michael wasn't sure what, if anything, his brother was thinking or whether Alex actually *could* think. He wondered what was going on behind that screenshot, that seemingly live image of the person who was supposed to be dead. But Michael wanted so badly to believe his brother was really there in front of him and not at Saint Michael's with every other dead relative.

Michael continued, "I'm sure that in my own final moments, I'll think of that terrible scene. I've been drawn back to it all my life. I know it'll be with me to my own end. It's shaped how I feel about death—and life. You know, how fragile and fleeting it all is."

Michael and Alex looked at each other in silence, nearly mirror images. "From that day on," Michael said, "I knew life didn't last forever."

Chapter 40

South Beach, Florida
December 5, 2009

Miami was steamy. Despite what every doctor and morning news show medical analyst advised, Michael always felt like the sun and a tan did wonders for his health. It certainly made him feel good.

Michael wanted to formally announce his decision regarding Alex's business to Donna and the Lesters. Since Donna was already vacationing in Miami, Michael flew down with Samantha and the Lesters. Michael called it an "off-site management meeting," which had Fat Lester confused and concerned until he realized that it didn't matter, because Michael was picking up the tab.

Michael booked their usual junior suite at the Setai in South Beach, where Donna was also staying. He then booked Fat and Skinny Lester at a discreet distance away in the South Beach Marriot. Although Michael had come to trust and cherish both Lesters, he could not envision Fat Lester lounging at the pool of the Setai, with its international clientele and its understated almost Zen-like atmosphere. Alex himself would have checked out before he even made it up to his room. It was, Michael thought to himself, perhaps one of the remaining differences between them.

DeVito's restaurant, however, at the foot of South Beach was anything but Zen-like. Danny DeVito wasn't in town, but Frank Sinatra's recorded voice filled the air while the waiters rolled by with eight-pound lobsters and sizzling Kobe beefsteaks that almost looked like they were worth the astronomical prices on the menu. The décor was a combination of Tuscan villa and 1940s Hollywood glitz. The deep-red Venetian crystal chandeliers softly illuminated the bright-white leather chairs, but mostly spotlighted a bevy of discontinued models: tall, young blondes accompanied by deeply tanned men twice their age.

Despite smoking restrictions, there was a whiff of cigar smoke in the air. This was a macho man's place, Michael thought to himself.

Donna approached the table wearing her oversized Dior sunglasses, despite the evening shade, and a short, tight white skirt showing off her shapely legs and slim ankles. Michael noticed that she attracted the leering glances of the open-shirted, gold-chain male crowd in DeVito's that night. He knew, just watching her stroll to the table, that it wouldn't be long before Donna lined up a new husband.

They sat out on the patio overlooking the crowd of partygoers, strollers, and the stream of cars on Ocean Drive. In the near horizon, the sand and the Atlantic Ocean were vaguely visible in the darkening night.

Their waiter looked like he had played for the Italian football team twenty years ago. "I'll have a dry Blue Sapphire martini and Greta Garbo here will have a Grey Goose cosmo." As Michael smiled at Donna, Fat and Skinny Lester, distracted and captivated by the parade of scantily clad women all around them, each ordered a Dewar's on the rocks.

"Samantha's just spending a quiet night in her room watching some movies and enjoying room service. She'll see you tomorrow at the pool," Michael said, looking at Donna. He was relieved

Samantha had backed out of the dinner, otherwise, he would have had to arrange a daytime meeting while she was shopping so he could make his announcement. He knew he would need to filter or at least carefully position any such conversation with his wife.

"She's also not crazy about DeVito's. Just a little too much testosterone here for her." Or, Michael thought, maybe just too many young blondes. Michael chose to keep that thought to himself.

After a round of drinks and the usual small talk, everyone dug into their first course. Michael took charge of the dinner conversation. Although keeping a low tone so he wouldn't be overheard beyond their table, Michael was confident and firm.

"We've all gotten through a lot in the past month. Together, we've collected the money due Alex, paid all the money out that Alex owed others—except, of course, for the two hundred thousand we charged Sharkey for being greedy. We've uncovered the three million that Alex had stashed away.

"I'm going to be sure that the money is distributed in a way that my brother would have wanted. Most of the money, of course, is going to Donna and George. But," Michael continued, looking at the two Lesters, "I'm also sure Alex would have wanted you guys to receive something in his memory. I'm going to sit down and work out the details next week with Donna, but I wanted you both to know that you'll be getting some part of that money."

Skinny Lester was the first to respond. "Michael, Donna, you both have been like family to us. I think I can speak for Lester, too, when I say that we didn't expect anything from the cash Alex left. Alex always paid us well. Better than we could have done anywhere on our own. I could have never done this well driving a taxi, which is the only thing that college ever really prepared me for."

Fat Lester finally had organized his thoughts. He said, "Other than my cousin here, Alex was my only family. No one else even talks to me. My own family thinks I'm no good. Alex always respected me, even through my booze and drug problems. I didn't even like myself. I don't know how he put up with me." A tear glistened in his eye and threatened to roll down his cheek. Fat Lester stopped speaking.

Michael continued, "There's something else I want to talk about. I want to keep Alex's business alive. I'm going to run it. Hopefully, I can do half the job that Alex did. I'm going to need your help, both of you," he said, looking again at Fat and Skinny Lester.

Michael then turned toward Donna. "Donna, we can discuss some of the numbers when we sit down together, but I'm offering you the opportunity to invest in the business a portion of the money Alex left you. This way, we can grow it further, and you'll hopefully have a steady stream of income."

"Michael," Donna said, "I'm shocked. What about your job? I never dreamed you'd want to do this. Other than being shocked, though, I think it's a great idea. I'm definitely in, at least as long as I get to keep a good portion of what's coming to me. I trust you, you're brilliant, but I don't want to totally roll the dice. You understand, don't you?"

"I do and don't worry. There's enough money to go around. Also, I'm going to invest some of my own money in this. As for my Gibraltar position, frankly, I'm bored and I expect to be fired any day now after the speech I gave in LA."

Michael then laid out his quick vision for the new enterprise. "We're going to have basically three lines of business. First, sports betting, college and pro football and basketball, and major-league baseball. Second, loan-sharking. Citibank is charging me nearly 30 percent on my credit card. From what I've been hearing and looking at how Alex did it, we can charge anywhere from 50 to 250 percent interest, depending on the borrower and how risky the loan. Finally, we'll do some limited horse racing—but if it involves big dollars and long shots, we'll lay it off using OTB just like Alex did so we don't incur the risk."

Both Lesters had their mouths open in shock. Skinny Lester

was the first to speak up with, "I'm in." Fat Lester added, "Good shit."

"By the way, I've been meaning to ask you, Michael, what else did you ever find on Alex's laptop besides the location of the cash?"

Michael had implied to Donna that he had hired experts to crack the user name and password mysteries and that the location of the money was simply in the files on the computer. He had never told her about Jennifer, let alone Catherine Saint-Laurent. He decided it would be better not to have anyone know that he and Alex spoke more now than they had before he was murdered.

"I found a lot of interesting stuff, at least for me. I don't think it would be too interesting to anyone else. The location of the money was the only big thing, of course."

"Michael," Donna asked, "I just have one question. This is a big change for you. How does Samantha feel about it?"

Michael, knowing full well he had some convincing to do, said simply, "She doesn't know everything yet ... exactly."

Rolling her eyes, Donna said, "You know, Michael, sometimes I think I see more of your brother in you every day."

Chapter 41

New York City
December 7, 2009

Michael was enjoying his walk up Fifth Avenue. Although the New York weather was frigid, with a sharp wind blowing in his face, the noontime sun took the edge off the cold. The city looked surreally clear. Michael was on his way to meet Richard Perkins, the chairman of Gibraltar Financial's parent company and Dick Applegarden's boss. They had a twelve thirty lunch at the 21 Club.

Although it was set up as an informal "let's just touch base" meeting, Michael knew there was no such thing. Perkins was not a "let's touch base" type of guy. He was sure that as soon as the order for drinks was taken, Perkins would announce that he had a "difficult mission to accomplish." He would go on to say, Michael speculated, that he knew how difficult a situation Michael had walked into and how hard he had worked to turn the company around. Finally, he would get right to the point: "Michael, the board has decided to request your resignation." He would then state how painful he knew this was for Michael and give him the option of leaving the restaurant or continuing with him through the meal.

Michael knew the playbook well. He had followed it himself innumerable times. As his mind wandered with thoughts about his tumultuous time at Gibraltar, Michael was brought back to the moment by the ring of his cell phone. It was Karen. "Hi, Boss. Are you all set for your lunch? I can't believe this is happening."

"Don't worry, Karen. I'm totally prepared. I've spoken to Rothberg. He even wanted me to wear a wire to tape the conversation. Listen, I haven't been happy. I knew when I made that speech that it would probably provoke them to fire me. I don't want anything from them, just a reasonable severance, and I plan on making sure you're keeping your job with a comparable position."

"Michael, please don't worry about me. I feel terrible for you. I know the board was so upset over your speech, but it has certainly been well received by the press. *Businessweek* and the *Financial Times* had great things to say about you—and Gibraltar. Everyone just assumes the board approved the speech ahead of time. So, it's made everyone look good. I just can't believe they're getting rid of you like this after all you've done for them."

Judging from her longer-than-usual pauses, Michael suspected that Karen must have been close to tears. "Just so you know, I'll be reminding Richard that you warned me to show the speech to marketing for clearance and that I just refused. It happens to have the added benefit of being the truth. But listen, this isn't about the speech. I did my best, and we did a lot of great things—the company is on a solid recovery and growth path. It's time for me to move on and get out of their hair."

Michael felt as if a tremendous burden was being lifted off his shoulders.

"What are you going to do next?" Karen asked.

"Oh, I don't know. Maybe set up a bookmaking operation in Queens." Michael could hear Karen chuckling. "I'll call you later, unless they disconnect my cell phone account while I'm in the restaurant."

Michael was walking west on Fifty-Second Street, approaching the black iron gated entrance with the politically incorrect jockey statue out front of the 21 Club. Just as he hung up with Karen, his phone rang again—Samantha.

"Hi, darling, are you okay? I'll love you even more if you're unemployed for a while. I'll have you home with me, you know."

Michael knew he could always count on Samantha. "Don't worry, there's nothing they can do that would surprise or throw me. I'm ready for this. But I'm just in front of 21—let me call you when I get out. I love you." As he walked through the entrance vestibule, he thought of JFK, who dined at the restaurant on the eve of his inauguration, and of Alfred Hitchcock, a regular patron and a master of mystery and intrigue. They were two of Michael's favorite characters. At the moment, he felt more attuned to Hitchcock.

———

Michael sat at his table as he watched Richard Perkins approaching. Richard was a former military officer, tall, always perfectly erect and proper. Today he was dressed in a conservative dark-gray suit and striped red-and-navy-blue tie. Despite the hard-driving Gibraltar culture, Michael had never heard Richard utter a profanity or even raise his voice. Nevertheless, Richard Perkins was positively frightening. Despite his extreme conservatism and overly straight-laced approach, Michael actually liked and respected him. At least he was predictable, consistent, and straightforward—rare traits in an ego-driven business world.

They were both comfortably seated at a quiet table in the Bar Room, which Perkins had obviously requested when his secretary made the reservation. Michael looked around at the restaurant, with its simple red-and-white checked tablecloths that belied its pricey reputation. It was filled with businessmen. With martinis on half the tables, it could have been a scene out of the 1950s.

It never ceased to amaze Michael how, despite the financial woes of so many businesses, senior executives thought nothing of treating themselves to exorbitantly priced drinks and meals. Having lunch at 21 while laying off hundreds of employees making middle-class wages seemed to reek of Marie Antoinette. Michael was glad he would soon be an entrepreneur.

"Shall we order drinks?" Richard asked Michael as the black-suited waiter appeared. Everything was going according to plan, Michael thought. He ordered a straight-up gin martini. He figured he didn't need to be at his sharpest today; he just needed to be able to listen and walk out with dignity when the meal was over. Perkins ordered bourbon on the rocks, a nod to his southern heritage.

As though an "On the Air" sign had lit up, Perkins got down to business. "You know, Michael, I've had a difficult mission to accomplish. With Dick's unfortunate death, I've had to lead the search for a successor. You walked into a very difficult situation. I know things were a lot worse than what was represented to you when you were hired. Frankly, we didn't know ourselves how bad things were until the numbers started rolling in after Dick's acquisitions had closed. The board, although we didn't always show it, knows how hard you have worked to turn things around. We also know how delicate a dance it was for you having to fix what your boss, our beloved Dick, created before you came."

"Thanks, Richard. It has been quite a rocky road, but I feel we have navigated through this as well as anyone could. I'm glad to hear that you recognized some of the built-in tensions and awkwardness that existed, particularly between me and Dick." Michael actually felt pretty good about Perkins's buildup to the climax.

"As you know," Richard continued, "Dick and some of the board were pretty upset with your speech in LA. I'm still not happy that you never cleared it for our approval. It's not the way we do things."

"I understand that, Richard, but you know it would never have been approved."

"That's my point, Michael." Richard was bearing down on Michael. "On the other hand, I'm big enough to understand that sometimes you need people who have the courage of their convictions. You have also become a sort of folk hero out there."

"I wasn't trying to be any sort of hero. I just wanted to bring to light a poisonous culture and way of doing business that I think is destroying the fabric of American industry." Michael knew that anytime he could frame an issue to Perkins in terms of preserving the American way of life, he would tap into Perkins's innate patriotism. But Perkins wasn't listening. He had a mission to accomplish before the appetizers arrived.

Michael saw the waiter approaching with two Caesar salads. "Michael, I asked you to meet for lunch today ..." Just then the two salads were placed on the table, breaking Perkins's train of thought and conversation. Uncharacteristically, he had misjudged the timing of the presentation of the salads. Michael wondered whether the waiter realized he had delayed Michael's "execution," however briefly.

The waiter took three steps away, but only to a nearby serving table to retrieve a large pepper mill. It was obvious that Perkins was getting impatient. "Michael, the board met formally yesterday, and after reviewing a number of difficult options, made a decision that, I believe, will not come as a total surprise to you."

"Don't worry, Richard. I've been around enough situations. I'm well prepared for any decision the board has made."

Richard seemed relieved. "I know that, Michael, and I appreciate it. Let me get to the point. The board has decided to promote you to the role of chairman. In other words, we want you to replace Dick. Congratulations."

Chapter 42

Queens Village, Queens, New York
December 8, 2009

D espite Michael's dislike of his former sister-in-law, he had invited Greta Garbone for drinks. Although dinner might have been more appropriate for the discussion he needed to have with her, Michael wanted to limit the time involved and keep a quicker escape as an easy option.

He asked Greta to meet him at a local bar in Queens Village at the intersection of Union Turnpike and Springfield Boulevard. The Black Rose was an old-fashioned neighborhood bar whose heyday had been forty years ago. Dim lighting, no food, just solid drinks. It had a dark charm, with its long wooden bar, red leather padding around the edges, and semicircular private red leather banquettes. It was just several blocks from where Michael and Alex had grown up and was a regular hangout for Alex in his younger days.

Michael had not been inside the Black Rose since he joined his brother there for drinks during a break from college. He still had a picture of Alex taken in the bar almost thirty years ago, looking like Frank Sinatra with a cigarette hanging out of his mouth and a drink in hand. Although a big drinker and smoker, Alex looked handsome, slim, and healthy then.

The Black Rose brought back memories of Alex and being young, when everyone he knew as a child, including his parents, was still alive and in their prime.

When Michael saw Greta walk through the door, the uncomfortable memories from the time when she was part of his extended family came rushing back. He was glad he had not made this a dinner meeting.

Greta had not aged well. "Greta, you look well," he lied.

"For God's sake, Michael, is that the best you can do? I'm not even forty for God's sake. I should hope I'm 'well.' Christ, that's how you greet a seventy-year-old." Arithmetic, Michael thought, was never Greta's strong point. He couldn't recall how old she really was, but he knew she'd passed forty several years ago.

Michael realized that even with just drinks, this evening was going to seem like an eternity. He was thinking that maybe he should have arranged instead to meet Greta at McDonald's for a quick burger or, even quicker, at Jiffy Lube while having an oil change.

Michael began, "Anyway, Greta. I wanted to fill you in on some things that have occurred regarding Alex."

"Have they found out who was behind his murder?"

"No, Donna hasn't heard anything new from the police. We might have had a much better shot if the kid who did it wasn't shot dead in the bar at the same time. You know sometimes these types of crimes don't get solved quickly. Whoever was behind this may have been a professional or in some type of organized crime. If that's the case, it could be years before someone talks or the cops get a good lead."

"Listen, Michael. Your brother was a terrible husband and treated me like shit in the divorce, but he wasn't a bad guy. I'd like to see them find the son of a bitch who hired that kid to kill him. After all, Alex was the father of my son."

"That's the reason I wanted to see you tonight, Greta. Alex was always concerned about George. It was his wish that George be taken care of as best as possible from whatever Alex could provide." Michael was trying to measure his words carefully with Greta, knowing she would always look for an opening to redress whatever ills she felt needed to be fixed from either her marriage to—or divorce from—Alex.

Michael knew that Greta was already aware of the cash found in Alex's home and the safe deposit box since George had been at Alex's house the day both were recovered. Greta also knew about Alex's laptop and that there could be something of interest on the computer without, of course, knowing anything about Alex's artificial intelligence program. Michael would have preferred that Donna not be quite so open to George's involvement.

"So, what did Alex leave for us?" Greta was intensely interested now.

Michael didn't have a lot of patience for Greta's approach but knew he had to stay calm or he'd be eaten up alive.

Keeping his voice low, Michael continued, "Greta, I'm going to be straight with you so we don't misunderstand each other or waste a lot of time. My brother's concern financially was for your son. He wanted me to be sure that George was provided for. Whatever happened between you and Alex is not something I can fix or even address. But I can take care of George with funds that, as you know, we have now secured. The amount left in Alex's estate was minimal, but George did get a share of that. This, however, is substantial."

"How much are we talking about?" It was clear that Greta needed a number.

"I'm prepared to put a million dollars aside for George. I'll give him one hundred thousand dollars immediately. I'll then pay him out a hundred thousand each year for the next nine years." Michael paused for Greta's reaction.

Greta's face tightened. "Michael, first of all, you got three million dollars the other day from the box and the freaking dining room floor. I'd expect George to get at least half of that, not a third. Second, he's got to get it all now. This is our—his—money."

"Greta, the money is being allocated the way I believe Alex would have wanted. Besides Donna, I believe that Alex would have wanted Fat and Skinny Lester to receive something. They've earned it, and they were as close to Alex as anyone, and for most of his life."

Greta started to interrupt, but Michael cut her off. "Now listen, Greta. Let me finish. We can't show any of this money. I'm probably the only one out of all of you who can spend what I want because I'm making a good, legitimate income on which I pay out over 30 percent in taxes. No one else around here is showing any substantial income. So, whatever George gets, he's going to have to be careful about what he spends. The last time I looked, he had no job. If I give him a lot of money—and I consider a hundred thousand a fortune for him—and he starts spending it, we're all screwed.

"By the way, not that I need to make an accounting to you, but I'm personally taking none of Alex's cash. George will take what I give him when I give it to him, as long as he's discreet in how he spends it. I'm not looking to be his father, but I'm also not going to let him be stupid. If he doesn't work with me on how he spends it, I'll cut him off."

"Michael, I don't want to fight with you. But honestly, I need money myself—I'm desperate. I owe people money. Things didn't go the way I thought they would." Greta was quickly changing her approach.

"What happened to that high-flying guy you were living with? What was his name, 'Merlin the Magician'?"

When it was apparent to her that Alex was not going to be her ticket to stardom, Greta had actually run off with a magician who, for a short time, was modestly successful in Las Vegas and traveling shows. But Alex had later told Michael that Greta's new lover had gotten into financial trouble and had borrowed from loan sharks. Alex knew because "Merlin" had secretly contacted him for a loan.

"I kicked him out a few weeks ago. He was a leech," Greta said.

Michael had no desire to hear any more details. "Greta, I'm here to simply carry out what my brother would have wanted, and he wanted Donna and George to be taken care of. I'm going to do that. But with George, I need to make sure that he is cautious about how the money is spent, for all the reasons you already know. He is too young and immature to be trusted with a large sum of money. But I can't help you with your own money issues."

"You always looked down on my family, Michael."

"I never really looked down on anyone. I'm just picky about whom I spend my holidays with. Some of your family were nice people, but I wasn't happy about being around drug addicts and ex-cons. My parents did a lot coming over as poor immigrants to make successes of themselves here."

"Your brother wasn't exactly a saint."

"My brother used his brains and his wits to beat the system—not to be a victim. But, you know, I'm not here to relive old times. George will get his money—on my terms. He's going to have to then take care of you, if that's what he wants to do."

Michael turned as his eye caught the attention of the barmaid. "Check, please."

Chapter 43

Westport, Connecticut
December 8, 2009

I t was nearly midnight, but Michael was still agitated from his meeting with Greta. He needed to vent to someone, and who could be more appropriate to unload on than Alex? So Michael sat down in his library, plugged in the laptop to conserve its power, and after keying in the user name and password, saw his brother appear on the brightly lit screen.

"Alex, sometimes when Samantha gives me a hard time over something, I say to myself, 'Next time around, I'm going to marry a bimbo.' You know, someone who just looks pretty but is stupid. Well, my meeting with Greta cured me of that fantasy."

"She's not so stupid." Alex appeared a bit defensive.

"Let me ask you, seriously, now that I have you like this, what in the world could have ever possessed you to marry her?"

"What do you mean, now that you have me 'like this'?" Alex became suddenly more serious.

"Well, I guess I mean you're not *physically* present, at least," Michael said.

"I wouldn't take anything for fuckin' granted. Your life, the one you consider to be the 'real' one, may be all in your head. Mine is on a computer, yours is in your brain. They're more similar than you think, except we know the limits of your brain. We don't know the limits of my computer yet, so don't get too cocky. I put a lot of money into this; I planned to get myself smarter in the process."

"I never thought about it that way," Michael said, feeling chastised, again.

"But anyway, you wanted to know how I could have married Greta? Actually, I thought I was marrying *Rosemary* Garbone. That's who she was when I first met her. I had already split with Pam. Greta used to come into Grimaldi's when I still owned it. Nice girl, on the make, looked pretty good then. We got along, you know what I mean? Then, as soon as we got married, she started in about moving to LA; she wanted to be some kind of actress and thought I was going to bankroll her and move out there."

"Did you ever say you would?"

"Not that I can fuckin' remember. What am I, nuts? I mean, maybe one night when we were both smashed. Who can remember every word you say to someone? I took her on a few trips out to LA before we were married. She'd say, you know, 'Wouldn't it be great to live out here?' I didn't even listen half the time. I probably said, 'Oh yeah, sure.' Who knows what I might have said. But there was no way. Everyone wears fucking sunglasses out there—it's crazy.

"So, we get married and she changes her name to *Greta* Garbone because she thinks she's going to be an actress. No education, no experience, no acting school, but we're supposed to pick up and go. She was nuts."

"What happened then?"

"What happened? Nothing happened. I told her she was crazy. I said that when you look like Angelina Jolie, then we'll move to Hollywood. I had her tits done for her, but I wasn't going to do everything. I said I'd pay for her to be a porn star, that was all. She got pissed off at that. I was only kidding, I think. In the meantime, I'm thinking, I've got to get out of this whole marriage thing with her. She was really crazy. I even told her something like that ... maybe not as politely."

"You two were married several years though."

"Yeah, well, shortly after I started thinking divorce, she got pregnant with George. So that was that for a while."

"Did you leave her for Donna?"

"No, I was just *dating* Donna—nothing serious, we'd just screw around—but I never left Greta. Later on, she left *me* for that Merlin the fucking magician. I didn't give a shit at that point. When Greta realized we weren't going to Hollywood, things got bad, even after George was born. I took her to Vegas for several days, and she goes to one of those magic shows or something. It was like a little act he had in the cocktail lounge of one of the casinos. She must have hooked up with him there."

"With the magician?"

"Yeah. I thought it was almost funny months later when she told me about it. She said it was 'magical.' I don't even think she realized what she was saying. 'Magical,' I told her, 'I bet it was, he's a fucking magician, after all.' He promised her all kinds of shit. He thought he was going to be big time too. He thought he was going to be on the big stage there. He wound up finally doing magic shows at kids' birthday parties in Queens. But that was later. So, she tells me she's leaving to go marry this guy. I told her to be my guest."

"What about Donna? You were seeing her while you were married to Greta?" Michael marveled at Alex's fluid concepts of marriage and dating.

"Yeah, but as I said, just on the side. It worked out; Greta took off with the magician, and then Donna and I got married. But Greta basically blackmailed me in the divorce settlement. I had to give her a lot, even though she's the one who wanted out. She was threatening to cause problems, said she'd go the cops or the *New York Post* about my business. So, we finally settled. I was giving her extra money every month. I didn't have to but—"

"So she was still dependent on you even after the divorce."

"More or less. More, really," Alex said.

"You kind of like it that way, don't you?" Michael watched Alex for a reaction.

"What do you mean?" Alex's eyebrows arched up.

"Well, to have people dependent on you?"

Alex paused, seemingly weighing the thought. "Maybe—I never thought about it. Anyway, it got worse for her. Next thing I know, Merlin's broke and borrowing money from me. He was into me for twenty grand before I finally had to cut him off. He told me that Greta was getting vicious, she was hitting him. He thinks she's seeing someone else too.

"Wouldn't surprise me. Even when she was with me, she was always looking around. I remember fuckin' Sharkey had his eyes on her. She was coming on to him. We had some big fights over that. When she doesn't have enough money—and she never does—she becomes a desperate woman. I felt bad for Merlin. He wasn't a bad guy. Let me tell you, you don't want to be broke and married to Greta."

"Did Greta have any idea that her new husband was borrowing money from her last one?" Michael asked.

Alex laughed. "I never told her; she'd have killed him."

Chapter 44

New York City
December 11, 2009
6:00 p.m.

Michael had planned what he hoped would be a festive and relaxed evening with Samantha.

Etheleen Staley was an old and trusted good friend. Michael had purchased much of his extensive photography collection from her gallery, Staley Wise, over the past twenty years.

Tonight was an exhibit of the former model-turned-photographer Ellen von Unwerth's sexy photographs. Von Unwerth had been a successful runway model and now had moved to the other side of the camera. Michael had his eye on one of her newest prints, "Follow Me, Paris."

Deacon Dan picked up Michael and Samantha in his silver Lincoln Town Car at their Westport home for the trip down to Soho to see the exhibit and then have dinner nearby at DaSilvano on Sixth Avenue in Greenwich Village. As they arrived at the corner of Broadway and Spring Street, Michael turned to Samantha. "It's like a different city down here—the young people, the look, the dress, and even the sounds are different from uptown. There's that edge here."

Samantha laughed. "I like the edgy feeling too, Michael. It's better than being *on edge*."

"I hope that's all behind us now," Michael said.

Michael was looking forward to settling down to some sort of routine again. He began to finally feel a sense of calm, perhaps accomplishment. He wanted to celebrate by purchasing a print and then heading off to dinner nearby.

Dan stopped the car and came around and opened Samantha's door. "Here you are, guys. Michael, I know this is your all-time favorite place."

"This—and Yankee Stadium." Dan and Michael had spent a good part of the last hour in the car talking about the New York Yankees. "Dan, we'll be about an hour, and then we'll go to DaSilvano. I've got a table for the three of us. I'll call you on your cell as we're getting ready to leave the gallery."

Michael and Samantha walked past Dean and DeLuca, an upscale grocery shop, entered the gallery building's small lobby, and took the elevator to the third floor. The elevator doors opened to the glass entrance of the gallery.

An opening at Staley-Wise Gallery was an event. The gallery was electrified with collectors and art aficionados, champagne, wine, sparkling water, smoked salmon, and fresh shrimp hors d'oeuvres. The noise level was high; the crowd numbered just over a hundred people, with a much greater proportion of women— most very tall, willowy, and blonde. The scene was black and white, from the photographs to the wall-to-wall elegant young ladies in their little black dresses and shiny stockings, each holding a glass of crisp, white chardonnay. It was apparent that Ellen von Unwerth had attracted a lot of her model acquaintances to the event.

Michael watched as von Unwerth worked the small crowd or, more precisely, the crowd worked her. Ellen von Unwerth was herself tall, probably six feet with her heels on, with a remarkable figure and a long mane of carefully disheveled silver-blonde hair. One would never guess that she was in her fifties.

As soon as Etheleen Staley saw Michael and Samantha, she approached them, giving them both a kiss on each cheek.

"Etheleen, I previewed the exhibit online. I know which print I want already," said Michael.

Michael and Samantha trusted Etheleen's professional judgment and advice implicitly. Michael knew she had a keen eye for the aesthetics and for art as an investment.

"You two are so funny," Etheleen said as Michael led them to the photograph he had selected. "Samantha loves to look and keep changing her mind, which I love. And you, Michael, seem to know what you want before you even get here."

The image he had selected was a sexy print showing, from the rear, a woman's black-stockinged legs approaching a table at a Paris bistro.

Etheleen nodded, signaling her approval. "Michael, I love this print. I knew you'd like it too. Ellen is a fabulous photographer."

"Just put it on my Amex and have it delivered to Elizabeth Goldfeder at GK Framing over on Hudson Street."

"I love it when you come in—and not just because you spend money. I know you love what you buy."

As Michael called Dan to let him know they'd be leaving in a few minutes, he overheard Samantha speaking with Etheleen. "You know, nothing makes Michael as happy as when he's here. No matter what kind of pressures he's under, when he comes to your gallery, he's smiling and happy again." *As usual,* he thought, *she's right.*

"Dan, we'll meet you right outside on Broadway in three minutes." Michael, ready to leave, turned back to Samantha and Etheleen. "Dan's right downstairs waiting, so I think we're going to take off for dinner. Thanks for everything, Etheleen. If you get tired of your own party, just head up to DaSilvano and join us for dinner."

Michael and Samantha walked past the spirited cocktail crowd, the front desk, and the long-limbed models in their short, black cocktail dresses. They exited the gallery through the heavy glass door and waited until the elevator reached the gallery's third floor. They entered the elevator, pressed the black "Lobby" button, and watched the overhead lights indicating they had reached the main floor.

Samantha exited first, followed closely by Michael as they walked through the small lobby and out through another set of heavy glass doors. Michael could see Dan in his car, sitting in the driver's seat, looking in his rearview mirror. Michael figured he was looking out for a police car since he was parked below a No Parking sign.

As Michael looked to the rear of Dan's car, however, he saw a familiar but eerie sight. It was a black Town Car, just like the one that followed him from the bank two days before. Although black Lincoln Town Cars were everywhere in New York, the driver of this one had the same black sunglasses as his recent pursuer. This time, however, there were two other passengers in the car, each looking more intimidating than the other.

Michael steered Samantha forward toward Dan's car, trying to get them both inside to safety as quickly as possible. As he moved toward the car, he saw the three doors of the black car open and three hulking but surprisingly fast-moving men leave the vehicle, doors still open behind them, and race toward Michael and his wife.

Before he or Samantha could reach the car, they were all over him. The first one came between him and Samantha, causing Samantha to fall against the side of the car. They grabbed Michael by his arms. He heard someone say, "Come with us quietly so we don't have to mess with your wife."

Before he could say a word, he saw a bright white handkerchief cover his face, enveloping him like a parachute. A strong hand was pressing the handkerchief over his nose and mouth. He tried to breathe, but when he inhaled, he was afraid he would ingest the cloth and started to gag. In that instant, he felt something strange. A warm flush swept over his face and body like a gentle tidal wave. He tried to move, but none of his muscles reacted. Nothing was working. He was helpless and going down.

Chapter 45

Michael had not yet opened his eyes. He was conscious, but he wasn't sure he was alive.

His stomach hurt. His face burned. His eyes stung. On top of that, his heart was racing, and he felt too light and dizzy. Michael wasn't sure he was attached to his body; it might be there, he thought, but he couldn't feel anything. He heard sounds; men were speaking, and he could hear words but couldn't understand them. There was the sensation of moving in a car, but time was a blur.

After what felt like an hour since he regained consciousness, Michael opened his eyes, and although he could perceive light and images, they didn't register in his mind. It was like looking at abstract art but without being able to use your brain. He couldn't conceive of ever having control of his senses and body again.

As more immeasurable time passed, some aspects of awareness seemed to slowly return. He began to comprehend isolated words, sometimes a phrase.

He knew now that he was alive but in trouble. He remembered

the white handkerchief and trying to get to his car. The handkerchief must have had chloroform or something like that in it, he thought. Michael had seen it numerous times in the movies. Did people really do this sort of thing? These guys obviously did. He began to feel his arms and hands and realized they were securely bound. This wasn't good.

"How ya doing, Michael?" the driver said. "Hey, our boy here is waking up," he said, half turning in the driver's seat to face Michael, who was seated in the right rear passenger seat. "Mr. Sharkey wanted me to extend his warmest greeting to you. He couldn't come with us tonight, but we've got a little tape recording he made just for you."

"Where's my wife?" Michael could only remember trying to push Samantha into Dan's car as he was being grabbed.

"Oh, your wife is fine. The driver, too. We don't fuck around with innocent people, just cheats who don't pay their debts." The driver seemed to be the only one of the three thugs who was speaking.

Michael could see that he was in the backseat of the black Lincoln Town Car. As he began to regain his ability to focus, he could see and feel that his hands and arms, just below his elbows, were securely pressed against his side and wrapped in duct tape, which went around his arms and chest. Although he had regained some feeling, he couldn't move.

"Are you guys crazy? Sharkey has a tape for me? The police can't be far behind."

With that, all three of the guys started laughing. The driver spoke again. "Yeah, the police are all looking for you, Michael. They're looking all over the city for a black Lincoln Town Car. That's like looking for a fuckin' yellow taxi."

Michael realized that, as stupid as they looked and sounded, their logic was pretty good. There had to be thousands of black Town Cars—the staple of the limo and livery services throughout the city.

"What's this tape about?" Michael asked. "And where are we going?" He wasn't sure he wanted to hear the answer.

"Where we goin'? Where the fuck do you think we're goin'? Out to fuckin' dinner?" Michael realized the driver was another schizoid personality. One moment he spoke like a nearly normal human being, the next second he was a thug.

Finally, one of the others spoke up. The one sitting next to Michael in the backseat said, "Morty, play him the fuckin' tape before we get there."

Michael had read that it was advisable for kidnap victims to try to converse with their captors or do anything to at least humanize whatever interaction they could. Reading the *New York Times* over a blueberry muffin in the morning, the strategy made perfect sense. Sitting in the back of the car, while imprisoned in duct tape and surrounded by three demented animals, it all seemed ridiculous.

"So, Morty, you guys work for Mr. Sharkey?" Michael figured he still had nothing to lose; maybe he could find an angle.

"I work part-time for Mr. Sharkey, you know, stuff like this at night. In the daytime, I work for a funeral home in Brooklyn. That's why they call me Morty, you know? Morty the Mortician. I drive the hearse. The jobs are alike, except on Mr. Sharkey's jobs, the bodies are still breathing—in the beginning anyway. You know what I mean?"

Michael was beginning to feel his legs and feet. If the conversation wasn't bad enough, when he leaned forward to look at his feet, what he saw made him shudder. When he looked down, he couldn't see his feet. They were embedded in a large metal pan of concrete that took up nearly the entire floor below his seat area. The concrete had set. Michael could not get his feet to even wiggle.

Michael looked out his car window. He could see out but imagined it would be hard for others to see in due to the dark tinted windows. Michael recognized the Triborough Bridge. They were leaving Manhattan and heading toward Queens. Not good in the scheme of things generally, let alone in this situation.

He looked out at the people in passing cars and those walking in the streets, all of them going about their daily, routine activities, unaware that Michael was on his way to a planned extinction. He thought about how bizarre it was to the victims—whether in a carriage on their way to the guillotine, a cattle train to Nazi death camps, gazing at approaching clotheslines from a crashing airliner window, or in the backseat of a Mafia hit man's car—to see the rest of the world going about the routine business of daily life.

Michael's mind had wandered. He was jerked back to reality by the clicking of a microcassette recorder. Morty was about to play Sharkey's message. "We call Mr. Sharkey 'KK.'" With that everyone in the car, except Michael, began laughing and grunting.

"Why is that?" Michael asked.

"Because he's the 'cassette killer.' Get it? KK?" They all broke up again, Morty almost swerving off the Grand Central Parkway.

Despite the fact that these three had total control over his remaining breathing moments, Michael felt the need to correct their spelling. "*Cassette* is spelled with a *c*, you assholes."

Suddenly the goon in the backseat with him violently pushed Michael's head into the passenger window. Morty became the momentary voice of reason. "Leave him." Then, however, he turned on Michael. "Maybe we didn't go to college, you little asshole, but *killer* has a fuckin' *k* in it. You know what else, you fuck? In fifteen minutes you'll be fuckin' dead, and we'll be having a big juicy steak. Now shut your fuckin' mouth and listen to Mr. Sharkey." Morty pushed the "Play" button on the recorder.

Michael recognized Sharkey's chilling voice, and although the language was familiar, the sound matched his appearance—corpse-like:

"Michael, my friend. I'm sorry things had to end this way, at least for you. You tried to fuck with me. That was a mistake. If you'd have lived as long as I have, you'd know all things end this way. It's just a matter of how and timing. You thought you won at Peter Luger's. Churchill or Hitler once said, 'All victories are fleeting.' You understand that now. You see, you always lose the final game. Good-bye, Michael."

Morty quickly turned off the cassette player. "Hey, Lump, I told you Mr. Sharkey was good. He's like a poet."

Michael looked at his newly identified captor in the front passenger seat, who still had not spoken. "Your name is Lump?"

Lump turned around, looked at Michael, and said simply, "Shut the fuck up."

Michael decided to push his already very bad luck. "You guys have to be kidding me. What's his name?" Michael nodded toward the thug who just moments before nearly pushed his head through the window.

"I'm Nicky Bats. What's it to you?"

Michael couldn't resist. "Are you guys in some fucking gangster movie or what?" The car broke up with laughter. He had always been good at lightening up a situation and finding humor where there really was none. Michael knew, however, that it wouldn't change what looked to be a voyage to the bottom of the sea, or at least the bottom of some pier in Queens.

The car had turned off the Grand Central Parkway and was now exiting the Whitestone Expressway, somewhere around Willets Point in Queens, a blue-collar neighborhood of old wooden houses, and boating and plumbing supply shops.

Michael knew his ride was coming to an end. He needed to try anything he could. "Listen, guys, I've got money. I can take care of you. Just let me out of this."

Morty made eye contact with Michael as they both looked into the rearview mirror. "Hey, I'd like to help you, but if we turned on Mr. Sharkey, we'd all wind up in cement. Besides, Mr. Sharkey's already got your money."

Chapter 46

New York City
7:00 p.m.

"Samantha, where exactly are you now?" Fletcher said as soon as she had told him what had happened.

Holding her cell phone tightly to her ear, Samantha looked up at the street signs, "I'm at the corner of Broadway and Spring Street. It's just crazy here now, Fletcher. The cops have closed off both streets, and they're diverting traffic away from the area." She pressed her finger to her free ear to block out the clatter from the police radios and stared ahead at Deacon Dan's car, its doors wide open and surrounded by marked and unmarked police cars. Uniformed officers and detectives swarmed the area, appearing to be questioning passersby.

"It had happened so fast. The whole thing took less than a minute from the time we stepped outside the building until their car took off--with Michael."

"What have the police said about finding them?"

"They said that without a license plate number, it's going to be tough—it was one of those black Lincoln Town Cars that all the livery drivers use. The detective told me that they're going to look at area surveillance tapes, but it would take hours before they could hope to find anything of value on them. By then, Fletcher, it'll be too late."

"Samantha, listen to me, do you know anyone who knows Michael's situation and would possibly have at least an educated guess on who might have kidnapped him? Anyone at all?"

"No, I don't even know most of the people he's been hanging out with now." Her mind raced through the people she met at Alex's funeral. "Fletcher, let me make a call. I'll call you right back." She dialed her sister-in-law.

Samantha imagined Donna lounging around her bedroom, trying to decide whether to eat dinner in or go out. She was relieved when Donna picked up on the first ring.

"Samantha, is that you?"

"Oh my God, Donna. Michael's been kidnapped. We're in the city. We were just leaving a gallery to go to dinner and these guys rushed out of a car; they covered his mouth with something and then, in a second, had him in their car. The police are here, but there are a million black Lincolns in the city. They'll never find him. I've already called our police chief friend, Fletcher, but I don't know what he can do; he's in Connecticut. I can't believe this is happening. They looked mean. They're going to do something awful to Michael."

"Okay, Samantha, try to stay calm. Do you want me to come to you?" Samantha was never close to Donna, but they had always gotten along.

"I don't know. But listen, is there anyone you can think of who might have done this—or who might at least know where they're headed?"

There was an unusually long silence. Samantha took the phone away from her ear to check in case the connection had been lost, but she could see the seconds still ticking off on the screen, indicating the call was still in progress. Then she heard Donna's voice.

"Samantha, I borrowed Michael's cell phone while we were at

Alex's wake. I planted a GPS tracker in it. Let me get on my computer and see if it's working."

"Donna, oh my God, that's ... crazy ... but that might be the best news I could have. Whatever you do, hurry. I don't think there's much time from the look of those guys."

"Okay, just hold on while I go to my computer."

"Please, Donna, hurry."

"I've got it open, and I'm putting in my password to the GPS site." After a short pause, she continued. "We're in!"

Samantha's mind was racing between her astonishment at Donna's nerve in placing the GPS tracker on Michael and her fear that it either wasn't working or that his phone had been thrown away.

"Now let me get to the right screens ... Samantha, we're in luck! Holy shit, I'm looking at a street map of Queens—actually, Flushing and Willets Point."

Samantha wanted to scream. "Donna, keep going, hurry."

"I see the red symbol for the 'subject,' which I pray is Michael's location. They're clearly in Flushing and heading to Willets Point."

"That's a start; can you zero in closer? Will it give you a street or anything?"

"I'm trying. Hold on, Samantha, I may have an even more exact location. I don't know for sure, but there's a good chance this is where he is."

"Oh my God, Donna, where?"

"It looks like they just got off the Whitestone Expressway at the Thirty-First Street exit, and they're now on Willets Point Boulevard."

"That's terrific, Donna—"

"Maybe not," Donna quickly interrupted.

"Why? What's wrong?" Samantha's heart dropped.

"They're only two blocks now from the water."

Samantha rushed to the NYPD detective who was standing several feet away. "Officer, I think I know where they may be!" Samantha repeated the location she had just received from Donna. She watched as the detective called the information into his police radio. She could hear the positive response from what sounded like a dispatcher.

The detective's voice was reassuring as he said, "We'll have units and a helicopter there in just a few minutes, maybe less, Mrs. Nicholas." But then he came closer. She noticed his expression change to one of confusion or, she thought, skepticism. "But, I have to ask you, how did you get this?"

"It's a long story, but I'd like to introduce you to my sister-in-law," she said as she handed the phone over to the detective. "She's tracking my husband from his phone."

―――――

After several minutes, Samantha approached the detective, who appeared to have finally put down his radio receiver. He handed back Samantha's cell phone.

"Is there any news? Have they found him?" she asked, trying not to be hysterical.

"We're close, ma'am. We've got several units now flooding the entire area, including the specific location we got from your sister-in-law."

Her cell phone rang. It was Fletcher again.

"Samantha, I've been trying to reach you. I pulled some strings with my old friends, and I'm in a NYPD helicopter. I understand you've got some GPS lead that he's in Willets Point near the water."

"Yes, my sister-in-law Donna—I know this is odd—has a GPS attached to Michael's cell phone."

"Why would she have that?" Fletcher asked.

"Fletcher, I don't have a clue. She said she'd explain it all later. You know, with all this stuff that Michael has gotten involved with, the world has become just terrifying. Fletcher, should I try calling Michael's cell?"

"No, whatever you do, don't do it now. If this GPS thing is real, we don't want them to throw the phone out the window or something."

Although Michael was from Queens, he wasn't familiar with the exact area he and his captors were speeding through. He knew he wasn't in a great area of Flushing as he saw the small, old, deteriorating factories and buildings, many of them abandoned. Morty, Lump, and Nicky Bats had also turned strangely silent.

Michael wondered whether they were beginning the detachment process, making it easier for even hard-core psychopaths to kill their prey. He knew his only hope was that their car would somehow be pulled over by an unsuspecting cop for speeding. It seemed highly unlikely, especially since he hadn't even seen a single police car since leaving the Triborough Bridge. His mind raced through all the possible escape strategies, none of which seemed to hold the slightest chance of success. Only sheer luck or complete stupidity would save him.

Morty, Lump, and Nicky Bats each seemed capable of the stupidity, except this was a task they likely performed without even having to think, like a plumber fixing a drain. They had done it so many times before, it was a routine, mindless, mechanical process.

Michael thought that he should at least try to keep them talking. "So, what do you guys think about the Yankees this year?" he asked no one in particular.

"Shut the fuck up," Morty said.

Michael could see that his ride was nearing an end. Willets Point was dark and deserted at this hour of the night. There was no reason for anyone to be here unless they were up to something sinister. He was torn between trying to mentally prepare for the end of his life and still trying to look for any chance of escape. The latter seemed more hopeless with each passing block and with each step closer to the approaching pier or boat or whatever was to be the method of dumping him in the water. He wondered how long it would take to drown.

The car began to slow down. Michael could hardly see anything through his window. Still, no one spoke. As the car came to a stop, Michael could see a simple iron lamppost, curved downward at the very top, an ordinary lightbulb appearing to be the only illumination in the area. It cast an ominous glow over what looked like an old-fashioned wooden pier. It reminded him of an Edward Hopper painting. There were no boats, just the pier, which seemed to go out to nowhere. Without any light other than the one at the foot of the pier, the water was invisible. But Michael knew it was there, and he knew he would feel it soon enough.

Morty, Lump, and Nicky Bats opened their car doors almost simultaneously. Morty left the car engine running, an indication, Michael thought, that this wasn't going to take long, at least for them. He came around and opened Michael's door from the outside. As Michael was helped out of his seat, Lump and Nicky Bats grabbed the cement block holding Michael's feet. Michael looked out toward the pier and could now see that the length of the pier was no more than ninety feet. *The distance from home to first in baseball,* he thought. This would be his last at-bat.

Chapter 47

The view from the helicopter was breathtaking. Fletcher could see the New York Mets Citi Field and the Triborough, Whitestone, and Throgs Neck bridges, all close by around him. In the near horizon was the majestic skyline of Manhattan. The night was dark, but the city's lights glittered everywhere on this cold evening. Directly below, however, there was little light. These Queens streets were not part of the great, powerful metropolis. They hid more than they revealed.

The NYPD Harbor Scuba Team was an elite corps of police divers trained to deploy into any New York City waterway within six minutes. Detective Eddie Nardelli headed the team of two divers riding in the NYPD Aviation Unit helicopter for tonight's rescue mission. Nardelli and his partner, fellow detective Kenny Rivera, were both in their black wetsuits, their scuba tanks already strapped on their backs. They were each armed with Smith & Wesson semiautomatic 9mm handguns with fluted firing pins capable of firing even after being submerged in the water, and they were ready to jump from the helicopter into the black murky waters around Flushing.

"Fletcher," Nardelli asked, "who is this guy?"

"He's a good friend from Westport. He's helped us out in the past. His brother was murdered by some hit guy a few weeks ago in Whitestone. I think the same people have got him now."

"Is he clean?" It was hard to hear over the whirring of the helicopter.

"I think so. He's a good guy. His brother may have been into some gambling stuff, but nothing serious."

Fletcher stared down at the local streets, which fanned out from the major arteries toward the surrounding body of water. "What is all this, just commercial stuff? What about the docks?"

Detective Nardelli waved his arm, motioning out to the streets directly below them. "This area is dead at night. It's almost dead even during the day. Just old abandoned factories and piers. The water's cold, dirty, and deep. If someone gets dumped down in these waters, unless he floats back up or you know the exact spot, you'll never find him. Divers with searchlights can only see a foot in front of them, even during the day. The water's probably close to freezing. Even if this guy's not tied up or anything and able to swim, once he hits the water, he'll be dead in two minutes."

"We're coming right over the Whitestone Expressway right over there," the pilot shouted. "I'm going to come in real low. We'll be right over Willets Point Boulevard. There's 119th Street, where they radioed these guys might be. Fortunately, there aren't too many cars this time of night. I see some of our guys approaching the area."

Fletcher could see the area the pilot was pointing out and the several flashing red lights from the patrol cars heading toward the water. "We have to find that car before they get to the pier," Fletcher shouted. His eyes strained as he tried to focus and interpret what he saw.

"Get the big spotlight right over there," Fletcher said, pointing to a spot where a solitary car with its lights on stood right next to the edge of the water. A single streetlight dimly illuminated the scene. There were people running, carrying something.

———

Morty looked at Michael as if he was one of the caskets he transported to the cemeteries in Brooklyn. During the night, his "packages" were not as neatly encased as the ones he moved during the day. He also missed the police escorts that accompanied the big daytime funeral processions. They helped him steer through the busy New York streets. At night, his "deliveries" tended to be to lonely, deserted parts of the city, so the police escort wasn't needed—not to mention that the cops wouldn't look favorably upon Morty's night work.

"Hey, Lump," he said, "where we goin' to dinner?" Morty figured they would be sitting down to either a thick T-bone or a bowl of spaghetti and hot Italian sausage in less than fifteen minutes.

Morty remembered the sound of approaching helicopters from his service during the first Gulf War. He had heard that sound in the distance again just a minute ago but put it out of his mind. Now it was louder. LaGuardia Airport was nearby, but helicopters here were pretty much only for rush-hour traffic reporters. It was too long into the night for that.

The chopper was coming closer; it was too low. And now sirens. They too were getting louder and closer. There was no way anyone could have followed them here, he thought. This had never happened before. Something was wrong. He felt a rush of energy, not fear but some strange excitement he hadn't felt in a long time. He looked at Lump and Nicky. They were still clueless. But suddenly, Nicky Bats looked at Lump; then they both looked right at Morty. The edge of the pier was less than twenty feet away.

Morty began to weigh the options in his mind. They could still dump Michael before anyone was going to get to them. But what if they were caught before they could get away? Kidnapping versus murder. Neither was good. How close were the cops? If they didn't finish the job, Mr. Sharkey would be very upset.

Morty saw the spotlight from the helicopter first. It caught the three of them carting the bound-and-concrete-anchored Michael. "Let's get the fuck out of here," Morty commanded. They dropped Michael hard on the ground and ran toward their car. Before they could enter, however, police cars appeared everywhere around them, blocking the car and even their own escape by foot.

The helicopter searchlight moved between Michael, helpless but alive on the pier and the three perps. Cops were getting out of their cars, guns drawn, shouting, "*Get on the ground, get on the ground!*"

Lump turned to Morty and said, "We should have dumped him. Mr. Sharkey's going to be pissed."

"That's the least of our fuckin' problems," replied Morty. And then he remembered the cassette still sitting in the car—and all the other recordings on it he had sworn to Mr. Sharkey that he had erased.

Chapter 48

Westport, Connecticut
December 12, 2009

Michael had spent most of the day speaking with the police and trying to juggle his responsibilities at Gibraltar. He had informed Richard Perkins and the security services at Gibraltar Financial about last night's terrifying events. Everyone assumed this might be somehow connected to the murder of Michael's brother. Fortunately, there seemed to be no suspicion that Michael's life had now become completely intertwined with his brother's.

Michael knew that once that connection was even suspected, his legitimate business career would end abruptly. Just juggling the two businesses would be a herculean task. Michael knew he couldn't do both for too long. Karen was already doing a great job covering for him.

Now, alone in the silence and subdued lighting of his library, Michael opened up Alex's laptop and once more visited with his brother. After the usual preliminaries of user name and password, Alex appeared on the screen.

"Alex, it's Michael."

"How are you, Michael?"

"I'm great. I've acquired a taste for chloroform." He then described the kidnapping in detail to Alex. "The police are looking for Sharkey. It's just a matter of time until they find him. They want him for at least three other murders that were identified on the cassette tapes found in Morty's car."

"He won't be that easy to catch. His friends will get him to Italy or Venezuela. Sharkey's a cheap thug, but he's connected. I heard he's sort of friends with the president of Venezuela, that guy Chavez. What about my murder? Who ordered the hit?" Alex was calm, almost expressionless.

"Of course they suspect Sharkey—but why would he want to get rid of you when you owed him seven hundred grand?" Michael said. "Obviously, the cops don't know about that."

"I agree. It wouldn't make any sense. There's more to it, or there's got to be someone else behind my murder."

"What about those kids that Donna said approached you months ago and wanted a payoff or a piece of the action?" Michael asked.

"Yeah, it makes sense that it's connected to that, but the question is, who was behind them? They were just doing someone else's errands."

Michael remembered a comment Morty made in the car. "What do you think Morty meant when he said to me that Sharkey already has my money?"

"Sharkey must have told him, or he was just fuckin' bragging that he somehow had your money or was getting it. It could have just been bullshit, or there's a connection or something going on that we don't know about yet."

Michael continued to marvel at the whole idea of being able to actually carry on a conversation with his brother—and about events that occurred *after* he died. Although Alex didn't have conclusive answers—no one alive did either, including the NYPD—he was making perfect sense and had good insights. Michael decided to see how far he could push the questioning; he wanted to test Alex's "memory."

"Alex, do you remember the time you came home late from a date or something and in the morning you had to confess that you'd lost your shoes?" Michael asked.

Alex became more animated. "Yeah, I remember. Christ, Mom was relentless. I told her that I forgot them. She wouldn't give up, just kept asking me how I could possibly just forget my shoes—in the winter, no less."

"What did happen to them?"

"I was in the hedges in Windsor Park with some girl, and a cop surprised us. We grabbed some clothes and ran, but neither of us got our shoes. It must have been even tougher for her when she got home. She was missing more."

Michael was impressed with the depth this artificial intelligence was showing. Obviously the program was sophisticated, but it was also evident that Alex and Russell had spent a lot of time feeding background experiences and personality characteristics into the system. Michael decided to press further, this time into the truly unknown.

"Alex, where are you now?"

"I'm right here with you, Michael."

"Do you understand that you're now a product of your computer and the software that you had Russell put together before you died?" Michael wondered if Alex would be offended or angered by this question.

"I know what the fuck you're trying to say, Michael. But you may not be as smart as you think when it comes to this. You know that expression, 'think outside the box'?"

"I do, but I've never heard *you* say it."

"My mind is a lot clearer now. I'm not drinking; I'm not eating a lot of crap. I'm getting a lot of fuckin' rest too since you don't seem to have the time to speak with me as much as I'd like. Actually, you seem to stay away now just like before."

"You've got to realize, I'm living two lives now—my old one and a good part of *your* old one—plus, until I open up about everything to at least Samantha, it's hard for me to break away in privacy and speak with you."

Alex shrugged on the screen. "Whatever."

Michael felt like he was in an endless exercise with Alex to either solve major or minor mysteries or to try to tie up a myriad of loose ends that weren't obviously connected.

"Alex, a few days after you were buried, I received a text message stating that an Apple device that evidently was missing had been found. It gave the location, which turned out to be Saint Michael's cemetery. Do you have any idea what that was about?"

"I'm no expert on all this technical shit, but there's some kind of connection between the spirit and the Internet."

"What kind of connection?" Michael asked.

"It might have something to do with what they call cloud computing, but I don't understand a lot of this yet. Give me time."

Michael decided to get back to more practical matters for which Alex seemed fully capable of providing guidance. He talked to Alex about his promotion to chairman after the death of Dick Applegarden.

"Michael, you know, of course, that this guy didn't die from that shit you're telling me. Something else happened." Alex's eyes burned through the screen, directly to Michael.

Michael didn't answer. He thought about Applegarden, his duplicity, and his rage after Michael's Los Angeles speech. He thought, the truth was, he didn't care about Applegarden and he wasn't sorry that Chairman Dick was dead. He knew that wasn't a nice thought, but all he cared about now was who was behind Alex's murder—and who was trying to kill him. He needed to get Alex back to what mattered.

"Alex, can I trust Donna?" Michael asked.

"Donna needs money. All my wives need money. She's afraid of being broke. It's too late for her to work anymore. She's okay as long as she has some security, but she'll do some crazy things if she feels she could run out of money. She's not a bad woman, but a little nuts and totally insecure when it comes to money."

"Would she kill for money?" Michael asked.

Alex stared straight ahead. His response took longer than any others. It was apparent that this question required much thought or complicated extrapolation from all the input and intelligence the system had accumulated. At first, Alex appeared to be unsure, but finally and firmly he answered, "Yes." Then, several long seconds later, he added, "But then again, all my wives would."

Chapter 49

Westport, Connecticut
December 12, 2009

Michael was a reluctant celebrity, although not as reluctant as Samantha. Nevertheless, he felt good, not only because he was at Mario's, but because he was alive. He and Samantha had spent hours discussing the kidnapping, their new life, and the future of Michael's new business. Now it was time to relax in their favorite hangout, even while continuing the challenging discussions.

Paul, the maître d', greeted them at the door with his familiar welcome and upbeat spirit. He seated them at their favorite table by the window, which looked out at the Westport train station. Michael enjoyed observing the harried New York commuters begin to file home at the end of the day. He took perverse pleasure in watching them, like watching the rush-hour traffic reports on television on your day off.

As Michael sipped his first martini and Samantha her sauvignon blanc, Tiger came by their table. Fletcher had been in earlier and told Tiger all the inside details about the kidnapping and rescue. Mario's regulars already knew most of the story from the local news stations. Michael was now well known in town. It was more notoriety than he wanted.

"Jesus, Michael. You guys had quite a night on Friday. Everybody in the bar was watching the whole thing on the late news. It was good for business, but, Christ, I was worried about you." But it was apparent that Tiger, in his own low-key way, enjoyed the story now that Michael was safely home. "The folks at the bar said, 'Wow, this guy always seemed so quiet. Who would want to kidnap him?'"

"Don't worry, Tiger. I'm going to keep him on a tight leash from now on," Samantha said.

Michael glanced at Samantha, knowing she was serious about the leash. He knew she was not on board with everything, particularly after last night. He also knew there was much she still didn't know—too much that he hadn't told her.

"Your brother must have been some character," Tiger said. "I always liked him when you'd bring him in for dinner. He was a nice guy—but you could tell he was probably into some things you couldn't talk about. The two of you were different that way, you know. You were, like, Mr. Clean."

Before Michael had a chance to speak, Fletcher and his wife, Angie, walked in the front door and over to their table. Michael hugged Fletcher. A few people at the bar and in the restaurant glanced knowingly at their table. It seemed as if everyone in Westport knew what had happened.

"I didn't know you were coming here tonight. Please join us, sit down," Samantha said, motioning to the other two seats at the table.

"We don't want to intrude on your dinner. This was just a spur-of-the-moment thing. Angie didn't want to cook," Fletcher said.

"Are you crazy? I think after saving my life, dinner together is a good thing." Michael was happy for their company. Fletcher and Angie sat down, ordered their drinks, and prepared to join their good friends for a quiet Westport dinner, secure amongst the locals they all knew or recognized.

"Michael," Angie said, "you are unbelievable. You must have been scared shitless in that car!"

Michael enjoyed Angie's colorful and direct speaking style. He appreciated her lack of affectations or patience for the more stuck-up, country-club types who populated many of the more prosperous Fairfield County towns. He knew she was someone you didn't want to cross—but a most devoted and loyal friend to those she loved.

"I was," Michael said. "I didn't see any way they'd find us in that Town Car. Even when I heard the sirens and the helicopter, I was already at the pier. I thought those guys were still going to throw me in."

Tiger returned and pulled up a chair to join in the minicelebration. "You know," he said, "Fletcher is now a real big shot. Before last night, he was just a small-town police chief. When everyone heard he was on that helicopter with the NYPD, he became Clint Eastwood."

Fletcher smiled but then turned serious. "Yeah, I had to call in some favors to get them to pick me up in the chopper and take me with them." He then turned toward Samantha. "But I have one question, Samantha. Why did Donna have a tracking device on Michael's cell phone?"

Samantha looked at Michael, who answered, "At Alex's wake, she borrowed my phone and secretly installed this GPS tracking software on it. She had done the same thing with Alex when he was alive. I don't think Donna knew whom she could trust. Until Alex was shot, I had never really spent that much time with her myself. It's pretty strange, but then again, so is Donna."

"She told me she'd explain. I know she was embarrassed, but thank God she'd done it," Samantha said.

Fletcher turned now to Michael. "Are you really taking over Alex's business? How the hell are you going to do that and run Gibraltar? Is this what you want to do at this point in your life?"

"You know, the truth is," Michael said to everyone at the table, "I'm tired of running things at Gibraltar. I'm tired of constantly finding ways to cut costs. I'm tired of cutting out everything that makes people feel good about where they work. I'm tired of getting rid of good, hardworking people and having to tell those left behind that they need to now just do the work of their fired coworkers. This isn't fun anymore. And I'm tired of answering to people who don't have a clue about the business and could care less about anything farther out than three or six months. And, by the way, to do all these unpleasant things, I've spent half of my life on an airplane or in some Marriott. This isn't a life."

"Wow, you're serious. You know, I never saw it that way," Angie said.

"Michael," Fletcher interjected, "you know that Alex's business is illegal."

"Everything that Alex did is done either by the state—like the off-track betting parlors throughout New York, which take the same exact bets as a bookie does, or by Citibank, in terms of the loan-sharking. Loan sharks charge more than Citi's 30 percent, but on the other hand, there's no collateral to fall back on. We can't put a lien or foreclose on someone's house or garnish their wages the way the banks do, so a loan shark charges a higher interest rate. It may be illegal, but it's only because our politicians are a bunch of hypocrites."

"Okay, and what about the IRS issue?" Fletcher asked. "Most of these guys get in big trouble when they're caught because they don't declare the income from these activities. How can you leave yourself vulnerable like that? You could wind up in jail."

Michael had obviously thought through a lot of this, surprising even Samantha with the depth of his research. "I've already spoken at length with my attorney, Larry Rothberg. We're going to find a safe mechanism to actually report all the income I make, mostly by reporting gambling gains and loan interest income through some type of corporate entity. I think I can also expand into some totally legal investments so that the line becomes very blurred. At least regarding the IRS, I'll be in total legal compliance."

Angie looked at Samantha. "And how do you feel about all this?"

"Well ..." Samantha at first hesitated and then said, "In the beginning, I couldn't imagine it. I thought for sure Michael was just settling Alex's affairs and then everything would get back to normal. But you know, Michael's right. Normal meant rarely being together, except on weekends. And even that was sometimes not happening with all the off-site planning meetings or the company-wide motivational weekends or the team-building nonsense that went on.

"He's miserable at the office. Over the past few weeks, I could see how Michael enjoyed this strange new life—and he was home at night, although late. And now with Sofia away at college, I'm alone. This should be a time for Michael and me to be together more. We can still make a lot of money—even more than before— and travel a lot as Michael will have a lot more freedom. Last night shook me up obviously. But I think this is something that may have more to do with Alex than with the business itself. I guess what I'm saying, Angie, is that I'm open to this ... I think." Samantha exhaled.

Michael's attention shifted to the television hanging over the bar. It was a news story about one of the numerous scandals surrounding the Catholic Church. It showed a film clip of an aging and embattled pope. Michael watched, his attention split between the conversation at the table and the newscast. It was then that something—someone, actually—caught his eye. The scene was a reporter standing on the famous Via Del Corso in Rome. Michael knew the street well; he and Samantha had walked past that exact spot a hundred times. The reporter was speaking, referring to how the average Roman seemed to pay little attention to the scandalous issues that the American press focused on.

Michael watched that one person who had caught his eye. He

was moving slowly, as though in slow motion—one of the passersby behind the reporter who was clearly caught on camera. Although it was a fleeting glimpse, Michael recognized him. It was Sharkey.

Michael started to speak, to announce that he had seen the man who had tried to have him killed, but quickly caught himself. No one else at the table had ever seen Sharkey, and it hardly seemed believable that he would show up in the background of an evening newscast from Rome, here in Mario's. Maybe, Michael thought, he was imagining it. Yet, didn't Alex mention Italy as one of the two likely hideouts for Sharkey? He noticed that Samantha was watching him, obviously curious about his evident distraction. He tuned back into the conversation.

"Michael, dear, if you can break away from the news for a minute, I was telling Ang and Fletcher that I'm open to this change, if that's what you really want," Samantha said, her voice elevated.

Michael was surprised, if not shocked. "I'm not sure that this is permanent—"

"Michael, really? Are you just trying to fool me or are you fooling yourself too? I'm so tired of hearing that this is just 'to settle your brother's affairs.' You are hooked. I can see it—and I hope that *you* can."

Michael looked at Samantha. "You're right, as always." He knew he was almost home free. Except, he thought, for the minor issue of Alex. But that, he knew, would have to wait.

"What about this promotion now? Are you going to run both businesses at the same time?" Fletcher asked Michael.

"I'll do it as long as I can. Gibraltar does provide a good cover. But I don't see it lasting for too long. I don't kid myself; this board wanted to fire me right after the LA speech. It wasn't just Applegarden—they were supporting him. The only reason they promoted me now was because of all the press. I mean, that speech was reported in the trades all over the world. They couldn't afford to get rid of me after the press hailed them as so courageous by letting me give that speech. The public doesn't know what really went on. The board will push me out when they can do it without taking a lot of heat. Plus, if I keep the Gibraltar job long-term, it doesn't change my life—I'd just have two jobs. I'm doing this partly to change my lifestyle and have a life. But I'd like to just finish up some things."

"It's ironic, isn't it? First, you just wanted to finish up some things with Alex's business. Now, you want to finish things up at Gibraltar," Angie said. "Michael, aren't you afraid?"

Angie struck what Michael had always thought would be a nerve, yet as he thought about his answer, he surprised himself. "You know, if someone had showed me a film of what I just went through, I'd say it's absolutely terrifying. And certainly, at times it was. But the truth is, I'm only scared at night. Fear doesn't come around during the day. Even as a kid. It's at night that you get scared, whether it's the ghosts and monsters when you're young, or mortality and other lesser problems when you get older. They come out at night, when you turn over in your sleep and it wakes you up."

Michael then turned to Fletcher. "So, what do you think?"

"I think you're crazy, but you know what, I think you'll pull it off. And, you know, I have to be careful to steer clear of anything that may not be exactly kosher since I'm still a police chief here, but that shouldn't be too hard. Most of all, I'll feel better when they arrest this Sharkey and when we find out for sure who's behind your brother's murder. Until then, you're still in danger."

"Until then," Michael said, pointing to the two big guys hovering at Mario's entrance, "I've got us some good private security."

Tiger rejoined the table. "I see some of your people at the door. Paul offered them a drink, but they wouldn't take anything. What are they—in rehab or something?"

Chapter 50

New York City
December 13, 2009

Michael was pleasantly surprised when his cell phone rang and the caller's name lit up: "Jennifer Walsh." His mind raced back to the scene at the Gansevoort Hotel.

"Hi, Jennifer, what's going on?"

"Well, Catherine and I would love to meet with you, as soon as possible. Catherine has a business proposition for you she'd like to discuss. Plus, we think you're a great guy."

Michael was intrigued. "Listen, I don't know what in the world I can do for you, but first of all, I certainly owe you a favor. Second, I can't think of nicer people to spend some time with. How about dinner at La Grenouille tonight?"

"That's perfect, Michael. Catherine will be so happy." Jennifer was upbeat.

"Good, I'll make a seven o'clock reservation."

"Michael," Jennifer paused, "you know Catherine is French—and ah, you know, a film type. They don't eat quite as early as we do—or, as you evidently do. Would nine thirty tonight be okay for you?"

Michael paused, thinking he used to be getting ready for bed at that time. "Absolutely, I'll make reservations for the three of us at nine thirty."

———

Michael arrived fifteen minutes early at La Grenouille. He had dined there several times before, although he was not a regular or "known" to the restaurant. Nevertheless, as he passed under the playfully lettered white canopy and into the entry and adjacent bar area of the restaurant, he was reminded of its reputation for gorgeous bouquets of fresh floral arrangements. Stepping into La Grenouille was like stepping back in time to a refined French culture. Nearly fifty years old, La Grenouille was the last of Manhattan's truly great classic French restaurants. It was a fitting choice for a dinner with the equally legendary Catherine Saint-Laurent.

Michael was efficiently and politely seated at a table near the entrance. He ordered a bottle of Pol Roger Blanc de Blanc, had the waiter pour him a glass while putting the bottle on ice, and waited for his guests to arrive. As he sipped his champagne, he observed the restaurant. It was nearly full, with most diners well along in the meal sequence.

He wondered whether the staff was concerned with his party's late start. It was clear that, unless another party entered, Michael's table would be there long after everyone else had left, especially since neither Jennifer nor Catherine had yet arrived. He remembered the cultural differences he had learned over the years. The French, Italians, Greeks, and Latinos never arrived on time. The Germans were efficiently if not brutally punctual.

Michael was punctual but, more than that, enjoyed arriving at a restaurant in time to select his favorite seat, order his cocktail, and settle in before having to wait for the inevitable delay in ordering drinks once the dinner party reached more than one or two people. He enjoyed his moments alone, sipping his champagne and taking in the beautiful room as he gazed at New York's beautiful people and speculated on what sort of "business proposition" a woman like Catherine Saint-Laurent could possibly have in mind for him.

After half an hour—and a half bottle of champagne—he heard a commotion coming from the bar and entry behind him. The heads at all the surrounding tables turned toward the sounds; raised voices behind him were all speaking fluent and rapid French. Michael gazed over his shoulder at the arrival of two glamorous blondes, surrounded by black tuxedo-clad waiters and the maître d', worshipping their way to his table.

Catherine Saint-Laurent was dressed in a glamorous yet discreet black cocktail dress; Jennifer in an elegant indiscreet white side-slit dress. Michael thought he might be imagining it, but suddenly the restaurant staff was staring at him, clearly impressed with the company he kept. Certainly the level of attention, solicitation, and eye contact had risen in the thirty seconds it took Ms. Saint-Laurent to arrive at Michael's table. Both beautiful women kissed Michael on each cheek in the traditional French style and sat down on either side of him.

After more sideways stares, the other diners resumed their meals, but their hushed whispers betrayed their continuing fascination with the French movie star. It was like sitting with Michael Jordon at a Chicago sports bar, Michael thought, except Jennifer and Catherine were a lot prettier to look at.

Michael quickly ordered another bottle of the Pol Roger, which arrived within ninety seconds. Three waiters surrounded the table, and in a whirl of crystal champagne glasses and white linen, bubbles were everywhere. Michael could not help admiring the view: a famous French and Hollywood star, and Jennifer, a younger, flashy, all-American beauty, somehow sitting at his table. It was a scene made in heaven.

After the buzz subsided and the formalities were over, Catherine Saint-Laurent raised her glass to Michael. "A toast to you,

Michael. We look forward to doing business together and, more importantly, to a long and great friendship."

After half an hour of conversation about Mick Jagger, French politics, the indiscretions of American politicians, the religious sanctimoniousness of the American voters, and speculation over the marriage of French President Nicolas Sarkozy and his wife, Carla Bruni, they ordered dinner. Michael chose the country pâté and grilled Dover sole with mustard sauce. Jennifer wanted red meat and selected the beef filet, while Catherine pleased the waiter with her selection of sautéed frog legs.

Michael had determined that he would let Catherine and Jennifer dictate the pace of the meal and determine when the discussion of business, whatever it might be, would be initiated. After they finished their appetizers and before the arrival of the main courses, Catherine spoke up, her tone changing ever so slightly.

"Michael," she began, "you are probably wondering about my so-called 'business proposition,' which Jennifer mentioned to you over the phone today. I am sorry for this great mystery. It is really not so complicated."

"I must admit, Catherine," Michael said, "I'm dying of curiosity."

Before beginning, she took a quick glance around the room to be sure no one was listening. Catherine's voice changed to a whisper as she leaned closer to Michael, ensuring she would be heard no further than their own table.

"I would never speak of this in public, but it has been true that my career has not been, as you say, so hot over the last ten years. The French idolize their aging female stars—but they do not necessarily create parts for them. My agent takes me to lunch in Paris simply to be seen with me. So, I have to create for myself the opportunity to revitalize my career. I have found a screenplay that, I believe, would be ideal for my 'comeback.' Unfortunately, I am not, as your Hollywood executives like to say, 'bankable' today. So I have had to raise much of the money myself to produce this film.

My connections in Paris and Monaco have been very generous, but I still needed close to a million dollars. Your brother was kind enough to be my final investor."

"How much was he going to invest?" Michael asked.

"Seven hundred and fifty thousand dollars. It was to be a loan for three years. Your brother was generous not to charge us what he would charge some other types of people. We had a special relationship with him. He was not an investor—but a very special friend."

Michael wished he had remembered to ask Alex more about Catherine when he was on the laptop last night. "Well, before we get into the financial terms, what's the movie about?"

Jennifer, who had been very quiet but listening intently, spoke up. "You'll love it, Michael. It's about a low-key but well-respected French executive who secretly gets involved in organized crime. It takes place in the streets of Paris and other beautiful places around the world. Catherine plays his wife, who struggles at first with her husband's change—and then embraces it. It's got a lot of murder, some discreet French sex, mystery, glitzy jet-setting, alongside "some tough, down-to-earth terror."

"I'm not a movie critic, but this sounds terrific." Michael's mind was racing with excitement over the whole situation—and his own career transition—which was in progress in such a glamorous way right before his eyes in this restaurant with these two beautiful women across the table. But his thoughts quickly went to the incredible irony of the movie's story line.

Showing her famous subtle smile, Catherine Saint-Laurent leaned in closer. He immediately felt her presence in that space usually reserved for intimate conversation. "Michael," she whispered, "perhaps this is something you can relate to, yes?"

"You have no idea," he said, and for the first time in weeks, laughed, flashing his own broad smile. As he leaned back in his chair, he felt a sense of relief, a loosening of the tension that had gripped him since his brother's murder. There was clearly more to this life, he thought, more than he could ever have imagined.

"So, we're hoping that you will consider honoring Alex's commitment. I understand here in America, all business is done with the pen and paper. In Europe, you know, things are different; although, I must confess, changing there too. There is no document from your brother. It was just his word. In that sense, perhaps only in that sense, Alex was a European. But I understand if this is something you are not comfortable to do …" As she concluded her lines, Catherine placed her slender, bejeweled hand over Michael's.

Michael, by his nature, usually had immediate instincts, which his experience had taught him to sometimes overrule until he had time to fully digest the information. But, as he had matured and gained experience, he learned that sometimes delaying a decision is fatal. He realized he needed to quickly get back in touch with Alex. Right now, he was in no mood to procrastinate. If he was about to make a mistake, so be it. He could always mitigate it somehow later. This felt too good.

Michael looked right into Catherine's stunning gray eyes. "They always say 'the devil is in the details,' but I believe we can figure them out very soon. I want you to know that I plan on supporting your venture and your comeback. I'll provide the seven hundred and fifty thousand on, I'm sure, comparable or similar terms as my brother had committed to you."

As soon as he said it, Michael knew that he had violated everything his cautious instincts had taught him. He had no idea yet about the exact terms; he was counting on either Jennifer or Catherine to be honest in detailing the terms agreed to by Alex. Who knew if those terms were reasonable? He knew his brother didn't give money away, to anyone. Nevertheless, he'd figure it out, soon. He needed to speak again with Alex. His brother would guide him.

Catherine flashed her movie-star smile, picked up her wineglass, uttered something unintelligible to Michael in French, then looked to Jennifer as they clicked their glasses. They both then looked to Michael, who held his glass first to Catherine and then to Jennifer, clicking each loudly enough to again attract the glances from the other diners, all so curious and smiling, feeling that surely they were witnessing something very important.

Chapter 51

New York City
December 16, 2009

Michael was back in his Manhattan office at Gibraltar Financial headquarters. Dressed in his navy-blue pinstriped Brioni suit, crisply starched white shirt, and pale blue Hermes tie, he gazed out the large window behind his desk at the buildings farther down Madison Avenue. His office was on the fortieth floor of the iconic Gibraltar Financial Insurance Building occupying the square block at Fifty-Ninth Street and Madison Avenue. From his perch, he could also see the swank green rooftop gardens and crystal blue pools atop some of the buildings. It was a rich view.

Seated around his desk were Karen and John Hightower, a "chief of staff" working for Richard Perkins, Michael's new boss. Hightower, in his early thirties, was an accountant whom Perkins hired to do all the things—and have all the conversations—that he was uncomfortable doing. Hightower was perfectly designed to get under Michael's skin; he was strictly a numbers guy, a little too young for his position, with no operating or real-world experience, and a Brit with more than a touch of undeserved arrogance. Michael knew beforehand why Hightower was here to see him.

"John, you don't mind if Karen sits in on our little meeting, do you? She can help us keep track of any follow-up issues or details."

Michael knew full well that Hightower, who was very status-conscious, did mind having a "secretary" sitting in on what he perceived as a confidential meeting. Michael never trusted Hightower and wanted a witness to any direct orders he received from him on behalf of Perkins.

"No, of course not," said Hightower, looking perturbed and not making eye contact with anyone else.

"Good. What exactly is on your agenda this morning?" Michael asked.

"Well, Mr. Perkins has reviewed the budgets of your division and those of the other divisions. We are still coming up short in terms of cuts and cost savings. In view of Wall Street's expectations—"

Michael cut him short. "How much do I need to cut out of my budget? Just give me the number, and we can save each other a lot of time."

Hightower looked down and said, "Twenty-three million, unless you could do more."

Michael laughed. "Unless I could do more? That's a new approach. You know that 80 percent of my budget is made up of personnel or related costs. So, it's basically about cutting more people; I'd guess that's about fifty heads."

"Mr. Perkins doesn't care how you do it."

"And this is on top of the cuts we already made in this budget back in October?" Michael continued, looking at Karen, who appeared to be fidgeting. "And what about my earlier offer to move my group's offices out of this palace and into much cheaper space in Queens?" Michael asked, knowing the answer.

"That offer will be rejected again, since the board signed a lease here for another five years. The other divisions would simply have to pick up your savings, and that's unacceptable, of course."

"Well," Michael persisted, "why in the world would the board in all its wisdom sign a lease extension *here*, one of the most expensive locations in the world, knowing full well that we're going to have to severely cut the hell out of our budgets?"

Michael could see Karen shifting nervously in her chair. She deliberately cleared her throat, an often-used signal between them that he was about to get himself in more trouble. Not that anyone cared for or about John Hightower, but Michael knew he would report every ugly detail to Perkins and the rest of the board.

"You know," Michael continued, "this is just a horrible economy. No business is going to show great results until this situation passes. I've already cut out a lot of the muscle from this organization. Any more will truly hurt our ability to recover when the economy rebounds." Michael knew Hightower couldn't care less. "If I was a shareholder in it for the long term, I'd be very concerned about this."

John Hightower was expressionless. Michael looked at his eyes and saw nothing, much like what he had seen in Morty the Mortician's eyes. At least, Michael thought, Morty had a sense of humor, dark and stormy that it was.

Michael wanted to ask why anyone would really need a chief of staff, but after looking directly at Karen and reading the concern on her face, decided to just drop his attack and finish up the meeting. "When do you need the revised budget?"

"There's no hurry. We've already taken the twenty-three million out of your next year's budget, so at your convenience, you can just send us the detail showing where exactly you made the cuts." Hightower appeared to be restraining the urge to smile. Perhaps, Michael thought, Hightower knew it wouldn't be wise to risk provoking him, especially considering Michael's reputation for verbal marksmanship. Even better, maybe he understood how close Michael was to literally coming across the desk at him.

Michael rose up from his chair abruptly. "I think we're done here, John. I'll have the revisions to you by the end of the month."

As Hightower walked out of his office escorted by Karen, Michael's cell phone rang. It was Skinny Lester. "Michael, I'm sorry to bother you. I just wanted to let you know that Fat Lester and I are contacting all Alex's customers, except Sharkey, of course. We're letting everyone know that we're back in business. So far, everyone's positive. A lot of questions about you, but everything's good. We're already getting a lot of football action."

"Hey, that's great, Lester. Keep going. Don't forget, make a list of whom I should meet with directly. I can do some with drinks, but the high rollers should be a dinner. You tell me the ones I should do alone and the ones you should join me on. I'd like you to join me whenever it makes sense, since I don't know any of these guys."

"You got it. By the way, someone from the NYPD called the office. He wanted your cell number. I hope it's okay, I gave it to him. He said he'd call you."

Just as Lester was speaking, Michael could see another call coming in on his cell. "I think that's them calling now. Let me take this call." Michael pressed the option on his phone that allowed him to hang up and take the new incoming call. "Hello, this is Michael Nicholas."

"Mr. Nicholas, this is Detective O'Gara from the First Precinct in Lower Manhattan. I believe you reported a stolen BMW a few weeks ago, which we found in the Hudson River."

"That's right. It was evidently taken from an auto repair shop where I thought it had been towed." Michael really had no idea if the car had ever made it to the auto repair place.

"Mr. Nicholas, as I'm sure you recall, we found a body in that car when we fished it out. We couldn't identify it at the time."

"I certainly recall. No one forgets a dead body in his car. Did you have any luck with the identification?"

"Yes, we did. The prints turned up a match. Did you know anyone by the name of Donald Mermelstein?"

Michael knew immediately the name was not familiar to him. It wasn't the type of name you'd forget. "No, I'm pretty sure I don't know anyone by that name."

"This guy lived in Las Vegas and had several addresses in Queens. No idea how he could have wound up in your car, not to mention the bottom of the Hudson?"

Michael wrote the name down on a pad on his desk so he could ask the Lesters whether this could have been anyone Alex knew. "No, Detective, I can tell you for sure, I've never heard the name before."

"He had at least one other name he went by—let me run another one by you."

"Go right ahead," Michael said.

"Okay, this one must be his professional name. How about Merlin? Merlin the Magician?"

Stunned, Michael knew that there was only one answer he could give.

"I certainly don't know any Merlin the Magician."

Chapter 52

Saint Michael's Cemetery, Astoria, New York

Michael rested the silver laptop on the black granite bench facing Alex's grave. The blue screen lit up, casting a surreal glow on the nearby tombstones.

"What are you doing here, Michael?" Alex didn't look happy.

"I don't know exactly. I left the office early so I could get here on my way home before it got too dark."

"But why? And why did you bring *me* here with you?" Alex said. He now looked confused, uncertain of his ground—perhaps literally, Michael thought. He wondered if he had made a mistake by returning to the cemetery with Alex.

"Something drew me here. Maybe I'm just trying to understand what's happened. This is all so unreal. I thought if I brought this *new* you to where the old you was, and just kind of put the two of you together, or at least closer, maybe I could find some answers, figure something out, and make sense of this or understand it."

"Michael, you're looking in the wrong place. There's nothing here."

"What do you mean, 'there's nothing here'?"

"Just what I said."

But there was so much still to ask. It was difficult to balance Michael's need for answers about life and death with the pressing, everyday mysteries—like how Merlin's body appeared in his car, and what were the details of Catherine Saint-Laurent's movie. It was time to shift gears, Michael thought, to get to more practical matters. Michael looked up. It was getting too dark, and he was in a cemetery.

"This movie that you were helping Catherine finance, do you remember what it's going to be about?"

"Of course, I remember. I don't throw around three-quarters of a million dollars without knowing what the hell it's about." Alex was back to his sarcastic, cocky self, Michael thought, somewhat relieved.

"Don't you think it's a bit ironic that the theme is about a business executive who gets involved in some type of organized crime?"

"It was about a *French* business executive. You're not fuckin' French yet, are you?"

"That's not the point. It's still hits pretty close to home, don't you think?"

"Michael, that script was written long before any of this shit happened, probably two or three years ago."

"That makes it even more unusual—and then to have it wind up in my lap. That's quite a coincidence."

"I told you before, Michael. There is more to this world than meets the eye. Things I couldn't imagine before … before this. There's so much you don't know."

It was true, Michael thought. *Too much that I obviously don't know.* As he stared into the screen, he wondered too, *Why aren't I comfortable showing all this to Samantha? Am I imagining this or am I dreaming? Am I having some sort of breakdown? I don't think so, but how could this be happening? How can it be real?*

He turned back to Alex, the only person—or soul—who could have the answer.

"Alex, are you dead or alive?"

Alex stared ahead, his face expressionless again. "I honestly don't know."

As Michael struggled to understand the meaning of his brother's words, the screen went dark and the laptop shut down. Michael wasn't sure if Alex disconnected himself or if perhaps Michael missed the low-battery warnings. He tried to restart it, but nothing worked. He shut the laptop and took a deep, slow breath and looked beyond Alex's gravestone to the older section of the cemetery.

And now he knew it was time. *Alex, I don't think it was just you that brought me here tonight,* he thought.

It had been over a decade since Michael walked away from this cemetery where his father and then his mother were buried. The two days were etched in his memory, yet despite being several years apart, they appeared as one, a single day in hell. His beloved uncle was nearby too. And too many others.

He turned away from Alex's grave and walked down the gently sloping hill to the site of the other graves of his family and several of their close friends. They weren't far away, he knew, in the older section, which had been filled up some time back.

Michael knew the way to the place he had avoided for so long. It was hallowed ground for him tonight. He looked at their gravestones, the fading white marble with their names etched into it, yet the edges were no longer as sharp. How quickly time dulls even stone, he thought. How ironic that something as elusive as a memory would be clearer than the names of the dead etched so deeply into granite.

These were the names he remembered seeing on the letters as they came through the mail, or engraved in a brass plate outside his father's Manhattan shop door, or on the checks he received faithfully each week while away at college. Now they were in stone. Yet, as he passed each grave, the memories of those buried below came vividly to life.

As he looked around at the maze of symmetrically positioned

stone markers framed by the cold, gray sky, each one representing a living being who had brought him joy, it came over him, like an ocean wave that you think will drown you until you realize that it's receded and you've survived.

It wasn't what he thought. This wasn't a place he hated. And it wasn't discomfort that he felt here. Except, perhaps, the unease you feel when you are content when you know you shouldn't be, in a place you think you don't belong. A place you don't want to go to but feel drawn to like nowhere else.

And all this time, he thought he was repelled by this ground, when instead, it was the strong pull back that he had been fighting. Maybe it was because most of the people that he had loved—and still loved—were here.

Now he realized it. He was at home.

Chapter 53

Greenwich Village, New York
December 17, 2009

Silvano Marchetto, the venerable owner of DaSilvano, the man who brought Florentine cooking to New York, approached the Lesters' table. Dressed in a pink V-neck sweater, his unruly white hair almost flowing over his bold, oversize silver-framed glasses, he had a patrician manner that appeared to barely contain a wild and unpredictable core. "I understand that you are friends of Michael's?"

"Yes, is everything okay?" Skinny Lester answered.

"*Si, si*, of course. Welcome. You gentlemen just don't *look* like most of his friends."

Skinny Lester looked at his cousin. "Jesus, Lester, you could've ditched those wrinkled jeans for once."

But the great Silvano Marchetto put his hand on Fat Lester's shoulder. "Relax, my friend, you are good. What I meant was that many of Michael's friends are, how do you say, uptight. Maybe the ones I have seen are more business associates. I can tell though that you two enjoy good food, good wine, and each other. That's all that matters. Enjoy your evening here." Marchetto gave a combination sigh and a low, guttural laugh as he moved on to the next table.

Fat Lester exhaled, his tension seeming to dissipate. Skinny Lester watched Marchetto and said, "Still, it's probably why they gave us a table in the back, near the bathrooms. This is a pretty fancy place. It's one of Michael's favorites."

"Do you notice how well Michael dresses when he goes out to dinner? He's always wearing a sport coat or a cashmere sweater. He's got cuff links on his shirts, you know—French cuffs. His suits look custom."

Fat Lester twirled his fork into his tagliatelle alla Bolognese, "That shit works for him. He's got to dress up for his day job. It wouldn't work for us. But Alex was a pretty sharp dresser too. You know, I looked in his closet once; he had at least fifteen custom-made sport coats from that Korean guy, Gung Ho, in Flushing. Although, now that I think of it, he was always saying that none of them fit."

"The Korean guy is Chung Ho, not Gung Ho," Skinny Lester said before his thoughts drifted somewhere else. "It was just a month ago that we were at Alex's birthday party. Same fifteen or so guys—Joe D, Shakes, Frankie the Bookie—and same table at Picc-ola's, every year. Even Tony the usher showed up this year."

"Yeah, I remember him from when Alex would take us to the Yankee games," Fat Lester said, smiling over the memory. "Tony was the usher at the stadium for forty years. Alex had his season box there for all those years, and this guy shows up at the dinner. He's got to be seventy-five. He said Alex was his nicest customer, always tipped him well and just treated him well. How many guys have the usher from the stadium go out of their way to show up at their birthday party?"

Fat Lester pointed his fork as he made his point. "And don't forget Michael. He's been coming the last few years, even though he skipped about twenty before that."

As the two of them sat together and enjoyed their pasta and a bottle of Chianti Classico late that night, they had a chance to reflect on the path that got them where they were, their years with Alex, and the prospect of life with Michael.

"Who the hell would have ever believed Alex would be gone and his kid brother would take over? I always thought Michael was kind of an intellectual. He was always reading books," Fat Lester said, a forkful of the Bolognese disappearing into his mouth.

"We knew Alex for over forty years. We've actually known Michael for almost as long, since we saw him when he was first born," Skinny Lester said.

"I would have never thought he'd want to do what Alex was doing. If he's still in it after all the shit that's gone on the last several weeks, he's no fuckin' baby anymore," said Fat Lester. "When Michael met with Sharkey at Luger's that day, I was outside the room. In the middle, I heard a commotion. I wasn't sure if maybe Michael was in trouble, so I opened the door just a little to check it out, be sure he didn't need help. Michael had Sharkey by the throat. He had him so hard that Sharkey's eyes were bulging out of his fucking head. I thought Michael was going to kill him right there. Sharkey had to beg for his life."

"Shit," said Skinny Lester. "I didn't know it was that bad."

Fat Lester stopped eating, which didn't happen often when he was attacking spaghetti. "Les, could you kill a man if you had to?"

Skinny Lester looked up from his meal, his forehead wrinkled from the pressure of the question. "I've thought about it over the years. I guess it depends on what you mean by, if I 'had to.'"

"Christ, just answer the fucking question."

"No, maybe in self-defense or something like that. Could you?"

"Yeah, sure. But, it's funny, only when I'm angry. Not when I think about it at all. I've come close a few times. You know, once when I had someone down, and I'm beating him. I got all wrapped up in it. I realized I could do it. I could finish him off."

"Why didn't you?"

"I don't know, Les. I've asked myself the same question, you know: Why did I stop? And it wasn't any of the assholes from the business. Just some guys here and there in a bar who pissed me off."

Fat Lester continued. "I miss Alex. He was a stand-up guy. Even when I had my problems, he never left me. You two guys were the only ones I could count on." Fat Lester's eyes glistened again with the hint of a tear.

But his face appeared to turn red as he switched gears. "Lester, who the fuck ordered the hit on Alex? Sharkey was real pissed at Michael, but why would Sharkey have wanted to kill *Alex* before any of this crap started or before Alex paid him his seven hundred grand that he won?"

"You know," Skinny Lester said, "there's an expression: when you're looking to solve a crime, when you can't find the money, look for the dame."

Fat Lester stopped chewing and just looked, dumbfounded, at his cousin across the table.

Skinny Lester, knowing he had obviously confounded his cousin, smiled and said proudly, "My shrink, Donald Connor, told me that."

Fat Lester's face turned an even deeper shade of red. "First, I don't know why you have to see a fucking shrink. All these Jewish guys, like Woody Allen, see shrinks. Is that why you see one?"

"Well, I am Jewish, Lester—and so are you. Maybe you should see Connor also."

"I don't need a fuckin' shrink, Lester. And by the way, I've never even heard of an Irish shrink—with that name, he sounds like a comedian. The Irish are already so screwed up themselves. They're dark—I think it comes from all that dark beer they drink. First they sit at the bar laughing and everything and then, when they're good and drunk, they go and sulk in the back room or they just go and blow their brains out. You don't see Italians or Greeks becoming shrinks or going to them."

"And why is that, Lester? Not that it has to do with anything."

Skinny Lester knew that his cousin had lost him in the dust in the conversation.

"That's because they drink grappa and ouzo, stuff that's healthier for you," Fat Lester answered. It appeared, however, that a light now went on in his head as though he realized he'd gone off on one of his semisensical tangents. More calmly now, he continued, "But what the hell does that expression mean anyway? You think there's a woman behind Alex's murder?"

"Listen, Lester. There's a lot of shit that's gone on in just a few weeks. Alex and Russell murdered, Michael kidnapped, that Merlin guy showing up dead in Michael's car in the river. There's also money flying around all over. Some money from Alex's will, then the safety deposit box and money in the dining room, lots of money. Anyway, Dr. Connor was actually quoting Freud—"

Fat Lester, obviously bewildered again, interrupted. "Are you going fucking nuts now? You're giving me this Freud shit?"

Unfazed, Skinny Lester continued, "What he meant was that most crimes like this are committed either because of money or a woman. Probably both, many times."

Fat Lester, looking serious now that he had absorbed the thought, said, "So, who are you thinking? What woman? How about that hairdresser Alex was seeing? Or maybe Donna found out about her and wanted to get back at Alex? What about fuckin' Greta? She hated Alex."

"I don't know. But Alex had a lot of women all around him, and he had a lot of money. I think the two are connected. Now we know Sharkey went after Michael, but that was separate from *Alex's* murder. So, we probably have more than one killer out there. And the cops haven't brought in anyone. They can't even find Sharkey now; he's disappeared."

"He probably just finished his spaghetti at Al Moro in Rome," Fat Lester said. "He used to tell me that when I went to Rome, that's where you and I had to eat. Like we were ever going to go to Rome. Even Alex never went to Rome. He was always either in Queens or maybe Miami. He never wanted to leave the country. I'd love to get to Italy."

"Maybe one day we can, Les," Skinny Lester said.

Fat Lester's eyes widened. "I'll bet the Italian food is good there."

Chapter 54

Flushing, Queens, New York
December 18, 2009

Michael was alone in Alex's office.

He closed the door separating Alex's office from the larger, open space containing the bank of phones and the other employees' desks. At this late hour, it was almost certain that the entire two-story building was empty. The Mediterranean deli on the ground floor had closed hours ago. It was another bitter cold and windy night. The only sounds were an occasional car horn and the wind howling down Northern Boulevard.

Both Lesters were out making their nightly rounds throughout the city, delivering the winnings to their customers, picking up what was owed, or simply going to their regular bars and hangouts and buying an existing or prospective client a drink.

Michael turned off all the lights in the outer office as he switched on his brother's old, simple desk lamp and watched as Alex re-emerged from his deep, dark sleep onto the Apple laptop screen.

Michael thought that tonight he would try to get Alex to talk about the stream of criminal events that had occurred in just a matter of weeks—the murders, Merlin the Magician's body in his BMW, and the intrusion into his own home. It was possible, he thought, that once Sharkey was captured, Michael would be safe—except for the fact that someone was still out there who had wanted *Alex* dead. Until that crime was solved, Michael could never be sure who was still in danger.

So far, Alex's conversations with Michael had certainly been thought provoking and, at times, helpful. But Michael was unsure whether he could achieve a true breakthrough of insight from Alex. It appeared that despite the surreal reality of Alex's image, facial expressions, and voice, most of what Alex provided was an output of various facts and his own life's experiences that had, at some point, been loaded into the artificial intelligence software. But Alex was asking questions and apparently beginning to figure out how to use what he was discovering on the Internet.

At times, Michael felt that Alex may have been learning more from Michael than the other way around. Maybe Alex needed to digest and calibrate that new information. Perhaps, as Alex said, he was *learning*—and faster and better than the real or original model. The question was whether Alex would be able to assimilate *new* information such as the events leading up to and after his death, filter that new input through the personality model based upon the real-life Alex, and then make informed deductions from that information that would be revealing in solving crimes that appeared to be connected.

"Good evening, Alex, it's Michael."

"I know."

"Alex, I need your help."

"I'm no good when it comes to marriages."

Alex was apparently regaining his sense of humor, Michael thought. "No, it's not about that. I'd never ask your advice about marriages."

"You never really liked my wives, did you?"

Michael was impressed. Alex normally would never have made

such a revealing or emotionally provocative statement to Michael unless he had already had several drinks.

"You're right. I disliked all three."

"Some of them weren't crazy about you, either," Alex said, with a smirk.

"I'm sure they weren't," Michael said. "Anyway, I kept my distance."

"You've got to remember, I wasn't a great husband either. I ran around on all of them. I was probably more faithful to my wives after they became ex-wives—well, except for Greta. I couldn't stand her any better after we divorced than when we were married."

"So that just left Pam. Did you see her while you were married to Greta and Donna?"

"Yeah, I guess so. I saw Pam more after we were divorced than I did before." Alex laughed. "She was more fun then. It was easier. I should have only divorced her and never married her, if that's possible. We had a great relationship once we divorced and were married to other people."

Michael had to think about that for a minute.

"Listen," Alex continued, "I should never have gotten married—to anyone. Marriage changes everything. I don't like feeling like I can't do what I want to do. And once you're married, people think you've got to do certain things—you know, you can't see other women, you can't see your friends or go out to the bars or do whatever shit you want to do."

That was certainly an interesting statement, Michael thought, one that Alex had made even while alive and married to Donna. *I couldn't live like that,* Michael thought. *How could two brothers from the same parents have such different concepts of women and marriage?*

"Alex, I think you'd have missed being married. After all, you did it three times. There had to be something there that made you want to do it."

"I like the sex the first few months. After that, it gets complicated.

But now maybe I'll try one of those computer dating sites. I should have an inside track, if you know what I mean."

"That'll really work well, Alex. Particularly once the poor woman googles you and finds out you have already been murdered."

"Women always want the guy they can't have. I can play really hard to get from here. I can't decide whether I'm going to join Christian Singles or Jewish Mingle.com."

"Are you crazy? First of all, you're supposed to use the one that reflects your religion." As he said this, he recognized the even greater absurdity of the entire conversation. "You don't play all sides."

"You can when you're dead." Alex was laughing. "Anyway, you want to talk about religion, *now*?" Michael sensed his brother was trying to provoke him. "Internet dating was made for me. I just need to figure out how to have sex."

But Michael was anxious to get to the discussion he really needed. "Alex, let's talk about all the shit that's gone on, starting with your murder." Michael then walked Alex through again all the events that had occurred.

"We know Sharkey was behind my kidnapping, but the rest of all this stuff is still a mystery. You must have some ideas as to who wanted you dead and who would have broken into my house. And who the hell took my car and put that idiot Merlin in it? None of this makes any sense."

"What do you care?" Alex asked in his typically flippant way.

"Until I know, I can't be safe. I've already got Sharkey out there after me until they catch him. But I don't know what else could be lurking. If someone else wanted you dead, maybe they'll want me out of the way too. It certainly could have been caused by your business."

Alex was silent for a few moments, appearing to think through his response. "Michael, I haven't told you everything."

Chapter 55

"Do you know who's behind all this?" Michael stared intently at his brother on the screen.

"Yes, I think I know now."

Michael thought he heard a noise coming from outside his office. He was anxious to continue with Alex, but he was just as fearful of even more urgent dangers. He got up to open his office door to see if anyone had possibly entered the main bullpen office outside his door. As he approached the door, he remembered Alex's gun, which he hoped was still in the desk drawer. Before opening his door, he slid open the drawer and saw the handgun sitting just where he had left it weeks ago on his first visit to Alex's office. He realized that he had no real idea how to use it but gripped it firmly in his hand. It was surprisingly heavy. Keeping the gun slightly hidden behind his back, he carefully opened the door leading out to his larger room.

Michael looked into the screen and said, "Hold on, I'll be right back."

The main room was dark except for the small blinking lights on several of the telephone consoles and the glow of the streetlights outside coming through the wooden blinds on the windows facing the street. Michael flipped the light switches on the wall right outside his office and the entire room was bathed in a fluorescent wash of bright white light. The room was still. Michael could see virtually every square inch. No one was there. He went to the main door to ensure that it was still locked. It was and everything seemed to be in order.

Michael turned the main room's lights off and returned to his office, once again closing the door behind him. He pushed in the button lock on the inside door handle, knowing it would certainly be useless should anyone really want to enter his office. The gun in his right hand was another matter, despite the fact that he wasn't sure whether it was loaded and exactly how to discharge it if it was. Like a lot of other things, he reasoned that he'd figure it out when it came to the point that he needed it.

With the doors locked and Alex's gun in hand, Michael turned back to Alex, who was still staring straight ahead. Michael looked at the gun again and tried to figure out how to open it to see if it was loaded. Frustrated, he placed the gun on the desk.

Michael stared in again at Alex. "Alex, you know who may be behind all this? You said you haven't told me everything. Tell me now."

"Michael, when you told me about Mermelstein, or Merlin, whatever the fuck his name is, winding up in your car, I realized that there was one person who both hated me and needed a way to get money." Alex paused.

Despite being anxious for Alex to continue, Michael couldn't resist a touch of brotherly sarcasm. "All three of your wives would qualify, Alex."

Alex almost seemed offended. "Donna didn't hate me."

"Okay, that's one," Michael responded.

Michael was beginning to regret having distracted Alex away from the main point when he heard another sound coming from the outside room. He picked up the gun again and placed his right forefinger on the trigger. He held the gun at his side, but was determined to now get Alex's answer without any further delay or distractions.

"Alex, who wanted you dead?" Michael said, his tone more insistent.

But the noise outside his office caught Michael's attention again. This time there was no question someone was in the main room. He looked at his door and saw a ray of light coming under the bottom of the door near the floor. Someone had turned on the lights in the next room. He wasn't alone. He hoped that it might simply be one of the Lesters coming back after their evening out, but his instinct told him otherwise.

Alex seemed unaware of Michael's distraction.

"Greta is the only one who really hated me, and she was desperate for money as you found out yourself when you met with her. But she's too fuckin' stupid to be able to pull any of this stuff off by herself. Mermelstein was even dumber, especially for a Jewish guy. But when you told me that Mermelstein's body ..."

Michael was watching his office door, unsure whether to stay inside and hope the intruder would leave after seeing nothing of value in the main room or to open the door or at least holler out, hoping to chase that person away. He now wished he had taken the time to check out the gun.

"Hold on one second, Alex. I've got a little problem here," Michael said, interrupting Alex.

He saw the door handle turning. Someone was trying to open the door from the other room.

Michael gripped the gun more firmly now, and still unsure whether it was loaded, pulled the hammer back, hoping he had properly cocked it. But he was determined to get Alex's answer before anything else got in the way. "Alex, someone's outside your office here. I don't know what's going on. But finish what you were saying."

"The gun in my desk drawer is loaded. Don't be afraid to use it, Michael."

"Okay, I've got it. Just finish about Greta as fast as you can before something happens here." The door handle was now turning rapidly back and forth. Someone was clearly trying to get in. Michael couldn't stall any longer; he had to deal with it. "Who's there?" he hollered out. "Lester, is that you?"

There was no response. The doorknob stopped turning.

Alex began to speak again. "Greta would have a lot to gain if I was dead. She knew George would get some inheritance, and she probably knew I had a lot of cash all over the place that he would also get a share of. She couldn't live on a portion of what I was giving George each month. She needed a lot of cash quickly to get her out of debt and live the fuckin' fake life she wanted.

"But she couldn't have done it alone or with Mermelstein's help. She had to have hooked up with someone else. Mermelstein was no longer any help to her. He was fuckin' useless. He had no balls and no money—not a good combination if you're hanging out with Greta. He probably wouldn't leave on his own, so she got rid of him."

The noises from outside the door and the turning of the door handle had stopped. Michael thought perhaps he had frightened away the intruder. Maybe it was just a small-time burglar who didn't expect anyone to be in the office.

"So you think Greta is behind all this?" asked Michael.

"Yeah, but it's not that simple. She can't do anything alone—let alone stuff like all this that's happened. Also, she doesn't get rid of any guy until she's got another one lined up."

"So, who would this other guy be?"

Before Alex could answer, everything went pitch-dark. The desk lamp and the lights from the outside office shining under the door all disappeared. Michael checked the telephone; it too was dead. Someone had probably tripped the circuit breakers, which were located in the other room. Alex and his laptop, which always seemed to need AC power, also went dark. Michael was trapped in a room with no windows, and someone was outside his door.

"Who's out there?" Michael shouted again. He decided not to mention he had a gun, at least until he could locate if not see his intruder. He waited in silence for a few seconds, which seemed to go on forever.

Finally, a voice from just outside his door broke the silence. "Michael, open the door. It's Greta."

Chapter 56

Rome, Italy
December 17, 2009
12:00 a.m.

Sharkey sat alone in the far corner of the front room of Al Moro Restaurant, a place reserved strictly for local Romans or others who were well connected to them, Vatican insiders, or powerful Italians.

The room was still half-full and discreetly quiet. Tourists and other diners were relegated to the back room. Sharkey sat and admired the scene, from the aging but well-put-together group of good-looking Italian men and women to the still life of the perfect Italian meal on his table: veal Milanese, spaghetti carbonara, and a bottle of Italian Barolo. He put down his knife and fork, savored a long swallow of the wine, and discreetly pulled out his cell phone. He needed to speak with Greta.

"Greta, it's me."

"Oh thank God. Where did they put you up?" Greta answered.

"I'm safe, but let's not get into details here on the phone. My good friends have taken excellent care of me." Sharkey was whispering so he wouldn't upset the decorum of the restaurant. He also wanted to avoid bringing unwanted attention from speaking English in a room usually forbidden to Americans.

"Sharkey, I have to get out of here. I have to join you. I'm too close to all of this shit. The cops won't take long to put us two together." Greta's voice held more than a hint of desperation.

"Greta, my love, I have left you plenty of money. Please stay calm. You will be all right."

"No, you don't understand, Sharkey. Money isn't going to help me with this. It's not about the fuckin' bills. It's about the cops. Michael will lead them to me; he's not stupid."

"Please, dear ..." Sharkey was trying to calm her, but he could see Greta could not be assuaged.

"No, Sharkey. I'm going to book a flight to Rome. I'm going to join you. I just have to find my fuckin' passport and get a flight. You've got to protect me. I'm fuckin' all alone here now."

Sharkey tried to control himself. He didn't like being cornered. He could feel his temper flaring, like a sudden shot of electricity coursing through his veins. He had felt this before many times, and he knew it wasn't a good thing. He wanted to raise his voice but couldn't here in Al Moro.

Getting himself in check, he whispered back to Greta, knowing that this would likely fan the flames even more. "Greta, this isn't the time to run. I can't get you out of the US; they will be watching the airports. You would need another name, another passport, or they'll find you."

"Can't your fuckin' pope friends help?"

"No. It was not easy for them to even help me, but to go beyond that is impossible. They won't even be seen with me in public here. I'm eating alone." Sharkey felt calmer, but his hands were starting to tremble.

"Shit. Sharkey, you're eating fuckin' spaghetti? You've got to fuckin' help me get out of here."

"No, Greta. Now is not the time to flee. Now is the time to fix our problem."

"What do you mean, fix our problem? What the fuck does that mean, Sharkey?"

"It means to take care of Michael. Quickly. Find him and kill him."

"Are you fuckin' nuts? I've never killed anyone. Your fuckin' Morty and his fuckin' friends took care of that. Now you think I can just go do it?" Sharkey could tell Greta was on the verge of hysteria.

"Now stay calm, Greta. You've already killed—Alex; that guy Russell, the handyman, or whatever he was; your dear Merlin. Maybe you didn't murder them with your own hands, but there is no difference. It's not a sin; it's part of life. The State does it, and the Church does it, dear."

"What the hell are you talking about? Yes, you did them for me, but we were in this thing together. You know I can't do this myself. You know how to do this shit."

"Greta. I didn't do it with my own hands, but it doesn't make any difference. You have my gun. You just find out where Michael is and shoot him until he's dead. Empty the gun into him and then walk away."

Without waiting for an answer, Sharkey clicked off the phone. Greta was beyond reason, he thought. She would have time to think about what he had suggested and would either come out even angrier at him—or be ready to kill Michael. It was time to calm himself down, enjoy the remainder of his meal, finish his Barolo, and then leave in time for his meeting at the hotel.

It was thirty minutes past midnight when Sharkey paid his bill with newly minted euros and walked out of Al Moro. As he walked by the Trevi Fountain on his way back to his hotel, he gazed at the young crowd, tourists from all over the world, gathered around the fountain, partying and throwing their coins into the water. He laughed at the innocence of the young, thinking their wishes would come true in such a way. He relied, he thought to himself, on higher connections.

Chapter 57

Just before one in the morning, Sharkey walked up the Spanish Steps. The Hassler Hotel, one of the finest in Rome, was at the very top. He would be right on time for his meeting in the quiet and virtually hidden hotel bar. Out of breath from the 138-step climb, Sharkey walked slowly through the hotel's lobby and turned to the right, where the simple but plush bar was located.

As he approached, he saw only two people: Nicoli the bartender, and sipping a grappa at a small table to the right, Monsignor Dominick Petrucceli, a close aide to Cardinal Angelo Lovallo, the right hand of the pope.

In typical Italian fashion, they embraced and kissed.

"Joseph, it is so good to see you again." The monsignor was unobtrusively dressed in civilian clothes, leaving behind even his priest's collar. "The cardinal wishes he could join us, but as you can imagine, under the circumstances, that would not be advisable. He is too well known in Rome and would be too visible. We both remember your gracious assistance with our problem in New York years ago. You saved the Church tremendous embarrassment. We will always be in your debt."

"Thank you, Monsignor. I hope you will send my warmest regards and respect to the cardinal. I'm sure he is happy to be back in

Rome with his reputation safely intact. Those young men were no friends of the Church—or of my own people. I was happy to take care of things. I certainly trusted Bishop McCarthy's word over that of those troublemakers."

The troublemakers in question were two young men in their thirties who claimed to have been abused by Bishop Kevin McCarthy while he was a priest at a parish in the Bronx twenty years earlier. They were killed in a horrific car accident and explosion just before they were to appear for their formal deposition. The initial police investigator at the scene labeled the accident "suspicious." He was immediately replaced before his report could even be completed.

Nicoli, the bartender whom Sharkey had met over twenty years ago here in the same bar, brought him his favorite limoncello. Nicoli placed the small, frosted glass of limoncello on the table for Sharkey. "Signore Sharkey, so good to see you again."

"How are you, Nicoli?"

Nicoli, a bartender and de facto late-night Italian philosopher, responded, "Life is good, Signore Sharkey. Expensive, but good." As he said it, his eyebrows arched and his eyes seemed to look up to heaven, seeking either help or forgiveness.

The monsignor and Sharkey turned back to each other.

"Before I forget," the monsignor said, handing Sharkey a thick envelope, "here are additional euros. This should hold you for quite a while. I suggest you place it in the hotel's safe at the front desk before going up to your room."

"Thank you, Monsignor. You and the cardinal have been very generous." Sharkey didn't open the envelope, confident in its weight alone, but slipped it quickly in the inside hip pocket of his black leather sport coat.

As Monsignor Petrucceli scanned the room, his face turned stern and his deep voice became a soft whisper. He leaned across the table, just inches from Sharkey's face. "Joseph, the cardinal has thought heavily about your situation and the information you provided to him. It is not up to him, of course, to tell you your business, but he has taken the complete matter under his advisement. He has asked me to communicate his thoughts to you tonight."

"You know how much I respect the cardinal. I welcome his thoughts and suggestions."

"Very well." The monsignor looked around again, and apparently seeing no one within earshot, he continued. "Joseph, just as the Church had a cancer that needed to be removed when you were so helpful, so now do you have such a disease that threatens your body and soul. This cancer must be eliminated."

"As you know, Monsignor, I have taken steps to do that. I have spoken this evening with a relative of the person involved. I expect that she will eliminate the threat. I will know for sure tomorrow. Otherwise, I will make different arrangements for him to be taken care of." Sharkey felt relieved that the cardinal seemed to be in agreement with his move to eliminate Michael.

But the monsignor continued, almost brushing aside Sharkey's comments. "Joseph, when there is a cancer, you must eradicate not only the actual diseased tissue but also the surrounding tissue, which may contain a future threat or the seeds of reoccurrence. Ah, when you find a cockroach in your bowl of spaghetti, you do not simply remove the insect and resume eating. You throw out the entire serving. Do you understand what I'm saying, Joseph?"

Sharkey took it in, trying to be sure he understood the exact message. He was getting confused with all the talk about disease, cancer, and spaghetti. "Monsignor, I believe the surrounding tissue is healthy."

The monsignor was clearly not used to resistance. "Get rid of the woman."

Minutes later, as Sharkey rested his head in the soft pillows in his room at the Hassler, he contemplated his situation. His best-case scenario was that Greta had taken his advice and shot Michael. She would certainly have easy access to him. Sharkey would then have to make arrangements with his contacts in Queens to quickly eliminate Greta. That would be simple; Greta would be an easy mark for his boys. But he would need to do that before Greta could be arrested for Michael's murder.

There would still be the matter of Morty, Nicky Bats, and Lump—and the cassette tape—all in the hands of the NYPD. But Sharkey knew better than anyone that evidence and witnesses have a way of disappearing given the right connections. It would just take some time and money, and Sharkey had plenty of both.

With fifty thousand euros in the hotel safe, the Vatican eternally indebted to him, and a strategy in place in his mind to begin resurrecting his future, Joseph Sharkey closed his eyes and slept like a baby.

Chapter 58

Flushing, Queens, New York
December 18, 2009
11:20 p.m.

"I have a gun." Greta's voice sounded frighteningly calm. Michael pulled his cell phone out of his pocket and dialed 9-1-1. He whispered into the phone, "Forty-three-oh-one Northern Boulevard, Flushing, second floor, help, quick. She has a gun."

Michael was literally and figuratively boxed in. He was only slightly relieved that the voice he heard was not Sharkey's or one of his henchmen. On the other hand, Alex had just warned him that perhaps Greta was behind a few murders already, and there was certainly no love lost between them. He knew he couldn't afford to have Greta hear him, or whatever savagery was on her mind might be expedited. He left the phone connection open. He heard the 9-1-1 operator talking, but instead of speaking directly to her, he let her hear his conversation with Greta, still behind the door.

"Greta, what do you want?" Michael shouted.

"I fuckin' hate you. You and your fuckin' brother ruined my life."

"What do you want from me, Greta?"

Michael was buying time, looking at Alex's gun, trying to figure out exactly how to fire it, while waiting for Greta's response. He could hear muted conversations on his cell and hoped that the police would be on their way.

"I'm going to kill you, Michael."

"Greta, listen, I know you hate me, but I'm not your problem, believe me. I'm just doing what Alex wanted me to do. Your son's being well taken care of."

"That doesn't do me any fuckin' good, Michael, and you know it."

As he listened, Michael moved away from behind the desk, which was located in the center of the room, directly behind the door. "Greta, if it's some cash you need, I'll give you some. Don't do anything stupid now."

"Oh great, Michael. *Now* you'll give me cash. It's too late for that. Besides, Sharkey wants you dead."

"I know he does, Greta, but what's that got to do with you?"

"You're not as smart as you think, Michael. I'd have thought a smart guy like you would have figured it out by now."

Michael's mind was racing as he quietly moved the desk to the right far corner and prepared to hide behind it. "Figured what out?" he said.

"Sharkey and I are together. He's taking care of me. We're going to get married once all this shit blows over."

Michael just exhaled, flabbergasted. The thought of Sharkey and Greta as a couple—and working together—never crossed his mind as a possible combination. It certainly could explain everything. Alex had just told him that Greta would have needed a capable accomplice to pull off everything that had gone down over the past month.

"So Sharkey hired that kid to kill Alex?" Michael asked.

"Of course. He knew he wouldn't be a suspect because Alex owed him all that money. We knew we'd collect either way, although you really pissed Sharkey off when you tried to screw him on what Alex owed him. Anyway, Sharkey got rid of Merlin for me too. Another loser."

"Why did he have Merlin put into my car? What was the point of that?"

"Sharkey called it 'poetic justice.' Sharkey knows poetry and stuff. He said since Merlin owed your brother money, it would make sense that you got the body. Plus, we both wanted to scare the shit out of you. I wanted to get to Alex's cash without you sticking your fuckin' nose into places you don't understand."

"Is that why you guys had someone break into my house?"

"Yeah—and we figured we'd scare the shit out of that stuck-up bitch you're married to—and that would be the end of you in this whole thing."

"Greta, you'll wind up in a prison for the rest of your life if you do this. What about George?"

"I'm in too deep already to stop now. And George is a big boy; he's taking care of himself first too. He learned that from your fuckin' brother. Now he's only giving me five hundred a month. It costs me that much to get my fuckin' hair done each month."

"But why do you have to kill me? There's no more money in it for you now."

"Sharkey wants you dead. Anybody that could testify against him is going to disappear one way or another."

Michael was on the floor off to the right side where he had quietly moved the desk. He lay down flat on the floor behind the desk. He still had Alex's gun in his hand but had decided it was too risky for him to begin firing since he didn't have a good sense of exactly where Greta was standing. It sounded like she had been nervously pacing or moving around during their conversation. For Greta, Michael was trapped in a very small box—it was just a matter of firing enough bullets to spray the entire office until one found its target.

Michael heard a series of earsplitting explosions and saw puffs of smoke, plaster, and debris coming through the wooden door and again on the wall behind where the desk had been. The gun was obviously an automatic since it appeared that Greta had already fired off at least fifteen shots in rapid succession.

He stayed silent on the floor, raising his head just enough so he could see the damage. He raised his gun and pointed it at the door where the bullets had poured through.

"Michael, how does it feel to be cornered? No fuckin' options? How does it feel to die? You're going to join your big brother."

Michael still felt the odds were not with him to begin firing. His gun had only five or six bullets. The odds of hitting Greta without a better fix on where she was were not good and not worth the danger of tipping her off to his precise location and the fact that he was alive and armed. He decided to stay silent and see if Greta continued to fire or tried to blast through the door. Then he figured he would empty his pistol into her.

Another volley of bullets exploded through the door, passing directly above the area where Michael was lying down. Suddenly, Michael heard a commotion and a crash coming from outside his office walls.

The police had broken down the main door. "Police! Drop the gun and raise your hands. Drop the gun. Drop the gun!"

Then there was an explosion of simultaneous, earsplitting shots, too many to count—some of the bullets piercing through the wall into Michael's office.

Michael waited for a few moments, reassured by the voices of the NYPD in the next room. He was still in his darkened office, lying on the floor. Light was coming through the many holes in the plasterboard. He summoned the nerve to finally shout. "Help! I'm in here."

"NYPD. Are you hurt? Do you have a weapon?"

Michael carefully replaced the gun back into the desk drawer. "I'm not hurt, and I don't have a weapon."

"Then just open the door and walk out slowly," a commanding voice shouted.

Michael stood up from behind the desk and took three steps to the bullet-riddled door. He opened it and gingerly walked out amid the debris. Red lights from the patrol cars outside were flashing through the second-story office blinds and covering the entire office with a surreal flickering red glow. In front of him, Michael saw seven NYPD uniformed police officers, some kneeling, others standing—and they all had their guns drawn and aimed squarely at him.

Michael's eyes were drawn down to the floor. Lying two feet in front of him, almost at his feet, was Greta Garbone, her face looking more at peace than he'd ever seen it. She did not appear to have been shot above her neck, although blood was slowly trickling out from her mouth onto the beige carpet. She was dressed in a navy blue jogging outfit that was punctured with bullet holes. Her blood moved in a steadily extending puddle around her head.

Michael knew a dead body when he saw one.

Chapter 59

Westport, Connecticut
Christmas Eve, 2009

I t was nearly midnight. Samantha and Sofia, who was on her holiday break from Notre Dame, were both asleep upstairs. Michael sat alone in his library, watching the snow fall outside his window and gazing at the reflections of the twinkling Christmas lights outside on the freshly fallen snow.

It was time to wish Alex a Merry Christmas.

As he booted up the computer, Michael thought of a long-past Christmas Eve. He was seven years old. Michael tried to sneak downstairs during the night to see if Santa Claus had brought him the bicycle he had hoped for. Just as he looked down to catch a glimpse of the tall Christmas tree in the living room from the top of the second-floor balcony, Alex appeared out of nowhere to whisk Michael back to his bed. In that brief moment just before Alex appeared, Michael was able to see the reflection of the bike's wheel and spokes. As he rested his head back on his pillow, he went back to sleep with the sure knowledge that Santa had indeed already arrived. It was like a story from a children's book.

While waiting for Alex to appear on the screen, Michael thought about how the years had changed everything. Michael was happy, but tortured with anxiety and, sometimes, fear. While he enjoyed the love and security of a close and adoring family, his life was a complicated mass of dual existences, unlawful activities, and corporate pressures. Overall, he characterized his emotional state as "ambivalent happiness," alternating between happy contentment and periodic terror. Sometimes he felt he just couldn't get a firm fix on where he was on the scale of life's emotions, satisfactions, and disappointments. Did it really just depend on how he decided to view things? Were those people who promoted "attitude" as the cure-all for everyone's ills really right? Could "choosing to be happy" really have some merit in making someone happy?

Before Michael's cynical, doubting side could answer, Alex appeared on the laptop screen.

"Merry Christmas, Alex."

"Thanks, Michael, but we don't celebrate that here."

"What a couple of months this has all been," Michael said.

"Yeah, well, it's been pretty fuckin' big for me too."

"I guess you're right, Alex." Michael continued, detailing for his brother the most recent events.

Alex looked directly into Michael's eyes. "Michael, you know, my life was a lot easier than what you've gone through the last several weeks. I had a few problems with some small-time thugs over the years, but it wasn't much more than being robbed and handcuffed to my elevator, maybe some punches and an occasional police raid. Nothing like this shit. This stuff was all caused by Greta and her fuckin' greed. I never had a problem with Sharkey until Greta got her claws in him."

"What the hell did Sharkey see in Greta?" Michael asked.

"Greta probably looked real good to Sharkey. He didn't have a whole lot of good-looking women around him that I ever saw. She's a bitch, but she was great in bed. Greta wanted to be a film star. She could have been a great porno actress, but she'd get pissed every time I told her that. I even offered to bankroll a porno film for her, but she thought that was below her. Anyway, that's all she needed to hook Sharkey. He was a desperate man, trying not to be old. She was young."

"Samantha is very nervous." Michael turned more serious. "She went along with this whole thing initially because I told her it was just temporary. She loves the money, and I think she actually enjoys some of the excitement and characters, but this other violent and threatening stuff is too much for her. It may be too much for me too. I need things to calm down. Plus, I can't afford any more of this type of publicity, even if I'm made to appear to be an innocent victim. Eventually, Gibraltar will get concerned that it's all a distraction."

"First, I told you this before, you've got to shield Samantha from—"

Michael interrupted. "I know, Alex, but I can't exactly shield her from my being kidnapped and nearly thrown off a pier."

"I didn't mean that. Listen, once they capture Sharkey, all that stuff should be over. None of that ever happened to me, not even close. Probably, with Greta out of the way, he won't care about you anymore. Also, he's gotta have his hands full himself in hiding wherever he is. I haven't been able to locate him, but we know he's not in Flushing anymore."

"Maybe I need to tell Samantha about … you." He was unsure how, but Michael knew this would stir a reaction in Alex.

"That will be a mistake. She's not ready."

Michael feared he was right. "You and I run our marriages differently. Samantha has been my partner."

"If I wanted a partner for a wife, I'd have married one of the Lesters."

Michael knew it was time to change the subject. Telling Samantha the complete story about the virtual Alex was more than just a passing thought though. It was becoming the elephant in the room, the one that only he could see. It was the source of a lot of his deception with Samantha. Maybe he needed to show Alex to someone else, to be sure he was real.

Michael continued, "I do have to say, though, your business is like a money machine. We've made a small fortune in the last month. And I'm amazed at some of your clientele. It's funny how some people that you'd never expect are big bettors; you've got a few pretty prominent customers."

"Speaking of people you wouldn't expect using bookmakers—in your case *being* a bookmaker—what about your corporate job? Are you going to hold on to that too?" Alex asked.

"I think I want to keep both things going now. Gibraltar is a good way for me to show plenty of legitimate income. You know, I think the two Lesters can run your business for a lot of what has to be done. I'm going to let them hire one or two more guys—and maybe a woman—so that we can expand a little more, and so Skinny Lester can do some of what you or I would do if we were there."

"Just be sure," Alex added, "that you remember to use Skinny Lester for his brains and Fat Lester for his muscle—or whatever that three hundred pounds is. Don't confuse the two. Don't put Skinny Lester in a physical situation, and don't make Fat Lester have to think."

"I wouldn't worry about Fat Lester doing too much thinking," Michael said.

"By the way, Michael, if you want to keep your little wife happy with all this, you should just take some of the extra fuckin' money you're now making and go to Tiffany's or that Cartier place on Fifth Avenue and buy her something fuckin' drop dead. You think you knew my wives—well, let me tell you, I know your wife. Get her something big. That'll shut her up."

Michael was getting tired. Although Alex had a good point about buying Samantha a large piece of jewelry, he wasn't looking to Alex, of all people, for marital advice. But it was interesting, he thought, that Alex came back to the subject of Samantha. *Was he worried I was going to reveal our secret to her?*

"We'll miss you for Christmas Day tomorrow," Michael said.

"You never came to my house for my Christmas parties anyway, you know," Alex said, mildly chastising.

"I know. You always had too many old relatives—and unsavory characters—for me." Michael realized the irony now in his remark.

"Well, you'll have plenty of those unsavory characters around you now." Alex laughed. "You'll make my Christmas crowd look like the Nativity scene."

"Alex, what do you miss? Anything?"

"I miss the big roast beef at Mario's when I'd come up to visit you. That's what I miss. Next time you're there, tell Tiger hello for me."

Michael thought for a moment and said, "That'll be a little hard to do. Merry Christmas, Alex."

Chapter 60

Paris, France
January 15, 2010

"There's something I haven't told you, Samantha. It's about Alex," Michael said.

It was nearly eight o'clock when they walked into the Hemingway Bar at the Ritz Hotel, an intimate, luxurious, dark wood-paneled room. The lighting was subtle and cast a soft, warm glow over the room. The mahogany bar and the small surrounding tables were filled with handsome men in their subtly colorful Hermes ties and powder-blue shirts. They were accompanied by impossibly beautiful women in their white Dior gowns with red Louboutin high heels, Cartier rocks on their slender fingers, and Bulgari jewels glittering on the gentle slope of their winter-bronzed breasts. There was a sea breeze of Caron perfume in the air.

"May I help you, monsieur? Madame?" asked Pierre, the always polite and almost friendly waiter. Michael and Samantha had been here many times before, so it was no surprise that they were addressed in English. Samantha was fluent in French;

Michael still butchered the language after too many years of lessons.

"A glass of rosé champagne for madame, and a dry gin martini, straight up with two olives, *pour moi. Merci.*"

Five minutes later, Michael watched intently as Pierre expertly poured from the familiar yellow-labeled bottle of Veuve Clicquot into Samantha's flute glass, a slight head forming and the thousands of tiny bubbles finding their way to the top of the glass.

Michael's anxiety calmed as he observed the polished silver tray carrying a chilled martini glass and a side dish of olives. More importantly, it held a tall blue bottle of Plymouth English Gin, another bottle of Martini & Rossi Extra Dry vermouth, and a clear, tall mixing glass with several ice cubes. Pierre performed his magic and again meticulously mixed, poured, and served Michael the perfect martini.

Michael and Samantha clicked their glasses together. "Here's to Paris, again," Michael toasted. He reached over and placed his hand on Samantha's.

"What is it that you were saying about Alex, darling?"

Michael took a deep breath. "He's still alive."

Samantha's facial expression reminded Michael of Alex's warning not to disclose the miracle he was about to reveal. Maybe it *was* premature. As he began to tell Samantha about his lunch with Jennifer Walsh and his discovery of Alex's laptop, it was obvious that Samantha was no longer even listening, let alone believing. His words sounded off-key, and the story seemed unrealistic and unimaginable, even to himself. He stopped in midsentence and let Samantha speak.

"Michael, you just need to try to relax," Samantha replied. "Between Alex's death and then running his business and Gibraltar, you've been under a lot of pressure."

"I'm fine, Samantha, really, I am."

"I think your feelings about Alex go much deeper than you will admit, even to yourself. You know, Michael, you're not as tough as you'd like people to believe—and that's a good thing."

"Samantha, I know this all sounds implausible—if not crazy— but I am as practical and critical as I have ever been."

"I'm sure you are, Michael. But how could anyone possibly believe this?"

"Samantha. I know this all sounds crazy, but you have to hear me out. You know how you're always telling me about psychics and things and that—"

"Yes I do, Michael, and that's when you talk to me about coincidences and how the psychics have great street smarts and manipulative skills."

"Samantha, I don't blame you. Who would believe that someone who is dead could be alive?"

"Michael, Alex was shot dead in front of Maria and a bar full of cops who, as you remember, shot and killed his murderer. There was a funeral, a casket, a burial."

Michael was realizing how absurd he sounded, and Samantha was even making *him* question everything.

"Michael, for the sake of argument, I will suspend judgment on all this and let you just show me."

"That's all I ask," Michael answered.

"So, where is my illustrious brother-in-law?" Michael detected more than a subtle hint of sarcasm in Samantha's voice, but he felt like he was on the brink of some great passage. Being able to bring Samantha into his secret miracle would make it *real*. Not that there was any question.

"Alex is on the laptop in our hotel room."

Michael was filled with anticipation as they entered their cozy suite at the Luxembourg-Parc Hotel on the rue Vaugirard on Paris's Left

Bank. Samantha changed into her black silk nightgown and the hotel's cotton robe as Michael opened up the Apple laptop and placed it on the coffee table between them. He carefully typed in the user name and password and waited as the home screen with its icons appeared.

In order to ensure that Samantha didn't have time to notice the flashing Jennifer, he immediately double-clicked on the familiar ancient gold cross icon and waited for the late Alex Nicholas to appear.

But something was wrong. Alex had always appeared within seconds. Michael was nervous. He could feel Samantha's eyes watching over him, and with each passing second, Michael knew Samantha was sure he had lost his way. Just when Michael was convinced that he had made a terrible mistake, the screen began to come alive. He felt a wave of relief as it lit up.

But instead of Alex, an unfamiliar visual appeared. Its hues were the same as the icon he had just clicked onto: antique gold, red, and blue. A large cross came into view, and then the robed figure of Christ, appearing like a saint, his arms outstretched as though welcoming new visitors. Along the left side was a listing of upcoming religious feasts. It was the official website of the Greek Orthodox Archdiocese of America.

"I don't understand ..." Michael was confused.

"Michael, what is this? Is this what—or who—you've been communicating with on the computer?"

"No, this has never happened before. Samantha, you have to believe me, I'm not imagining things. I'm fine." But Michael recognized the sympathetic look he saw on Samantha's face. He knew what was coming next.

"I'm sure you are, Michael. As soon as we get home, I will book you an appointment with the finest psychiatrist in New York."

Chapter 61

For the first time since Alex was murdered, Michael was angry with his brother. "Was this some kind of joke?"

"I warned you, Michael; she wasn't ready."

"Well, we'll never know, will we, since you didn't show up, so to speak? She thinks I'm crazy now."

Alex appeared unfazed. "That's not a bad thing; I always wanted my wives to think I was a little fuckin' crazy. That way, they were never sure how far to push me."

"That may have worked well in your relationships—God knows, you've had enough of them. But it doesn't work that well for me. Samantha's going to try to send me to a psychiatrist when we get home."

"Samantha will be okay, and a few sessions with a good shrink probably wouldn't hurt you. You've got some problems, you know."

"*I've* got problems?" Michael sensed he was being provoked. Or was Alex trying to dodge the issue? "Okay, whatever, but why were you so set against my telling Samantha about you? Why are you so sure it would be a mistake?"

"Michael, I can only tell you what I know now. There could be more than this, but in any case, think about it. Once word gets out about everything, it will be chaos. Your life will be even more fuckin' nuts."

Alex had a point, Michael thought, but he suspected that Alex was holding back. "You know more than you're telling me."

Alex appeared to be struggling now, his cockiness gone. "To be honest, I'm not sure. I know intuitively that telling anyone else yet will be a mistake. What exactly is behind that, I don't know. I can't always tell where my feelings come from. This is some of what I still don't understand. Maybe it's just like how *you* don't understand when you get a feeling about something. But, Michael—"

Michael could see that Alex was struggling with something. "What, what is it?"

"You have to understand, *I'm not a computer.* I'm just communicating with you through one."

"Alex, this is all mind-boggling. I don't know what to believe sometimes. It's all so crazy. I mean, I'm happy—I'm overjoyed—that you're here. It's all so hard to understand, to believe."

"Michael, you're going to find that all the lines are becoming blurred. Life, death, the spirit, the Internet. This is going to take some time for all of us to understand."

Michael felt like he was on overload. "I guess so."

"But I do have another reason of my own on why you need to keep all this secret for now, and it's my own logical one."

"What's that?" Michael asked.

"Russell's not around to explain how he configured all these artificial intelligence programs, but now that we have proven that it works, once all the fuckin' geeks get their hands on this, they'd be able to figure out how to duplicate it."

"And what's so bad about that? We can bring immortality to others," Michael said.

Now Alex was returning to his old self as a wicked little smirk crossed his face. "Exactly, but we're going to make *money* on this. *A lot of money.*"

Michael felt emotionally drained. Tonight it all seemed overwhelming.

"Michael …"

"Yes, Alex?"

"Listen, once you're done with that psychiatrist your wife sends you to, you need to do one other thing."

"What's that?"

"Find the best patent attorney money can buy."

Chapter 62

Westport, Connecticut
July 15, 2010

As Samantha slept upstairs, Michael mixed himself a martini and settled into his library. Since his aborted attempt months earlier in Paris to reveal the new Alex to Samantha, this was the setting for most of Michael's meetings with his brother.

He glanced at one of his favorite family photographs, a picture of Alex in front of their childhood home, a Tudor on an attractive, tree-lined street in Queens. Alex was standing with Skinny Lester. They were both dressed in white tuxedos, looking young, fit, and healthy. Behind them was Alex's restored 1957 white Chevrolet convertible. It was a classic, even thirty years ago.

Michael picked up the framed photograph from the bookshelf and studied it. He vividly remembered looking through the viewfinder and taking the photograph, while standing in the quiet street in front of their home. His brother and Lester were taking a moment before stepping into the car, so the little brother could snap a picture with his new Brownie camera.

There was something in that scene that stirred Michael's

emotions. Perhaps it was the innocence of the times. Or maybe it was because his brother's dreams of being a professional athlete were still in front of him. Or was it just a carefree moment, full of glamour and promise for the subjects and the photographer?

Michael didn't know what it was that moved him, but he knew that long ago, his camera had captured the one moment he wished could have lasted forever.

He took his first sip from his Baccarat martini glass and felt the warmth stir in his stomach as the clear drink found its way down. Then he gently opened his laptop.

Alex spoke first. "I see that you're headed for Paris again?"

Michael was surprised. "Yes, we leave tomorrow night. How the hell did you know that?"

"I've gotten a lot better with this technology shit. Anyway, I noticed it on your e-mail; it was your American Express travel confirmation."

Michael couldn't read anything into Alex's expression, but he suspected that his brother was enjoying his ability to penetrate Michael's communications more than he let on.

"Well, that's a little frightening. Please don't start e-mailing me the death notices of every athlete and famous person who dies, like you used to when you were …" Michael hesitated. "You know."

"Alive?"

"Yes, I guess so, for want of a better word."

"Michael, I'm more alive than many of the living. You should check out my Facebook page by the way."

"You're kidding. You're on Facebook?"

"Yeah, I never paid much attention to it when I was really alive, but now I'm hooked. You would be amazed at how you can follow everyone on it."

"Oh, Christ. I hope none of your friends—let alone your wives—ever discover your page."

"Don't worry, they'll have no way of knowing it's really me. There are other guys named Alex Nicholas. I listed my occupation in my profile as 'astronomer.'" Alex appeared to take a deep breath. "I'm learning, Michael, I'm getting fuckin' stronger, you know?"

"That's interesting. Things are happening so quickly, Alex, for you and for me. This is all so strange—so real, yet so unreal."

"Michael, you have no idea. There's more I want to tell you, but not now. This still isn't the time. Not yet. Just be patient. Anyway, how's my business going?"

Michael's head was spinning. He had never envisioned the degree to which technology would allow Alex to link up with the rest of the virtual world. It seemed that every few weeks, Alex would make another connection or find a new link to the world from which everyone thought he had departed. Again, Michael needed time to absorb the ramifications; he needed to think. He was thankful that Alex changed the subject.

"It's going very well. You know, it's mostly baseball right now, although we cleaned up on the Kentucky Derby. I think we cleared nearly half a million last month."

"Sure, you and Donna and everyone are making a pile of money off my business, and I'm not collecting anything here."

Michael laughed, but he knew Alex meant it. "I'd pay you a royalty if I could."

"Yeah well, don't laugh, Michael, because you can. Ha, you're so smart."

"What do you mean? How the hell am I going to pay you anything?"

"Well, smart guy, did you ever hear of PayPal?"

"Oh Christ. You can't be serious," Michael said.

"I'm going to set up a PayPal account. Don't worry, I haven't actually figured that out yet because I'd have to link it to either a checking account or a credit card. Those things would be a little tough at the moment—although I expect to get a credit card offer online any day. You know those banks. They don't care if you're dead, as long as you can pay. Anyway, don't worry about it just yet. Ha."

Michael could see that, perhaps more than ever, Alex was enjoying himself. *Has he settled in?* Michael thought to himself. *And, if so, where is* in, *exactly?*

Alex turned somber, his face tightening up. "What's going on with Sharkey? Is there anything new?"

"Fortunately, he's dropped off the face of the earth. The NYPD has had a warrant out for his arrest for months now, but there's no sign of him. Skinny Lester agrees with what you guessed earlier, that he's left the country, and that since he had connections in Italy and Venezuela, he's most likely in one of those two places. And I know this is going to sound odd, but I thought I may have even seen him in the background of a CNN interview going on in Rome."

"I think you watch too much fuckin' television. That would be pretty coincidental, don't you think?"

"I thought so too, I mean, what would be the odds that—"

"About a thousand to one, assuming he is in Rome. No odds at all if he's not. I wouldn't take either side of that bet." Michael realized that mentioning odds to Alex was like waving a red cape in front of a bull.

"In any case, it's certainly been nice and calm with him out of the way," Michael said, still wondering whether he imagined the whole thing with Sharkey on the television at Mario's. Or was it just another strange occurrence, a clue offered by some unknown person or thing to the myriad of puzzles that had surrounded Michael's life?

Alex suddenly appeared to be looking away, his attention was somewhere else. Michael couldn't tell whether it was something not visible on the screen or whether he was simply thinking.

"I don't like not knowing where the fuck he is. I've tried to find him, but he's too stupid to use a computer, and I can't find any cell phone trace of him. But, I'll keep trying. He worries me, Michael," Alex continued, although Michael sensed that Alex was still thinking about Sharkey. "Speaking of the Lesters, how are they doing?"

"They both miss you. It's strange to see them; *your* friends, but guys that I knew as a kid and then hardly ever saw again for thirty years. Now I see or talk to them every day—like you did, I guess. They're doing a good job, too. Things have settled down. I've got good people around me both at Gibraltar and in your business. That's what's made it all possible for me. You know what it's like; you had two jobs at once, too."

A flash of recognition crossed Alex's face as he spoke. "Between the restaurant and the bookmaking, I had no day job—just two night ones, for several years. It was fuckin' good though because none of my wives would ever know where the hell I was. I could stay out all night, working. Then I got bored with Grimaldi's, and it became a pain in the ass, always having to watch everything, bartenders stealing from you and shit. So, I finally sold it to Maria."

"Well, Gibraltar won't last forever for me. Sometime, I'll get out or they'll force me out."

"So what happens then? Do you go to a bigger job or a bigger company?"

"I don't know. When you're on top, you always assume your career is on the upswing. But for all you really know, you may have peaked and your next step may be down. You don't know until it's too late—and you're looking back on it." Michael watched Alex's expression. He had lost him. He remembered how brief Alex's attention span on Michael's corporate life had always been.

"Anyway, I'll never have another CEO position. I'd never get through a background check again, at least not for something at that level." *Time to wrap up this topic,* he thought. Alex's eyes were wandering.

But to Michael's surprise, Alex came back with, "Why not? You haven't been arrested or anything, have you?"

"No, but now they get these security firms to do background checks before they hire you. They'll find all the news stories about your murder, my kidnapping, and the stuff at my house. There's too much smoke to ignore. Then they'd start interviewing people. It wouldn't take long for them to figure something out. I'd be eliminated—and they'd never tell me why. My life has changed, you know."

"Yeah, well so has mine." Again, Alex was bored with the discussion. Just as he would have while alive, he moved on to a new topic—no smooth transition, almost like a short circuit. "Have you looked at the other things on my laptop?" he asked.

"Like what?" Michael asked, puzzled.

"Like what? Like Jennifer's thing. Have you clicked on her icon? You couldn't have missed it. Her fucking blue eyes even light up on it."

"Oh, that. I promised her I wouldn't." Michael realized he'd actually forgotten about Jennifer's private show on Alex's computer. "Or to be more precise, I promised her I wouldn't let it get out."

"That's not what I asked you. Did you open it?"

"Not yet." Michael wasn't sure he wanted to view it. "I promised her I wouldn't."

Alex laughed; it was his bullying laugh. Michael recognized it from those times when Alex's darker side showed itself. "That's the fucking difference between you and me. Who gives a shit what you promised? This will be the best sex you've ever seen."

"Are you in it?"

"No, it's Jennifer, alone. With some of her favorite toys."

Chapter 63

Paris, France
July 17, 2010

While the Parisians were preparing to evacuate their city for their traditional summer holiday, Michael, Samantha, Angie, and Fletcher were enjoying a week on the town. For Michael, it was a combination of work and play. He needed to meet with several of Gibraltar Financial's Paris-based clients, and he took the opportunity to bring Samantha along to their favorite city before they headed off to the traditional summer holiday in Saint-Tropez. Adding to the fun, Fletcher and Angie decided to meet up with them for a few days of Paris shopping, dining, and celebration. For Michael, it was a time to cherish just being alive.

Situated in a chic, cobbled courtyard leading to a meticulously renovated seventeenth-century hotel, Ralph's—a new restaurant and the latest extension of Ralph Lauren's classic American, high-style empire—was already a hit in Paris.

Michael and Fletcher both relished cheeseburgers. Michael wouldn't be caught dead ordering one while in the company of his French Gibraltar clients. But the burgers at Ralph's were popular with the begrudging Parisians. It was lunchtime, and while Samantha and Angie looked on, two splendid burgers made from Black Angus steers raised at Ralph Lauren's own ranch, appeared in front of Michael and Fletcher.

Just as the waiter was leaving the table, Bertrand Rosen, the French financier and head of the highly touted investment firm Rosen & Sons, approached their table.

"Monsieur and Madame Nicholas, such a pleasure to see you again."

Michael was surprised that Rosen remembered meeting them; it had been years ago. Rosen gushed over Samantha and kissed her hand, and after a few words of small talk, he moved on. Before biting into his burger, Michael said to those at the table, "Why don't I trust that guy?"

As Michael devoured his burger and everyone enjoyed a robust glass of French Bordeaux, the conversation turned to the events resulting in Greta's death. Maybe, Michael thought, they all needed the emotional distance that a few months provided to put things in perspective.

"Would you have shot her if you had been confident of hitting her?" Fletcher asked Michael.

"I really didn't want to shoot her. Not so much because I just didn't want to kill her or anything. After all, it would have clearly been self-defense—not only legally but morally."

"So, what was the problem? Why the hesitation?" Samantha appeared to be seeking insights into her husband's thinking, as though it was a question she had wanted to ask but never had.

Michael stopped for a moment, seemingly bringing his thoughts to a concise conclusion. "I didn't want to kill her—or even discharge the pistol—because I knew it would change everything. It would change how the police looked at me and the whole situation. It would open up a whole Pandora's box of issues. Even if I had to acknowledge that I had a gun, it would have looked a lot different. And how could I prove that I had fired in self-defense instead of just wanting her out of the way? Before I opened the door, I placed the gun back in the desk drawer."

Angie watched her friend intently. "Leaving all that aside, could you have shot and killed her?"

Michael did not hesitate. "Absolutely." As soon as he said it, he saw Samantha flinch.

"Did the police ask a lot of questions?" Fletcher asked.

"They did. Listen, they're not interested in the gambling part or anything about Alex's business. After all, some of the big guys in that precinct and some other top cops in the city are customers. All they cared about was ensuring they covered themselves on shooting Greta—that they correctly assessed the situation that led up to firing on her.

"It was actually pretty straightforward. They got my 9-1-1 call and had overheard my conversation with Greta while I left the phone on. I was trapped in my—Alex's—office. She had cut out the power from the breaker box inside the front door, and when they walked in, she was holding a gun and had obviously been firing into my office trying to kill me. When they ordered her to drop her gun, she just turned toward them with the gun and, intentionally or not, pointed at the cops. That's all they needed to shoot her, eight times."

"Did they ask about why she was trying to kill you?" Fletcher asked, clearly knowing how the police would have to approach the situation.

"Yeah," Michael went on. "But it really wasn't that hard to explain. Greta was a jilted wife with a whole set of her own problems. She was pissed at me as the executor of Alex's estate; she wanted to receive money herself instead of it going to George. She was heavily in debt. Her former live-in boyfriend was found in the Hudson River, and on top of that, she was living with Sharkey, who's already a fugitive from justice. It all actually fit together very cleanly for the cops. Plus, it's the missing piece of the puzzle of who was behind Alex and Russell's murders. It was all logical and believable— and had the added benefit of being the truth. She had motive and, with Sharkey, the means to pull it all off.

"This was like a bonanza for the cops. Now, all they need to do is find Sharkey and it's all wrapped up. Greta was a killing waiting to happen. No one is going to challenge the cops on either how they reacted to the situation they walked in on or the character of the person they shot. It's open and shut."

"You know," Fletcher added, "it conveniently rescued you from a lot of potential problems. If she'd just been arrested instead of killed, she could have exposed a lot of difficult issues—from the cash to Alex's business."

Just as everyone, including Michael, was digesting his account, Michael's cell phone rang. It was Karen, calling from New York. Michael excused himself and walked out to the courtyard. "Hi, Karen."

"Hi, Boss. I just wanted to check in before the day got going here. I thought you might like to know that late yesterday I received a call from a writer at the *Economist*. They want to interview you for a story about how you keep a company going during a major downturn. They said they wanted your ideas on things like how to avoid destroying a company through layoffs and things despite the demands of Wall Street for financial performance even during hard times."

"They should talk to that Brit asshole from Richard's office—John Hightower—and ask him," Michael said while gazing at the parade of beautiful Parisian women filing past him in the courtyard.

"I think they want *you*. It's all a result of that LA speech. I'll set up a meeting in your office and put it on your calendar. I'll keep it under wraps again from marketing so you won't have to have them involved."

"No, not this time, Karen. Let's go through the proper channels. Let marketing know. If they want to send a communications person over to be there for the interview, it's okay with me."

"Michael, is the alcohol content greater there in Paris than at home? Or did I just reach the wrong number?"

"No, Karen. I'm fine. Listen, I'm not looking to be a total cowboy. Plus, I can only get away with so many things, and I gave Richard my word that I wouldn't give unauthorized speeches. This isn't a speech, but the *Economist* is too high profile to potentially have pushed in his face if I say something the board doesn't like. Right now, I've got enough going on, so I don't need to rock the boat any further. We'll play this one straight."

"I hear you, Boss. It certainly makes my life easier, not to mention my own job security."

"All the client meetings went reasonably well. I've e-mailed our account reps with a summary of each one. Tonight Samantha and I are having dinner with Catherine Saint-Laurent."

"You do live quite a life, Boss. I don't know how you do it or how you manage to know some of these people. Don't forget you also have a conference call with the *Financial Times* the day after tomorrow, and your driver will be at your hotel tomorrow morning at eight for the trip to Orly Airport. Be sure they don't take you to de Gaulle."

"I've got it. I'm all set. I'll speak with you when I get to Saint-Tropez." Michael turned off his cell phone and resumed his lunch inside.

It was a festive celebration evening at Chez Dumonet. This time, however, Michael achieved celebrity status at the bistro when he and Samantha were accompanied in the door by the stunning—even by Paris standards—Jennifer and the legendary Catherine Saint-Laurent.

After their hectic entrance, the greetings by Nono and Guillaume, and the now-familiar stares of the other diners, Michael and his party settled into his favorite table directly in front of the bar.

Michael quickly changed the tone when he sat down and exclaimed, "I was sitting right here, Catherine, when I received a call from Alex to say hello. During that call, he was shot dead."

"God, that seems like it was a lifetime ago. So much has happened in the last several months," Samantha said. "It's amazing how something you don't ever think about can happen and then change your life in a way you never could have dreamed possible."

Michael looked at his wife, and after reflecting on her words, said, "Life isn't always destined to go on the way it seems like it will. Events can change it in a split second, or we can will ourselves a different life—or both can combine to change our course. Yet, at times, it seems like nothing can change the path we're on. You realize how silly that concept is."

Catherine spoke up, a glass of the house champagne in hand. "I miss your brother, Michael. But I must admit, this tragedy brought me the opportunity to meet you and now Samantha. I want to thank you for keeping the commitment that Alex made to me. Your money completed the financing we needed. Casting is done, and we expect to begin shooting in September in Cannes."

Michael smiled and turned toward Jennifer. "I also owe Jennifer for her selflessness in seeking me out and helping me unlock the mystery of Alex's special computer. Without her, I don't know how I could have figured out where Alex had hidden not only his secrets but some of the money necessary to pay off his debts and continue his business. I have to confess, the first time we met at that lunch, I thought you might be a nut. Thank you, Jennifer."

"By the way," Jennifer asked, "was all that 'artificial intelligence' stuff any help other than finding Alex's hiding places?"

Michael thought it was interesting that Jennifer asked the question. He was, in fact, anxious to get some privacy, open up the laptop, and talk again to Alex. He could feel Samantha staring at him, watching for his reaction, but he diverted his eyes to his plate of smoked salmon and said, "No, not really. I mean, it was interesting, but I don't think the technology has come far enough yet to have any lasting impact, other than recording some information. Maybe someday all this artificial intelligence science will be meaningful—probably just a matter of years."

"Oh, that's a shame. It certainly would have been interesting to have Alex around again," Jennifer said. As she flashed her all-American perfect white teeth and those all-too-familiar blue eyes, Michael wondered if Jennifer believed him. But just before he answered, he caught Samantha's eyes still watching him.

"Unfortunately, I think Alex died about five years too soon to be able to live forever."

Chapter 64

Saint-Tropez, France
July 19, 2010

Michael and Samantha landed at Nice Airport from Paris and boarded a private helicopter to take them from the airport to the landing pad near their hotel in Saint-Tropez. The ride was a favorite of theirs. The twenty-minute flight was mostly flown at only five hundred feet, just above the deep-blue Mediterranean waters, until the actual approach to Saint-Tropez, when the craft had to rise high above the hills.

As they approached the hotel from the air, Michael thought about the routines they had established on these stays and how much he looked forward to another year of doing the same thing they had always done.

He and Samantha usually awoke about ten in the morning; had a breakfast of freshly squeezed orange juice, warm croissants, and strong French coffee; and then arrived at the pool by noon. They would then split a bottle of wine, usually rosé, at lunch and leave the pool for their room by six. Dinner was at nine after a five-minute ride on the hotel's shuttle to the quaint port town, and then back in bed by one in the morning.

And for now, Michael looked forward to getting settled in their familiar room and heading straight to the pool and the hot sun.

The pool at the Chateau de la Messardiere was a mosaic of various shades of tiny blue square tiles jutting out over the Picasso-blue Mediterranean Sea. Michael was lying alongside a twentysome-thing young woman who, at five foot ten, would be at least three inches taller with her spiked heels, a would-be model with long blonde hair and her small, firm breasts basking in the hot sun.

The reflection from the tiny droplets of perspiration on her breasts could be seen from all angles around the pool. The only impediments to the perfect Playboy-esque view were the tiny tur-quoise triangular piece of fabric between her slim thighs and the large Gucci sunglasses concealing her eyes. Her long, toned, and tanned legs parted ever so slightly across her lounge chair, a fruit drink and a copy of Russian *Vogue* nearby on her side table. She and Michael never exchanged words.

Michael noticed Samantha eyeing the odd but not uncommon poolside combination. She appeared to be mildly amused as she said, "I told you, money does buy happiness, however brief."

Several chairs to their right, an older but just as alluring French woman, also topless, sipped champagne. According to Mustafa, who had been in charge of Messardiere's pool for a decade, she was a French film star, no longer in demand but still well known and recognized. Mustafa knew everyone who stayed at the Chateau. He knew who was important to the hotel and who wasn't. Samantha and Michael were always well taken care of, mostly because they were longtime customers, generous tippers, and generally well liked—for Americans anyway.

Although they came in handy to shield his eyes from the strong

Mediterranean sun, Michael always said that his sunglasses were necessary at the Chateau's pool so that he could gaze at the "scenery" without appearing to be a voyeur. This summer was clearly no different.

Samantha and Michael took their usual reclining lounges at the very center, facing both the pool and the Mediterranean. Mustafa ensured that those same two chairs were reserved and waiting for them each morning, along with Michael's copy of *Le Monde*. Michael continued to struggle with his French, but he could at least make out the gist of most articles, especially if they had pictures. He usually dozed off before he finished a few pages.

As Michael gazed out at the pool scenery and the Mediterranean in the distance, he reflected on the events of the last eight months. It was hard to believe that, through it all, he had not only retained his position at Gibraltar, but with the death of his boss, Chairman Dick Applegarden, he had actually been promoted.

Yet Michael wasn't sure how he felt about his unexpected success. He wondered if, deep down, he really wanted to have been fired from Gibraltar. Although he was certainly now riding high, he chafed at the shortsighted corporate strategies he had become a part of. He felt somewhat satisfied yet more stressed than he had ever been.

Michael's daydreams were interrupted by the familiar ring of his cell phone.

"Hi, Boss. Just a reminder that you have a conference call with the *Financial Times* reporters in less than an hour. They know you'll be on your cell."

"They don't know where I am, do they?" Michael didn't need the press reporting that he was vacationing in Saint-Tropez. It wasn't good press relations and could always lead to an ugly article on corporate excess or even just a passing reference on page 6 of the *New York Post*. Michael still struggled himself with the amount he was getting paid compared to the average Gibraltar employee.

"No, I just implied you were in Europe on business, but one of the ground rules for the interview is that there are to be no questions about exactly where you are. I didn't say it, of course, but they may have reason to believe that you're in acquisition discussions somewhere. You didn't hear it here though." Karen was something else!

As Michael continued to speak into his cell, now gazing up at the sky from a full, flat reclining position on his chaise, three young ladies in their mid to late twenties, each almost six feet tall—and none wearing tops—walked by his chaise lounge. Michael's head was about four feet from their knees. Thank God, he thought, that he had his shades on. All were deeply tanned, their bodies slim and built where it counted, their legs long and shapely yet still lean—and glistening in the late morning sun. They strolled by, chatting and totally oblivious to the fact that Michael had nearly dropped his cell phone in awe.

Michael's mind wandered from his conversation with Karen as he speculated on the practicality of adding Playboy Publishing to Gibraltar Financial. That would certainly be a colorful discussion with the reporters and his own board. As he glanced over at Samantha, who was settling back in her chaise after a visit to the poolside ladies' room, he was reminded that her still shapely, slim, and sexy body was enough stimulation for any man.

"Boss, did I lose you?"

Michael laughed out loud at his own meandering thoughts. "No, I'm still here, Karen. Just thinking about what a great life it is that we lead."

"Did you say 'we'?"

"Yours is pretty good too, Karen. We're all so lucky. But I was really wandering off. Sorry."

No sooner had he said it than a woman's scream pierced the colorful but calm surroundings. Staff and security men rushed into the ladies' room near the pool. A young woman came rushing out of the entrance in obvious distress, crying and shrieking, *"Elle est morte! Elle est morte! Mon Dieu!"*

Samantha turned to Michael. "Someone's dead in the ladies' room! Oh my God. I was just in there."

Everyone around the pool and the casual diners in the adjacent outdoor restaurant stood up and watched as the scene of raw terror played out in front of them. After an initial few moments of silence, everyone began whispering to each other as the rumors passed amongst the small crowd of stunned vacationers now gazing in horror as word spread that the attractive French blonde who, just ten minutes earlier, was poolside basking in the sun was now lying dead in one of the ladies' room toilet stalls, her throat slit.

"Michael, I just spoke with her this morning. We both had the same blue wrap on; she also bought hers at the hotel's boutique. We were just laughing about it. I was leaving the stall, and she was going in." Samantha was shaking.

Michael had noticed the woman earlier when she was topless around the pool. He also remembered thinking that she resembled Samantha—a little younger but the same blonde hair and similar trim figures, height, and weight. Both spoke French around the pool. If she was wearing the same exact cover-up as Samantha, the similarity would have been even more striking. Michael hoped that for the moment at least, these thoughts wouldn't enter his wife's mind.

"Why would anyone want to kill her? And here at the Chateau? She had no jewelry on, no purse. It couldn't have been a robbery." Michael could see his wife's mind going to the same terrifying and dark place. "Michael, she resembled me, didn't she?"

"Yes, she did."

Chapter 65

Saint-Tropez, France
July 19, 2010

Dinner at the Hotel Yaca restaurant in town was tense. Samantha and Michael could not help but look everywhere for potential killers.

Michael realized that it was more difficult to identify or "profile" dangerous personalities in a foreign country. As familiar as the South of France was to them both, Saint-Tropez, nevertheless, attracted a diverse population of Arabs, North Africans, Eastern Europeans, and Russians who, even to sophisticated American eyes, were menacing in appearance. He sat, watching the multiple entrances to the dining area.

Michael had already booked the next flight out of Nice. A helicopter would be waiting for them on the landing pad near the hotel at seven in the morning to take them to the airport. They had to make it alive through the night in Saint-Tropez.

Michael had done everything he could to at least minimize their vulnerability. He hired a security guard to watch over them until they boarded the plane in Nice and a private car to take them to and from dinner instead of the hotel's SUV-shuttle. The ride in and out of Saint-Tropez in the dark night for dinner was nerve-racking.

The local police accepted the possibility that the murder might have been a case of mistaken identity—and that Samantha could have been the real target. They promised to watch the hotel during the night and appeared to be periodically checking in on them and their security guard here at dinner. If Samantha was a target, however, the problem could easily follow them home.

Michael noticed that Samantha had consumed more than her usual share of rosé, although she had hardly touched her meal. It was time to head back to the hotel for what he knew would be a restless night.

They entered room 548, the same room at the Chateau they had stayed in each year for over a decade. The hotel's turndown service had ensured that the lights were dimmed, the room was in perfect order, and soft, classical music played on the alarm radio. The familiar comfort of their surroundings provided at least some balance to the underlying fear and vulnerability he knew they both felt as they prepared for bed.

The security guard sitting on the couch in the hallway outside their door also offered some additional peace of mind. Michael, however, always worried about private security guards. How could anyone really know, especially in a foreign country, whether your assigned guard had been compromised? Or whether local influence and a few thousand euros had turned him into your killer?

To Michael's delight, Samantha always slept naked. As she approached their immaculate king-sized bed, Samantha noticed something different from any other evening's turndown. A single, elaborately gold-wrapped chocolate lay on her pillow. Perhaps a nice touch from the Chateau's management, knowing her anxiety from the murder and the possibility that she was the intended target. Michael thought it slightly odd that he hadn't received one on his pillow.

Samantha placed the chocolate on her bedside table, turned down the comforter, and tucked herself under the covers. Michael watched her fluid moves and prepared to join her.

But as Samantha adjusted her body to her desired position, Michael saw her suddenly stiffen as she placed her hand under her pillow and pulled out a small note card, similar to the ones the staff would leave each night with the morning's weather forecast. Michael hoped the housekeeper had accidentally misplaced the card. But as he watched Samantha grip the edges of the Chateau's embossed stationery, he knew immediately that it would contain no weather forecast. Samantha, her hands trembling, read the note out loud, and Michael watched as though gazing helplessly at a deadly accident unfolding in front of him:

"Samantha, sorry we missed you today.
Next time we'll check passports first.
You are going to die."

Samantha tried to scream. Her mouth opened, but no sound came out. She looked at Michael, her face contorted with terror. Michael grabbed the card out of her hand and put his arms in a protective embrace around her. Where could they turn for safety if someone could penetrate their room and bed? He picked up the phone to call the front desk—the line was dead. He then went to the door and unlatched the lock. Cautiously, he opened the door and looked for the security guard. The couch outside the room, where the guard had been sitting, was empty. Michael quickly retreated back into their room, bolting the door from the inside.

Michael looked around at the room. There was only one other exterior door, the one leading to their fifth-floor terrace. Going out the patio door meant a five-floor jump—plus, who knew if anyone was hiding out there? Michael quickly went to the heavy glass door and secured the lock, for what it was worth.

Just to be sure there was no one else in the room, he opened each of the four closet doors while holding a heavy brass bedside lamp in his other hand. Each door opened to a view of Samantha's shoes or other clothing. He looked at Samantha and realized that they needed to get out of the room.

"Samantha, grab your robe; let's get out of here. We've got to get to the front desk so they can get the police. Where the hell is our security guy?"

"Michael, I don't know—and why doesn't the phone work?"

"Whoever left the note must have disconnected the phone." Michael checked the phone plug as he was speaking. The cord had been cut, thereby removing the plug that needed to be connected to the wall outlet. He rapidly moved past the bed and went into the bathroom and then into the separate toilet room. The wall phone near the toilet was also dead.

Michael dialed the hotel's main line from his cell. No answer. "Where the hell is everyone?"

"Michael," Samantha pleaded, "let's just get out of here. I can't stay any longer. Whoever is after us has been in this room. They know we're here."

The front door was the only way out of the room.

Michael slowly reopened the door and peeked out to the hallway. The couch was still empty. The elevator door was no more than ten feet away. "Let's take the elevator. There's no way we're going down the stairway."

Samantha raced out the door and pressed the "down" elevator button, illuminating the tiny red light. The overhead lights indicated that the elevator was on the main floor. As Michael checked out the hallway and all the doors leading to it, Samantha watched the lights indicating the elevator's agonizingly slow ascent to the fifth floor.

Michael wondered what the elevator door, when it opened, would reveal. He knew Samantha was thinking the same thing. The elevator stopped at the fourth floor, further delaying its arrival and adding to the drama of who might be awaiting them when the doors opened. The groaning sound of the elevator opening and closing its doors and making its way up to the fifth floor was accentuated by the overall silence of the fifth-floor hallway.

"Something is wrong," Michael said. "But we're not the only ones here. Where's the goddamned guard?"

"I don't know, Michael." Samantha was in tears. "I just want to get on that plane and get home."

Finally, the elevator arrived at their floor. The door opened, revealing nothing unusual at first glance or eye level. But as Michael looked down, it was clear that more terror loomed as he stared at the crumpled body of the security guard lying in a pool of blood.

Samantha saw him one second later. "Oh my God!"

"Let's get in and get to the lobby." Michael was calm and his tone subdued, despite his own near internal panic. He had to exhibit some almost unrealistic sense of sanity or Samantha would break down in fear.

"Michael, are you crazy? I can't get in there. Let's take the stairs." Just as Samantha spoke, a door slammed shut—either the door to the stairway or a guest room. There was no more time to think about choices.

"No, we can't go down those stairs. Whoever is out there will be expecting that. Our odds are better here. I know it's crazy, please—just get in and close your eyes." Michael had no idea which was better. The thought of getting in the elevator with the murdered security guard seemed, in the split second he had to weigh such bizarre choices, only marginally preferable to stepping into an unknown, probably dark, stairway with innumerable opportunities for entrapment and more surprises.

He walked into the elevator first, stepping nearest the bloody, lifeless body and onto the wet, red-and-yellow bloodstained carpet. Michael pulled Samantha in with him, shielding her view from the gory scene at his feet. He pushed the button for "Lobby," put his arms around Samantha, and held his breath, hoping the door would not open again until they reached the lobby.

Michael watched the floor indicator lights just above the elevator door. First "5," then "4" flashed green, but as the elevator approached the third floor, it slowed to a sudden stop.

"Shit, what do we do now?" Samantha said to Michael.

"We've got to play it by ear. There's no plan. If it's bad, I'm going to try to throw myself at him right away while you get the hell out. It could be anyone though."

The elevator had stopped at the third floor. "Jesus, how long does it take for this damned door to open?" Michael whispered.

The elevator had a door on both sides. This time, the door on the opposite side would open. "Whoever walks in is going to have to literally step over this body," Michael said. "They're going to have one helleva shock."

"Yes, unless they're the killer," Samantha said, her voice breaking up.

The door opened to a mature, well-dressed French couple that Michael recognized from the pool. They immediately gave a welcoming nod of recognition as they took their first step into the elevator. Michael put both hands up, his palms open, in a gesture to warn them to stop so they wouldn't trip over the body. Michael's gaze shifted quickly back to Samantha who appeared paralyzed, her mouth partly open, as though she were about to speak. The couple finally looked down at the security guard's body in a bloody mess on the floor and then back up at Michael and Samantha, who were still dressed in their white terry cloth evening robes.

As he pulled his wife back from the elevator, Jacques Foucoult, a Paris solicitor, turned to Michael. "My God, what has happened?"

Michael shouted out, "Someone has killed the guard and is trying to kill us. Please, call the police. Hurry!" The doors closed, leaving Michael and Samantha alone again with the body. The only sounds were the creaking of the elevator mechanism.

Michael held Samantha firmly but kept his eyes glued to the indicator lights. "Okay, just three floors to go."

"What then, Michael?"

"I don't know, I don't know."

He felt like time was frozen. The distinct metallic odor of fresh blood and alcohol seemed to overwhelm the musty elevator air. The lobby indicator light flashed on, and the elevator came to another abrupt stop. The doors opened to a still life of perfect quiet, order, and a strange serenity.

Michael and Samantha quickly exited the bloody elevator. The lobby was empty. Not a soul was visible, even behind the front desk. Their slippers left bloody footprints on the white marble floor as they walked toward the front desk of the abandoned lobby. Michael felt the sticky bottoms clinging to the floor.

Holding Samantha's hand tightly, Michael walked past the reception desk on the right, then the abandoned concierge desk on the left, hoping to find anyone, if not the familiar face of the concierge, Alain Piezza. But the entire lobby was empty. Samantha looked outside the front glass doors. "Michael, look, there's something going on outside."

Michael looked out beyond the front doors. "It's the police!"

It was clear that a small military presence was waiting. A militia of heavily armed uniformed police officers, some carrying submachine guns, some with sniper rifles aimed at Michael and Samantha, were standing and then cautiously approaching the lobby. Sure enough, there was Piezza, accompanied by two of the approaching officers, pointing out Michael and Samantha as guests. The officers continued their approach but began waving for Michael and Samantha to rush and join them outside to safety.

Samantha ran toward them, now leading the way. Michael could not believe his eyes. A minute earlier, he had believed that a safe escape from the Chateau was almost impossible.

The lead officer, Captain LeClerque, needed information from them. *"Parlez-vous français, monsieur?"*

This was no time, Michael thought, to try to communicate in his pathetic French. Even Samantha, who usually insisted on speaking French in France, quickly answered, "No, we're Americans."

"No problem, I spent a year in New York City." The captain needed to assess the situation inside the hotel. "What did you see inside?"

Michael described the evening's horror, beginning with the note under Samantha's pillow and ending with the harrowing ride down the elevator with their security guard dead on the floor. The police were obviously already aware of the earlier murder in the pool bathroom.

"Our officers have surrounded the hotel's grounds. No one can get in or out. We will now go into the Chateau, floor by floor, room by room. Please, stay here behind the barricade. We will need you later. This officer will stay with you." Captain LeClerque motioned to a junior officer, who moved closer to Michael and Samantha, stretching his long arms out to them in a protective manner.

But just before leaving them, Captain LeClerque placed his hand on Michael's shoulder. "I must compliment you, monsieur."

"Yes, thank you, but why?"

"For an American, your text messages have been in perfect French. I never would have guessed—"

"Text messages? From me?"

"Why yes, of course. The messages were from a phone listed under the name 'Nicholas.' This is how we were notified of the problem in the Chateau. You are also quite modest, again, for an American. I compliment you, sir."

Michael turned and exchanged glances with Samantha, who then whispered into Michael's ear, "But you didn't send—" before she stopped in midsentence.

LeClerque continued, "If we had not been notified so quickly, the killer surely would not have fled before completing his work. You both are very fortunate."

Michael finally spoke, "Yes, I'm sure." He looked cautiously again at Samantha who wore what appeared to be a puzzled—or was it a troubled—expression. But, Michael realized, he wasn't sure at all *what* Samantha was thinking. For now, it was best to leave it alone and let her draw her own conclusions.

"By the way, Monsieur Nicholas, if you don't mind, I was curious how you were able to locate my private mobile number. And to do this under such intense pressure, *voilà*, I am amazed."

Michael didn't know what to say. "Ah, Captain, the wonders of technology."

"What was that all about? Did you send him a text?" Samantha said, once they were out of earshot.

"Of course not. I never even heard of him until five minutes ago."

Michael stared into Samantha's eyes; he couldn't tell what she was thinking. He wasn't even sure himself what to make of the captain's revelations, but he knew better than to bring up Alex's name. *Not yet. Not until she's ready to believe.* Samantha, he knew, needed time to reach her own conclusions.

Twenty minutes passed. The scene outside the Chateau was surreal: klieg lights, news cameras, police, and locals gathered in a controlled mob scene. Officers were now filing out of the hotel and returning to their places back behind the barricades. Michael watched as Captain LeClerque appeared busy receiving reports directly from the returning officers and an ongoing stream of police radio messages. He was nodding his head up and down with a restrained smile as he approached Michael and Samantha.

"We have him," the captain said to Michael and Samantha. "He was heading off the grounds toward the water. We suspect an accomplice was waiting on a boat to pick him up."

"Oh, what a relief," Samantha said.

"We have not been able to locate any such ship, however," LeClerque added.

"So someone else is still out there?" Michael said, his optimism quickly evaporating.

"Yes, I'm afraid so," LeClerque said. But the captain seemed preoccupied; he was looking down at his phone. "This is most un-usual, monsieur."

"What is it?" Michael said as Samantha drew near.

"We believe there was a speedboat that was waiting for our killer. Witnesses saw a—what do you say?—a cigarette boat at the beach. We suspect it took off when they realized that we appre-hended our suspect. But for the past several minutes, I have been receiving GPS coordinates from a fast-moving ship in the bay. They have been in the form of more text messages. We have tracked the source, and they appear to be coming directly from the boat. This is all very strange." He looked up at Michael as though he was wait-ing for an explanation.

"Our navy patrol ships are rapidly approaching these coordi-nates. They have the speedboat—a cigarette boat—in sight now and will be overtaking it shortly. I suspect that we will then have our remaining criminals."

"But why would the boat be both fleeing and sending you its location coordinates?" Michael said, innocently.

"Monsieur Nicholas, criminals are frequently stupid."

Chapter 66

It was nearly three in the morning before Michael and Samantha were allowed back to their room to catch a few hours' sleep before their helicopter took them back to Nice for their late-morning flight home to JFK.

Michael had spent an hour with the French police, who, in a dignified but persistent manner, questioned him and sat—absorbed if not fascinated themselves—as Michael recounted the events, beginning with Alex's shooting. The French officials, however, wanted to keep it simple. They needed to ensure that they caught the perpetrators of the crimes just committed that day on French soil, and it appeared that they were satisfied they had done just that.

Just as Michael and Samantha were finally tucked in bed, the phone rang. Reaching for it, Michael wondered what else could befall them in their final hours in Saint-Tropez.

"Monsieur Nicholas, this is Captain LeClerque. I am so sorry to disturb you."

"Yes, Captain. It's not a bother. What can I do for you?"

"I have news for you. I thought it might put your mind at ease. After all, we want to be sure you come back to Saint-Tropez again next summer."

"Of course, don't worry, Captain. I just hope next summer is a little more peaceful. What news do you have for me?"

"As you know, we captured the man we believe committed the murder at the pool and who murdered your security guard in the elevator. We also captured another person who was piloting the boat for the killer's getaway. They are both Russians. We are familiar with them, although until now, we had no grounds to detain them. They are professionals. There always seems to be a market here in Saint-Tropez and this part of France for Russian hit men.

"Nevertheless, monsieur, they are in our custody, and I do not expect them to be released any time soon. Between the surveillance tapes from the hotel and the eyewitness accounts from the guests and staff, I believe we will have these two behind bars for a long time. I am also pleased to tell you that we are sure they acted alone. No one else here was involved in carrying out these crimes."

"Did you find out why the speedboat was sending you its coordinates?" Michael asked.

"It's funny that you ask. I also was very curious too, of course. The driver on the boat claims he knows nothing about it. He claims that he set the GPS locator for his intended escape route to Marseilles, but that he had no idea that any location signals were being transmitted—let alone, of course, to me. I must confess to you, that I am without a clue as to how this could have occurred.

"But as I said, criminals are not always smart. This could have been a series of errors and coincidences. He may have unwittingly set the device to transmit his location and somehow perhaps in a manner only the gods can explain, those signals came to me. Perhaps, as they say, a 'twist of fate' or maybe just a mystery of this Internet that everyone is watching."

"Perhaps, Captain. Our world, it seems, has become very complex."

"But, monsieur, there is something else. The message I received from you earlier, warning me of the situation at the Chateau and requesting help—"

"Yes, I must admit I don't know how—"

"Monsieur, they have all vanished. I attempted to show the messages to our magistrate, and there is no trace of them. Poof, they are gone."

"I wish I could explain any of this, but I can't. I never sent those messages," Michael said. As he thought about this new and strange sequence of events, Captain LeClerque spoke again.

"Perhaps, monsieur, for some occurrences there are no answers. But there is one more thing I need to tell you. As you say in America, there is good news and bad news. The good news is these criminals have been caught. As I indicated, they acted alone and are now and for a long time secure in our prison."

"Yes—and the bad news, Captain?" Michael asked.

"The bad news, sir, is that, as I said, they are hired, professional hit men. Someone we don't know paid them to do their work today. We do not believe this person is in France. So, unless there is more than one team of assassins, which is highly doubtful, you should be safe here. And we will be watching you and your wife carefully until you board your plane in Nice. But, monsieur, it seems that someone with resources wants to bring harm to you or Madame Nicholas, or both of you."

Michael listened thoughtfully. The captain's conclusions weren't a surprise. "*Merci*, Captain. I appreciate your help today, and I look forward to being back here in Saint-Tropez next year. *Au revoir.*"

"Good night, Mr. Nicholas."

As soon as he hung up, Samantha lifted her head from the pillow and asked Michael, "What did he say?"

"He said the two involved will be locked up for a long time. They've got surveillance tapes and eyewitness accounts. They were Russian hit men who acted alone here."

"Did he say anything else?" Samantha asked.

"Just that he felt we were safe now and to have a good trip in the morning." Michael turned over, closed his eyes, and tried to sleep.

Chapter 67

4:30 a.m.

I t shouldn't have been a surprise, but Michael was wired, wide awake. He had left Samantha asleep, gently closing the bedroom door behind him and settling into the comfortable white cotton, thick-cushioned couch in the suite's sitting room. Here he logged onto his computer.

In seconds, Alex appeared on the screen. "*Buenos dias.*"

"I'm in France, Alex; Saint-Tropez is in France, not Spain."

"I know. I still don't see what the fuck you like about that country. They're all so serious and stuck-up, although they do have some good-looking women."

"Someday I'll explain it. I need to speak with you. Some horrible things have happened here that I suspect you already know about." Michael then filled Alex in on the details of the afternoon and evening, ending with the call from Captain LeClerque. Alex appeared to listen carefully but said nothing.

"So, how the hell did you figure out what was going on, and how did you send all these texts?" Michael asked. "Not to mention—in perfect French."

"The French part was easy—it's called iTranslate; it's an Apple app," Alex said, a look of satisfaction spread across his face.

"I'll have to check it out, but that's the least of it," Michael said, aware of the irony of getting technology lessons from Alex.

"The rest of it is not so simple. Some changes have been happening. I don't know whether you're aware of them or not. For example, I'm hardly sleeping anymore. It's funny, I hardly ever slept when I was alive—not that I'm dead, obviously—and now it's the same. I don't sleep."

"What do you mean?"

"The best way to explain this is that if I were just a computer, my systems, my software, whatever the fuck it is, it's all still working even though I may be resting. It's like I never shut down completely anymore. So, I'm always working, following things. It also means I'm tired a lot. Just like I always used to be. I feel like I'm still running around all night but without the booze."

"But how about the messages to the captain, and how are you finding out almost everything that's going on all the time?"

"A lot of things are at work here, Michael—hotel surveillance cameras that are transmitting images, captured text messages between the two hit men, GPS signals—they're all out there, in cyberspace or whatever the fuck you call it."

"But, Alex, *how do you get them*, and how do you sort through everything that's flying around in order to find what's happening in a specific situation, like mine yesterday?"

"There are filters, things like I can type into my mind (except I don't actually type), if that's what it is, that allow me to search for what I need. It's like when you do a Google search or you program a search mechanism to inform you about certain things."

Michael felt a rush of adrenaline—or was it stress, or fear?—he wasn't sure. "I just don't know how all this—and I mean everything, *including you*—how it's all possible. I mean, *am I dead myself* and I just don't know it?"

"No, Michael, you're not dead. *And neither am I.*"

Those words seemed to sear through Michael's brain. He was even more confused. "Alex, I just don't understand—"

"Listen, I don't fuckin' understand it yet myself. It's like there's some ether world out there, things we couldn't imagine before and that I can't intelligently explain even today. But I know that all these systems and software are allowing me to see and do things and make connections."

"Connections? What do you mean?"

"The more I learn, the more powerful I get. I can see the things from the old world, the one we grew up learning about in school or church, the stuff I never believed in. What we called your soul or spirit. Then, there's this new virtual life, cyberspace or whatever, with Internet messages and videos and all that, flying all over the place."

Michael sat, fixated. "Jesus. How is this all possible?"

"And, Michael—this is even stranger—somehow, the two come together."

Michael noticed that Alex was beginning to close his eyes, and like a fatigued driver, seemingly catch himself and perk up.

"Michael, I'm getting a bit tired."

"Okay, maybe all these questions put a strain on you. Can you just hold on another few minutes? I need to understand some things, like how much danger Samantha and I are really in right now."

"Yeah, I'm fine, don't worry—although a few amphetamines wouldn't hurt right now."

"Alex, what troubles me is that it's clear these guys were just hired guns. The person who employed them is obviously still out there," Michael said, watching Alex's face and looking for a reaction, a sign that everything would be okay.

But Alex looked somber. "Joseph Sharkey is behind everything. You and I both understand that. Sharkey is hiding in Rome; I've tracked him. He's got a problem now though. He hired these Russians without the knowledge of his hosts—his protectors—and when they find out about it, they're going to be pissed as hell. They're going to come down on him like a ton of bricks.

"These people don't like messy scenes in places where rich people like you hang out. Their style is more like, you know, poison pills or a switchblade through the side of the heart where you have to search for the entry wound—murders that look like natural causes or accidents. Things that don't generate publicity."

Michael listened, amazed again at Alex's knowledge. "So what does this mean for me?"

"It means you're safe for now. His protectors couldn't afford to let Sharkey ever be caught and arrested; he knows too much. Plus they owed him a favor, so they took him in. But they'll put a lid on him now; he won't be able to do a thing."

"Alex, who are these people? Who's hiding Sharkey?"

Alex hesitated and seemed momentarily uncertain. "I know their names and where they work. The names won't mean anything to you, but where they work will."

"For Christ's sake, Alex, where are they?"

Alex laughed, his dark sarcastic laugh. "You're close on that one. They're inside the Vatican."

"You're kidding. This can't be good for me. And what was the big *favor* they owed him that would cause them to get in bed with him at all?"

"Years ago, Sharkey took care of a big problem for the Church in the Bronx. Some kids were about to testify against a priest who molested them. Sharkey had them killed in a car accident. That's why the Church—or at least some big shots there—have been doing his bidding and are now protecting him."

"The Catholic Church?"

"Yeah, some monsignor and a cardinal. And it may go higher than that."

"How can it go any higher? You mean God?"

"Well, maybe not that high, but possibly the pope. At least it's possible that he may have some knowledge of all this, unless they're keeping it from him."

Michael was speechless. But more than ever, he was feeling the stirring of a new emotion. Something he hadn't really experienced since his immersion into his brother's world. Michael was angry.

"You mean to tell me that a cardinal inside the Vatican walls is helping a guy like Sharkey simply to return a dirty favor that he did for them?"

"It looks like Sharkey went to them after your kidnapping was botched and the cops had all the evidence they needed to put him away forever. So Sharkey called in a favor with this cardinal and the monsignor, who were the ones involved in covering up the problem in the Bronx. Maybe they really felt obligated to help him. More likely, they were worried that a desperate Sharkey would trade information on what he did for the Church in return for some kind of leniency and, in the process, implicate them. They would have had a fuckin' mess on their hands."

"I can't believe this, Alex."

"Michael, I've just forwarded a confidential document that I've captured. It's a transcript of an electronically recorded conversation within the Vatican. It looks like someone is bugging the rooms there. So, sign out with me and then check your e-mail."

"Alex, this is all so unbelievable. I don't understand how you find out all of this."

"Michael, stop trying to understand everything that goes on here."

"Alex, when you say 'here,' where exactly do you mean?"

Alex gave him a comforting, relaxed smile, and said, "Just read your e-mail—and have a safe trip home."

Michael clicked out of the program and logged onto his personal Internet account. He checked his inbox and noticed the name of the sender of the most recent message, delivered just two minutes ago. It was *anicholas@aal.com*, his brother's old e-mail account. He clicked on the message and watched as it appeared on his screen. It was an excerpt of a recorded and translated conversation. The initial notes indicated that the conversation between Monsignor Dominick Petrucceli and Cardinal Angelo Lovallo occurred yesterday:

"My son, you are troubled."

"Yes, my Father. This American is evil. He has no redeeming qualities. He has no conscience, no moral direction whatsoever. And yet, we are in debt to him. It is disturbing. It causes me to question—"

"Your faith? Dominick, do not question your faith. After all, we are all mortals, imperfect. You and I, in doing God's work and trying to protect our Church, have erred. Each misstep leading to another. Now is the time, however, to reverse our course and permanently eliminate the cancer of which we have spoken and been heretofore unable to contain."

"What do you mean, my Father?"

"Jesus said if the vine is to grow, it must be trimmed. Joseph Sharkey must be transferred from his hotel to an apartment here within our Vatican walls. A secure apartment."

"Secure, Father?"

"Yes, Dominick. Secure. One from which he will never leave."

Michael continued to stare at the transcript, embedded inside Alex's e-mail. Without warning, however, the transcript and the entire e-mail disappeared. Seconds later, his computer shut down, the screen going black. He immediately switched it on again and waited until his Internet connection was restored. He logged into his e-mail account, but Alex's message was gone. He clicked onto "deleted" mail and then "trash," but the e-mail had vanished.

Michael at last felt a sense of relief as he prepared to shut down the laptop and go to bed. Feeling secure now that Sharkey was contained far away, Michael looked forward to the morning when he and Samantha would board the Air France flight from Nice to JFK, as safe as any other passenger.

Although the desire for sleep was finally pulling at him, Michael continued to stare at the blank screen, unwilling to hit the "shut down" key, wondering about the miracle that had brought his brother back to him and into his life as never before.

Amazed yet unsettled, Michael wondered about the future and about Alex Nicholas. He thought about his brother's growing capacity to reason and to utilize the powerful resources and interconnections of the Internet. He tried to make some sense of where Alex's resurrection fit within the context of his—or anyone's—religion or spirituality.

But, most of all, he wondered where this strange miracle was headed.

Without any answers but content with the present moment, Michael finally turned off his computer and went to bed.

Chapter 68

Fifty thousand feet above the Atlantic Ocean, it all began to crystallize for Michael.

Just because Sharkey is being held in the Church's custody doesn't mean I'm safe, does it? Michael asked himself. He knew it was a rhetorical question. *Although these priests don't like Sharkey and may either never let him out or even kill him, that doesn't mean they still don't need to do something about me. I know too much. So does Samantha. Eventually, they'll wipe us all out.*

He sipped his glass of chardonnay, watched Samantha quietly absorbed in her Sudoku, and thought more about his situation. He recalled some of his most challenging corporate turnaround roles. There was a predictable pattern to how he had approached them. Unlike the traditional wisdom, he had not started out with guns blazing from day one. His style was to spend an initial period of time carefully assessing his situation and then finally developing a plan and moving forward.

Michael realized he had approached Alex's business and the threats it had presented in much the same way. He had taken the necessary actions to stabilize the business while protecting himself and his family.

Now, he knew, it was time to move out from under the defensive position he had maintained. It was time to fight, to take the initiative, to root out the threats and eliminate his enemies, particularly if those enemies were bad people.

Michael opened up his laptop and began to type a memo to be sent as soon as he arrived home this afternoon:

Memorandum to: Richard Perkins
From: Michael Nicholas
Date: July 20, 2010

RE: Business expansion into Italy

Richard, I believe that the global economic crisis has opened up an opportunity to aggressively expand Gibraltar Financial's market position in Europe. Although we already have significant market share in France and the United Kingdom, the changing political conditions occurring now in Italy provide us with a window of opportunity to expand rapidly in that country.

I will have our analysts prepare a detailed preliminary analysis for your review. In the interim, I will make plans to travel to Rome in order to meet with senior political and business leaders there.

In addition, I will need to have introductions to senior Vatican officials, perhaps beginning with the head of the Vatican Bank. Before proceeding with any business initiatives in Italy, we will need to ensure that we have the blessing of the appropriate Church officials. I understand that at least one member of our board is well connected inside the Vatican. Any assistance you could provide in opening those doors would be appreciated.

Michael

He then pulled out his BlackBerry and, after disabling the WiFi feature, typed a message to Karen DiNardo that would be sent as soon as he hit the ground:

Karen,

I expect to travel to Rome shortly for a series of business meetings designed to allow us to expand into Italy. There are two key Church officials there whom I will ultimately need to build a relationship with in order to secure their support. Please (discreetly) research these two Vatican officials for me: Cardinal Angelo Lovallo and Monsignor Dominick Petrucceli.

I will need to know everything about them, including their backgrounds, precise duties within the Church, and most importantly, their personal habits, interests, and exactly where they actually reside. Be sure to include their photographs in your report.

Please keep this confidential.

Thanks,
Michael

Satisfied, he switched off his BlackBerry, adjusted his seat to the fully reclined position, and pulled up the soft down comforter. For the first time since last November, Michael Nicholas knew he would sleep soundly.

Coming Soon, the sequel: *Death Logs In.*

For previews of upcoming books by
E. J. Simon and more information
about the author, visit
www.EJSimon.com.

Author's Note

Death Never Sleeps is a work of fiction. The names, characters, places, and incidents described in this novel are the product of the author's imagination or have been used fictitiously. Any resemblance to actual persons, businesses, events, or places is purely coincidental.

Acknowledgments

I am indebted to my editor, Debra Ginsberg, an accomplished and successful author in her own right, for her extensive critique and her incredibly insightful suggestions and ideas.

In addition, I am grateful to my friends and family members, who were kind enough to read the early manuscript drafts and offer their constructive observations and support; to my beautiful daughter, who was continually asking for more pages to read; to Reba Hilbert for her proofreading and marketing copy expertise; to the dedicated professionals at Writer's Relief, who have tirelessly assisted in the marketing of the manuscript; and to Hilary Oran, who believed in this story and was instrumental in setting me on the correct course at a critical juncture in its development.

E.J. SIMON was the CEO of GMAC Global Relocation Services (a division of GM) and the Managing Director of Douglas Elliman, the largest real estate company in NY. He is a consultant to many leading private equity firms and has held senior-level positions at prominent financial services companies. He is a world traveler, food enthusiast and lives in Connecticut. DEATH NEVER SLEEPS is his first novel.

CPSIA information can be obtained at www.ICGtesting.com
Printed in the USA
LVOW12s1440301014

411270LV00001B/196/P

9 780991 256402